BLOOD CITY ROLLERS

BY V. P. ANDERSON
ILLUSTRATED BY TATIANA HILL

LABYRINTH ROAD | NEW YORK

Text copyright © 2024 by V. P. Anderson
Cover art and interior illustrations copyright © 2024 by Tatiana Hill

All rights reserved. Published in the United States by Labyrinth Road, an imprint of Random House Children's Books, a division of Penguin Random House LLC, New York.

Labyrinth Road and the colophon are trademarks of Penguin Random House LLC.

RH Graphic with the book design is a trademark of Penguin Random House LLC.

Visit us on the Web! rhcbooks.com

Educators and librarians, for a variety of teaching tools, visit us at RHTeachersLibrarians.com

Library of Congress Cataloging-in-Publication Data
Names: Anderson, V. P., author. | Hill, Tatiana, illustrator.
Title: Blood City rollers / by V. P. Anderson; illustrated by Tatiana Hill.
Description: First edition. | New York: Labyrinth Road, 2024. | Series: Blood City rollers; 1 | Audience: Ages 8–12 | Summary: After ice-skater and Olympic hopeful Mina wipes out at her biggest competition she gets recruited by a squad of vampires who need a human player to complete their Paranormal Roller Derby team.
Identifiers: LCCN 2023031314 | ISBN 978-0-593-48571-2 (trade pbk.) | ISBN 978-0-593-48569-9 (hardcover) | ISBN 978-0-593-48570-5 (lib. bdg.) | ISBN 978-0-593-48572-9 (ebook)
Subjects: CYAC: Graphic novels. | Roller derby—Fiction. | Vampires—Fiction. | Competition—Fiction. | Friendship—Fiction. | LCGFT: Sports comics. | Vampire comics. | Graphic novels.
Classification: LCC PZ7.7.A496 Bl 2024 | DDC 741.5/973—dc23/eng/20230712

The artist used Photoshop to create the illustrations for this book.
The text of this book is set in 9.5-point Tucker Script.
Interior design by Juliet Goodman

MANUFACTURED IN CHINA
10 9 8 7 6 5 4 3 2 1
First Edition

TO ALL THE TEAMS THAT "RECRUITED" ME
OVER THE YEARS AND REALIZED THEY GOT
MORE THAN THEY'D BARGAINED FOR:
YOU'LL NEVER BE RID OF ME NOW!

—VERONICA

TO ALL THE DERBY SKATERS WHO FIRST
WELCOMED ME TO THE SKATE PARK AND
SHOWED ME HOW WONDERFUL THE SKATE
COMMUNITY COULD BE

—TATIANA

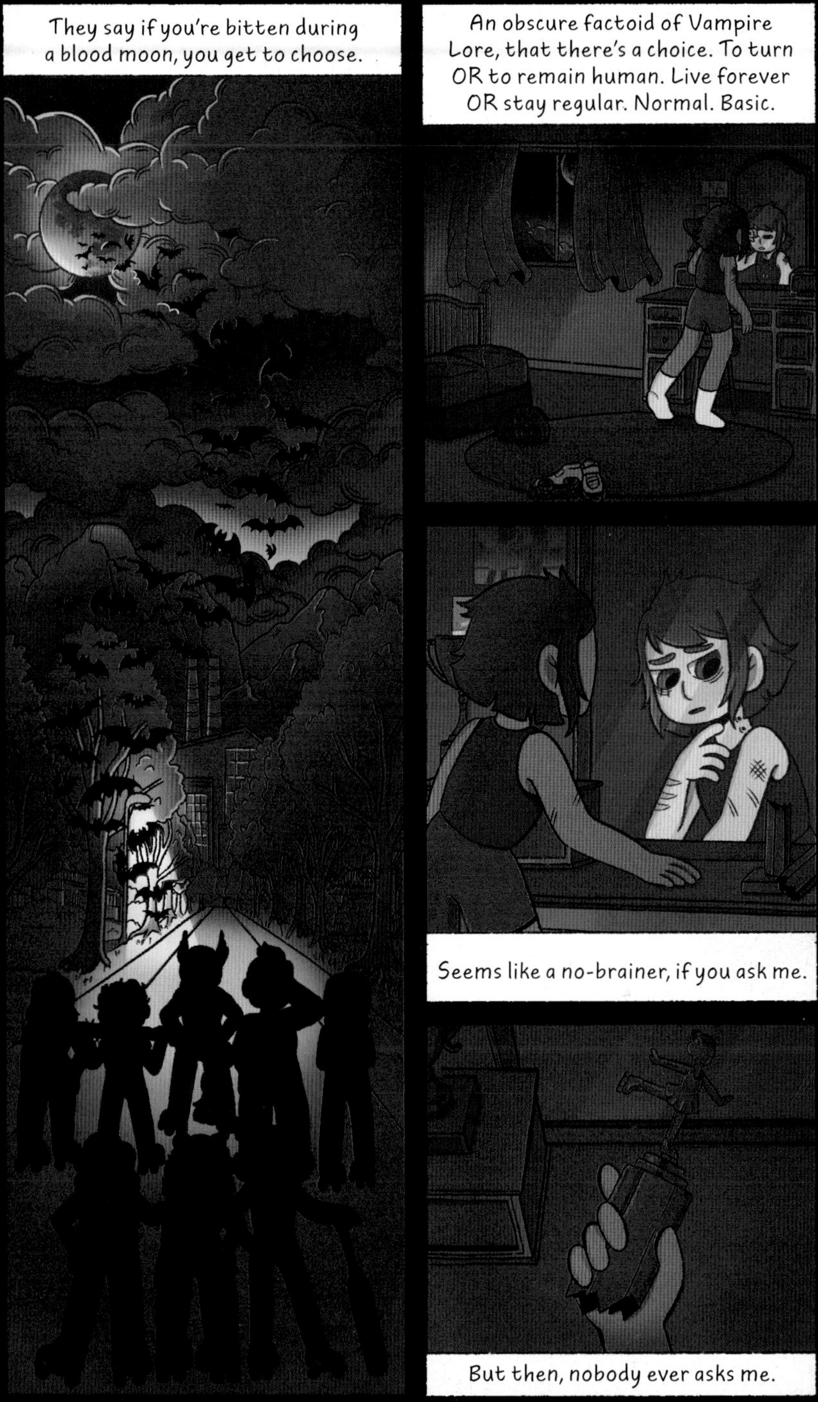
They say if you're bitten during a blood moon, you get to choose.
An obscure factoid of Vampire Lore, that there's a choice. To turn OR to remain human. Live forever OR stay regular. Normal. Basic.
Seems like a no-brainer, if you ask me.
But then, nobody ever asks me.

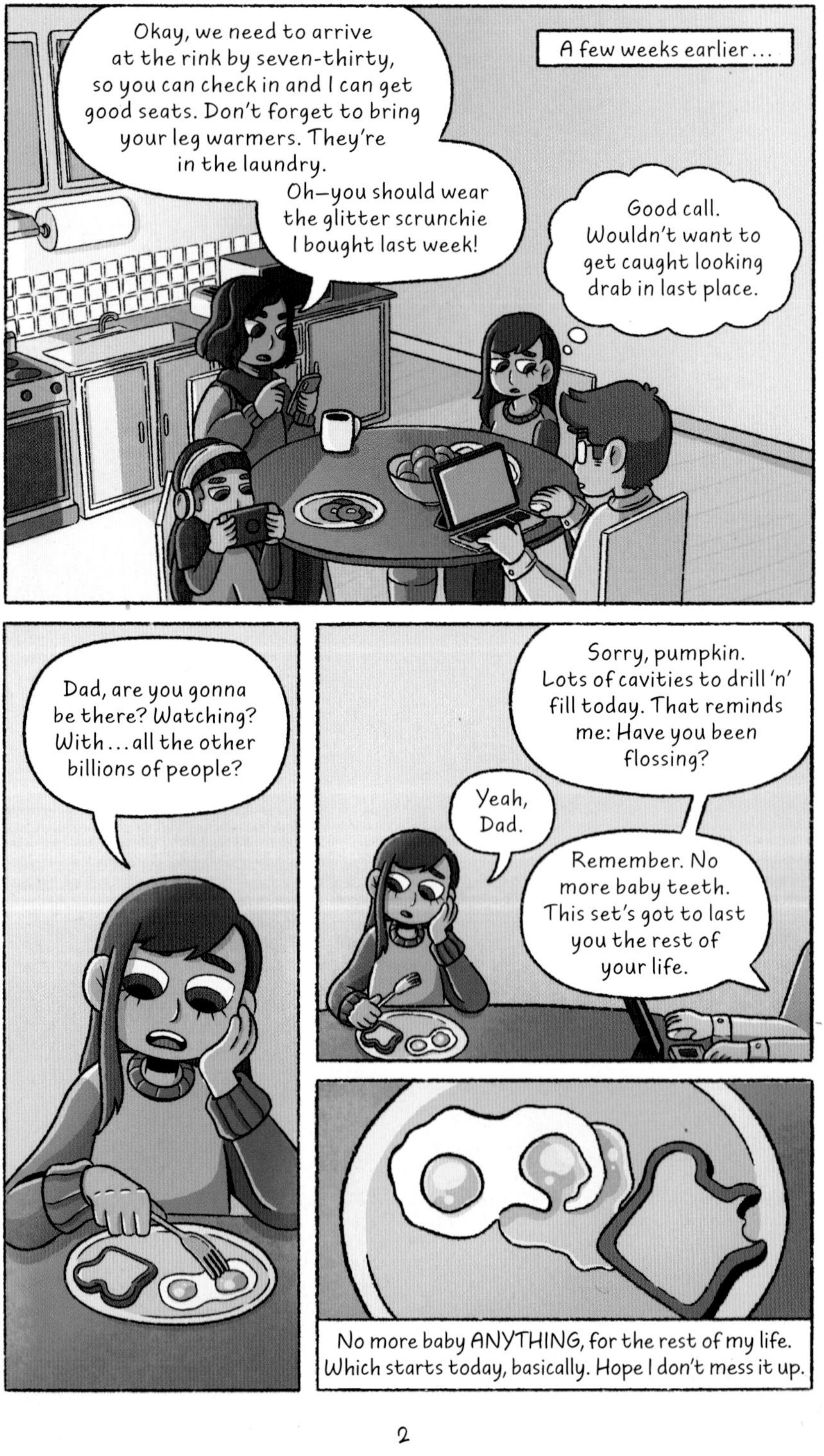
A few weeks earlier...
Okay, we need to arrive at the rink by seven-thirty, so you can check in and I can get good seats. Don't forget to bring your leg warmers. They're in the laundry.
Oh—you should wear the glitter scrunchie I bought last week!
Good call. Wouldn't want to get caught looking drab in last place.
Dad, are you gonna be there? Watching? With... all the other billions of people?
Sorry, pumpkin. Lots of cavities to drill 'n' fill today. That reminds me: Have you been flossing?
Yeah, Dad.
Remember. No more baby teeth. This set's got to last you the rest of your life.
No more baby ANYTHING, for the rest of my life. Which starts today, basically. Hope I don't mess it up.

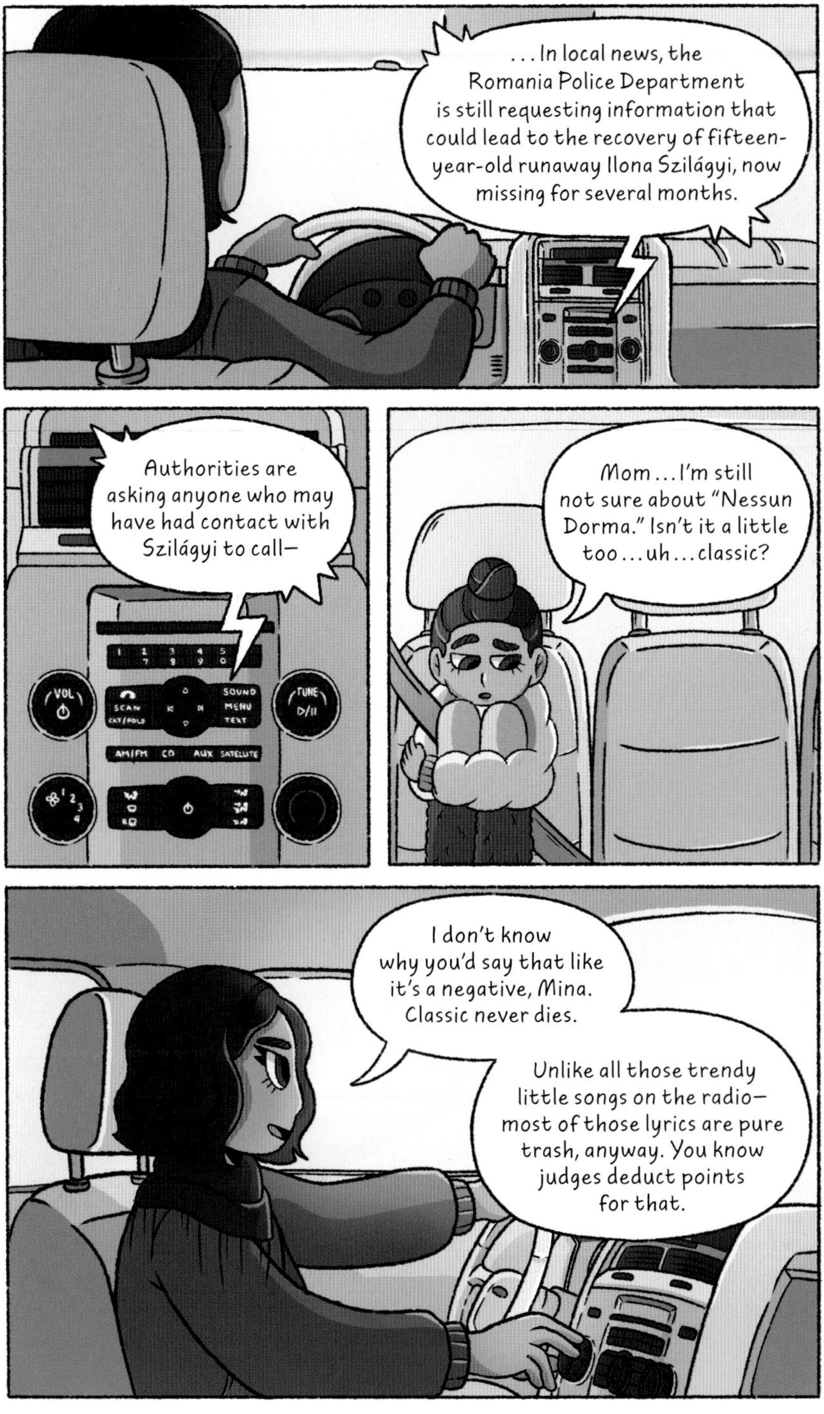
...In local news, the Romania Police Department is still requesting information that could lead to the recovery of fifteen-year-old runaway Ilona Szilágyi, now missing for several months.
Authorities are asking anyone who may have had contact with Szilágyi to call—
Mom...I'm still not sure about "Nessun Dorma." Isn't it a little too...uh...classic?
I don't know why you'd say that like it's a negative, Mina. Classic never dies.
Unlike all those trendy little songs on the radio—most of those lyrics are pure trash, anyway. You know judges deduct points for that.

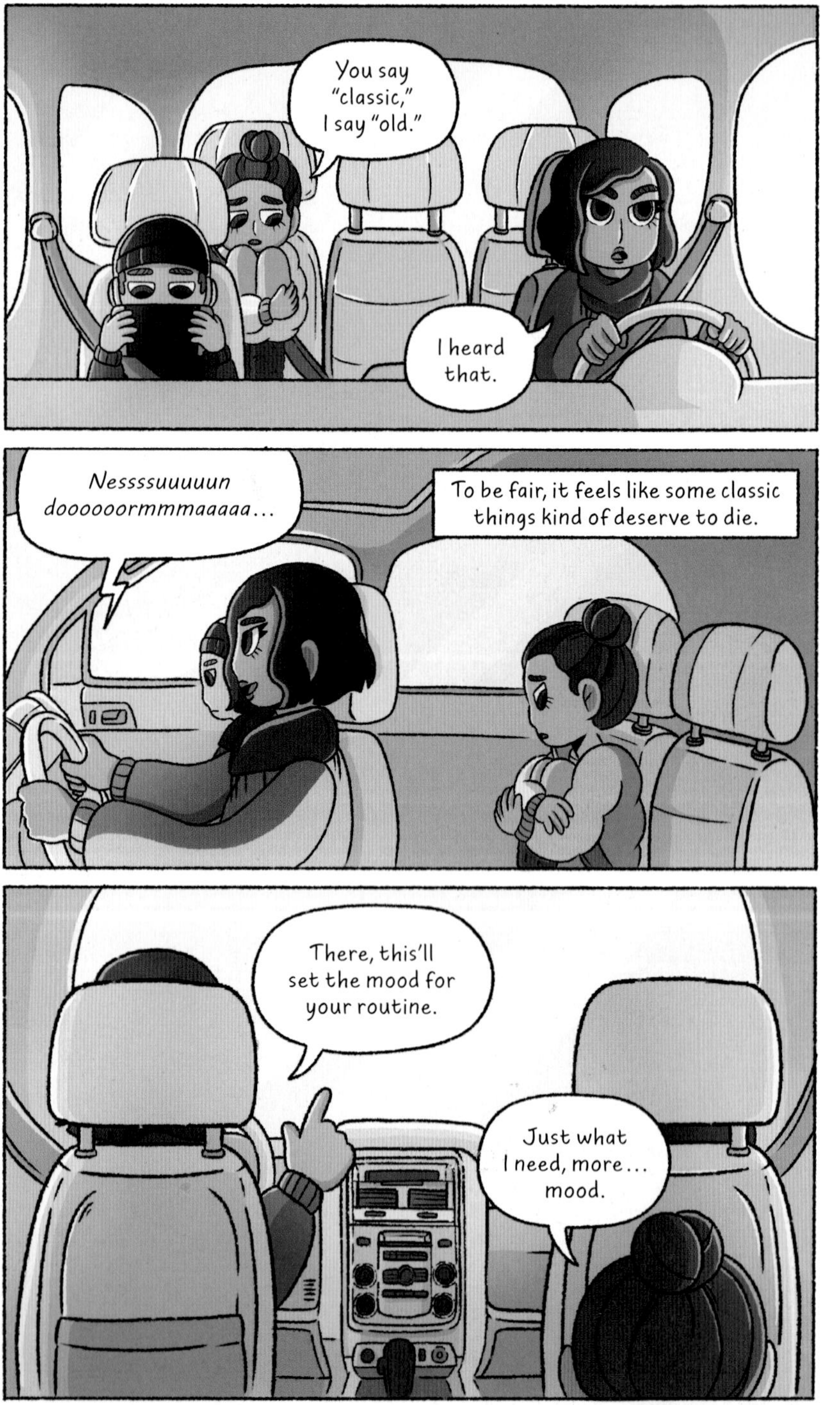
You say "classic," I say "old."
I heard that.
Nessssuuuuun dooooormmmaaaaa...
To be fair, it feels like some classic things kind of deserve to die.
There, this'll set the mood for your routine.
Just what I need, more... mood.

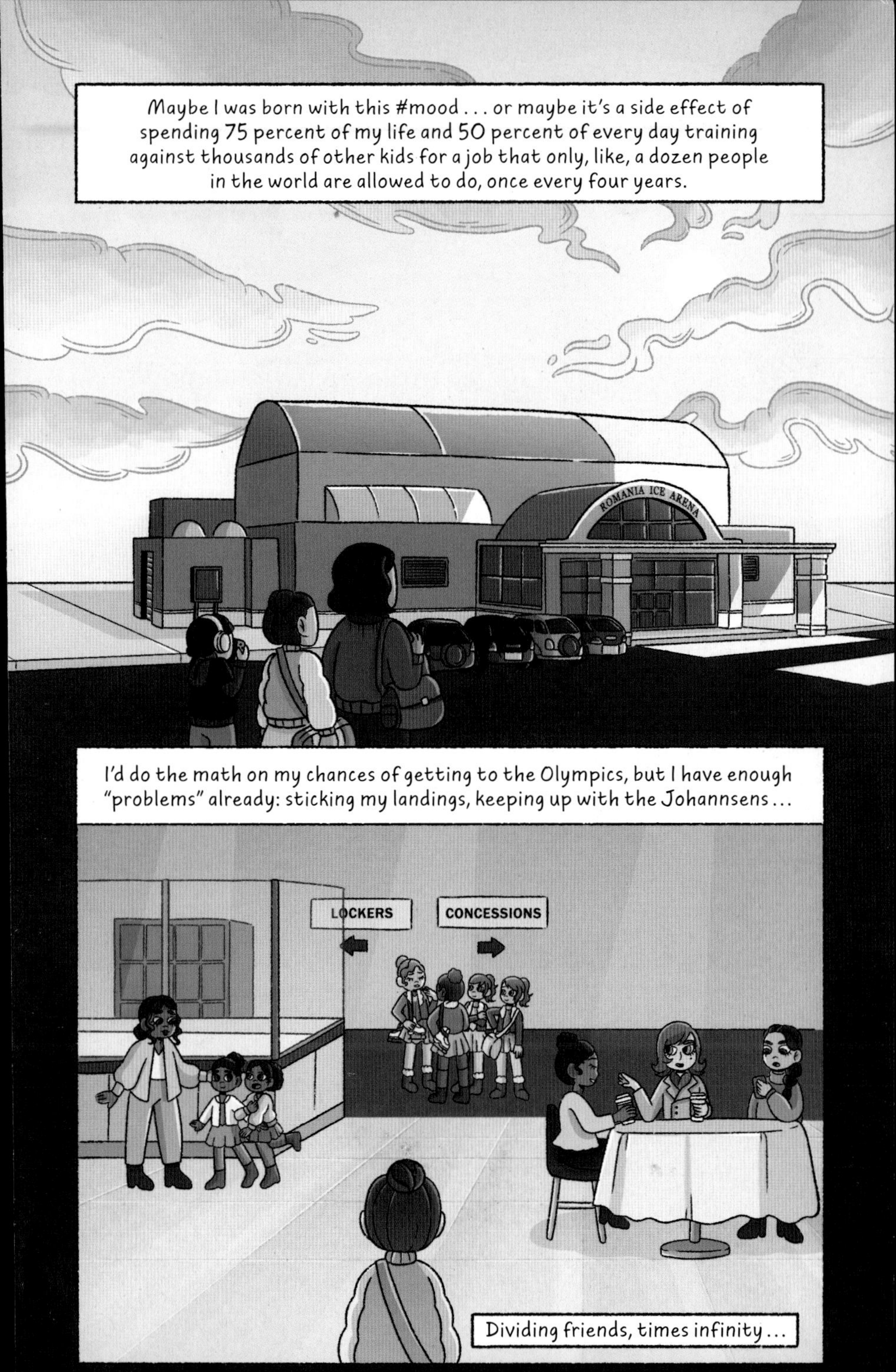
Maybe I was born with this #mood . . . or maybe it's a side effect of spending 75 percent of my life and 50 percent of every day training against thousands of other kids for a job that only, like, a dozen people in the world are allowed to do, once every four years.
ROMANIA ICE ARENA
I'd do the math on my chances of getting to the Olympics, but I have enough "problems" already: sticking my landings, keeping up with the Johannsens . . .
LOCKERS
CONCESSIONS
Dividing friends, times infinity . . .

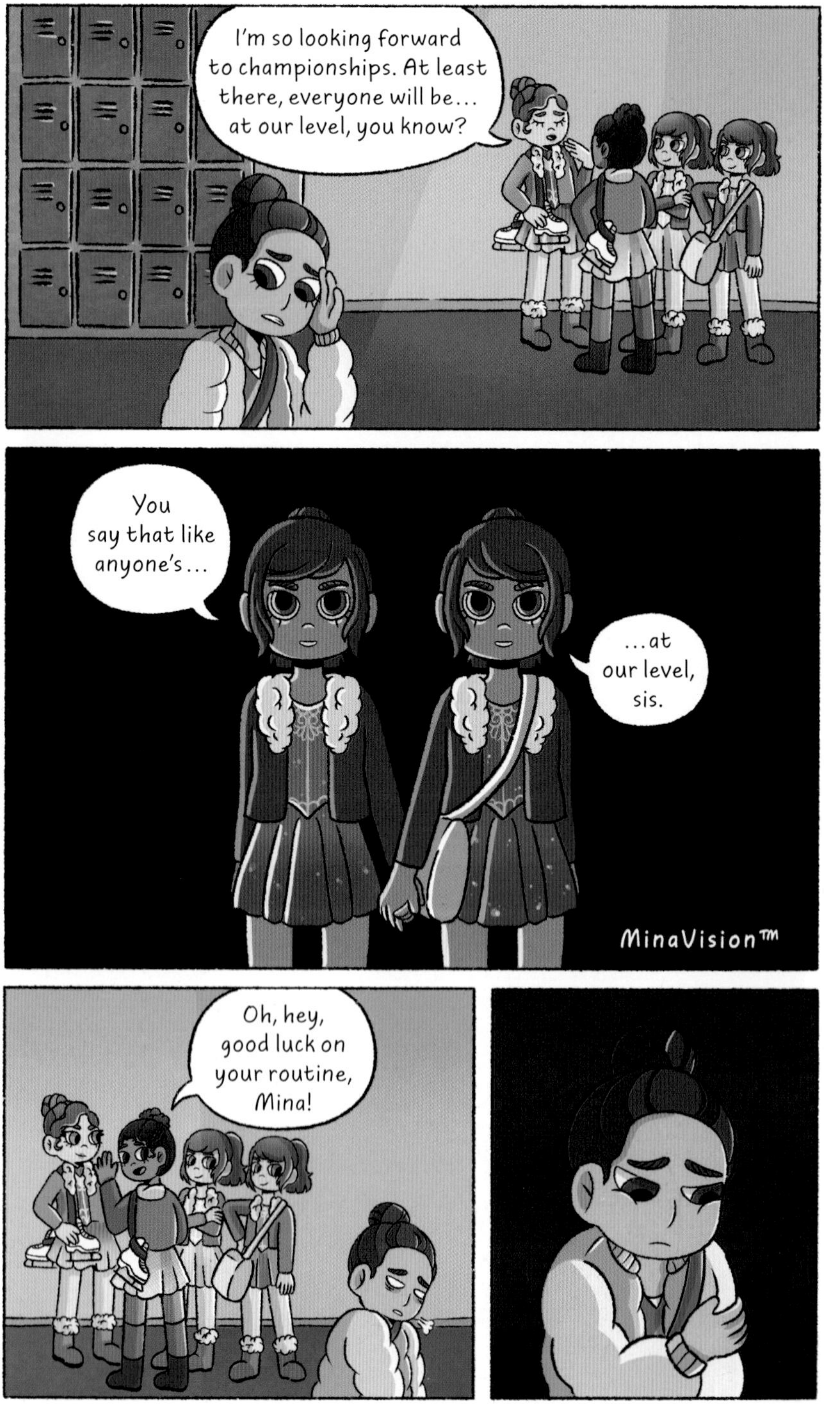
I'm so looking forward to championships. At least there, everyone will be... at our level, you know?
You say that like anyone's...
...at our level, sis.
MinaVision™
Oh, hey, good luck on your routine, Mina!

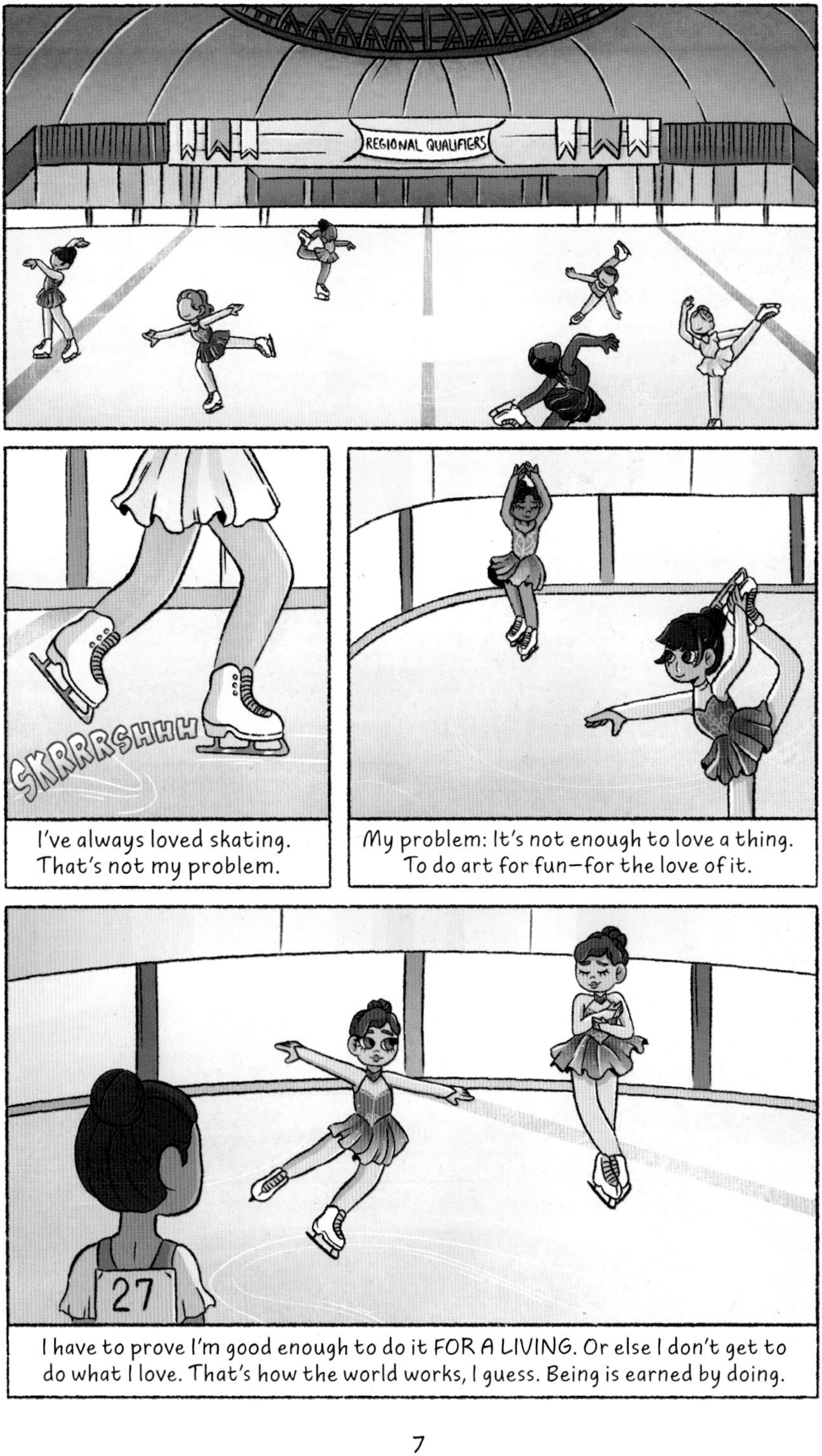
REGIONAL QUALIFIERS
SKRRRSHHH
I've always loved skating. That's not my problem.
My problem: It's not enough to love a thing. To do art for fun—for the love of it.
27
I have to prove I'm good enough to do it FOR A LIVING. Or else I don't get to do what I love. That's how the world works, I guess. Being is earned by doing.

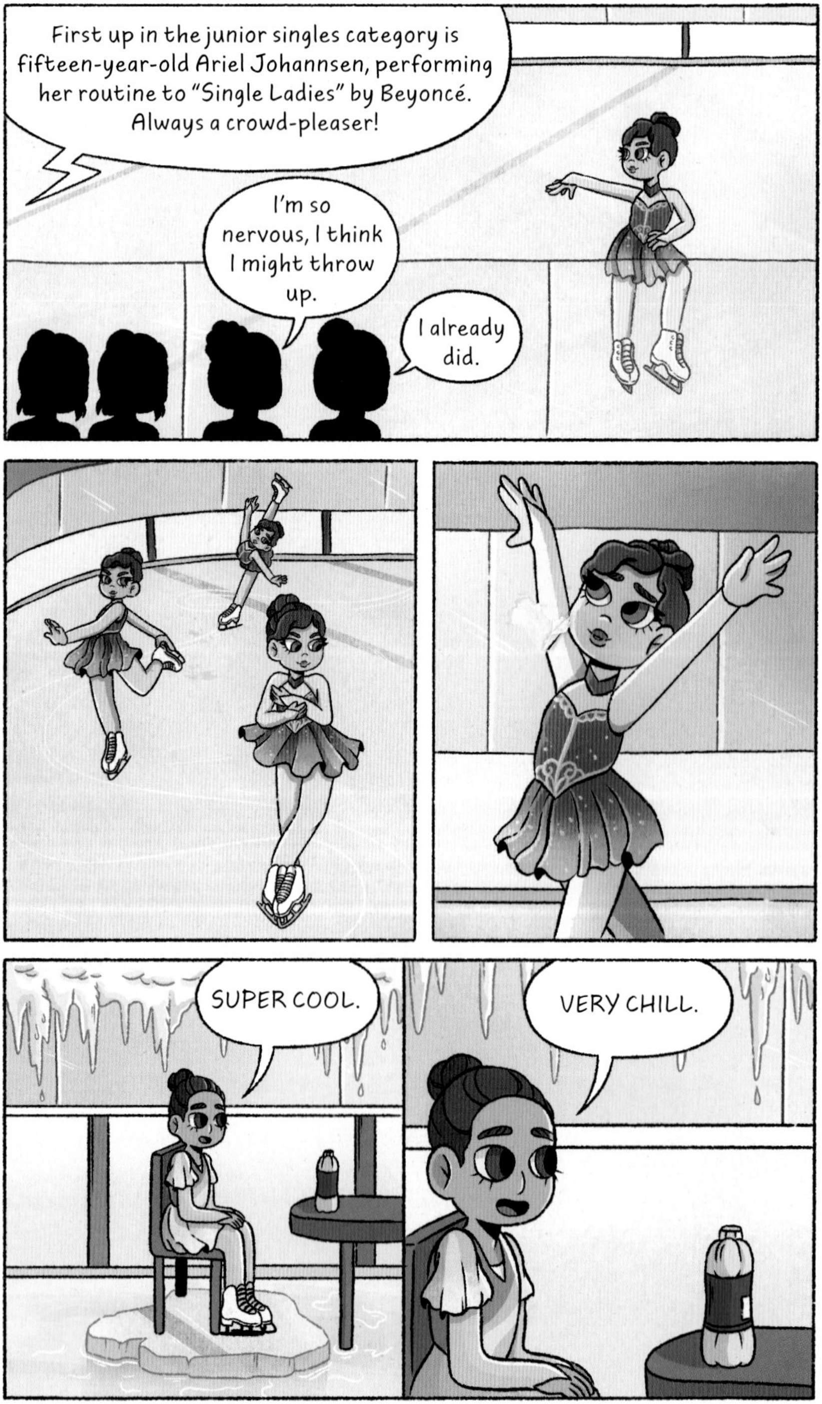
First up in the junior singles category is fifteen-year-old Ariel Johannsen, performing her routine to "Single Ladies" by Beyoncé. Always a crowd-pleaser!
I'm so nervous, I think I might throw up.
I already did.
SUPER COOL.
VERY CHILL.

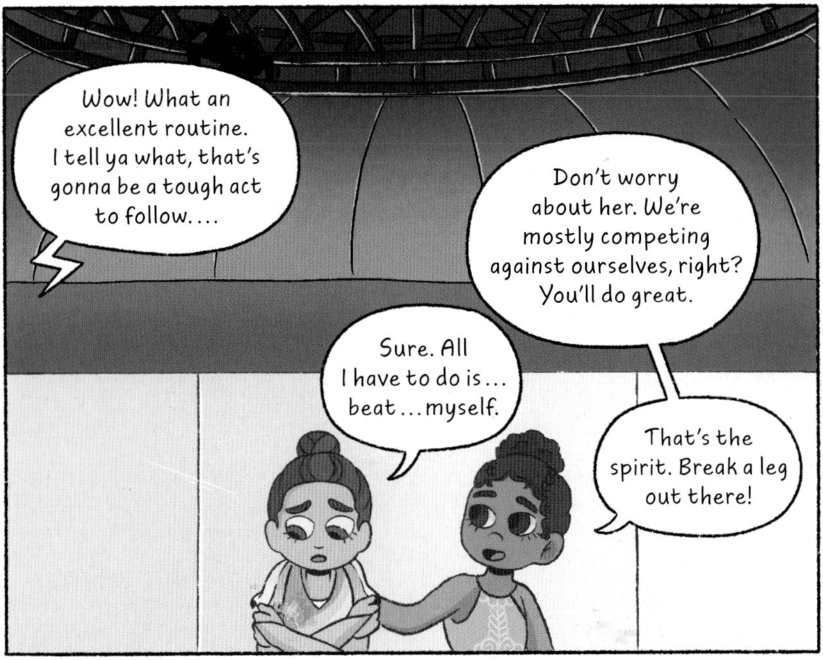
Wow! What an excellent routine. I tell ya what, that's gonna be a tough act to follow....
Don't worry about her. We're mostly competing against ourselves, right? You'll do great.
Sure. All I have to do is... beat... myself.
That's the spirit. Break a leg out there!

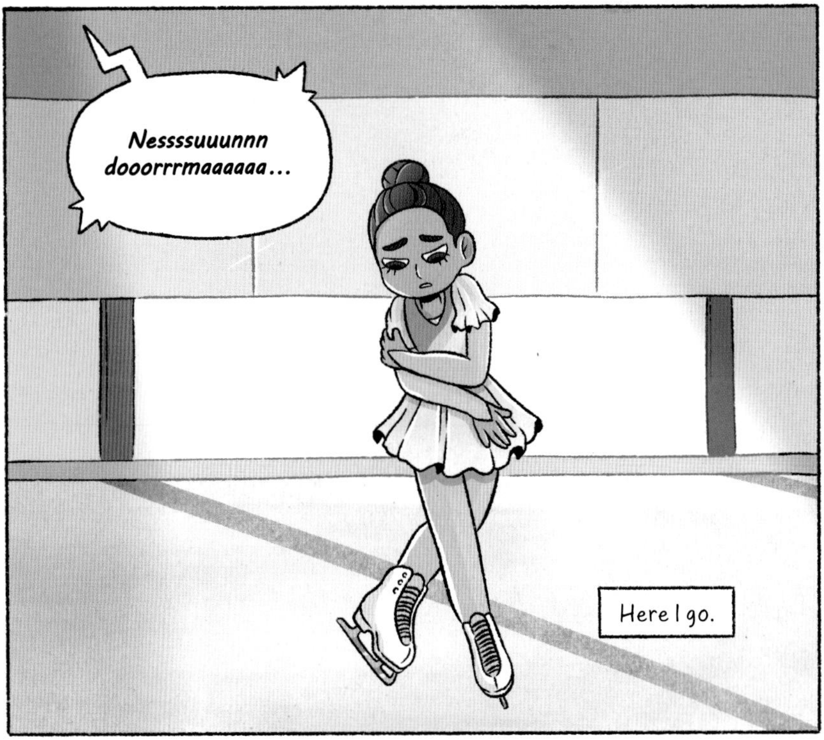
Nessssuuunnn dooorrrmaaaaaa...
Here I go.

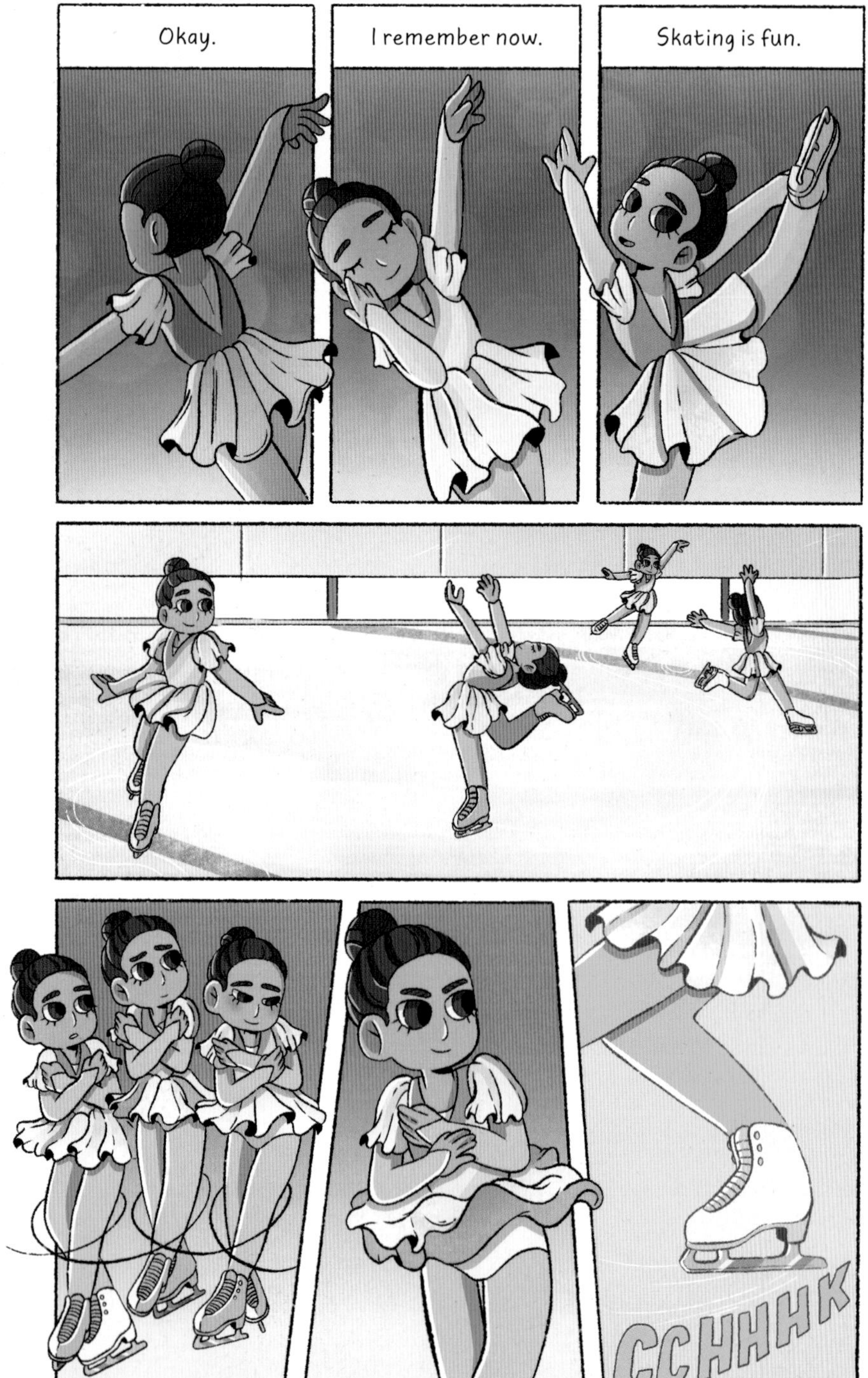
Okay.
I remember now.
Skating is fun.
CCHHHK

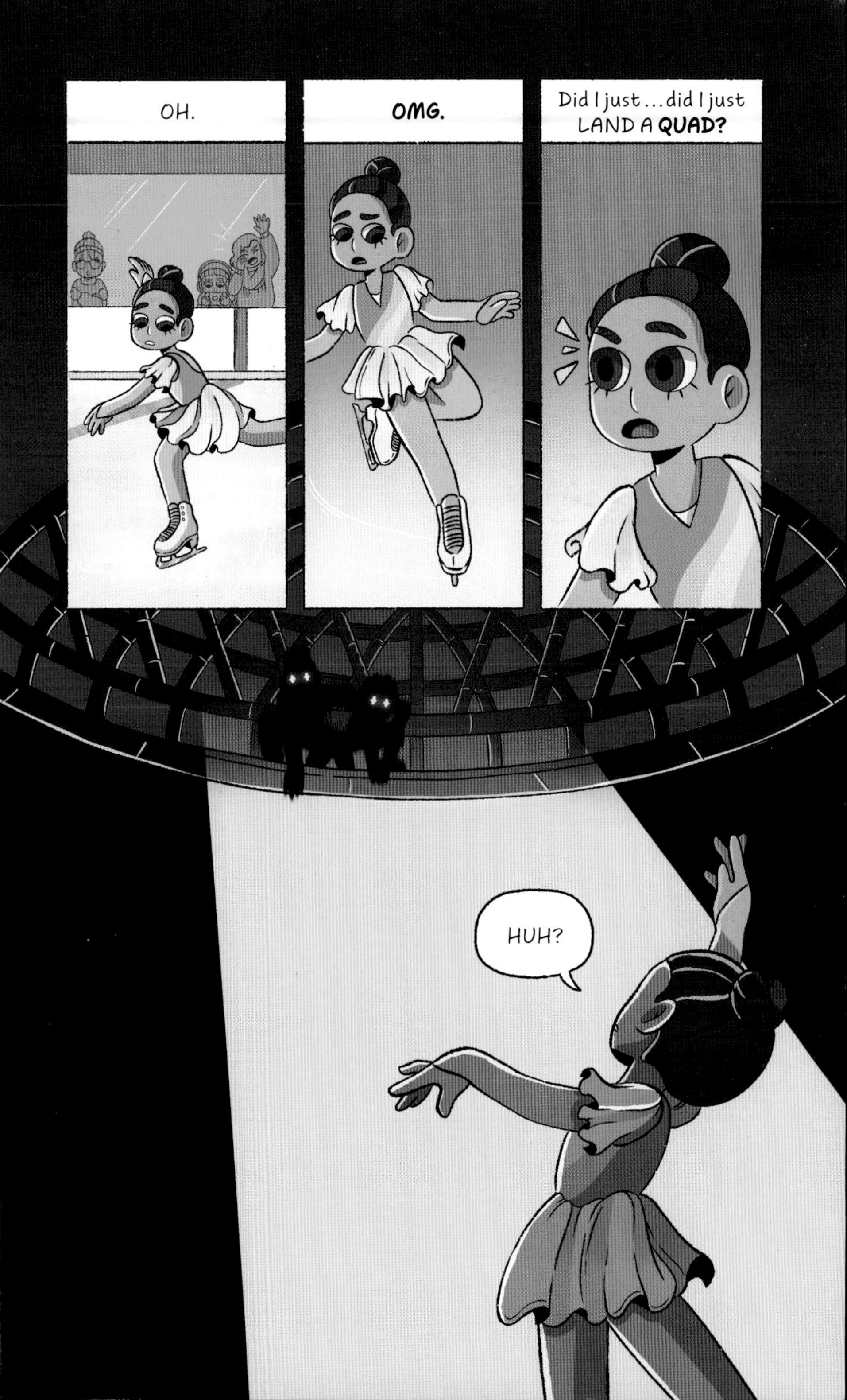
OH.
OMG.
Did I just . . . did I just LAND A QUAD?
HUH?

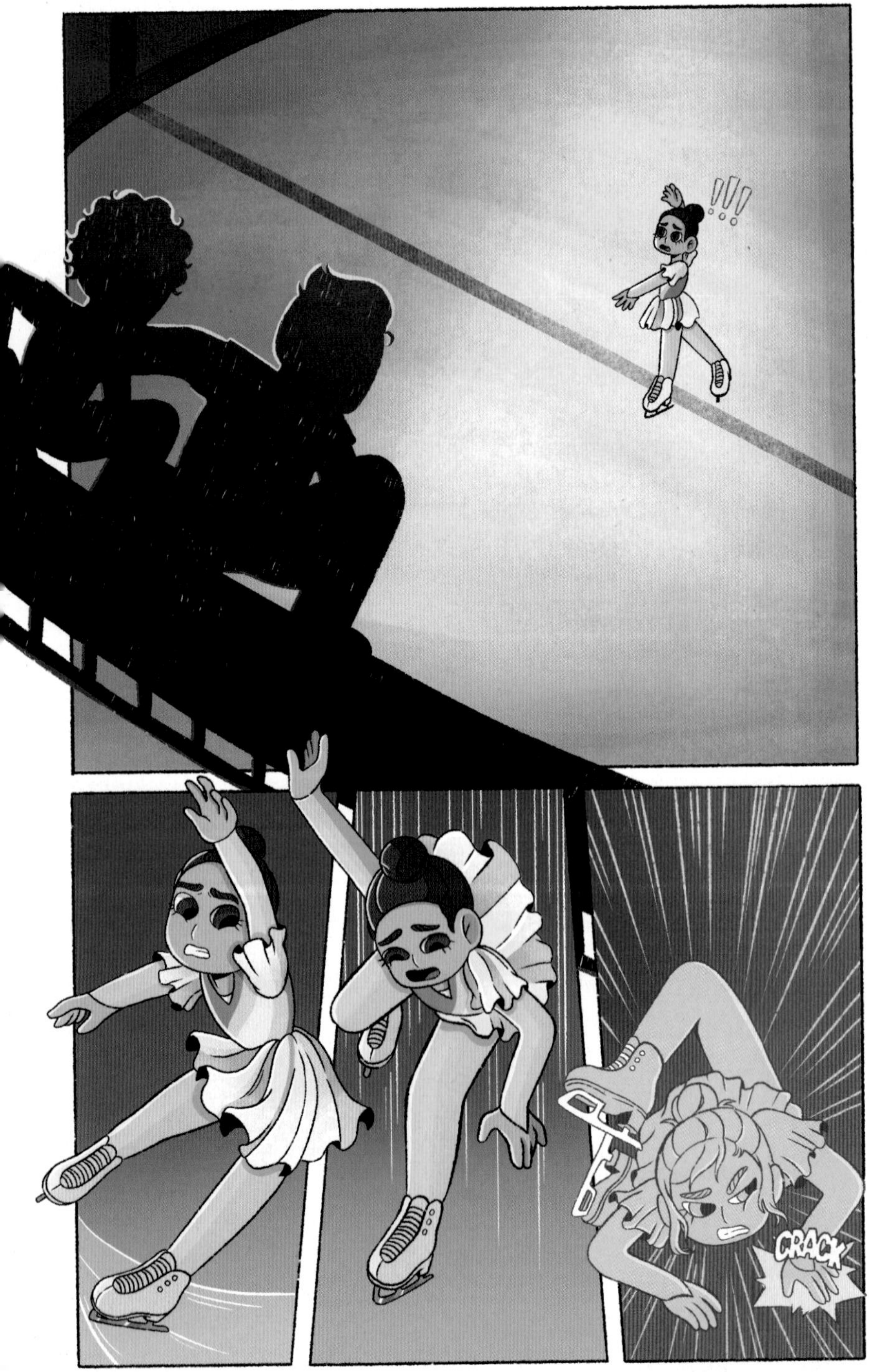
!!!
CRACK

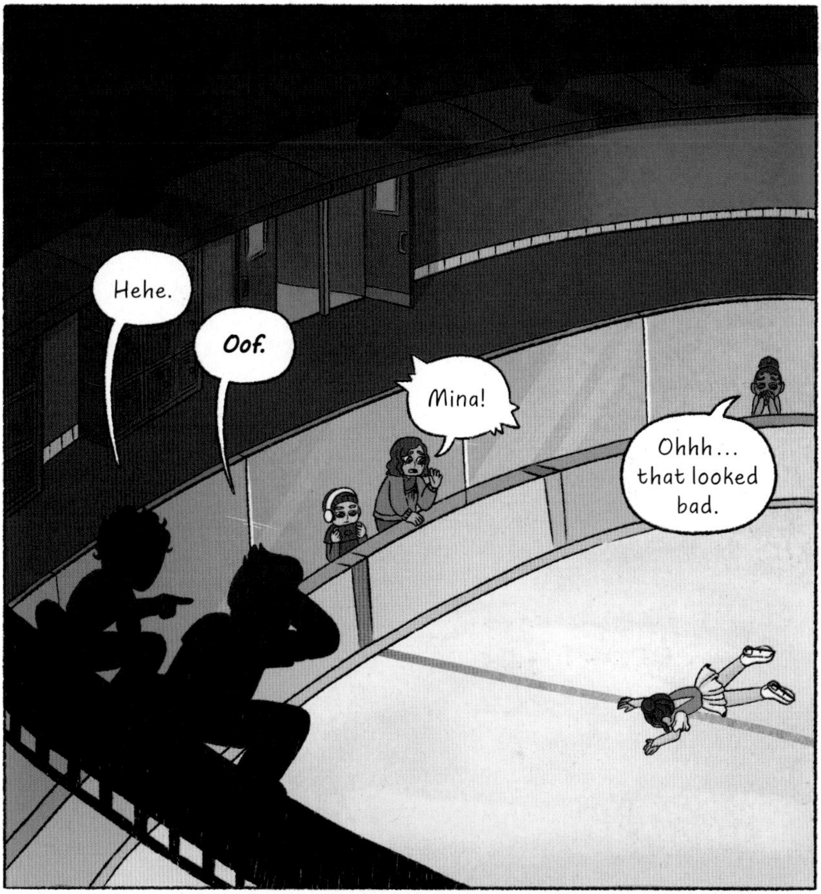
Hehe.
Oof.
Mina!
Ohhh... that looked bad.

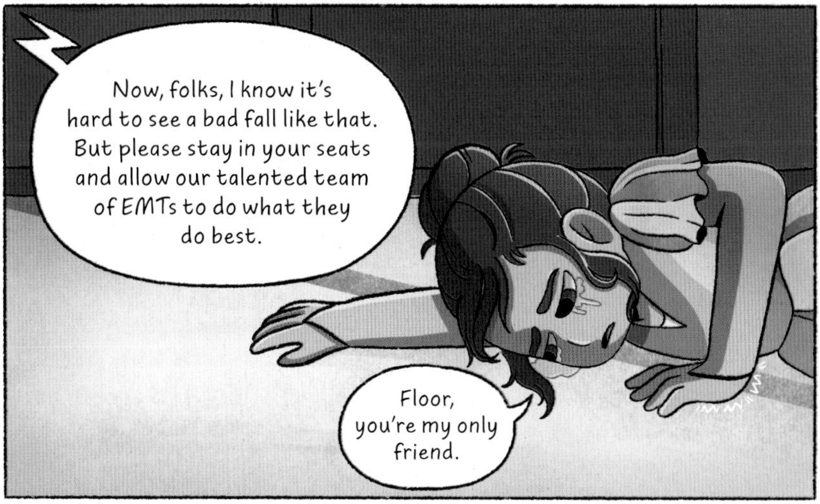
Now, folks, I know it's hard to see a bad fall like that. But please stay in your seats and allow our talented team of EMTs to do what they do best.
Floor, you're my only friend.

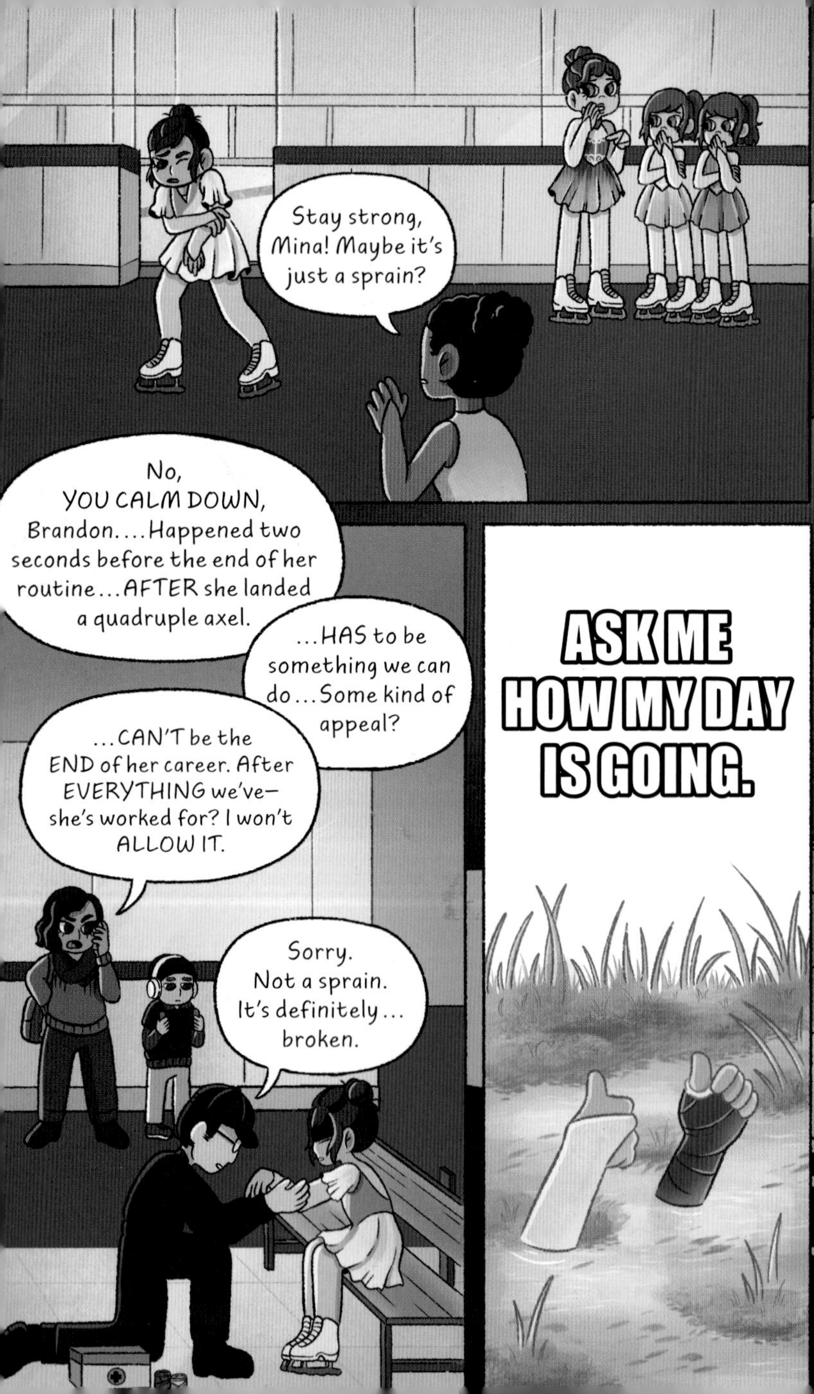
Stay strong, Mina! Maybe it's just a sprain?
No, YOU CALM DOWN, Brandon. . . . Happened two seconds before the end of her routine . . . AFTER she landed a quadruple axel.
. . . HAS to be something we can do . . . Some kind of appeal?
. . . CAN'T be the END of her career. After EVERYTHING we've— she's worked for? I won't ALLOW IT.
Sorry. Not a sprain. It's definitely . . . broken.
ASK ME HOW MY DAY IS GOING.

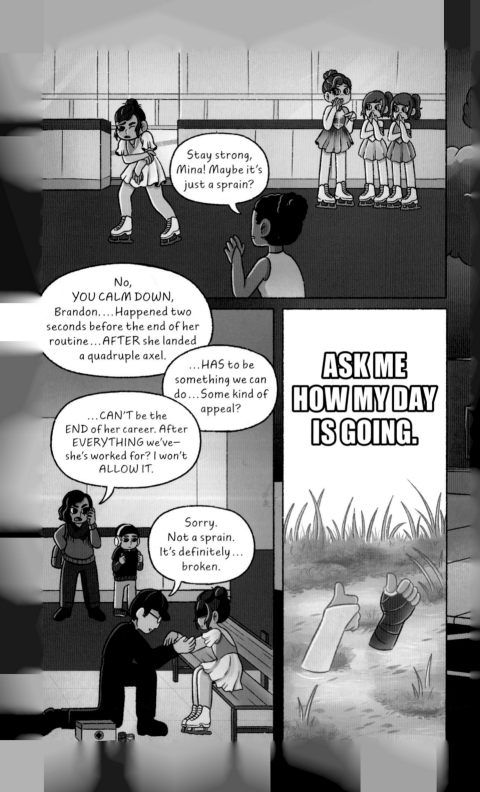

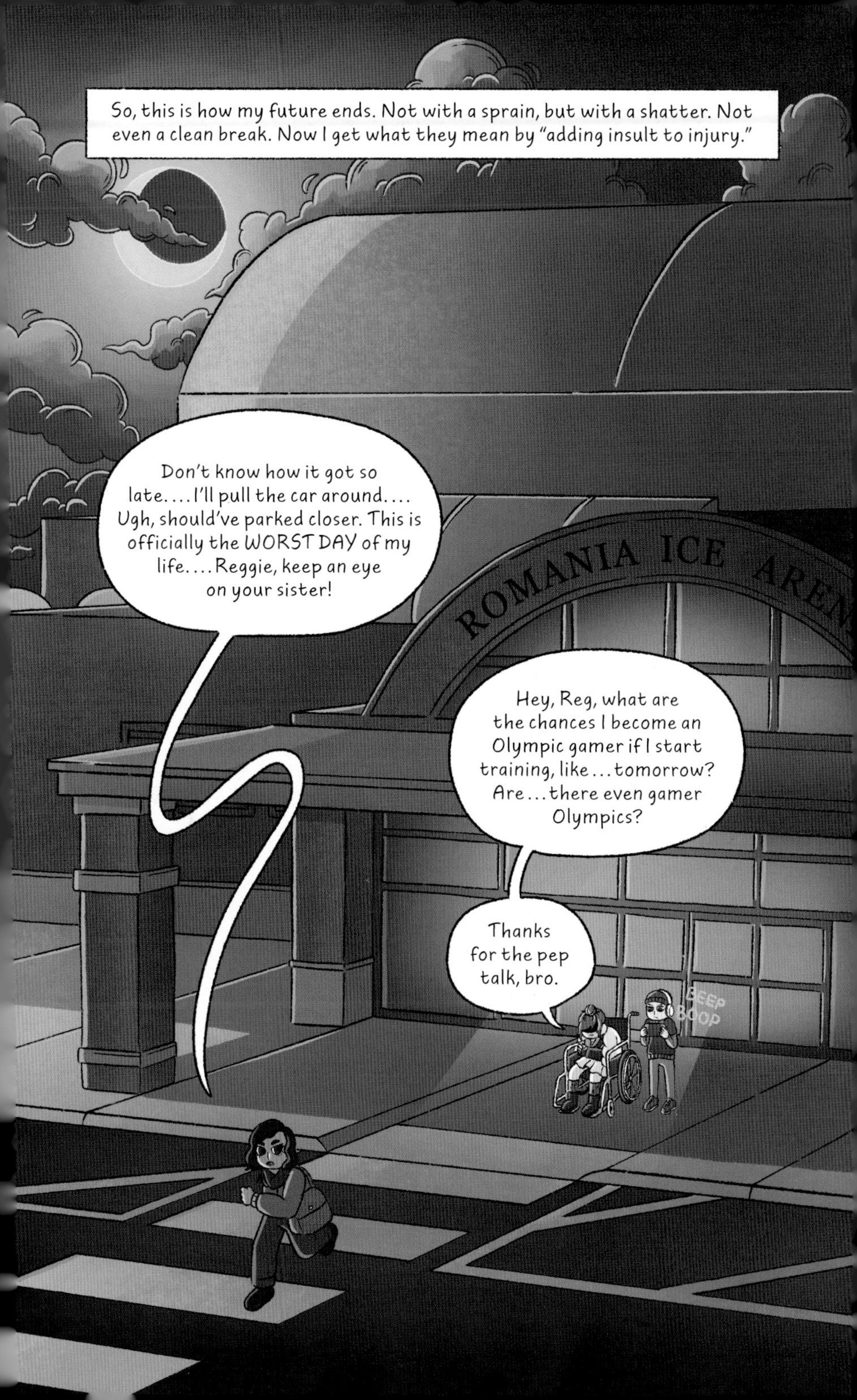
So, this is how my future ends. Not with a sprain, but with a shatter. Not even a clean break. Now I get what they mean by "adding insult to injury."
Don't know how it got so late. . . . I'll pull the car around. . . . Ugh, should've parked closer. This is officially the WORST DAY of my life. . . . Reggie, keep an eye on your sister!
ROMANIA ICE AREN
Hey, Reg, what are the chances I become an Olympic gamer if I start training, like . . . tomorrow? Are . . . there even gamer Olympics?
BEEP BOOP
Thanks for the pep talk, bro.

SIGH. Ten years of my life, and all I have to show for it is this... plastic trophy. It's not even real metal, let alone gold. #Fail.

At least you tried? JK, LOL, nobody cares.

MinaVision™

PARTICIPANT

Sniff. Wait. What the—?

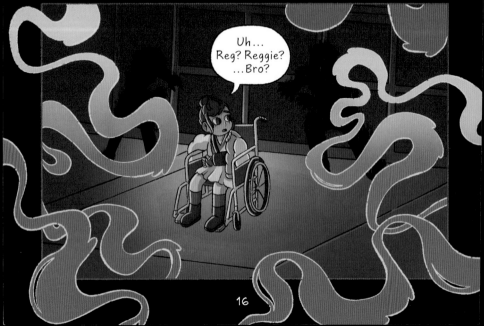

Uh... Reg? Reggie? ...Bro?

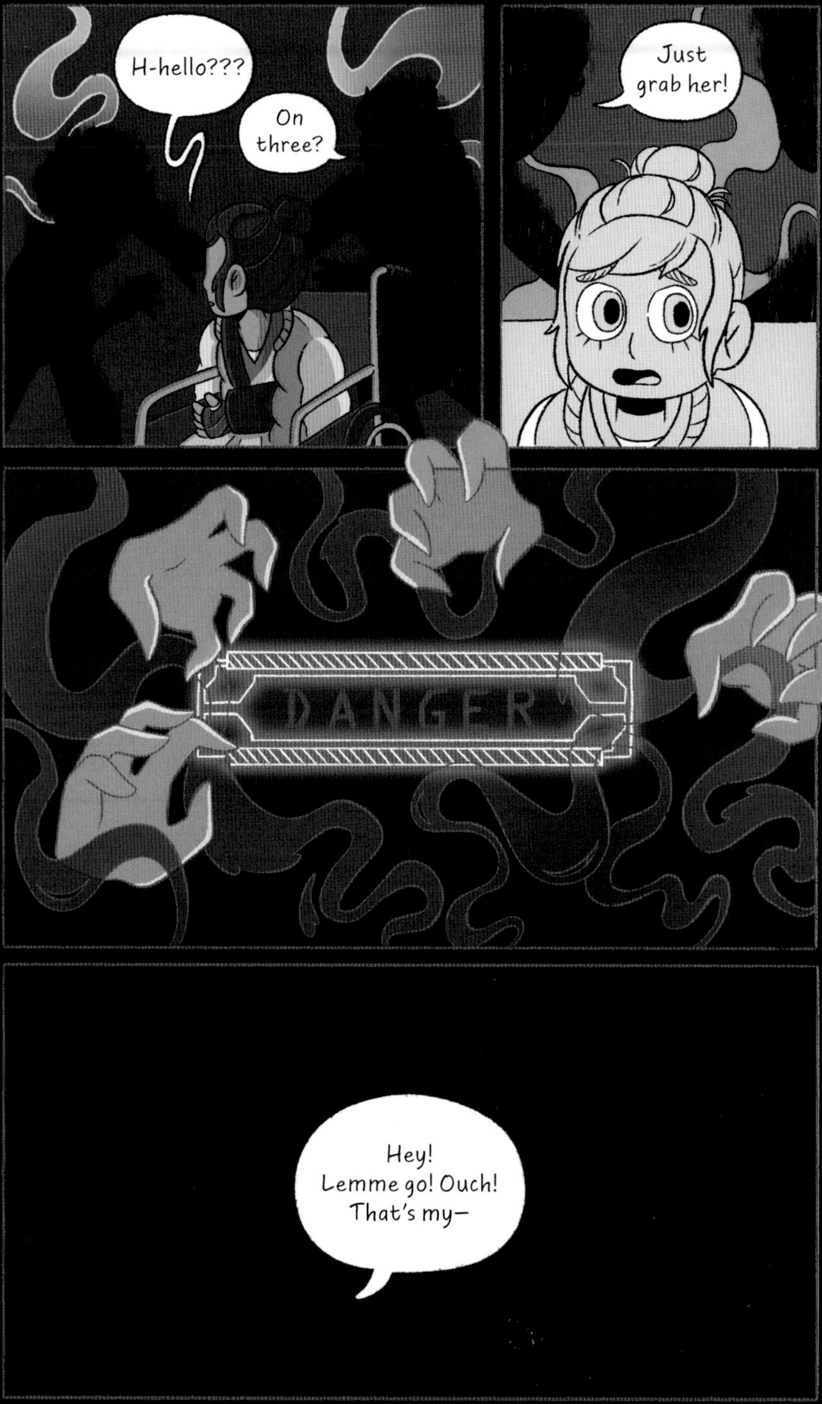
H-hello???
On three?
Just grab her!
DANGER
Hey!
Lemme go! Ouch!
That's my—

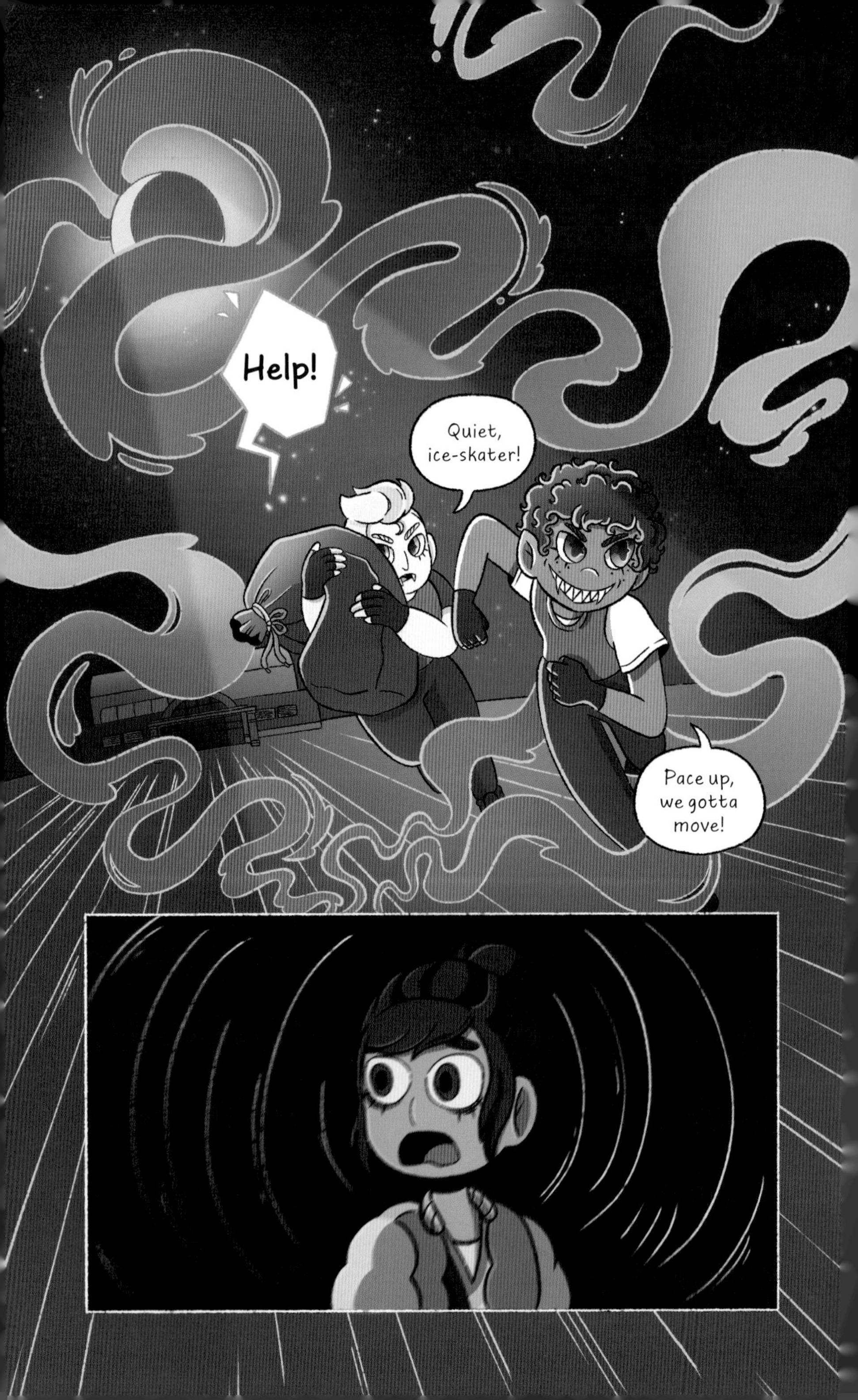
Help!
Quiet, ice-skater!
Pace up, we gotta move!

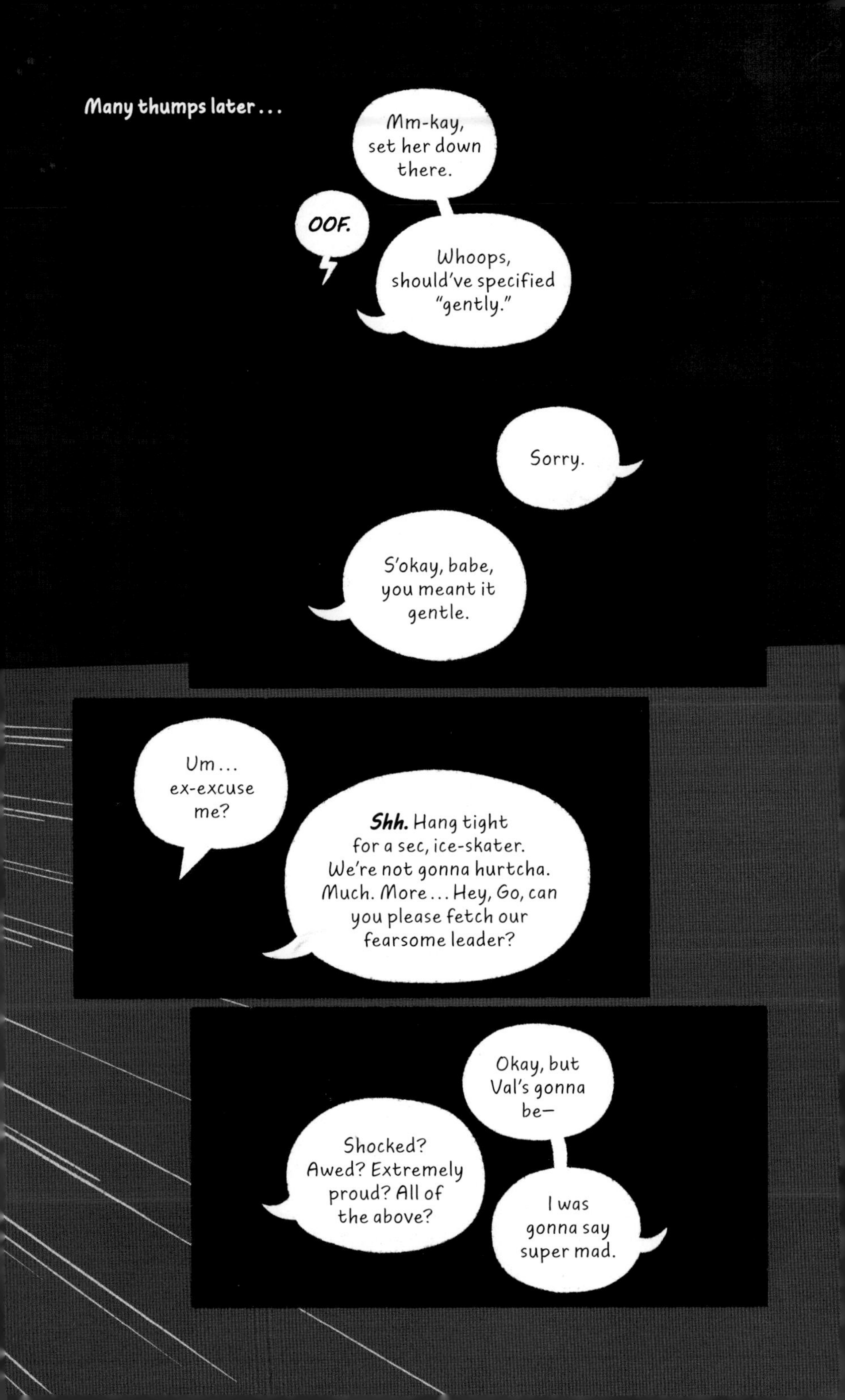
Many thumps later . . .
Mm-kay, set her down there.
OOF.
Whoops, should've specified "gently."
Sorry.
S'okay, babe, you meant it gentle.
Um . . . ex-excuse me?
Shh. Hang tight for a sec, ice-skater. We're not gonna hurtcha. Much. More . . . Hey, Go, can you please fetch our fearsome leader?
Okay, but Val's gonna be—
Shocked? Awed? Extremely proud? All of the above?
I was gonna say super mad.

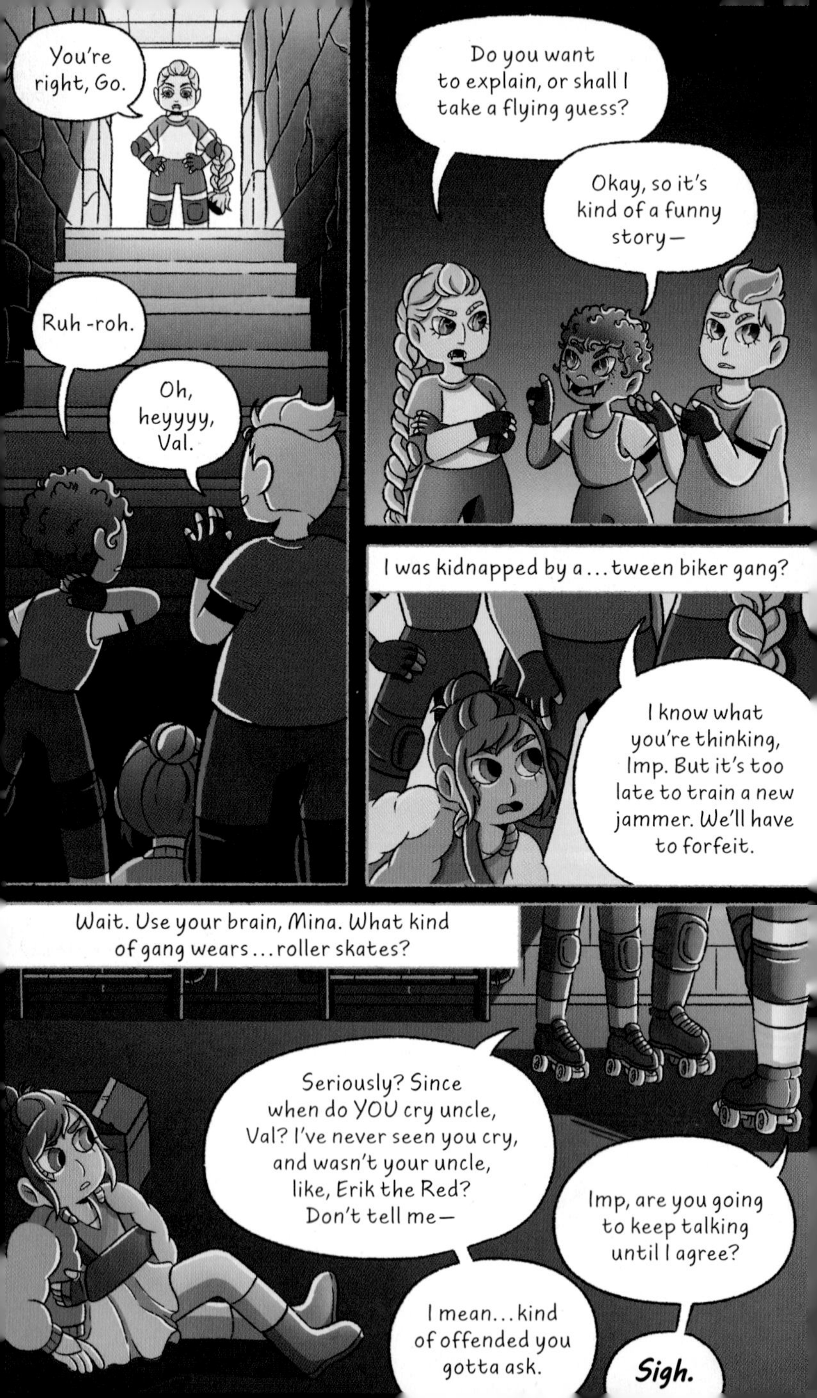

You're right, Go.
Ruh-roh.
Oh, heyyyy, Val.
Do you want to explain, or shall I take a flying guess?
Okay, so it's kind of a funny story—
I was kidnapped by a . . . tween biker gang?
I know what you're thinking, Imp. But it's too late to train a new jammer. We'll have to forfeit.
Wait. Use your brain, Mina. What kind of gang wears . . . roller skates?
Seriously? Since when do YOU cry uncle, Val? I've never seen you cry, and wasn't your uncle, like, Erik the Red? Don't tell me—
I mean . . . kind of offended you gotta ask.
Imp, are you going to keep talking until I agree?
Sigh.

Fine. Let's give her a taste. See how she does.

!!!

Uh, I'm sorry? Taste...of... what?

We saw her skate. She's the one. I promise.

What is your name, kid?

M—Mina. Mina Murray. ...N—not a kid.

I'm thirteen?

Yeah, but she's been training for the Olympics since she was three.

It's true. We heard her mom yelling that on the phone, a bunch of times.

It seems there is NO ESCAPE...from Mom's Olympic Goals, at least.

All right, Mina. So. The first rule is: There's NO sorry in roller derby.

Sorry? I mean . . . sor—there's no . . . in WHAT NOW?

$iG^{\mu\nu}(\rho) = \frac{1}{1-J_2}\left\{\frac{\overline{m}+\rho}{m^2-\rho^2}\left(P^{3/2}\right)\right.$

$\sqrt{3}\sin^2 O_{x^2}$

$\sqrt{2}\left(\cos\frac{6\pi}{4}\right)$

$\cos\frac{\pi}{2} + \frac{3\pi}{2}$

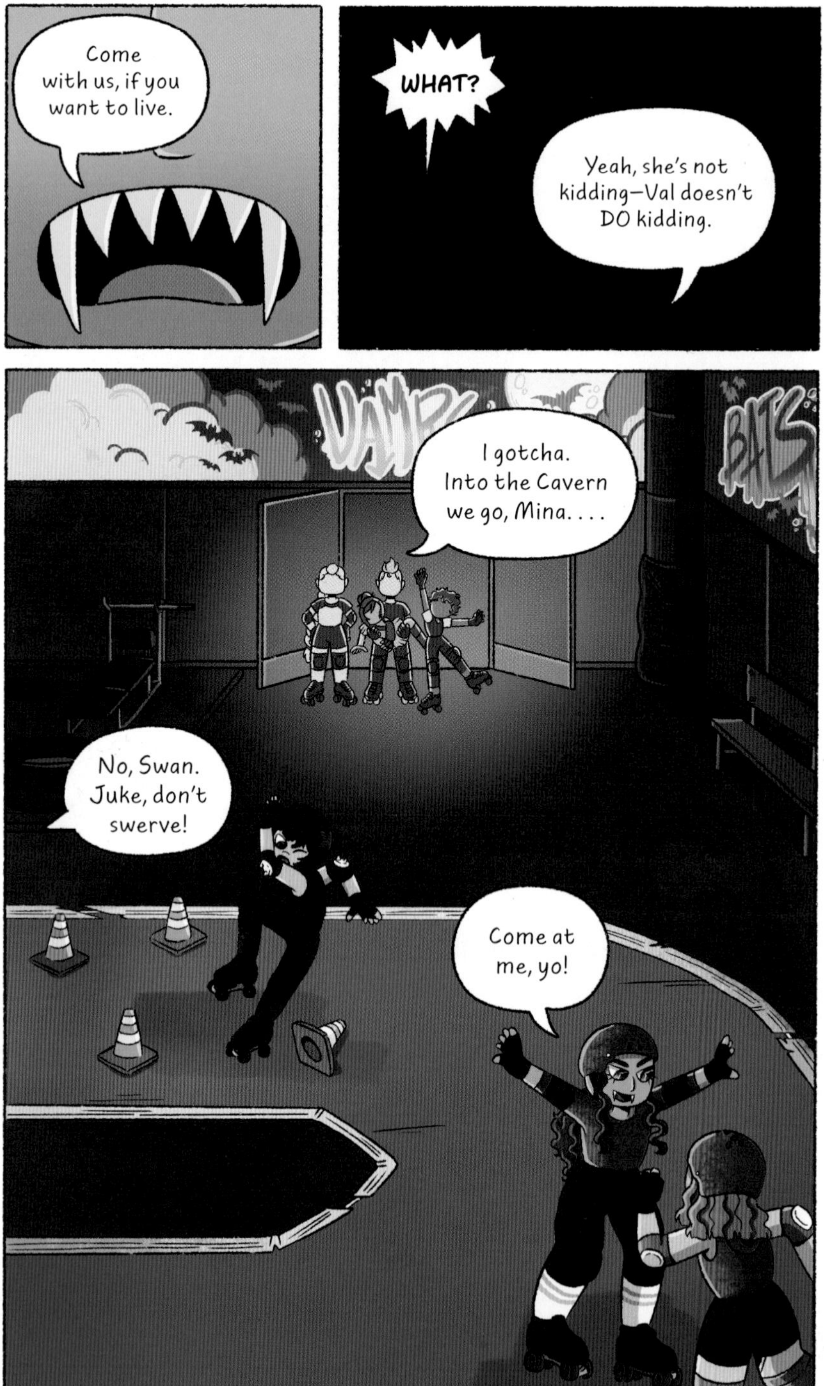
Come with us, if you want to live.
WHAT?
Yeah, she's not kidding—Val doesn't DO kidding.
VAMP
BATS
I gotcha. Into the Cavern we go, Mina. . . .
No, Swan. Juke, don't swerve!
Come at me, yo!

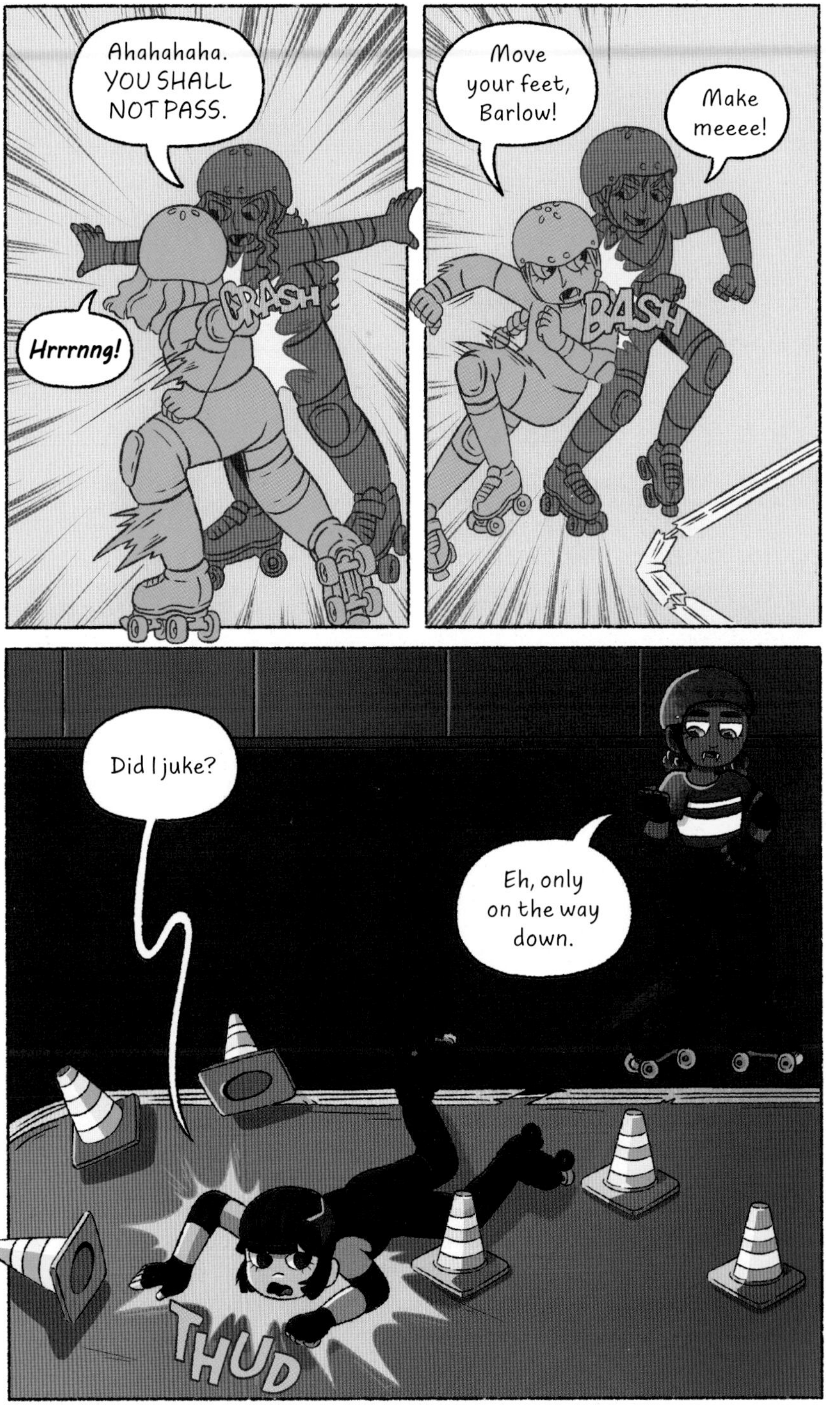
Ahahahaha. YOU SHALL NOT PASS.
Hrrrnng!
CRASH
Move your feet, Barlow!
Make meeee!
BASH
Did I juke?
Eh, only on the way down.
THUD

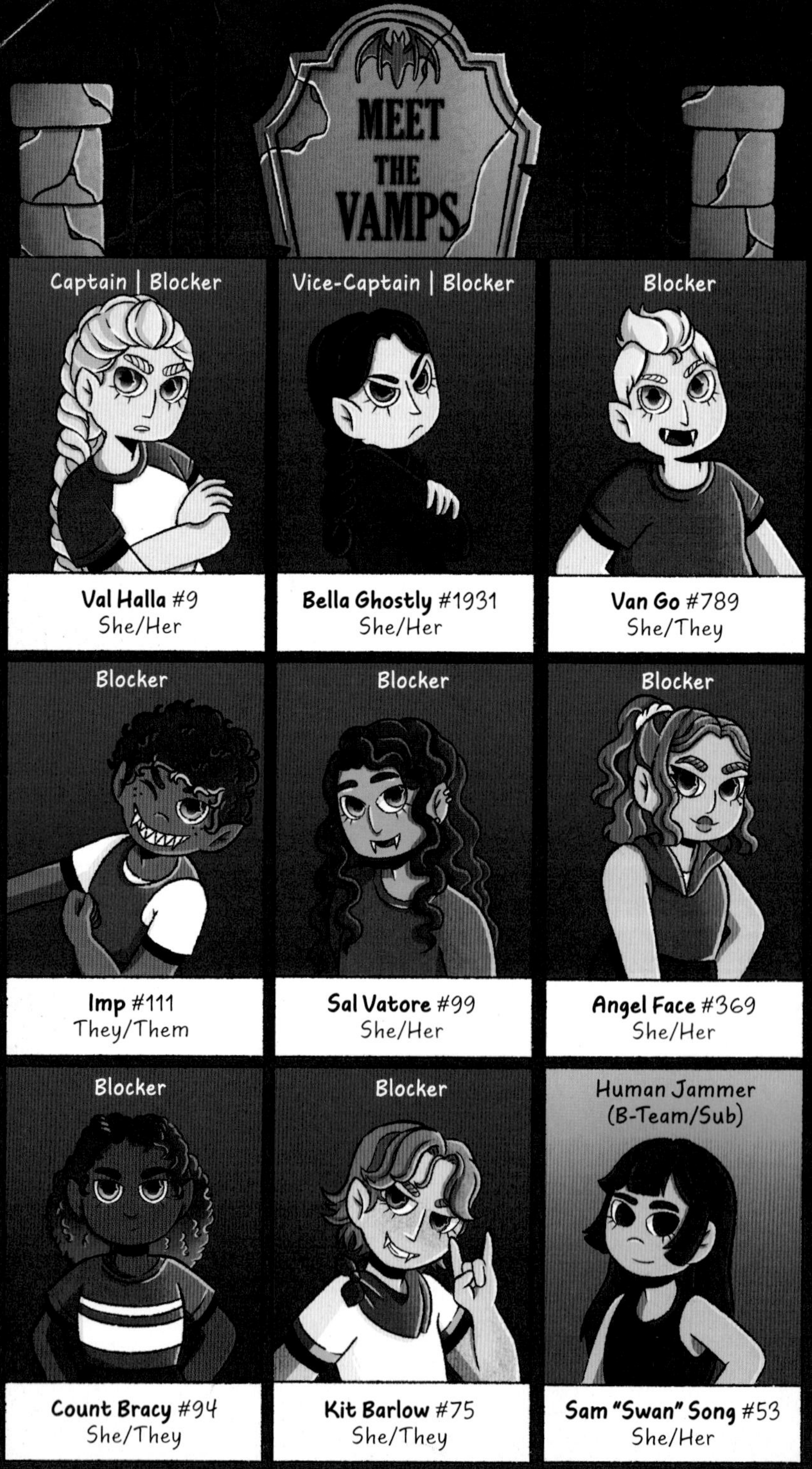
MEET THE VAMPS
Captain | Blocker
Val Halla #9
She/Her
Vice-Captain | Blocker
Bella Ghostly #1931
She/Her
Blocker
Van Go #789
She/They
Blocker
Imp #111
They/Them
Blocker
Sal Vatore #99
She/Her
Blocker
Angel Face #369
She/Her
Blocker
Count Bracy #94
She/They
Blocker
Kit Barlow #75
She/They
Human Jammer
(B-Team/Sub)
Sam "Swan" Song #53
She/Her

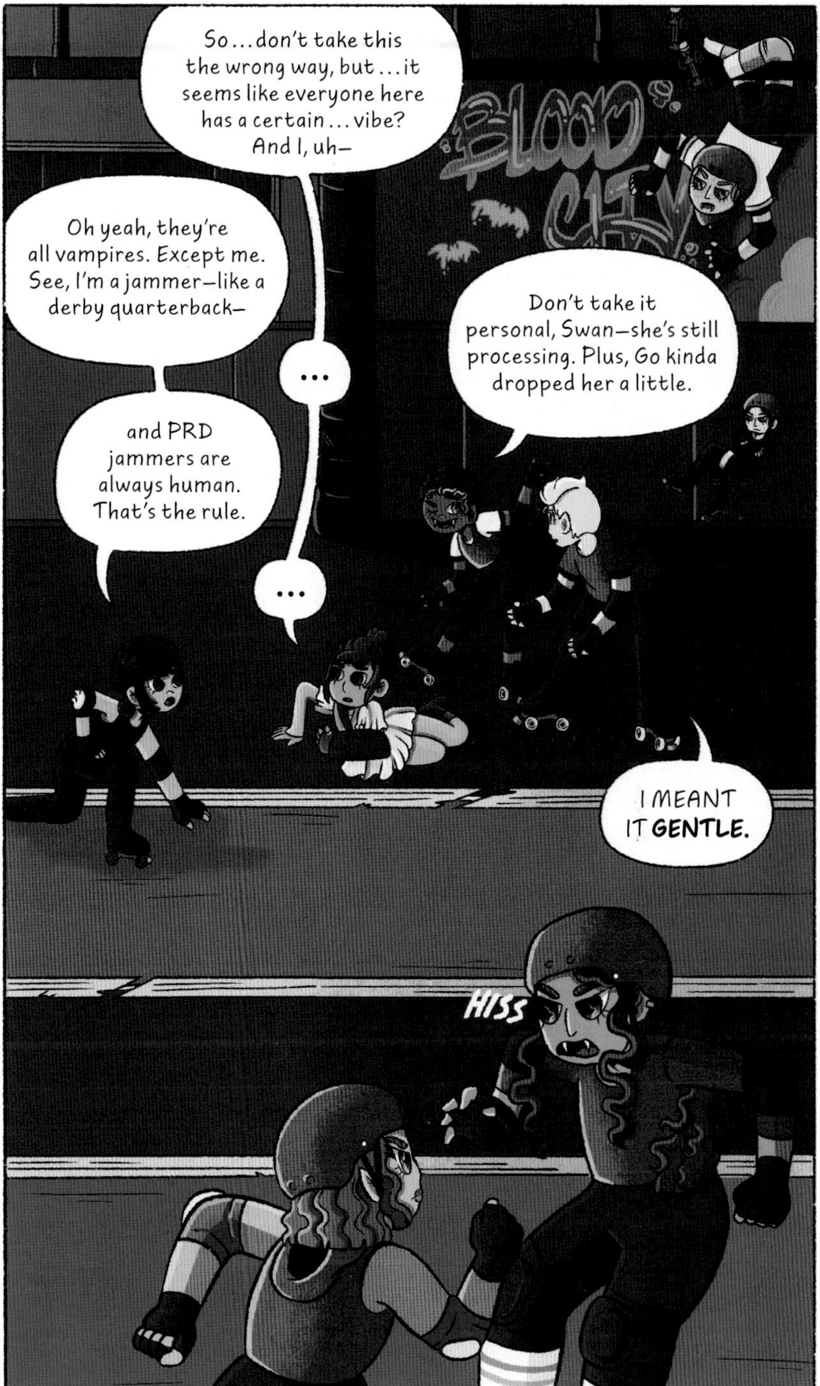

So...don't take this the wrong way, but...it seems like everyone here has a certain...vibe? And I, uh–
Oh yeah, they're all vampires. Except me. See, I'm a jammer–like a derby quarterback–
...
and PRD jammers are always human. That's the rule.
...
Don't take it personal, Swan–she's still processing. Plus, Go kinda dropped her a little.
I MEANT IT **GENTLE.**
HISS

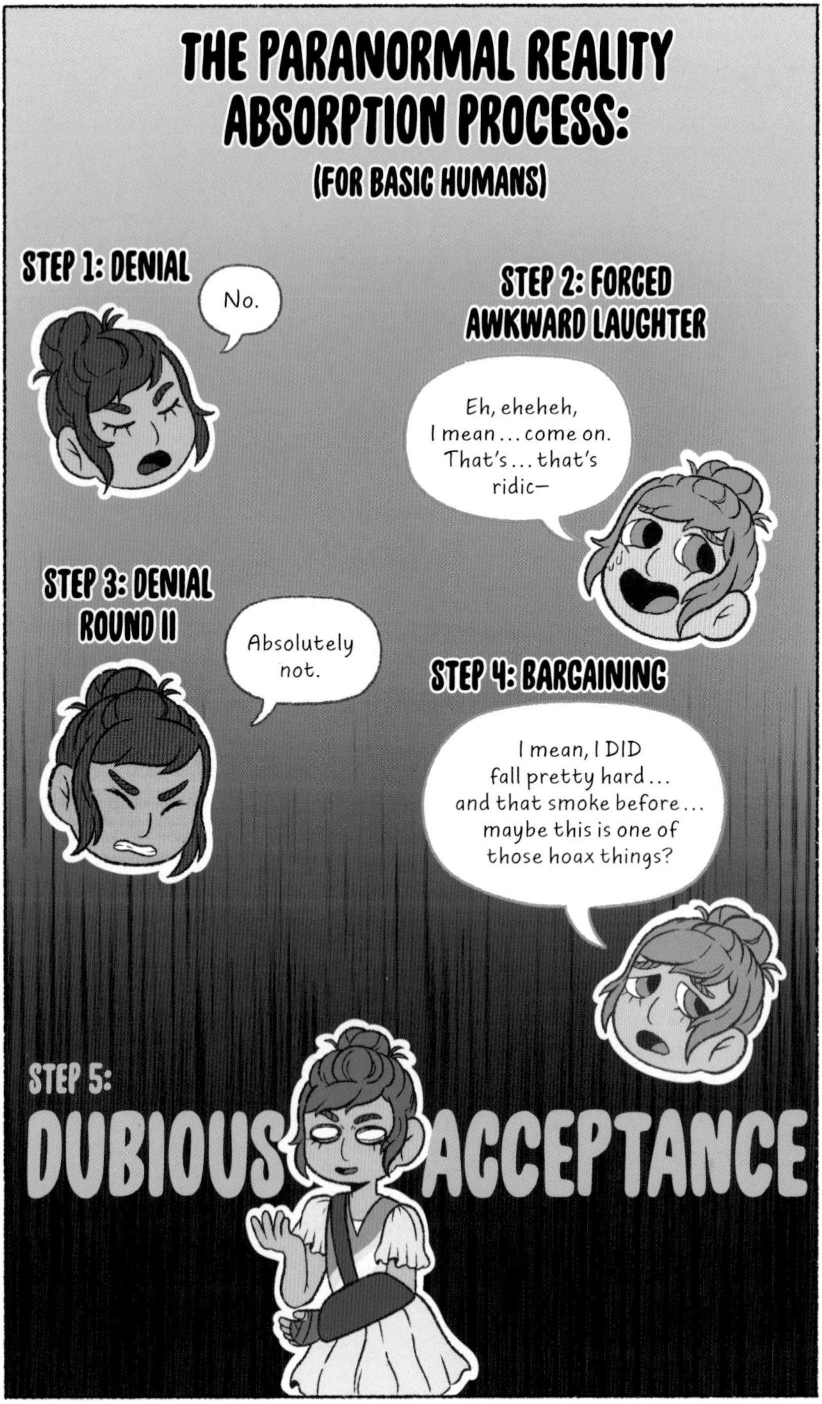
THE PARANORMAL REALITY ABSORPTION PROCESS:
(FOR BASIC HUMANS)
STEP 1: DENIAL
No.
STEP 2: FORCED AWKWARD LAUGHTER
Eh, eheheh, I mean... come on. That's... that's ridic—
STEP 3: DENIAL ROUND II
Absolutely not.
STEP 4: BARGAINING
I mean, I DID fall pretty hard... and that smoke before... maybe this is one of those hoax things?
STEP 5:
DUBIOUS ACCEPTANCE

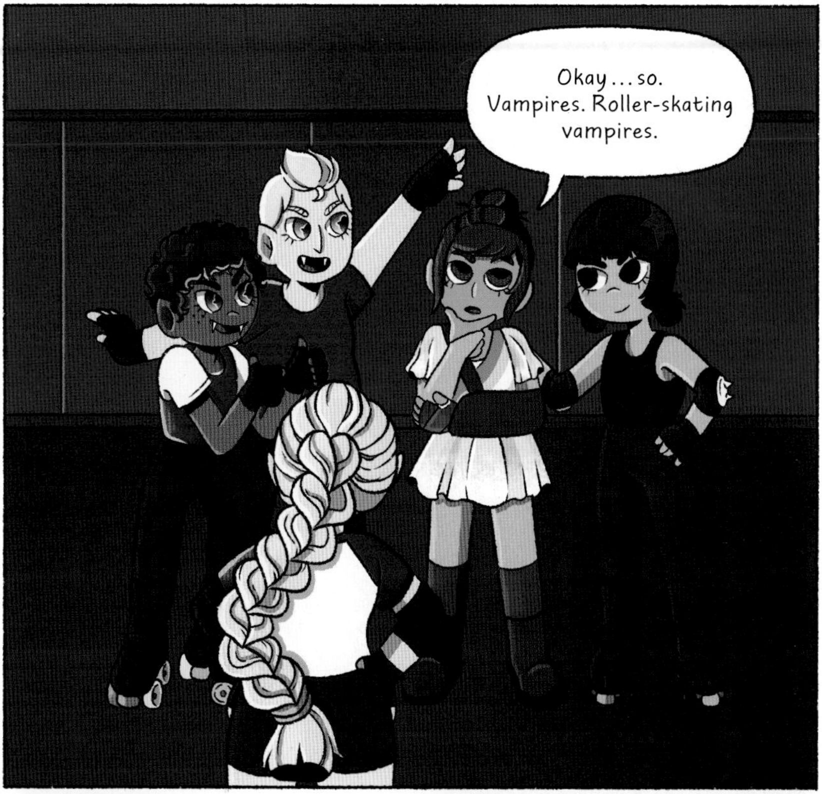
Okay ... so.
Vampires. Roller-skating vampires.

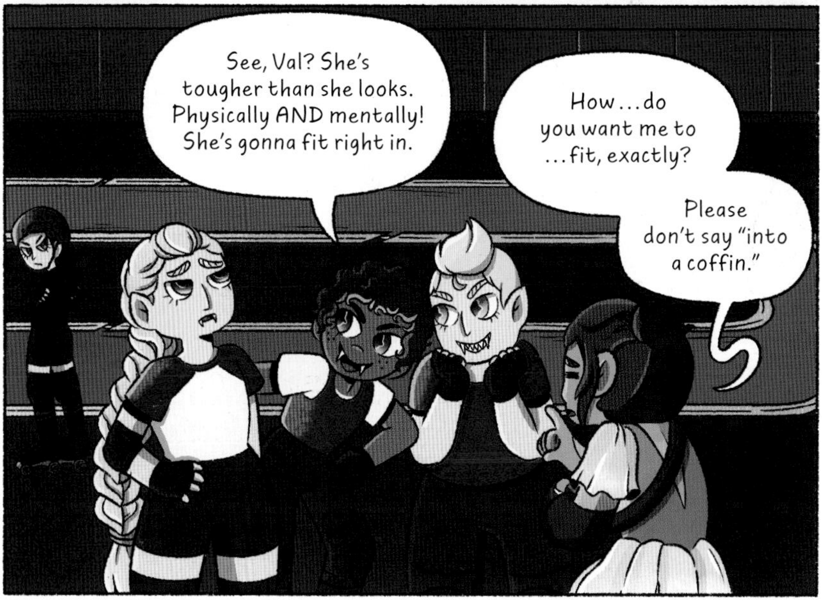
See, Val? She's tougher than she looks. Physically AND mentally! She's gonna fit right in.
How...do you want me to ...fit, exactly?
Please don't say "into a coffin."

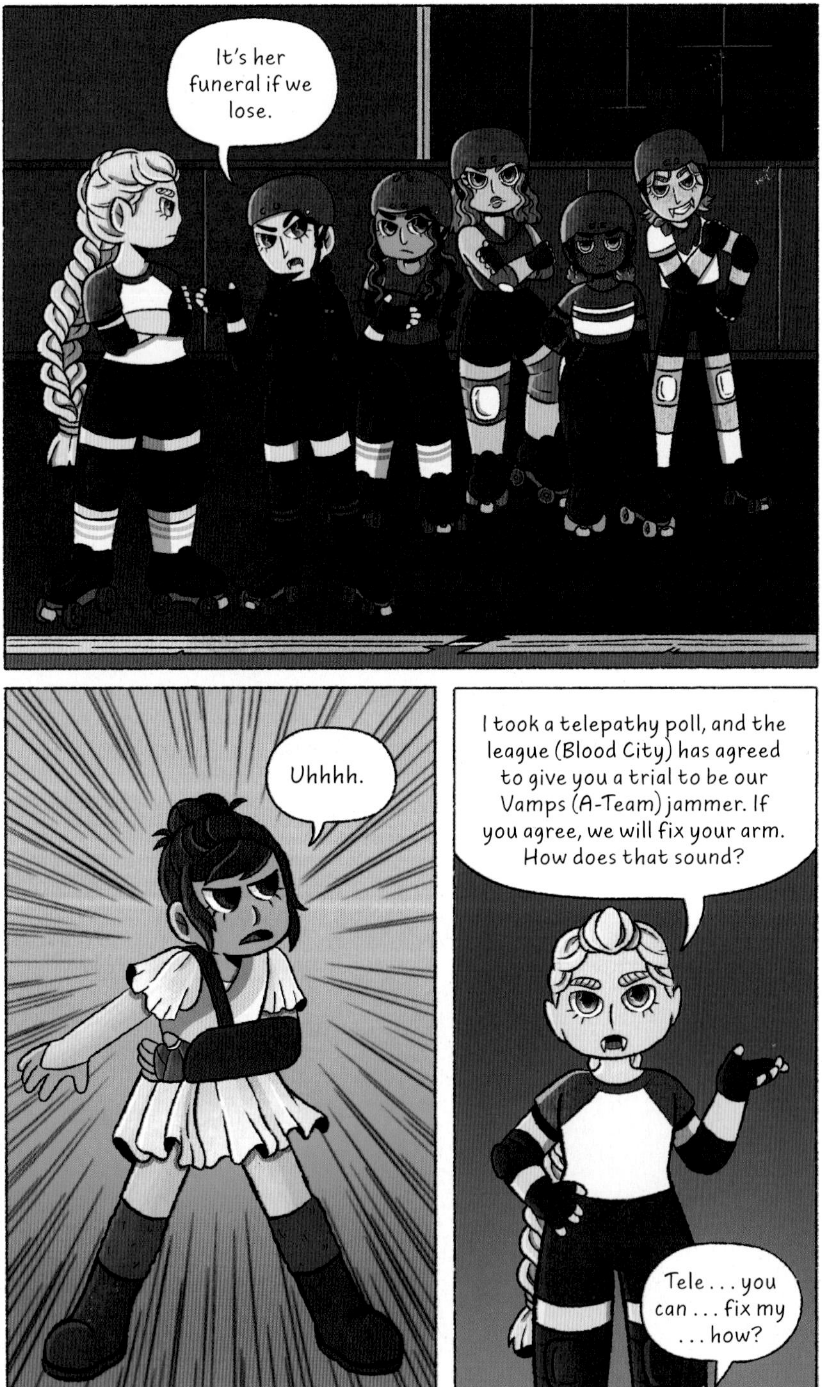
It's her funeral if we lose.
Uhhhh.
I took a telepathy poll, and the league (Blood City) has agreed to give you a trial to be our Vamps (A-Team) jammer. If you agree, we will fix your arm. How does that sound?
Tele . . . you can . . . fix my . . . how?

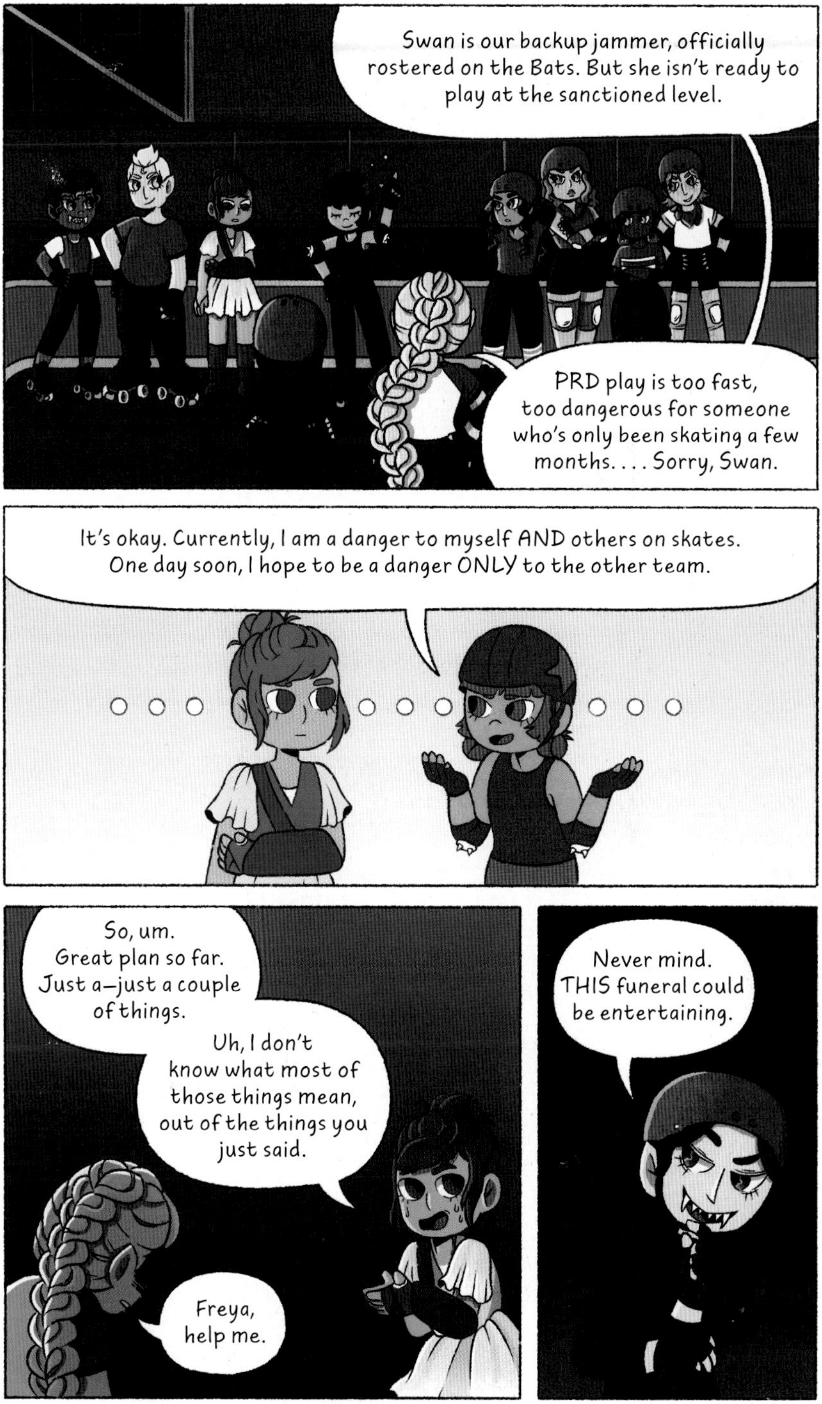
Swan is our backup jammer, officially rostered on the Bats. But she isn't ready to play at the sanctioned level.
PRD play is too fast, too dangerous for someone who's only been skating a few months. . . . Sorry, Swan.
It's okay. Currently, I am a danger to myself AND others on skates. One day soon, I hope to be a danger ONLY to the other team.
So, um. Great plan so far. Just a—just a couple of things.
Uh, I don't know what most of those things mean, out of the things you just said.
Freya, help me.
Never mind. THIS funeral could be entertaining.

'ay attention,
ecause I don't
njoy repeating
myself.

PARANORMAL ROLLER DERBY (PRD)

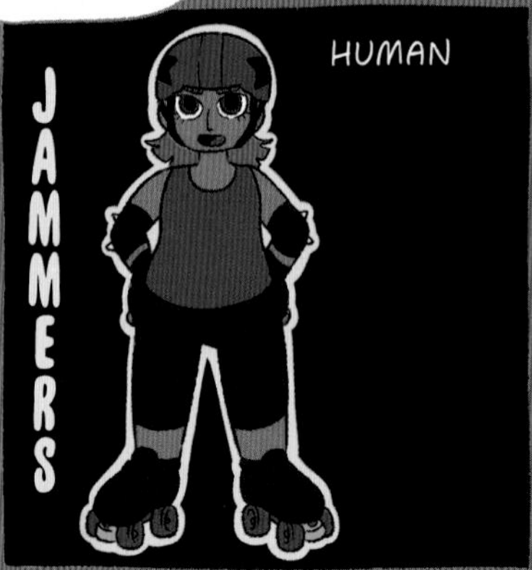
JAMMERS
HUMAN

Each PRD-sanctioned team is required to have ONE human jammer. Jammers rely on their extra-human teammates to help them score points . . . and survive the bout intact.

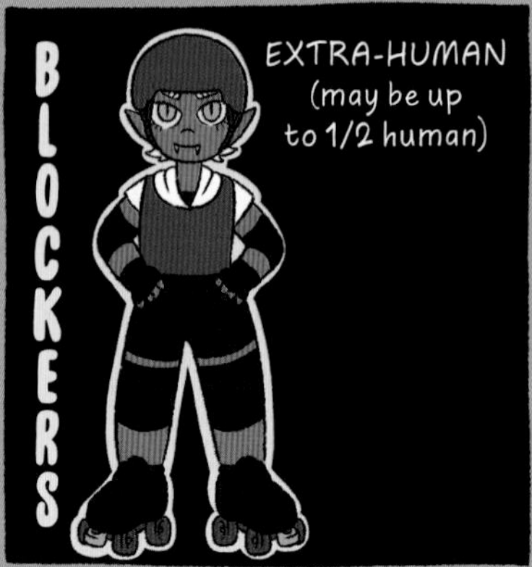
BLOCKERS
EXTRA-HUMAN
(may be up
to 1/2 human)

Each team has two blocking "lines" (four blockers = one line). Blockers play in "packs" to move their jammer around the track while also blocking the opposing jammer from scoring.

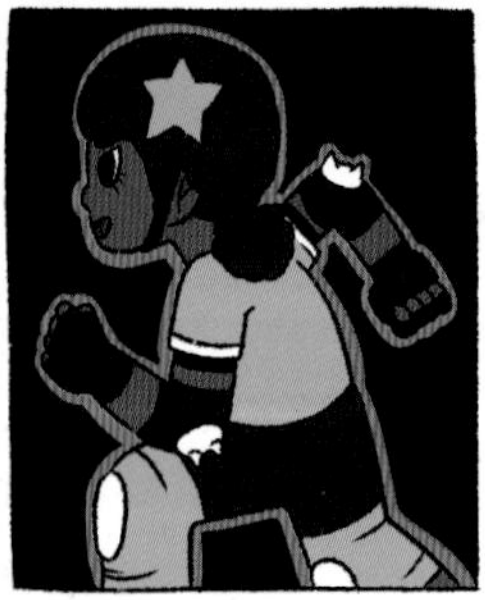

90 SECONDS

SCORING

Sanctioned PRD games ("bouts") are played in ninety-second heats ("jams"). For every opposing player a jammer passes in the pack, that jammer scores one point per lap. Pass an oppo blocker, get a point. Don't die in the process.
Easy enough, right?

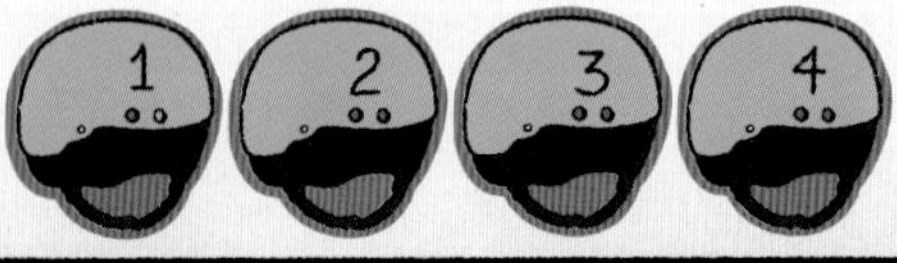
1
2
3
4

THE TRACK

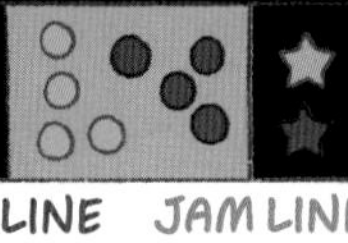
LIMIT LINE
JAM LINE

The track is where the magic (and the mayhem) happens. Blockers start in the "engagement zone" (EZ) and then pursue jammers around the track. Jammers begin behind the "jam line." Once they enter the EZ, jam is ON.

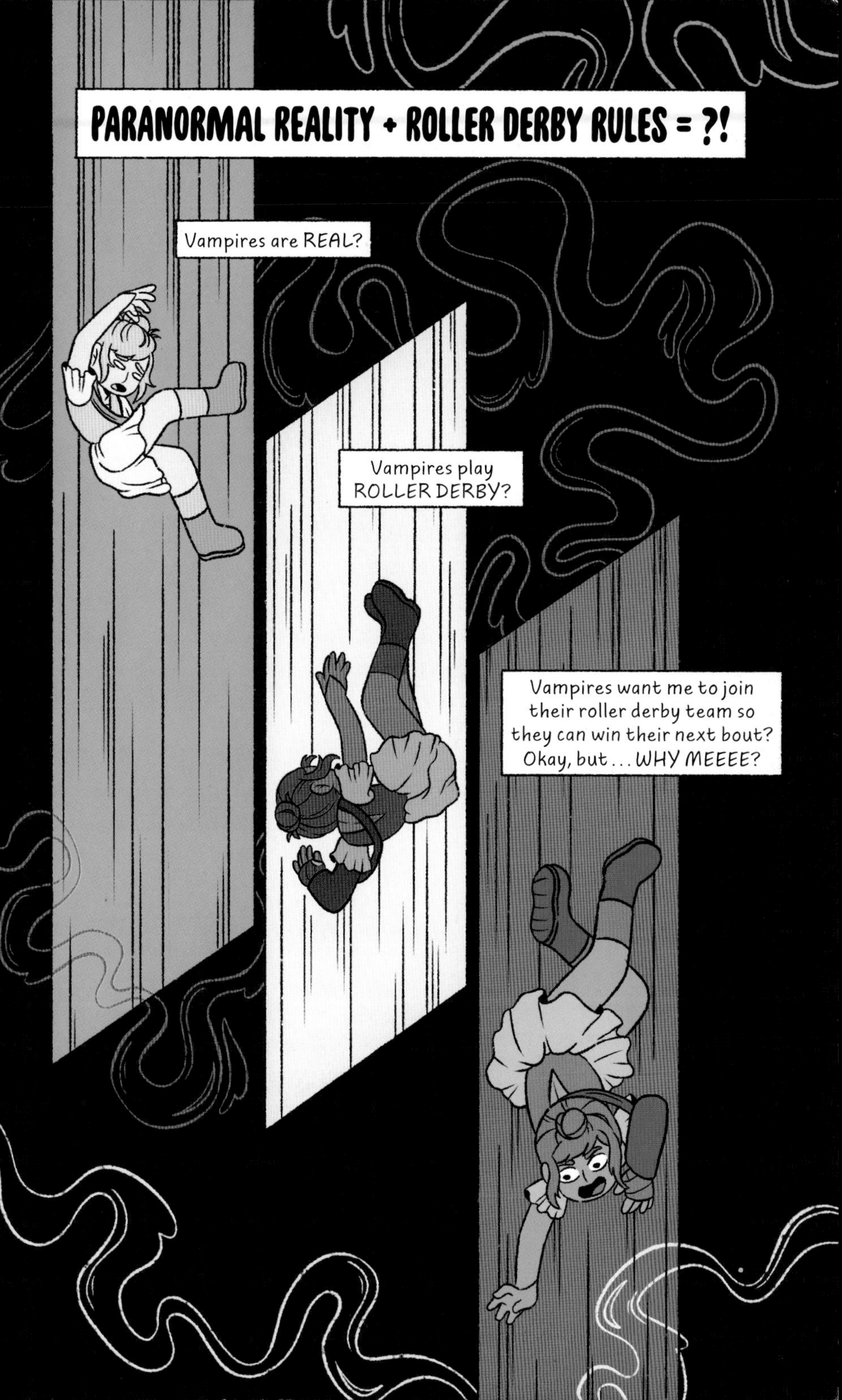
PARANORMAL REALITY + ROLLER DERBY RULES = ?!
Vampires are REAL?
Vampires play ROLLER DERBY?
Vampires want me to join their roller derby team so they can win their next bout? Okay, but . . . WHY MEEEE?

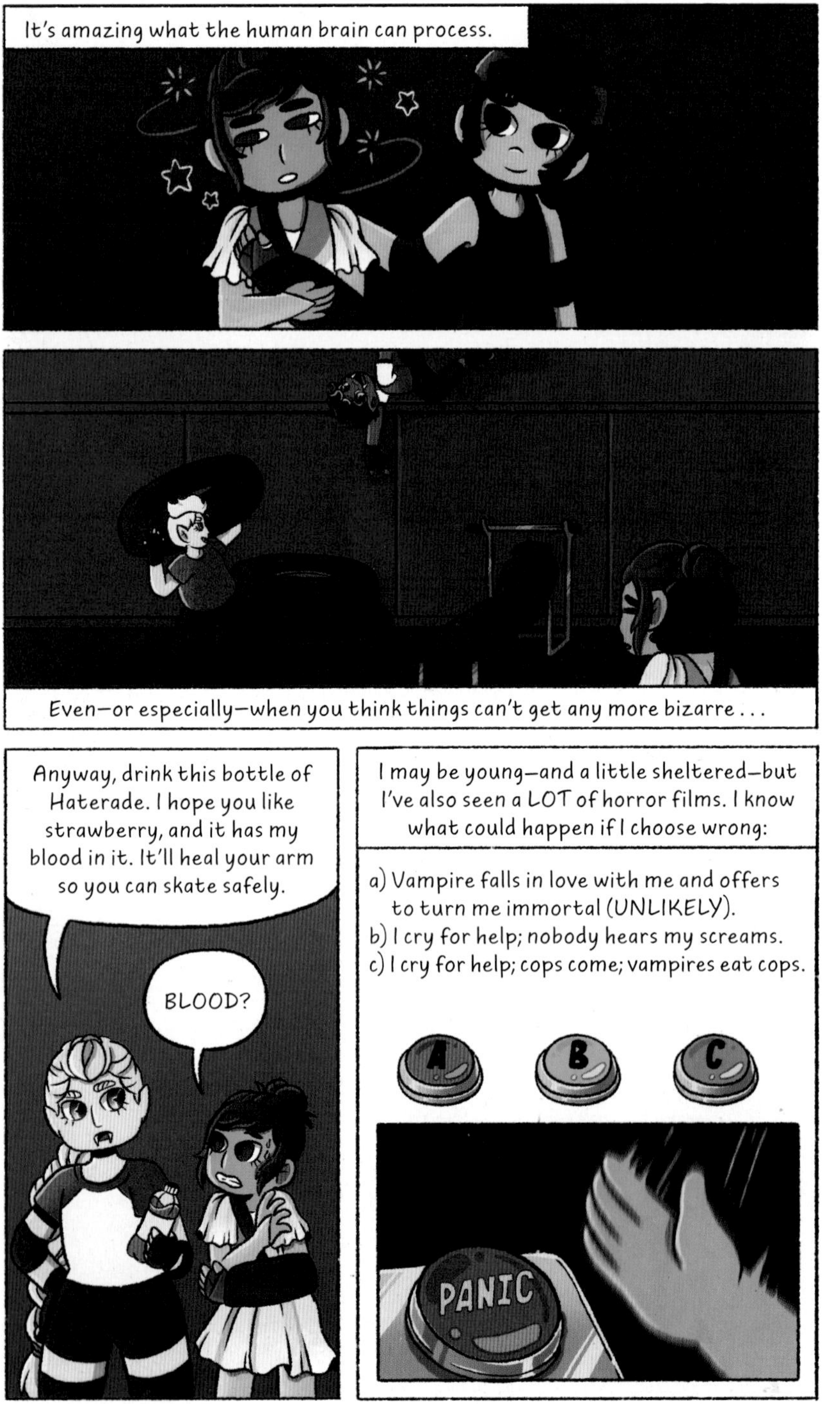
It's amazing what the human brain can process.
Even—or especially—when you think things can't get any more bizarre . . .
Anyway, drink this bottle of Haterade. I hope you like strawberry, and it has my blood in it. It'll heal your arm so you can skate safely.
BLOOD?
I may be young—and a little sheltered—but I've also seen a LOT of horror films. I know what could happen if I choose wrong:
a) Vampire falls in love with me and offers to turn me immortal (UNLIKELY).
b) I cry for help; nobody hears my screams.
c) I cry for help; cops come; vampires eat cops.
A
B
C
PANIC

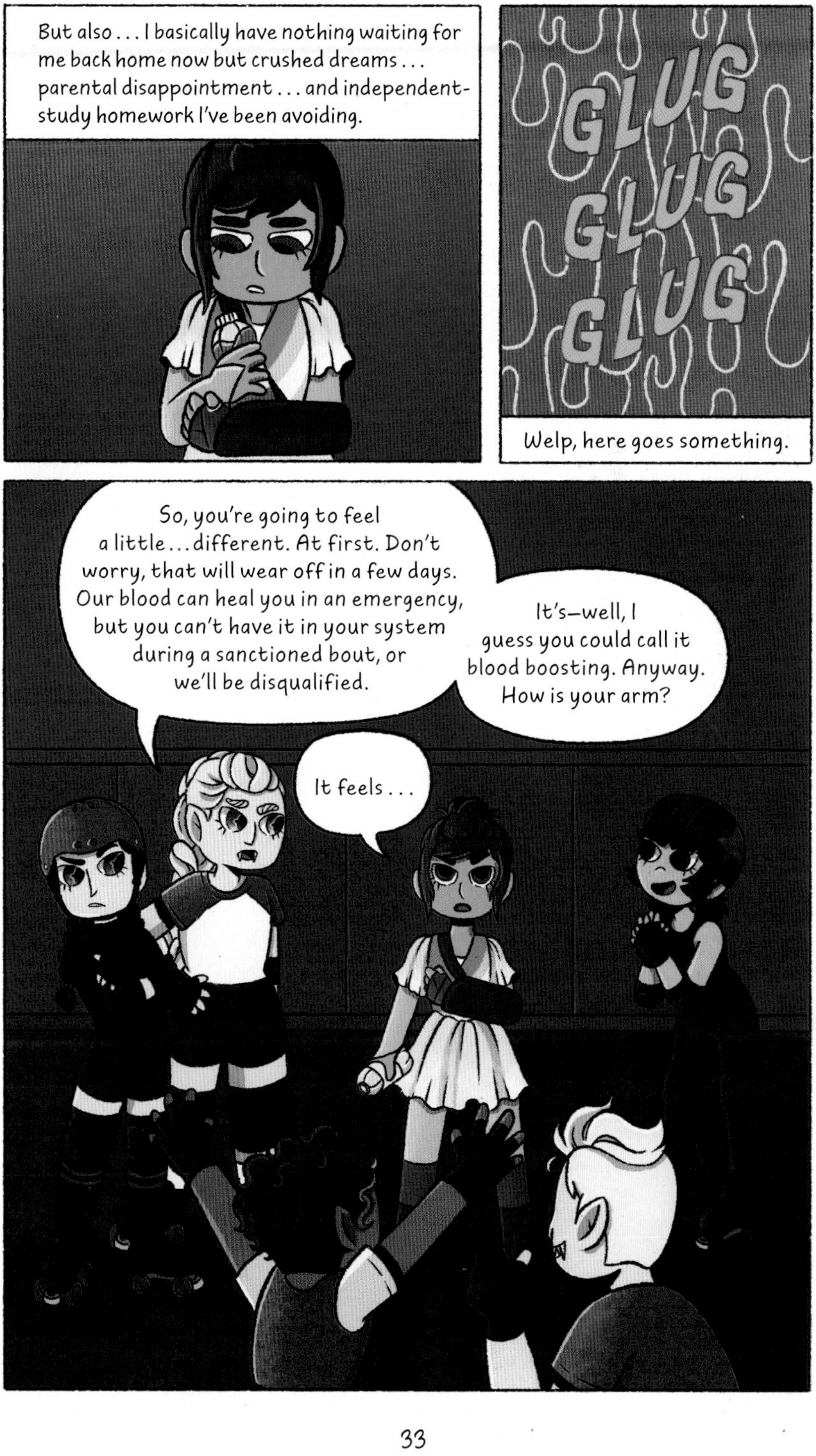
But also . . . I basically have nothing waiting for me back home now but crushed dreams . . . parental disappointment . . . and independent-study homework I've been avoiding.
GLUG
GLUG
GLUG
Welp, here goes something.
So, you're going to feel a little . . . different. At first. Don't worry, that will wear off in a few days. Our blood can heal you in an emergency, but you can't have it in your system during a sanctioned bout, or we'll be disqualified.
It's—well, I guess you could call it blood boosting. Anyway. How is your arm?
It feels . . .

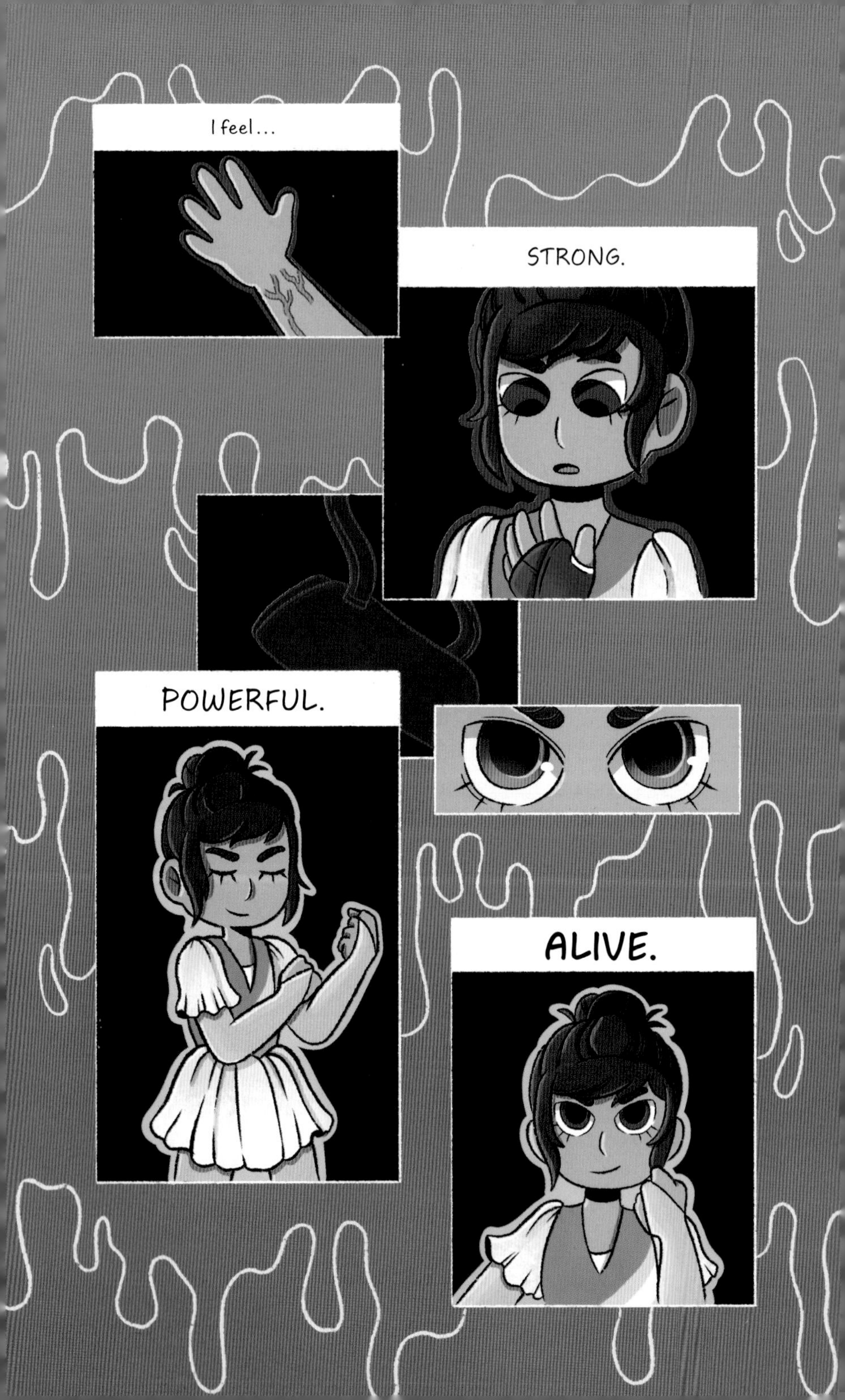
I feel...
STRONG.
POWERFUL.
ALIVE.

JAMMER TRYOUTS

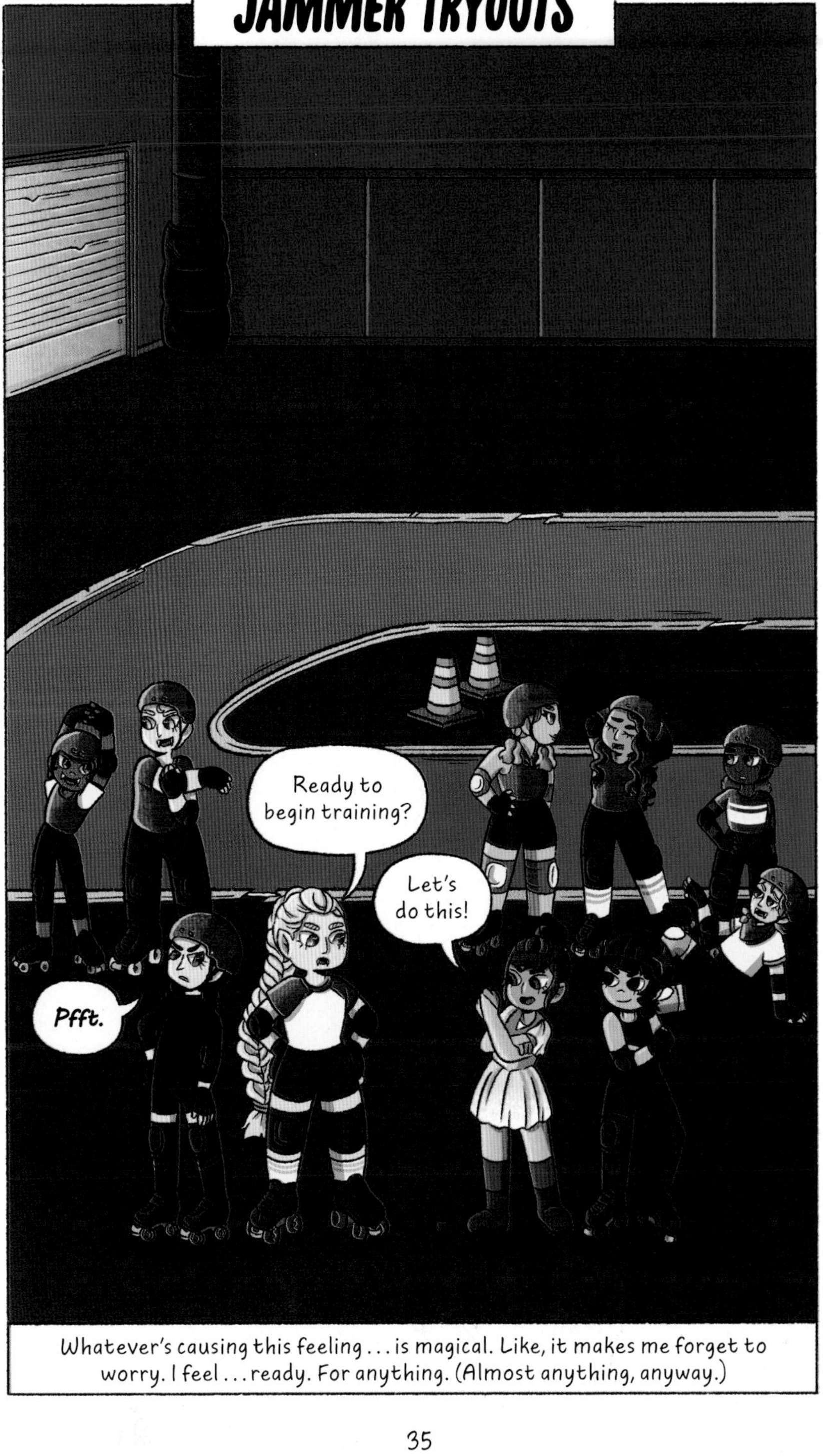

Ready to begin training?
Let's do this!
Pfft.

Whatever's causing this feeling . . . is magical. Like, it makes me forget to worry. I feel . . . ready. For anything. (Almost anything, anyway.)

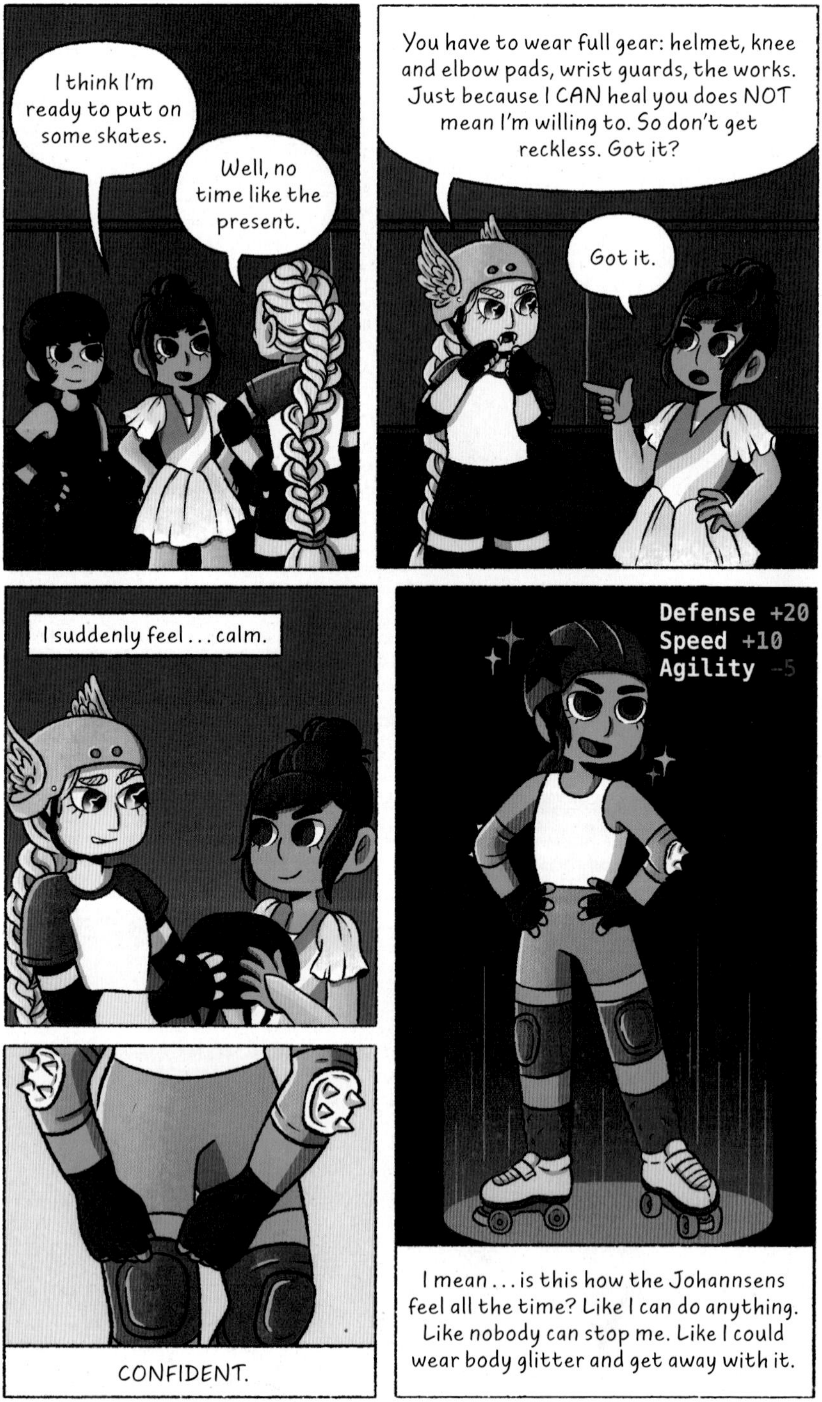
I think I'm ready to put on some skates.
Well, no time like the present.
You have to wear full gear: helmet, knee and elbow pads, wrist guards, the works. Just because I CAN heal you does NOT mean I'm willing to. So don't get reckless. Got it?
Got it.
I suddenly feel... calm.
Defense +20
Speed +10
Agility -5
CONFIDENT.
I mean... is this how the Johannsens feel all the time? Like I can do anything. Like nobody can stop me. Like I could wear body glitter and get away with it.

HOW TO SKATE LIKE A DERBY PLAYER:

1. Derby skating is similar to ice-skating . . . but instead of two blades, you have eight wheels. Also, eight blockers are actively trying to push you around.

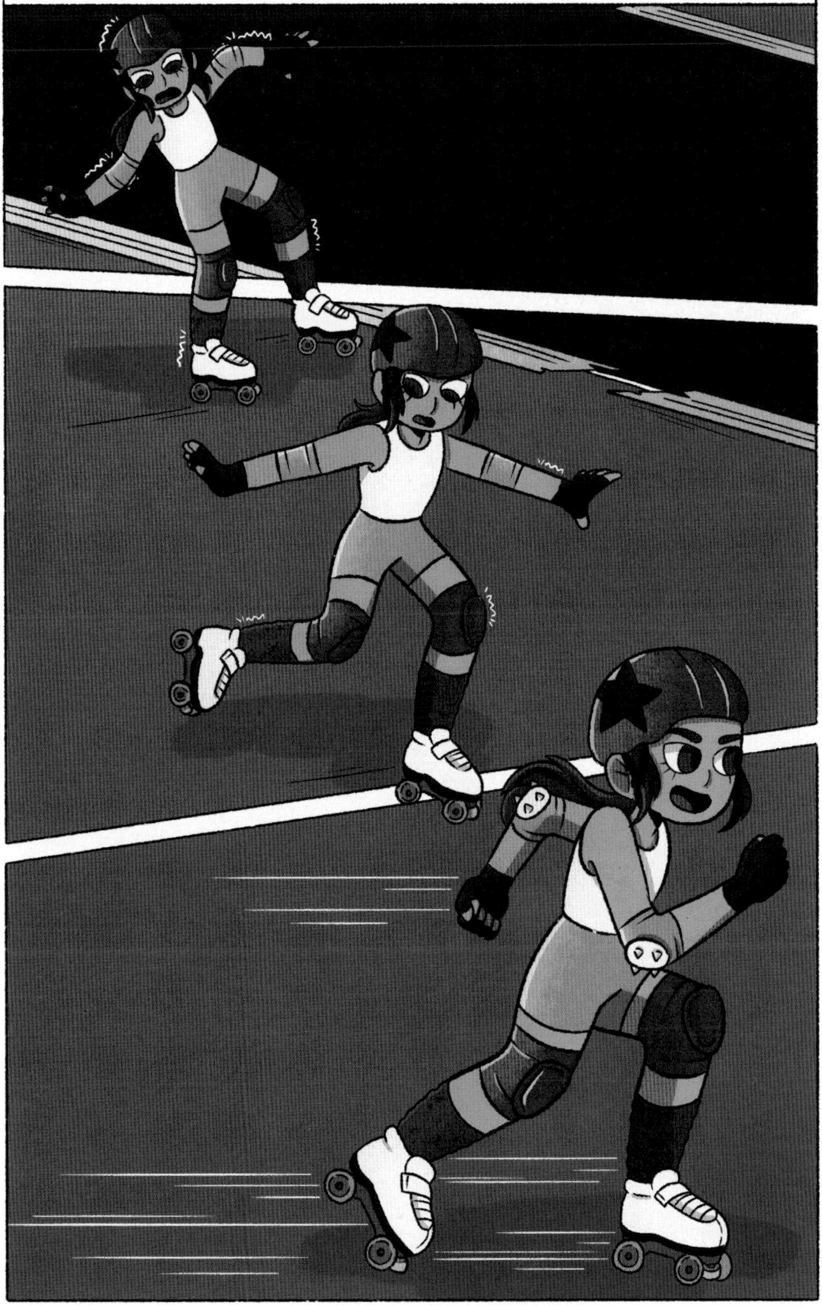

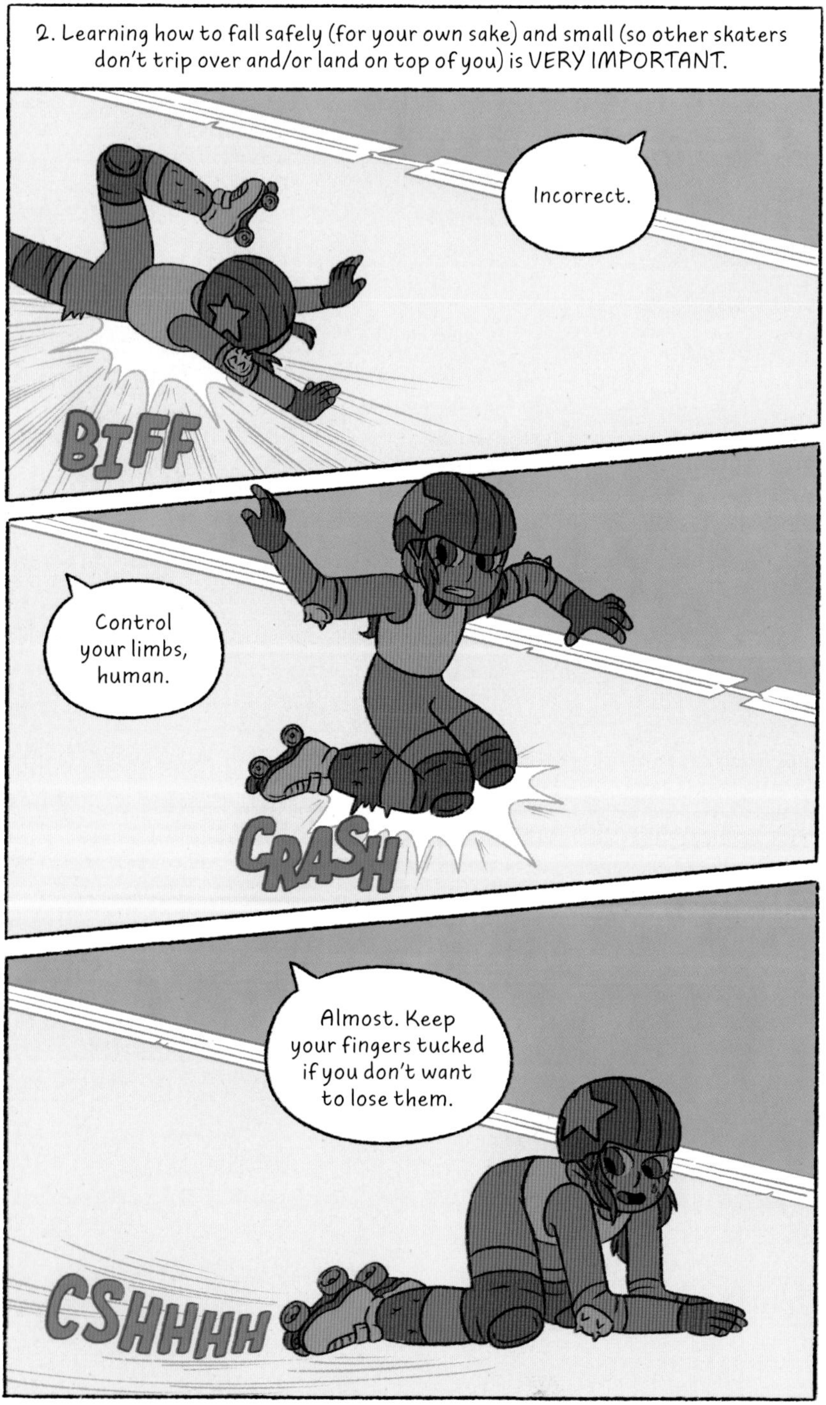
2. Learning how to fall safely (for your own sake) and small (so other skaters don't trip over and/or land on top of you) is VERY IMPORTANT.
Incorrect.
BIFF
Control your limbs, human.
CRASH
Almost. Keep your fingers tucked if you don't want to lose them.
CSHHHH

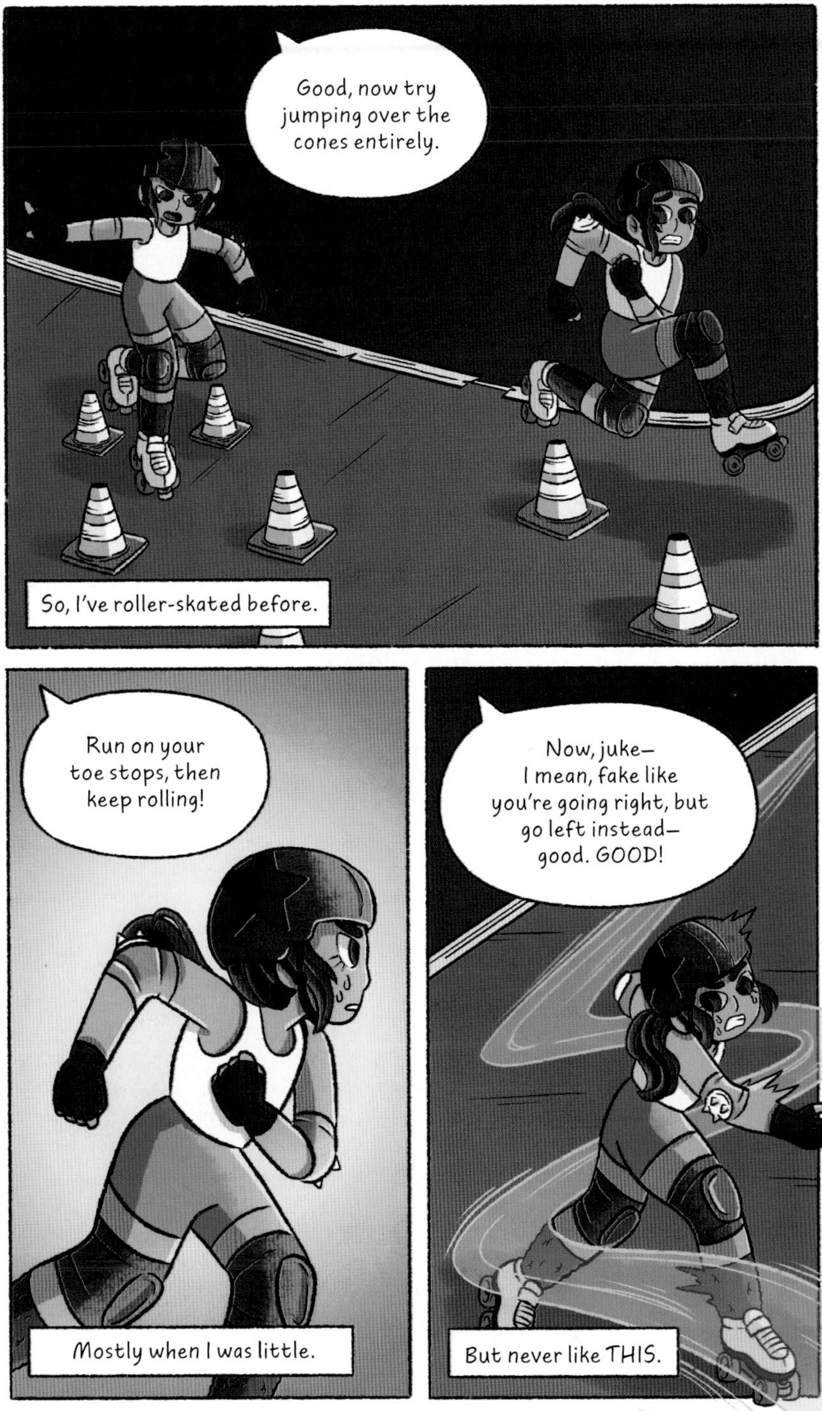
Good, now try jumping over the cones entirely.
So, I've roller-skated before.
Run on your toe stops, then keep rolling!
Mostly when I was little.
Now, juke— I mean, fake like you're going right, but go left instead— good. GOOD!
But never like THIS.

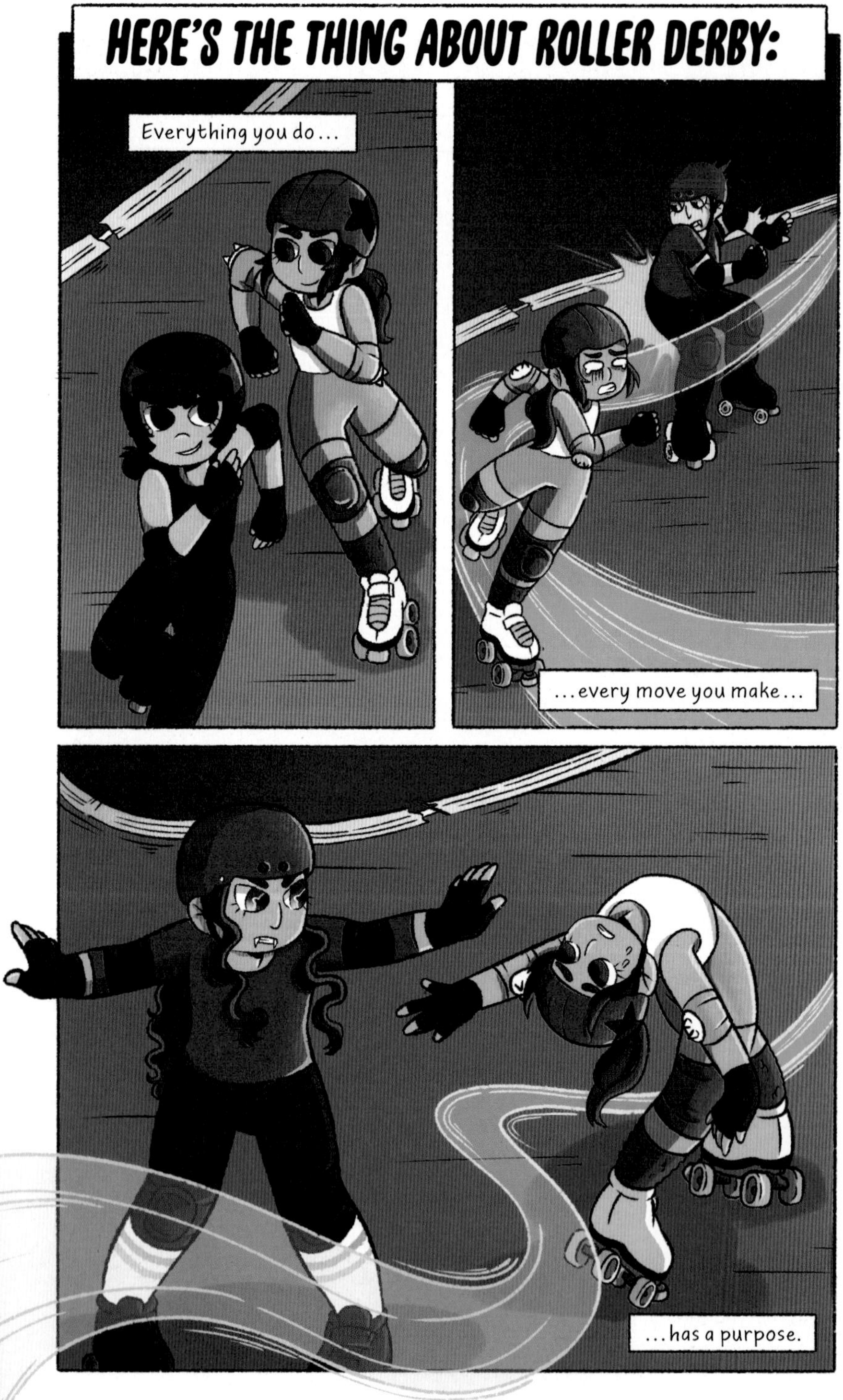

HERE'S THE THING ABOUT ROLLER DERBY:
Everything you do...
...every move you make...
...has a purpose.

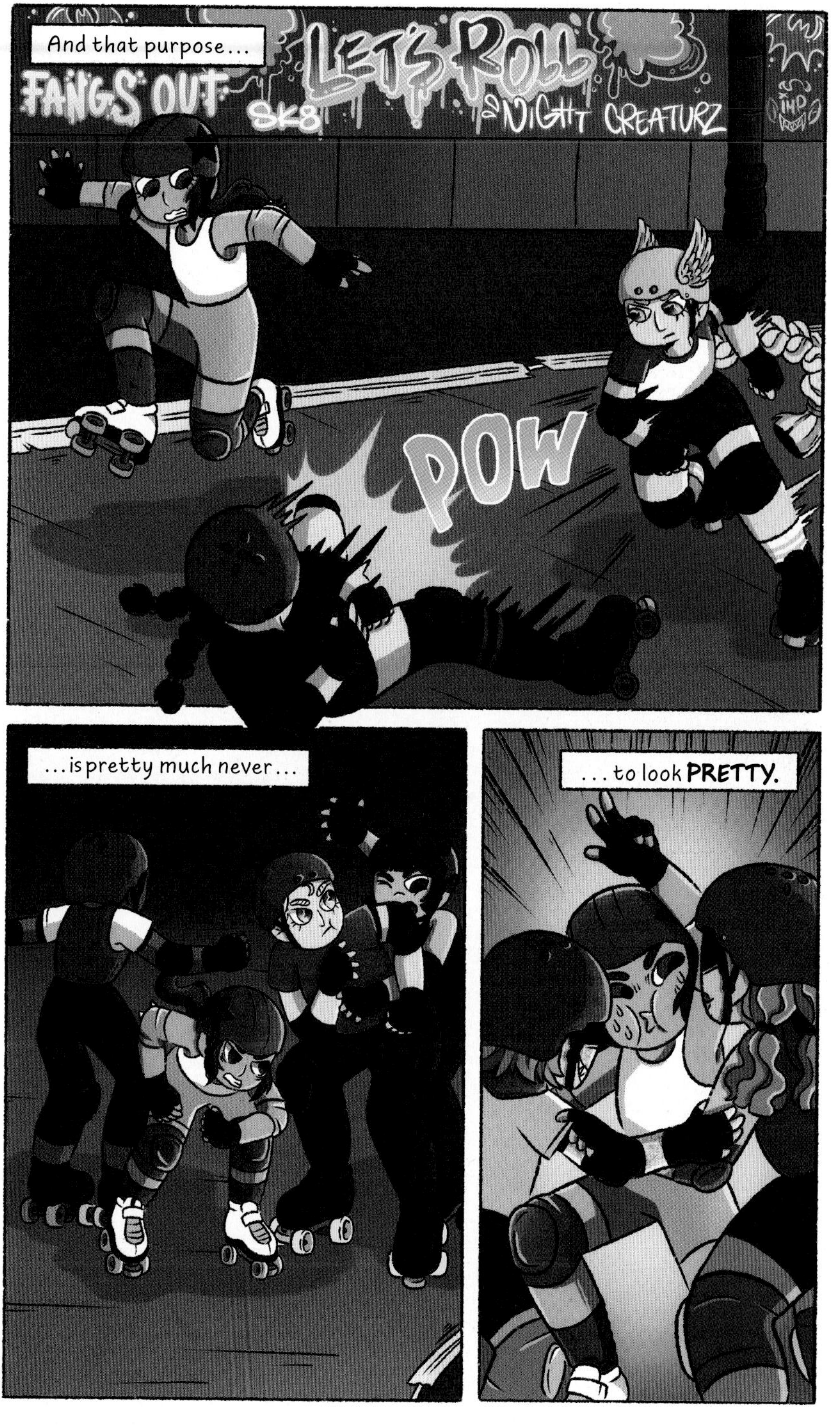
And that purpose...
FANGS OUT
LET'S ROLL
SK8
NIGHT CREATURZ
POW
...is pretty much never...
...to look **PRETTY.**

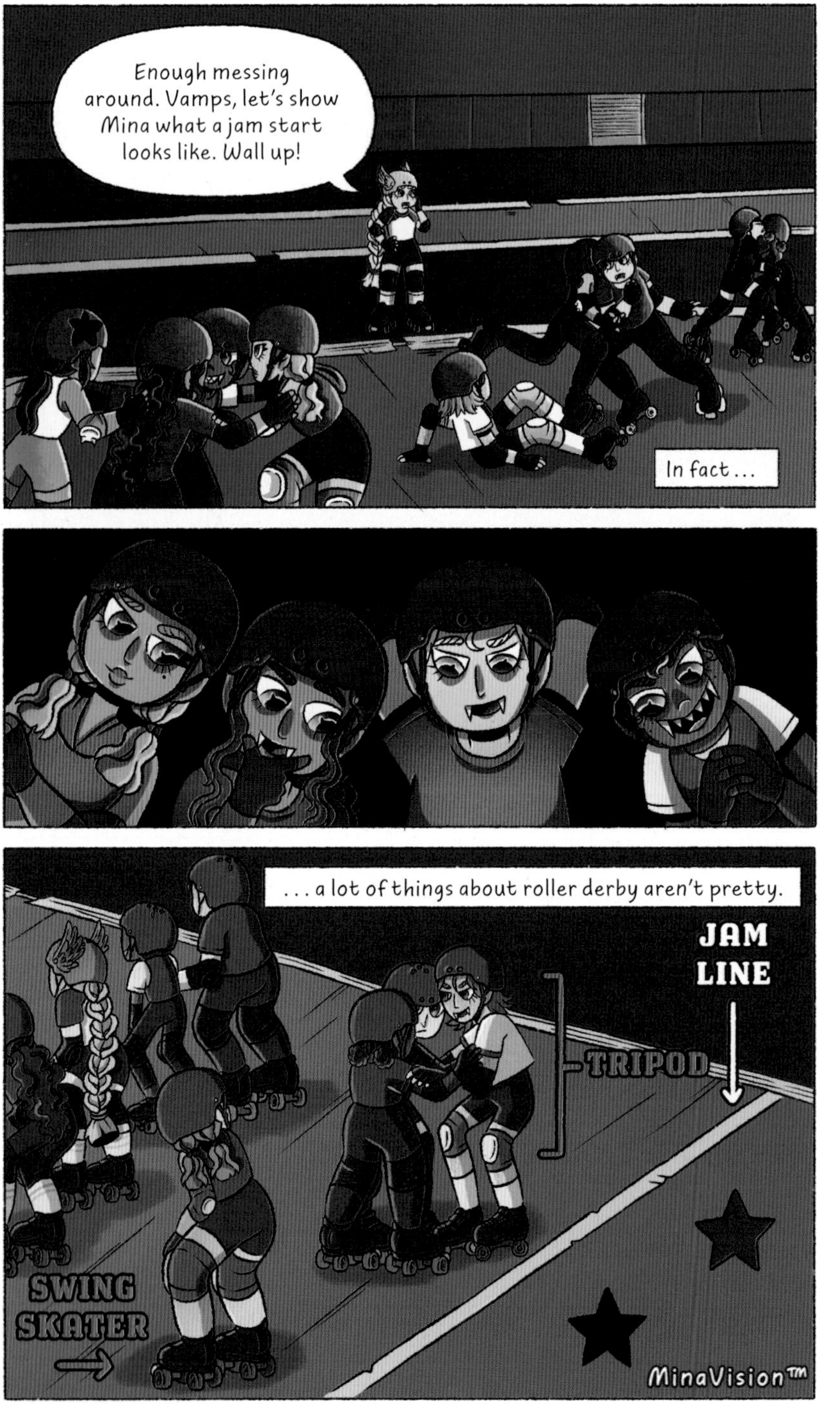

Enough messing around. Vamps, let's show Mina what a jam start looks like. Wall up!
In fact . . .
. . . a lot of things about roller derby aren't pretty.
JAM LINE
TRIPOD
SWING SKATER
MinaVision™

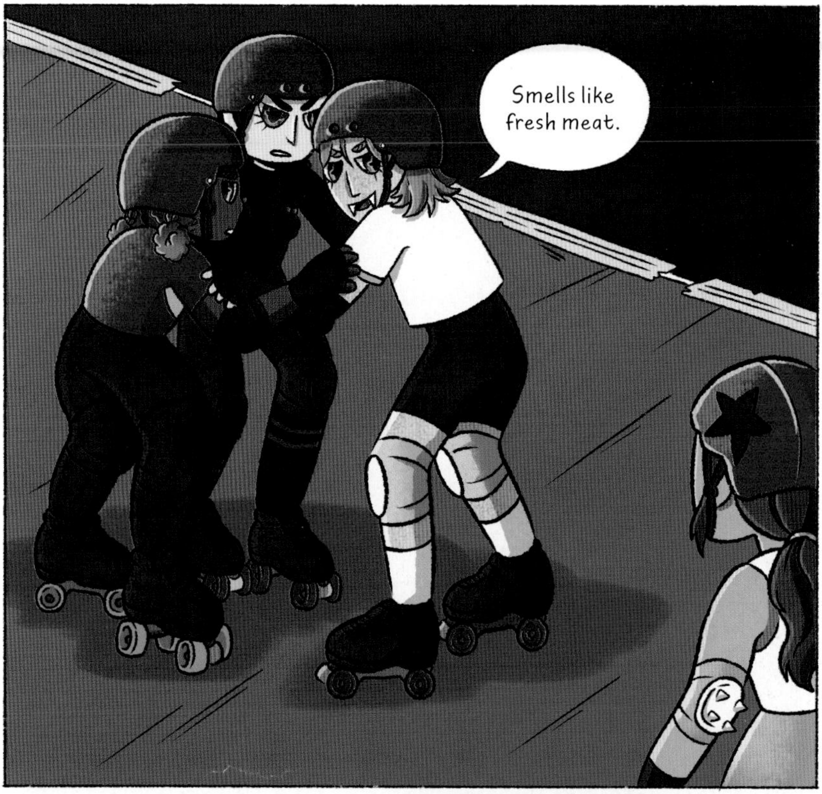
Smells like fresh meat.

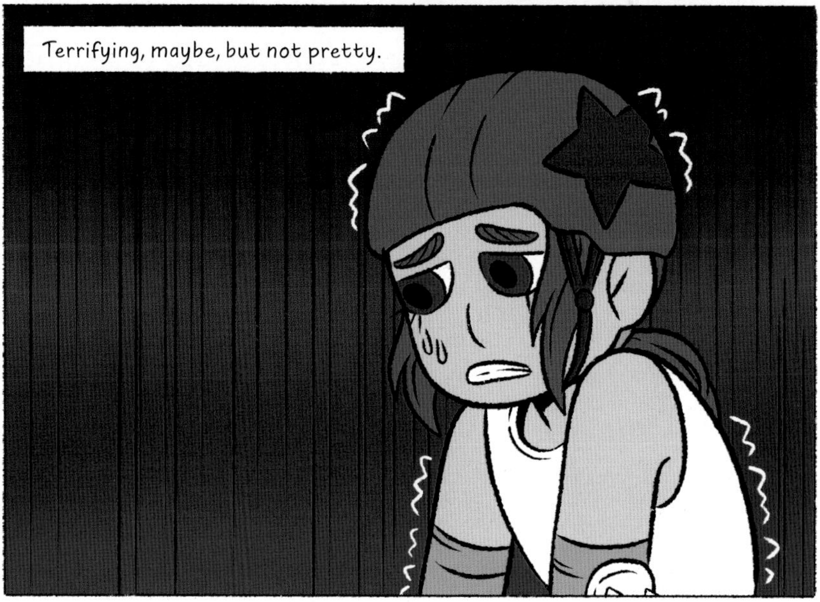
Terrifying, maybe, but not pretty.

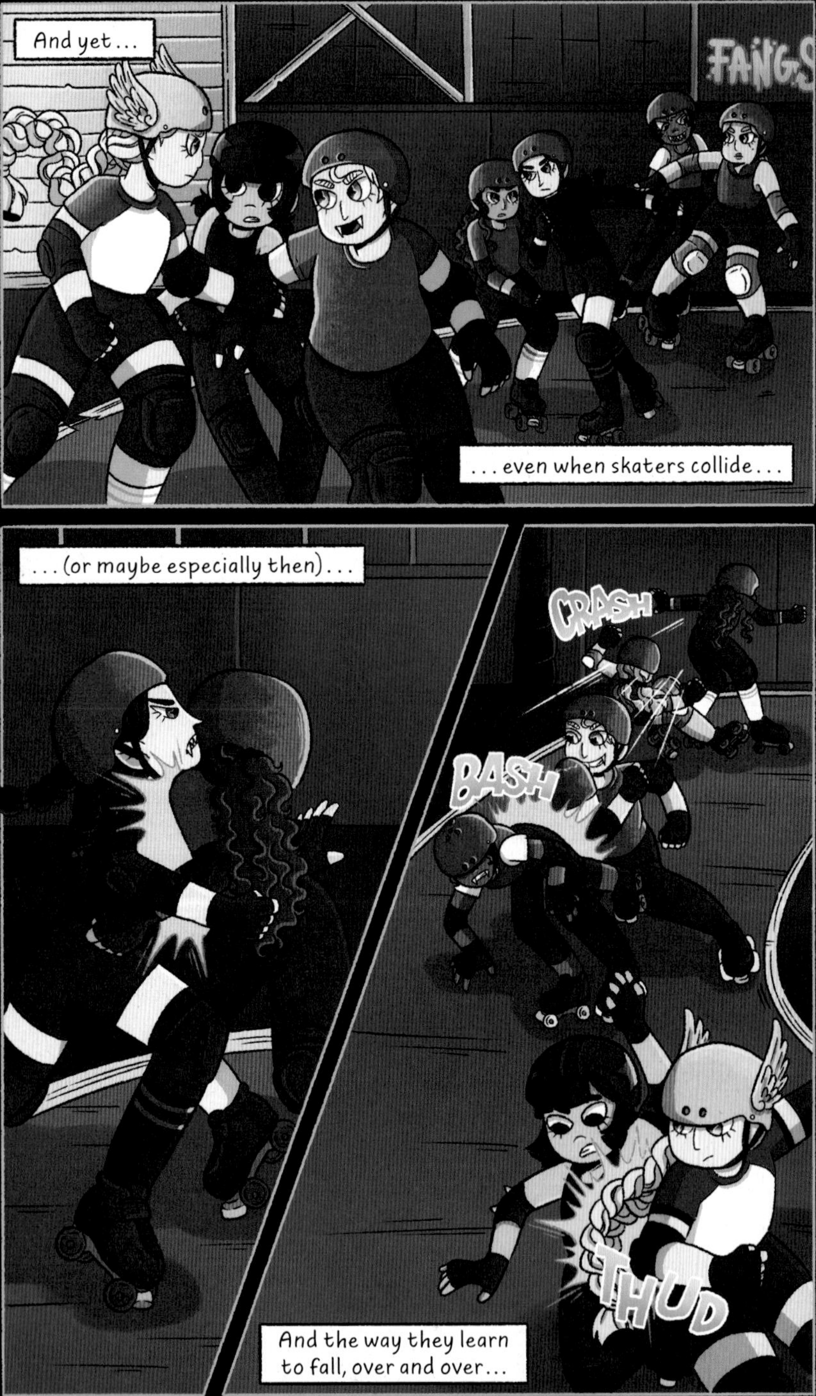
And yet...
FANGS
...even when skaters collide...
...(or maybe especially then)...
CRASH
BASH
THUD
And the way they learn to fall, over and over...

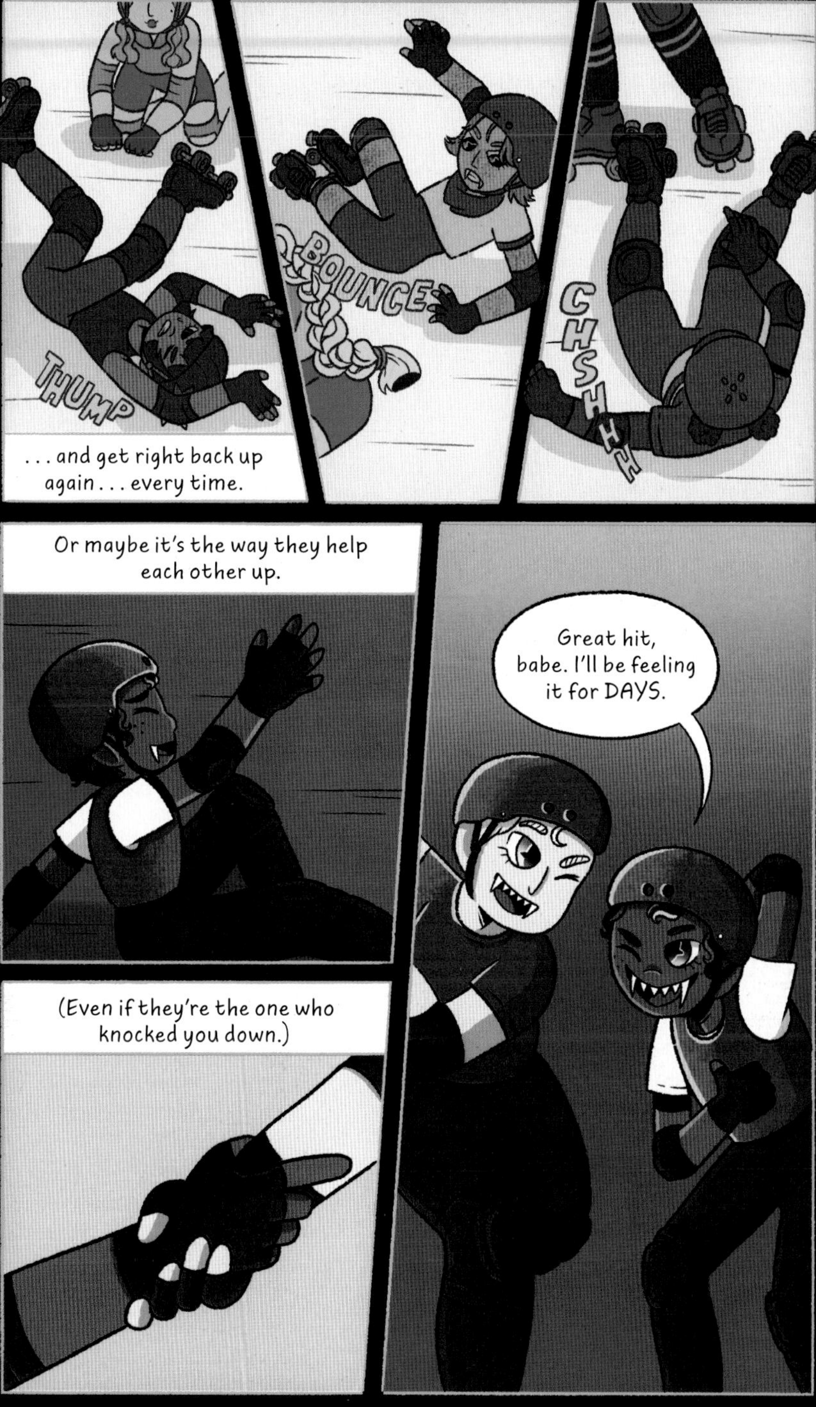
THUMP
BOUNCE
CHSHHH
. . . and get right back up again . . . every time.
Or maybe it's the way they help each other up.
Great hit, babe. I'll be feeling it for DAYS.
(Even if they're the one who knocked you down.)

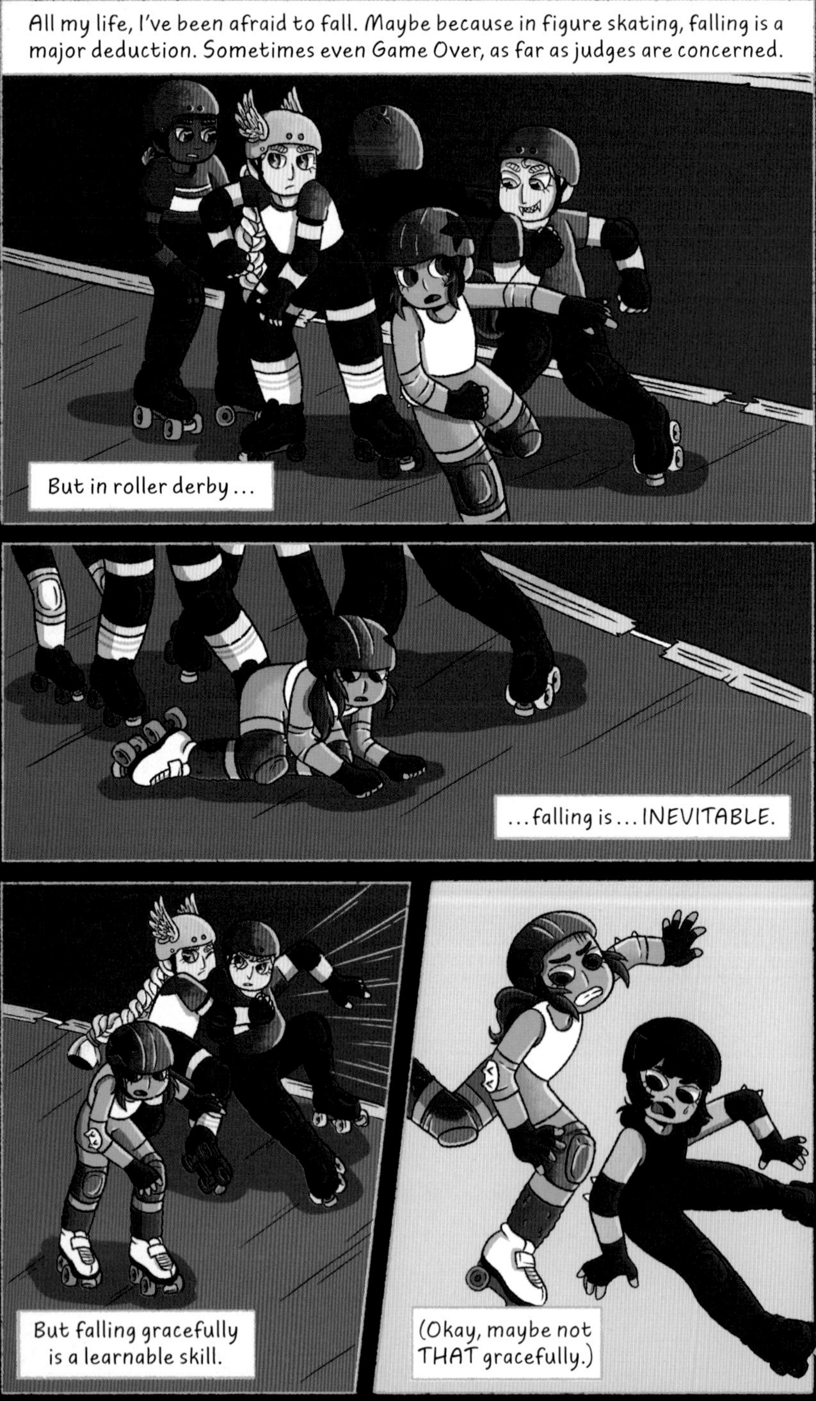
All my life, I've been afraid to fall. Maybe because in figure skating, falling is a major deduction. Sometimes even Game Over, as far as judges are concerned.
But in roller derby . . .
. . . falling is . . . INEVITABLE.
But falling gracefully is a learnable skill.
(Okay, maybe not THAT gracefully.)

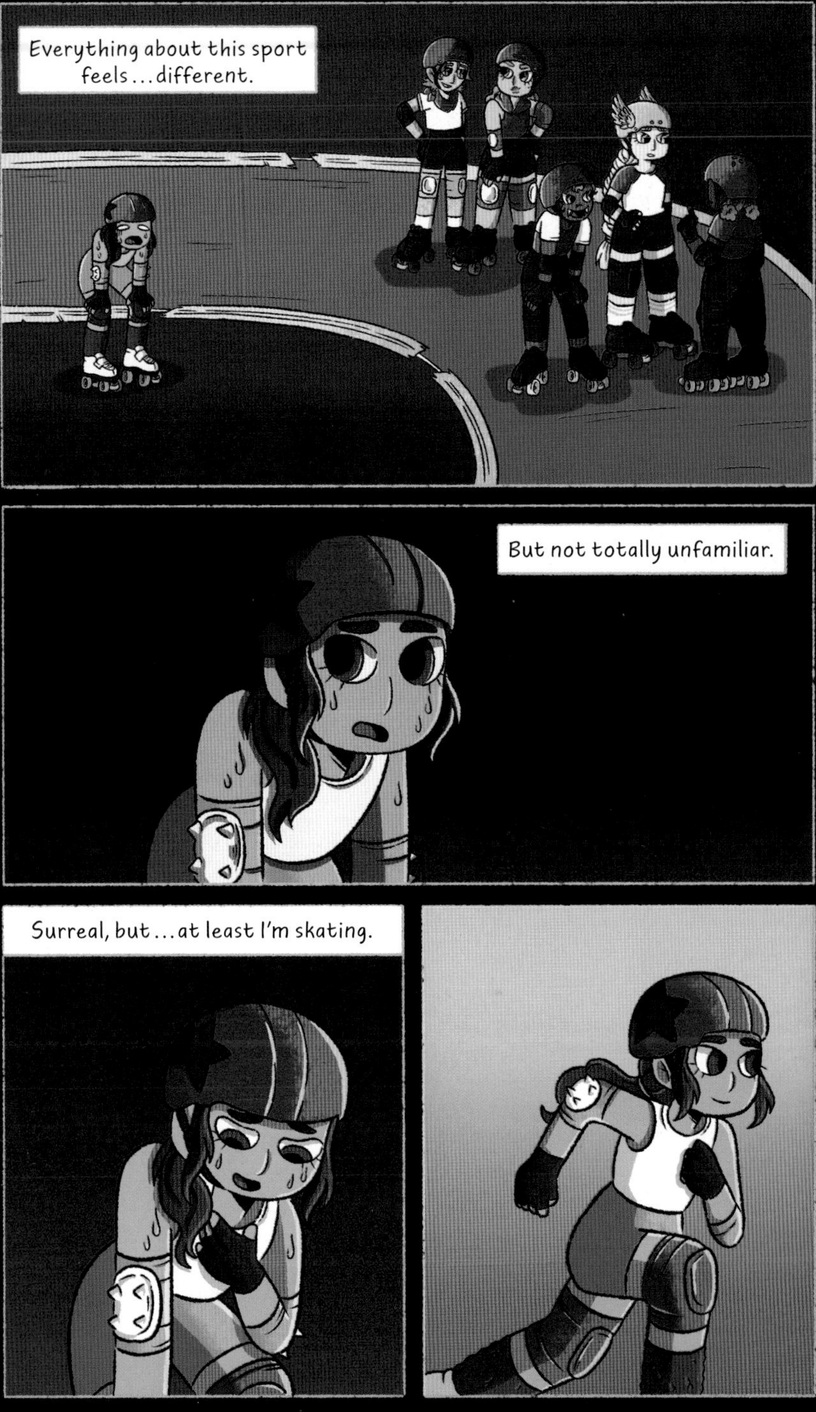
Everything about this sport feels... different.
But not totally unfamiliar.
Surreal, but... at least I'm skating.

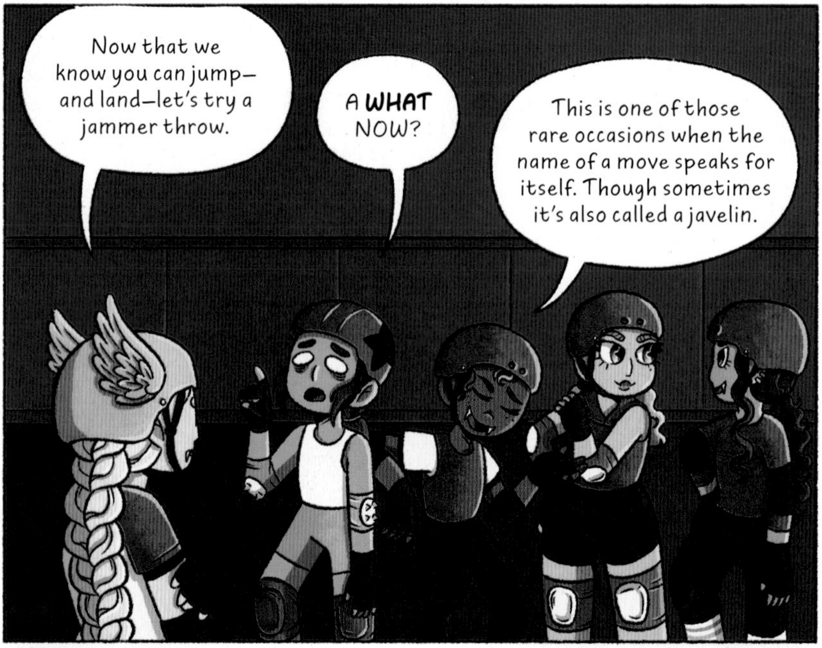
Now that we know you can jump—and land—let's try a jammer throw.
A **WHAT** NOW?
This is one of those rare occasions when the name of a move speaks for itself. Though sometimes it's also called a javelin.

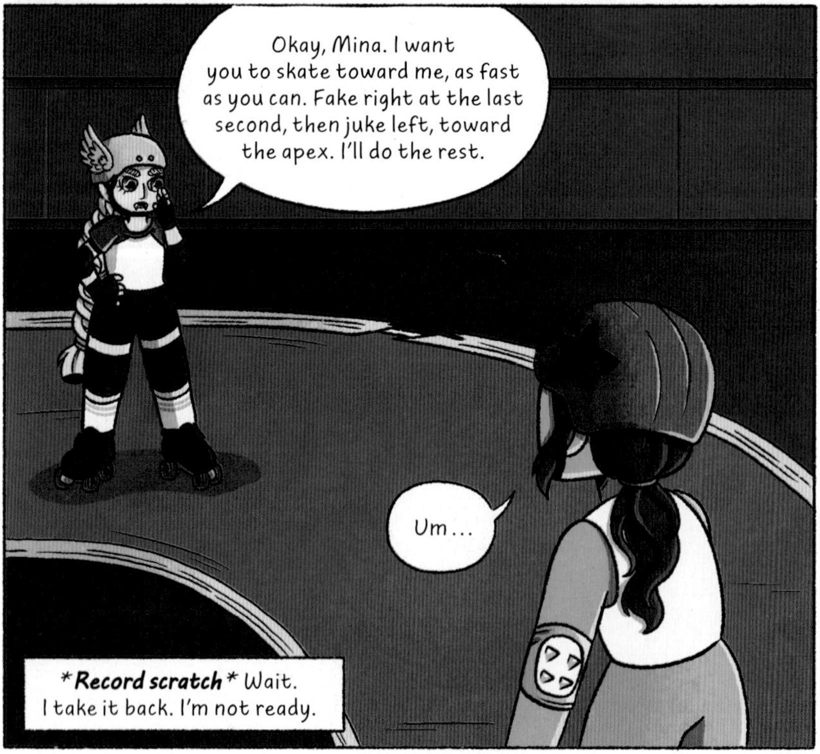
Okay, Mina. I want you to skate toward me, as fast as you can. Fake right at the last second, then juke left, toward the apex. I'll do the rest.
Um...
* ***Record scratch*** * Wait. I take it back. I'm not ready.

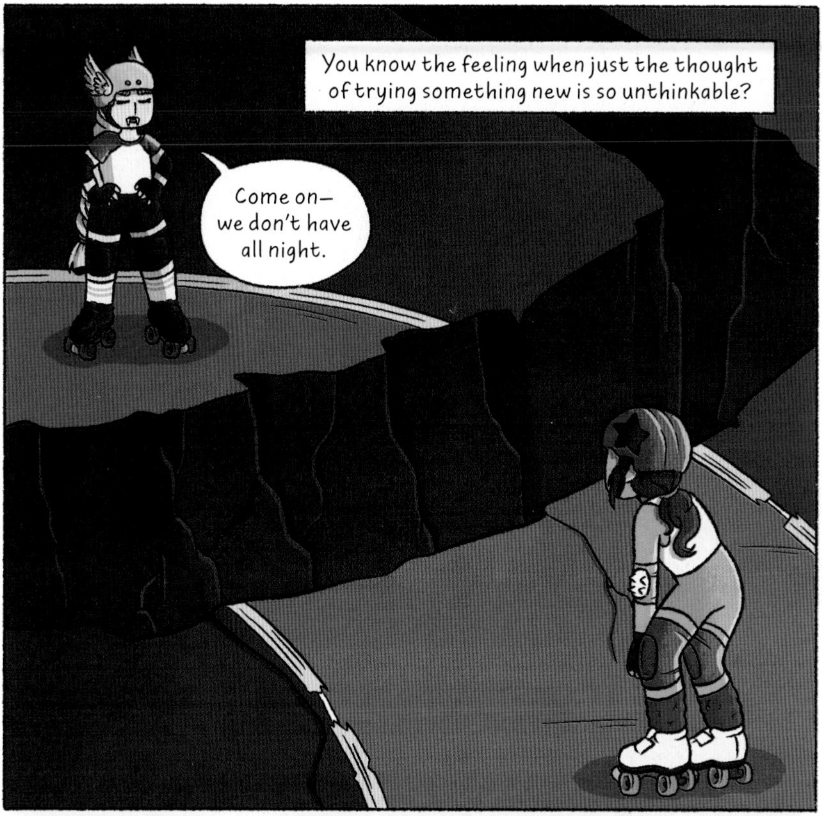
You know the feeling when just the thought of trying something new is so unthinkable?
Come on— we don't have all night.

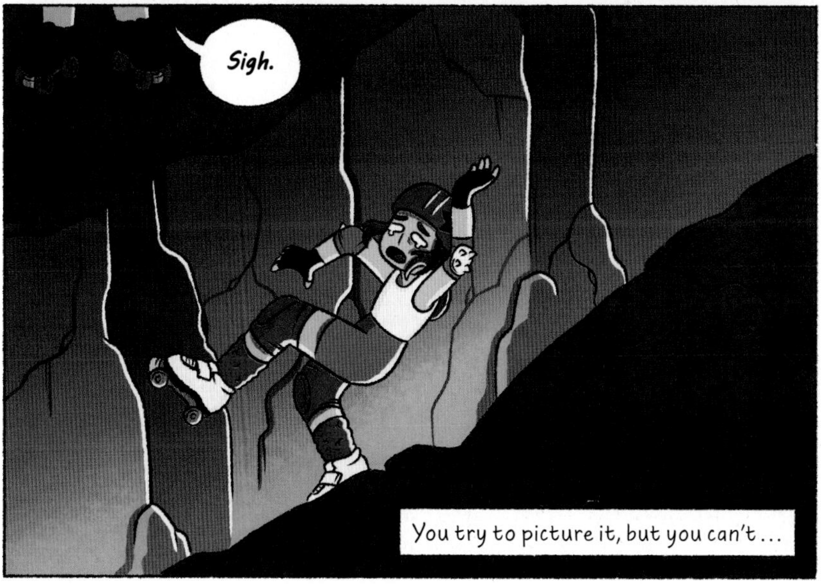
Sigh.
You try to picture it, but you can't . . .

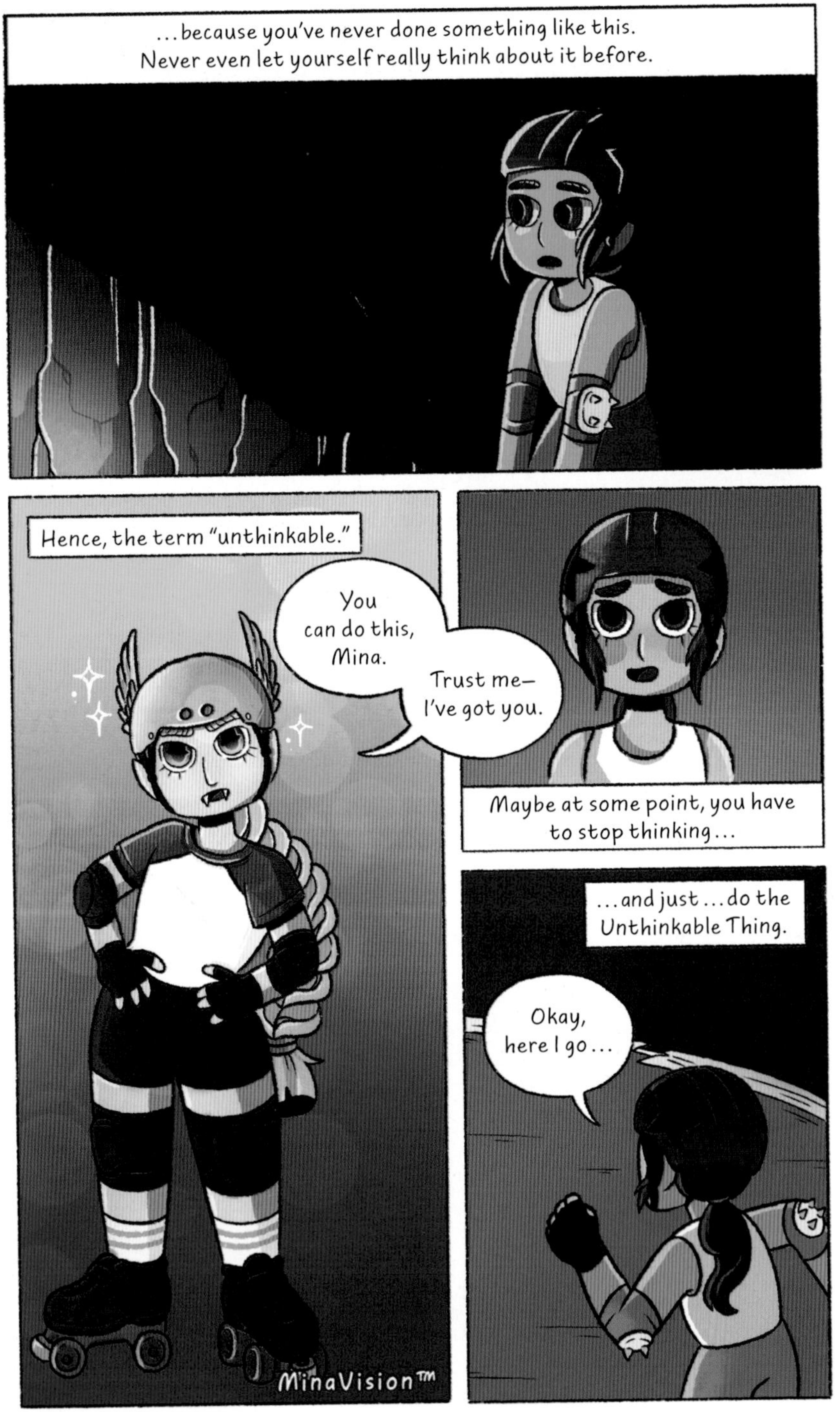
...because you've never done something like this. Never even let yourself really think about it before.
Hence, the term "unthinkable."
You can do this, Mina.
Trust me— I've got you.
MinaVision™
Maybe at some point, you have to stop thinking...
...and just ...do the Unthinkable Thing.
Okay, here I go...

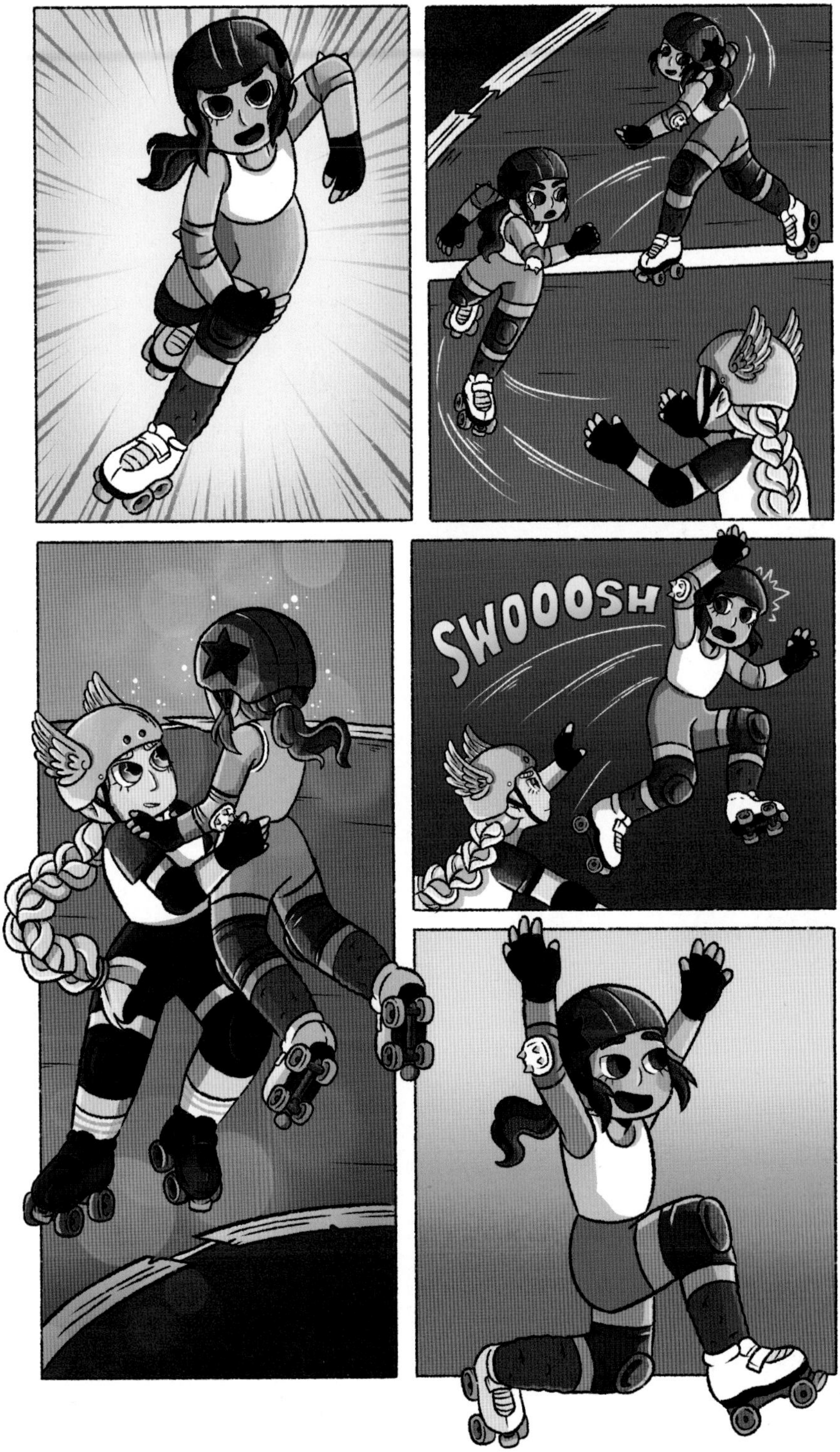
SWOOOSH

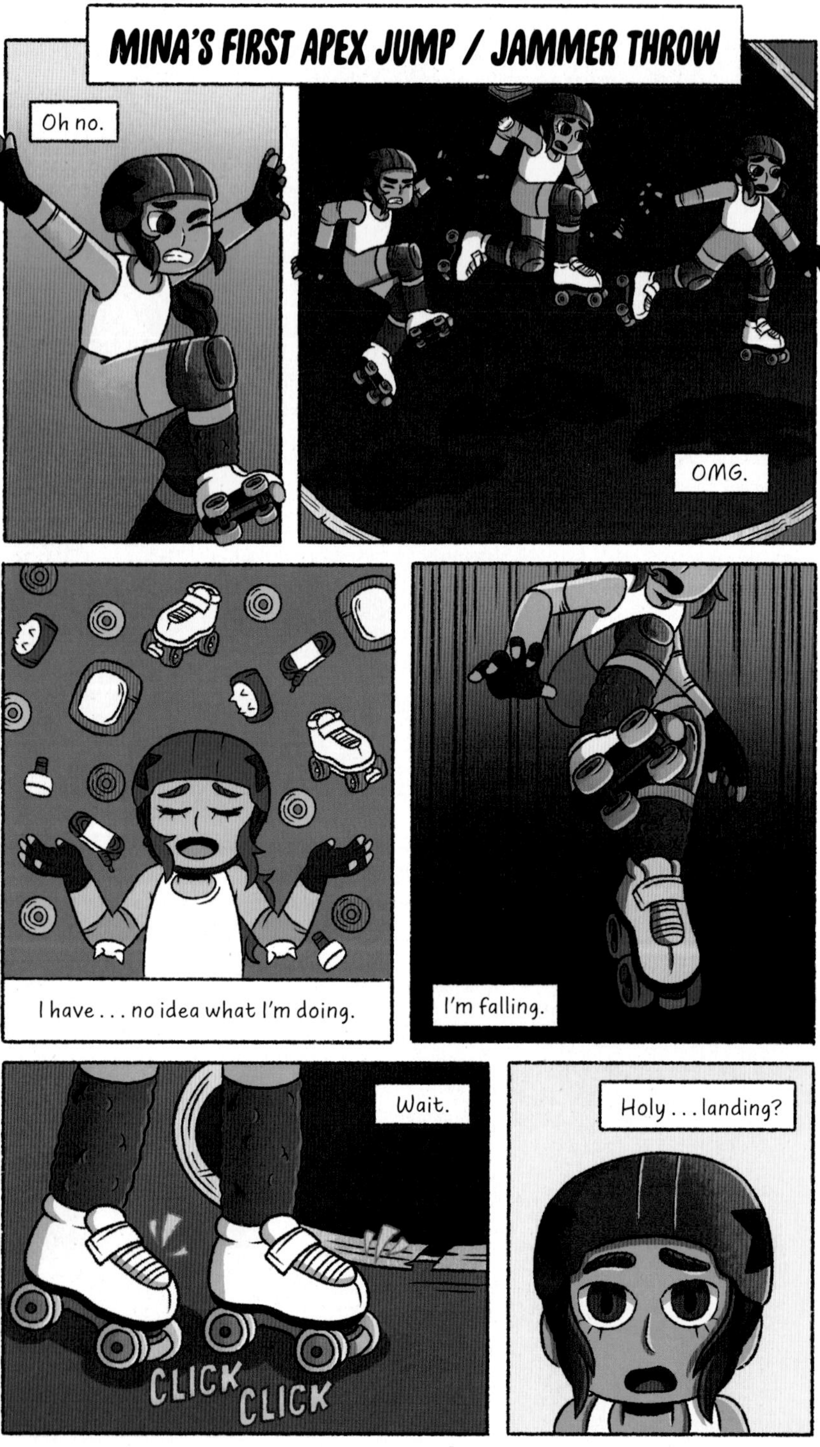
MINA'S FIRST APEX JUMP / JAMMER THROW
Oh no.
OMG.
I have . . . no idea what I'm doing.
I'm falling.
Wait.
CLICK
CLICK
Holy . . . landing?

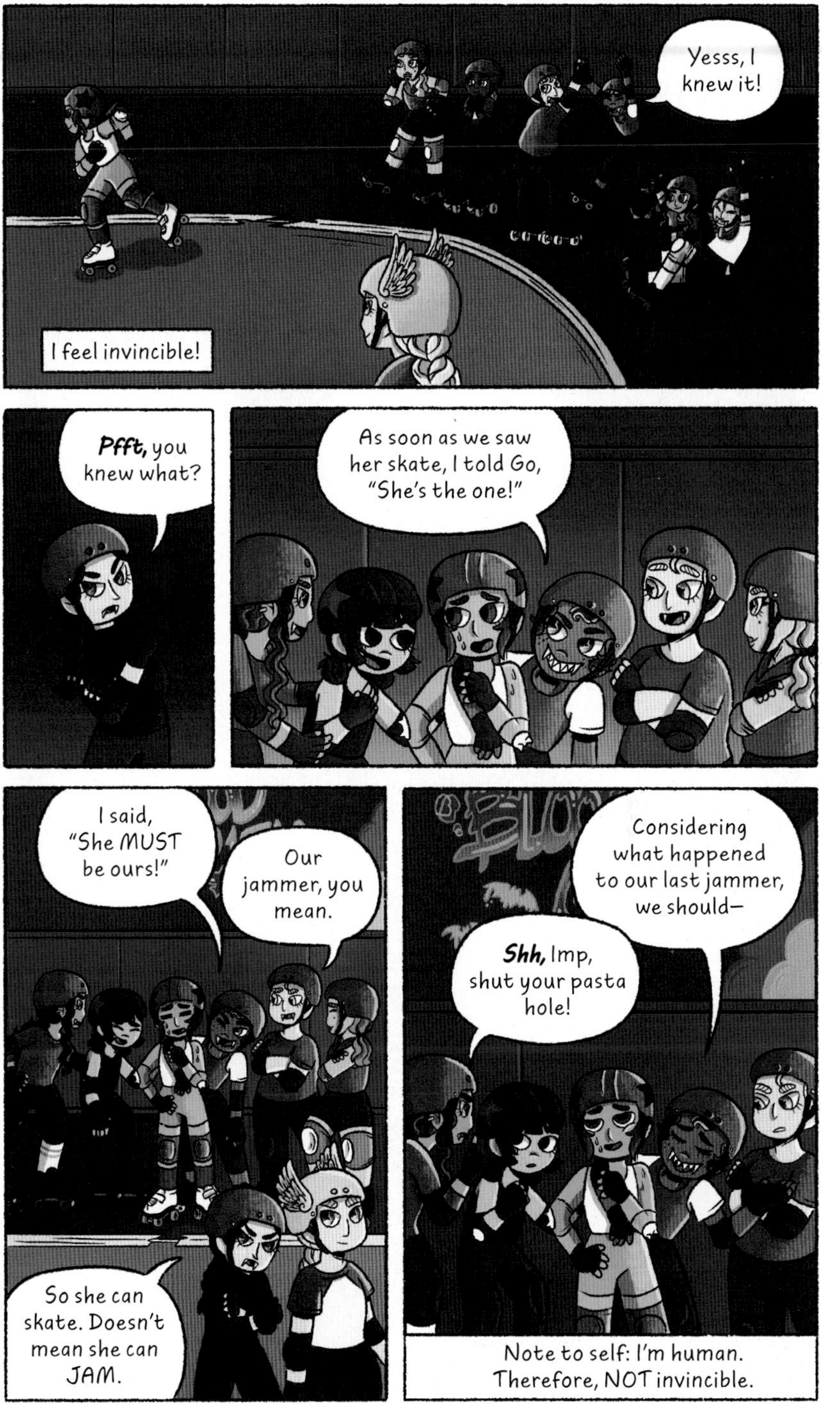

Yesss, I knew it!
I feel invincible!
Pfft, you knew what?
As soon as we saw her skate, I told Go, "She's the one!"
I said, "She MUST be ours!"
Our jammer, you mean.
So she can skate. Doesn't mean she can JAM.
Considering what happened to our last jammer, we should—
Shh, Imp, shut your pasta hole!
Note to self: I'm human. Therefore, NOT invincible.

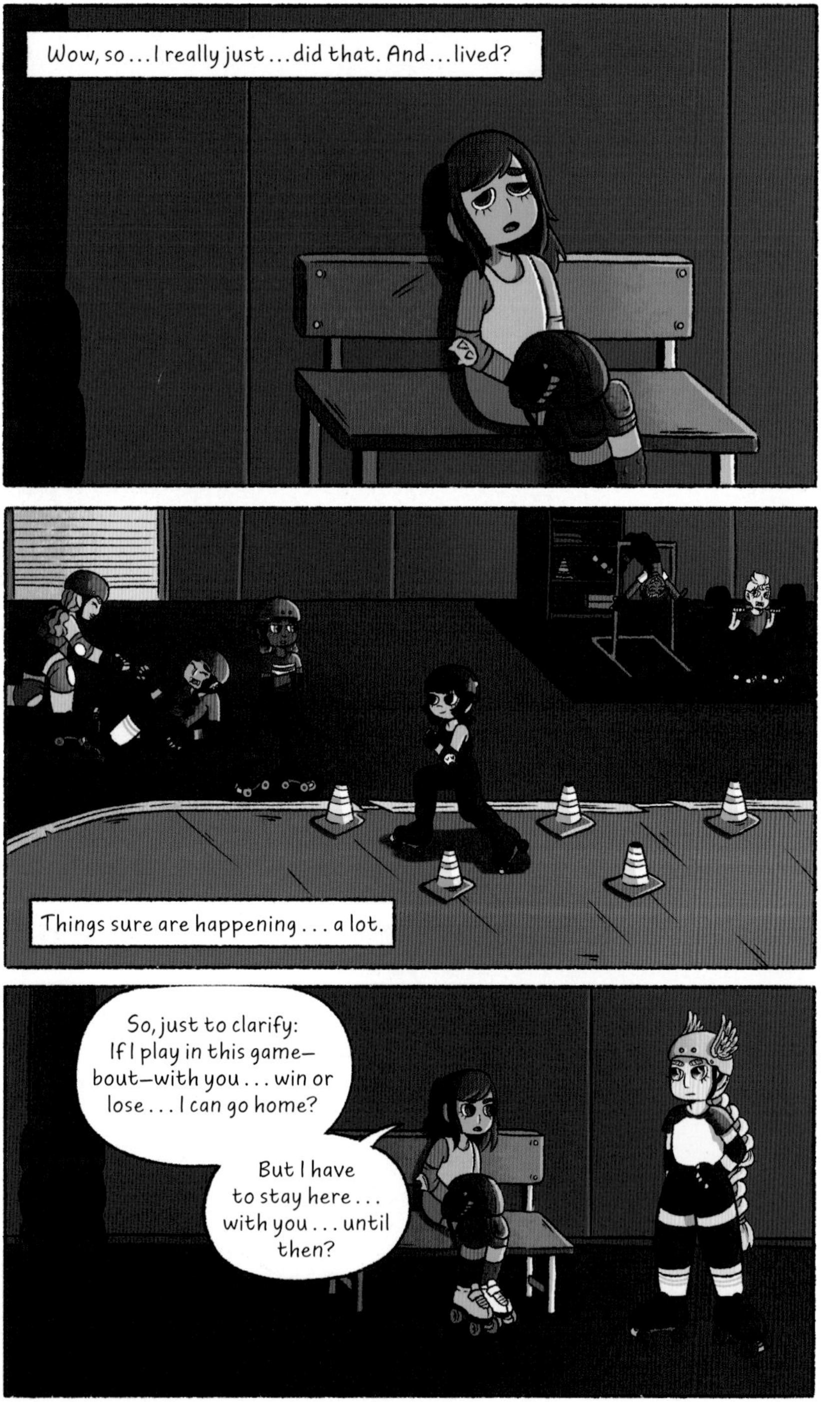
Wow, so . . . I really just . . . did that. And . . . lived?
Things sure are happening . . . a lot.
So, just to clarify: If I play in this game—bout—with you . . . win or lose . . . I can go home?
But I have to stay here . . . with you . . . until then?

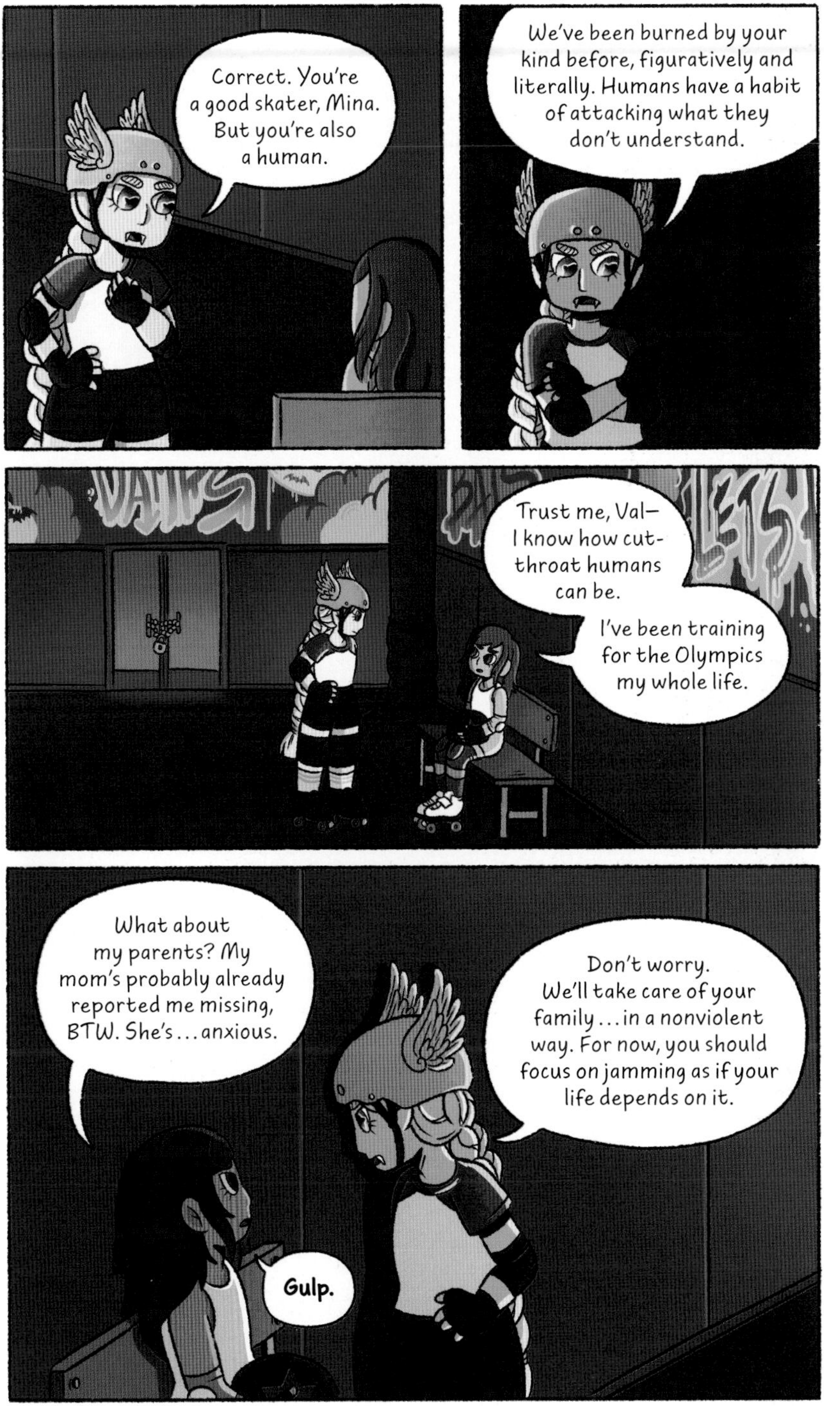
Correct. You're a good skater, Mina. But you're also a human.
We've been burned by your kind before, figuratively and literally. Humans have a habit of attacking what they don't understand.
Trust me, Val— I know how cut-throat humans can be.
I've been training for the Olympics my whole life.
What about my parents? My mom's probably already reported me missing, BTW. She's... anxious.
Don't worry. We'll take care of your family... in a nonviolent way. For now, you should focus on jamming as if your life depends on it.
Gulp.

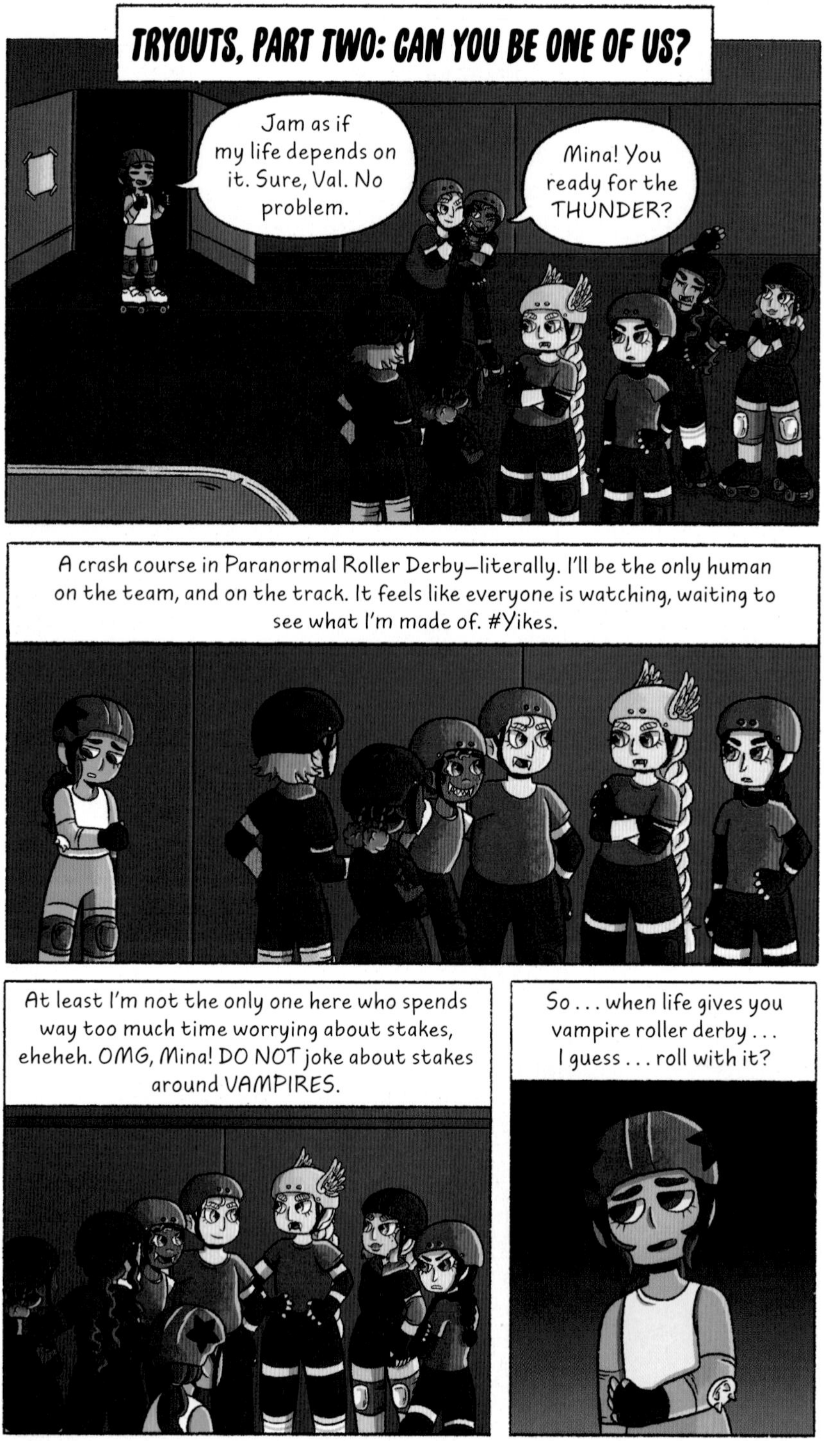
TRYOUTS, PART TWO: CAN YOU BE ONE OF US?
Jam as if my life depends on it. Sure, Val. No problem.
Mina! You ready for the THUNDER?
A crash course in Paranormal Roller Derby—literally. I'll be the only human on the team, and on the track. It feels like everyone is watching, waiting to see what I'm made of. #Yikes.
At least I'm not the only one here who spends way too much time worrying about stakes, eheheh. OMG, Mina! DO NOT joke about stakes around VAMPIRES.
So . . . when life gives you vampire roller derby . . . I guess . . . roll with it?

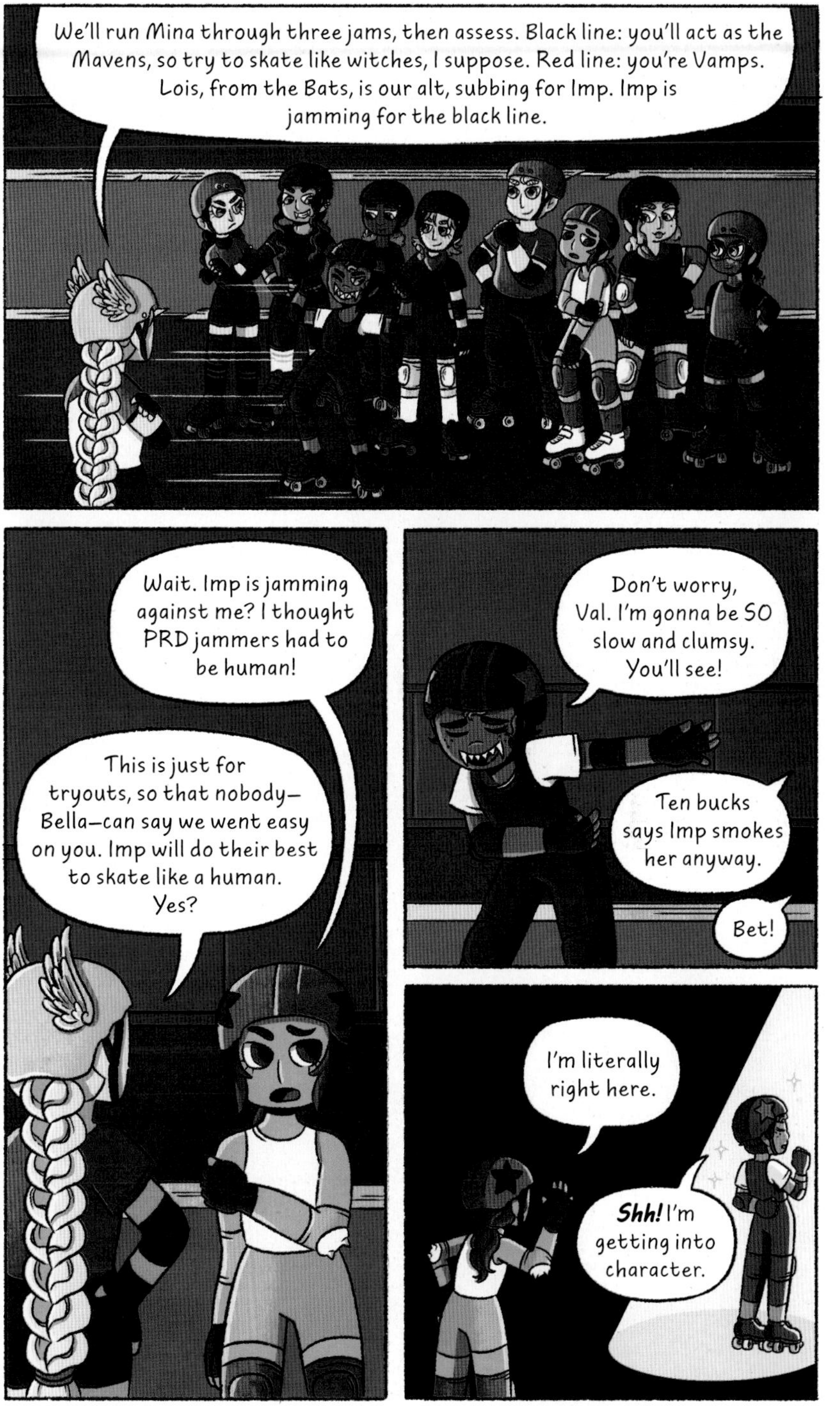

We'll run Mina through three jams, then assess. Black line: you'll act as the Mavens, so try to skate like witches, I suppose. Red line: you're Vamps. Lois, from the Bats, is our alt, subbing for Imp. Imp is jamming for the black line.
Wait. Imp is jamming against me? I thought PRD jammers had to be human!
This is just for tryouts, so that nobody—Bella—can say we went easy on you. Imp will do their best to skate like a human. Yes?
Don't worry, Val. I'm gonna be SO slow and clumsy. You'll see!
Ten bucks says Imp smokes her anyway.
Bet!
I'm literally right here.
Shh! I'm getting into character.

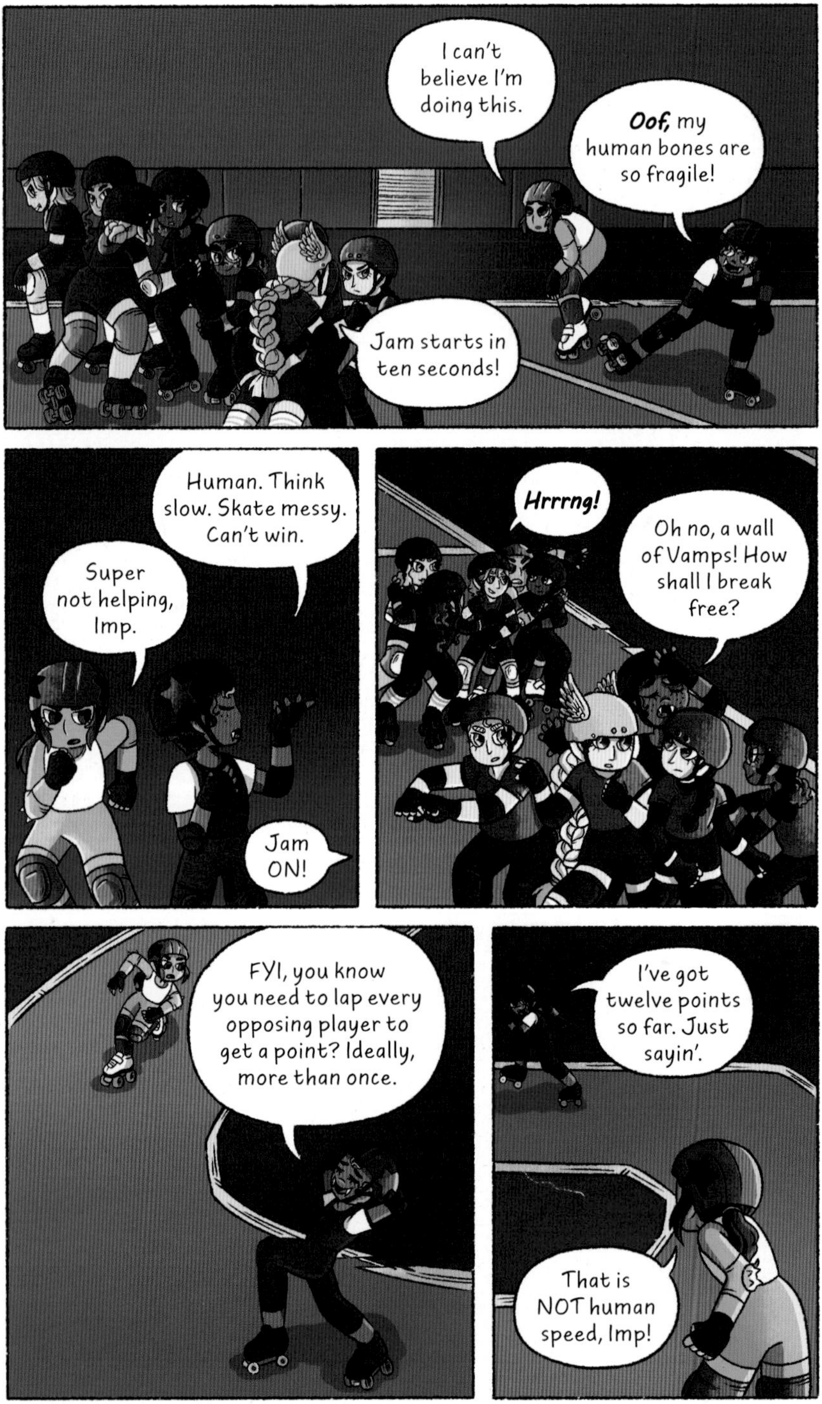
I can't believe I'm doing this.
Oof, my human bones are so fragile!
Jam starts in ten seconds!
Human. Think slow. Skate messy. Can't win.
Super not helping, Imp.
Jam ON!
Hrrrng!
Oh no, a wall of Vamps! How shall I break free?
FYI, you know you need to lap every opposing player to get a point? Ideally, more than once.
I've got twelve points so far. Just sayin'.
That is NOT human speed, Imp!

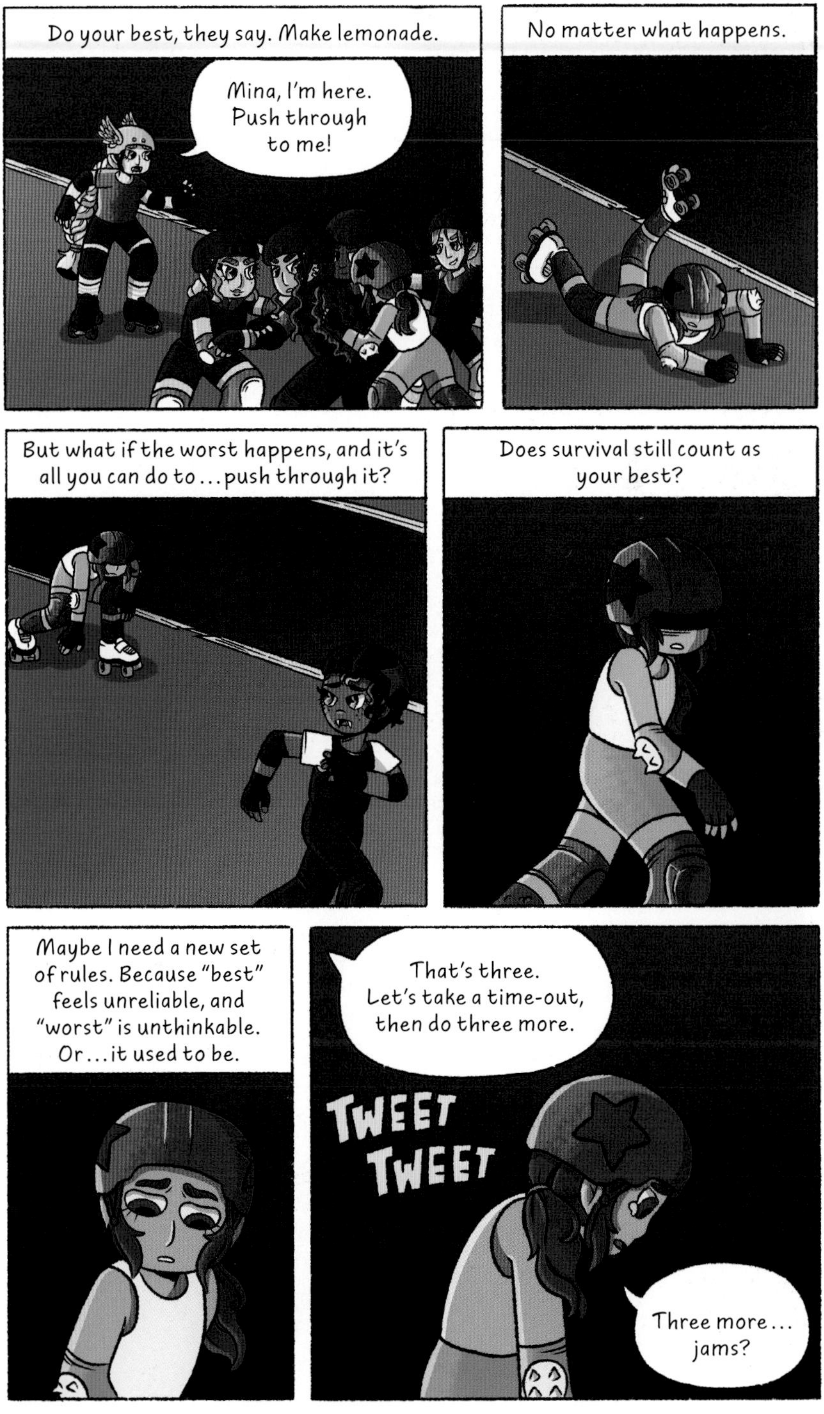

Do your best, they say. Make lemonade.
Mina, I'm here. Push through to me!
No matter what happens.
But what if the worst happens, and it's all you can do to . . . push through it?
Does survival still count as your best?
Maybe I need a new set of rules. Because "best" feels unreliable, and "worst" is unthinkable. Or . . . it used to be.
That's three. Let's take a time-out, then do three more.
TWEET
TWEET
Three more . . . jams?

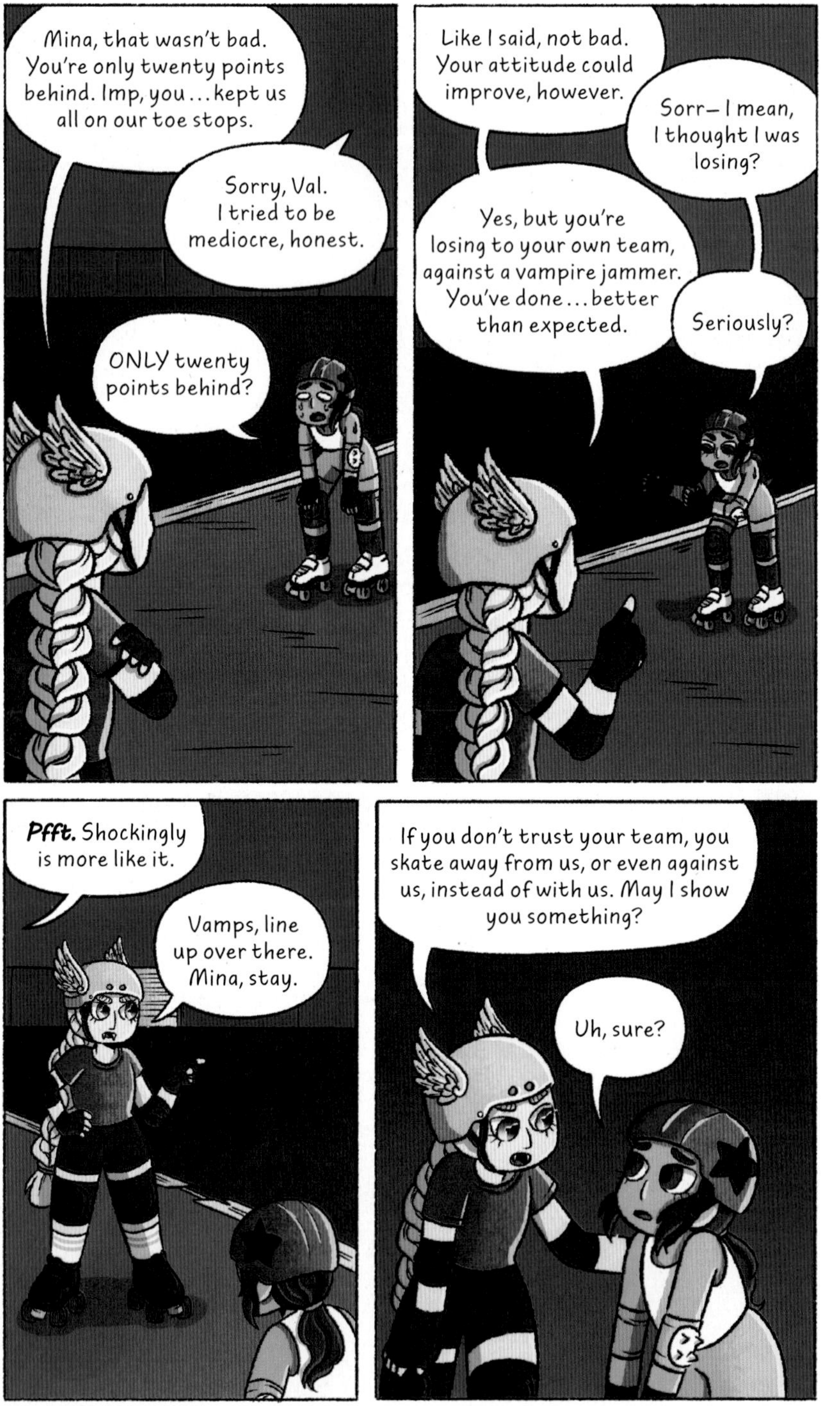

Mina, that wasn't bad. You're only twenty points behind. Imp, you... kept us all on our toe stops.
Sorry, Val. I tried to be mediocre, honest.
ONLY twenty points behind?
Like I said, not bad. Your attitude could improve, however.
Sorr— I mean, I thought I was losing?
Yes, but you're losing to your own team, against a vampire jammer. You've done... better than expected.
Seriously?
Pfft. Shockingly is more like it.
Vamps, line up over there. Mina, stay.
If you don't trust your team, you skate away from us, or even against us, instead of with us. May I show you something?
Uh, sure?

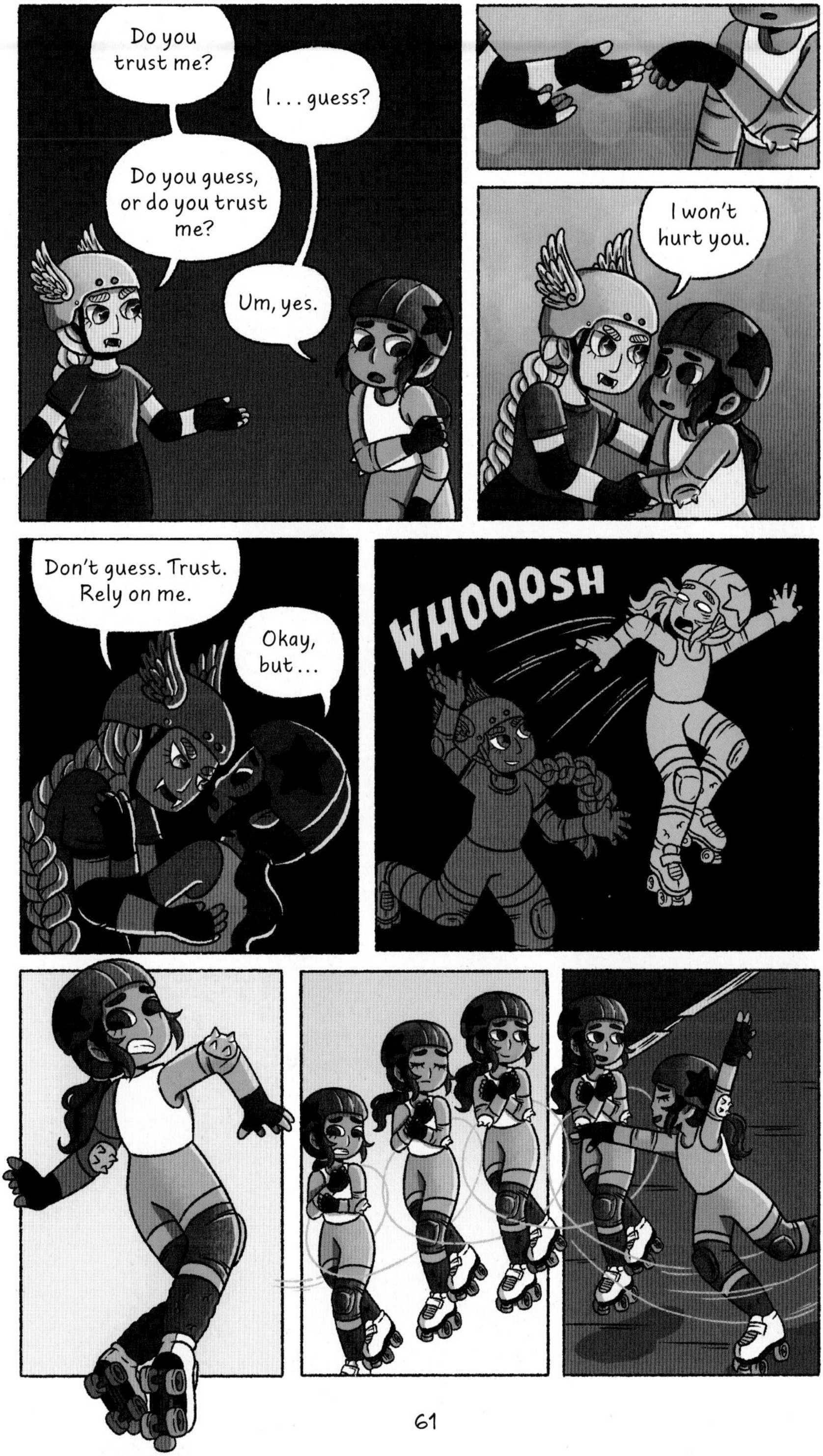
Do you trust me?
I . . . guess?
Do you guess, or do you trust me?
Um, yes.
I won't hurt you.
Don't guess. Trust. Rely on me.
Okay, but . . .
WHOOOSH

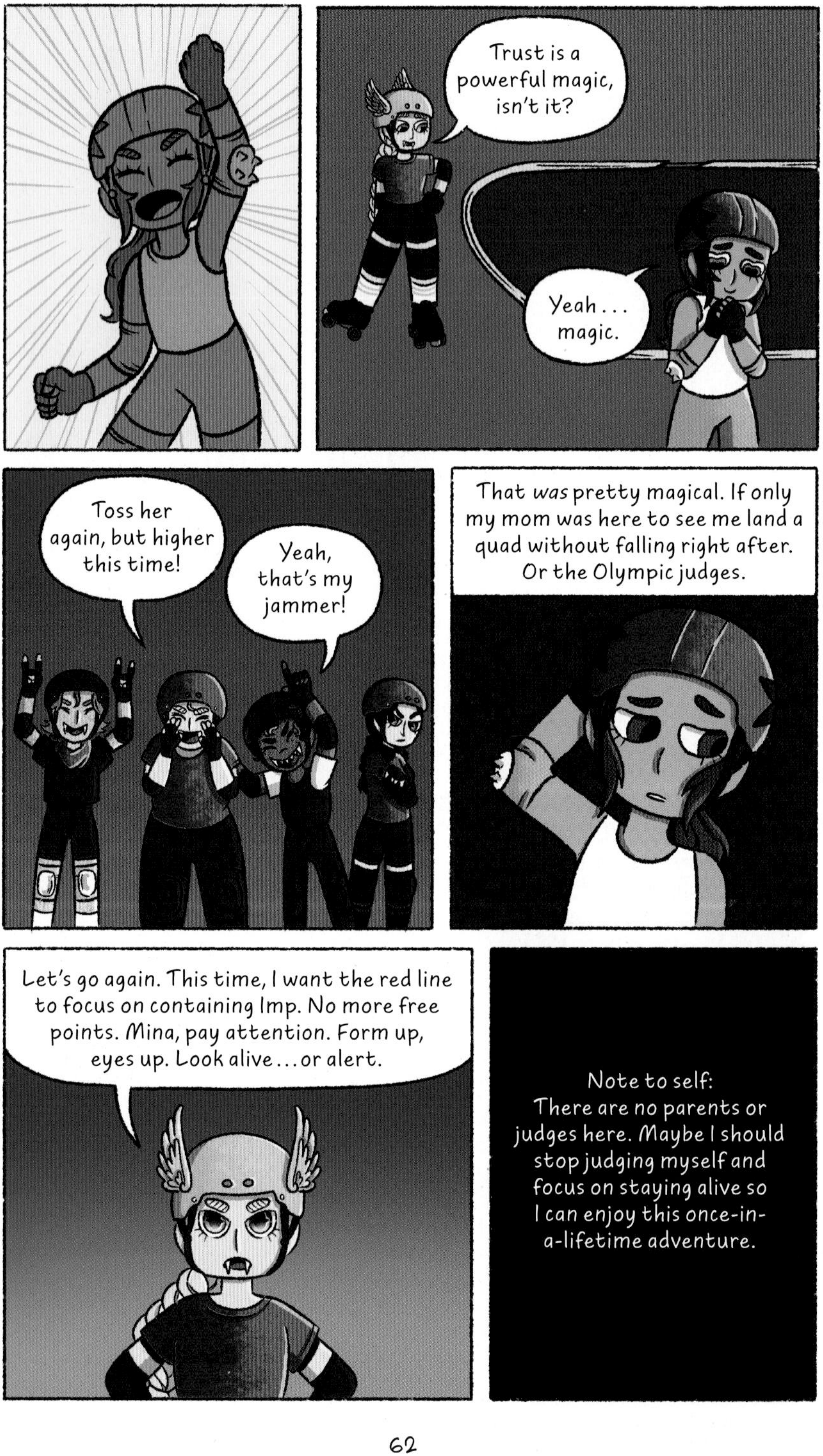
Trust is a powerful magic, isn't it?
Yeah . . . magic.
Toss her again, but higher this time!
Yeah, that's my jammer!
That *was* pretty magical. If only my mom was here to see me land a quad without falling right after. Or the Olympic judges.
Let's go again. This time, I want the red line to focus on containing Imp. No more free points. Mina, pay attention. Form up, eyes up. Look alive . . . or alert.
Note to self:
There are no parents or judges here. Maybe I should stop judging myself and focus on staying alive so I can enjoy this once-in-a-lifetime adventure.

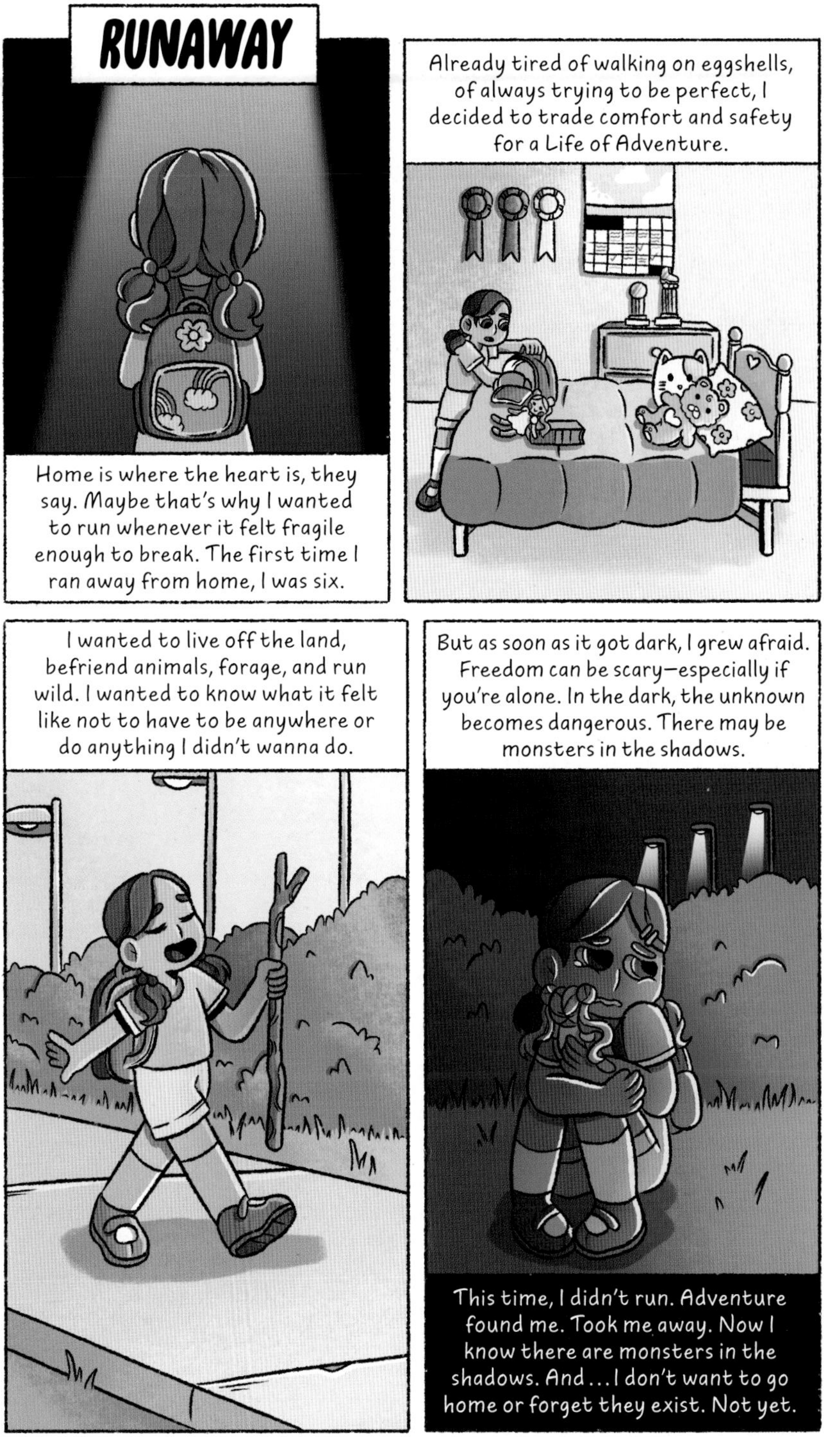
RUNAWAY
Home is where the heart is, they say. Maybe that's why I wanted to run whenever it felt fragile enough to break. The first time I ran away from home, I was six.
Already tired of walking on eggshells, of always trying to be perfect, I decided to trade comfort and safety for a Life of Adventure.
I wanted to live off the land, befriend animals, forage, and run wild. I wanted to know what it felt like not to have to be anywhere or do anything I didn't wanna do.
But as soon as it got dark, I grew afraid. Freedom can be scary—especially if you're alone. In the dark, the unknown becomes dangerous. There may be monsters in the shadows.
This time, I didn't run. Adventure found me. Took me away. Now I know there are monsters in the shadows. And . . . I don't want to go home or forget they exist. Not yet.

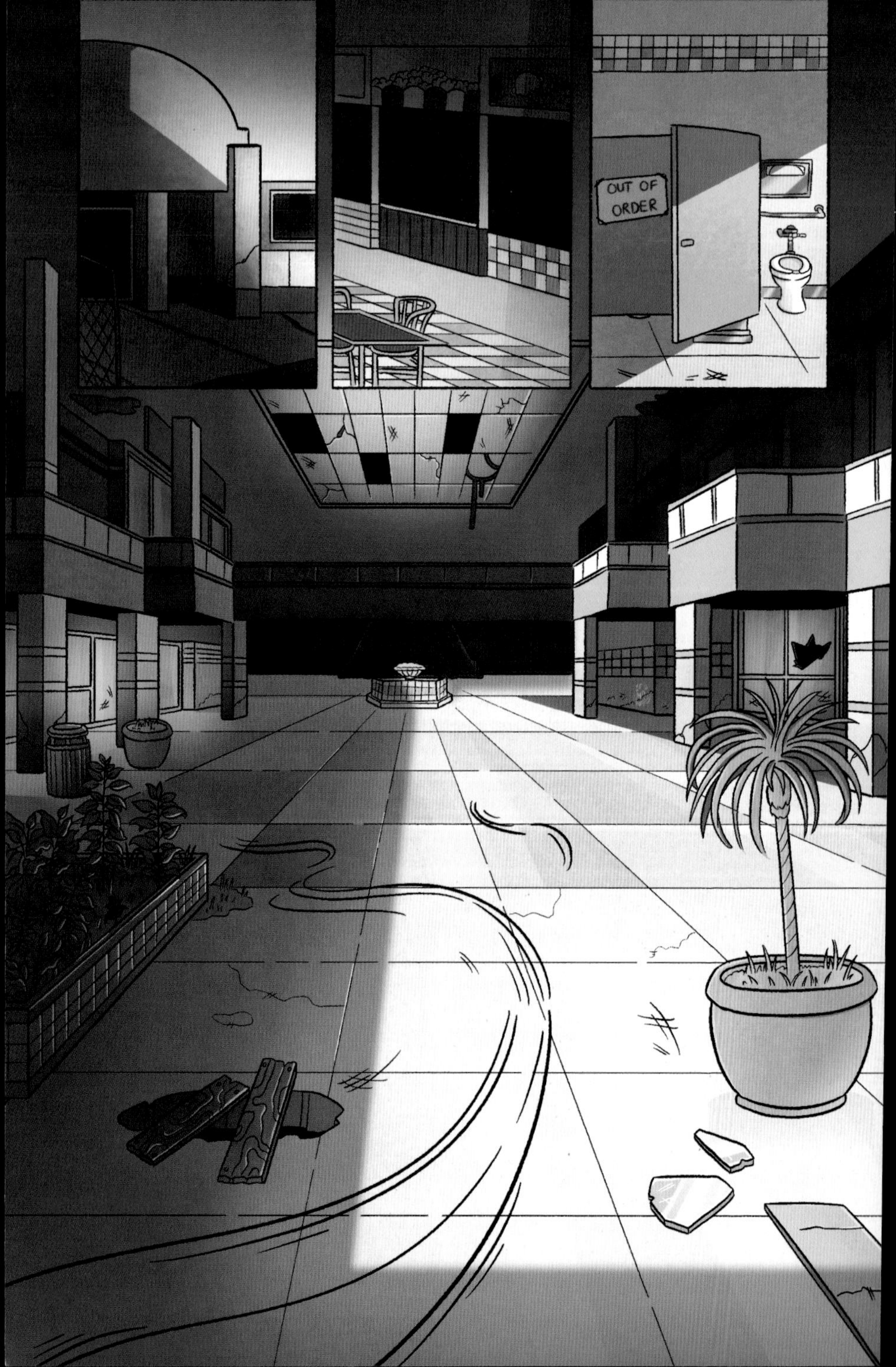
OUT OF
ORDER

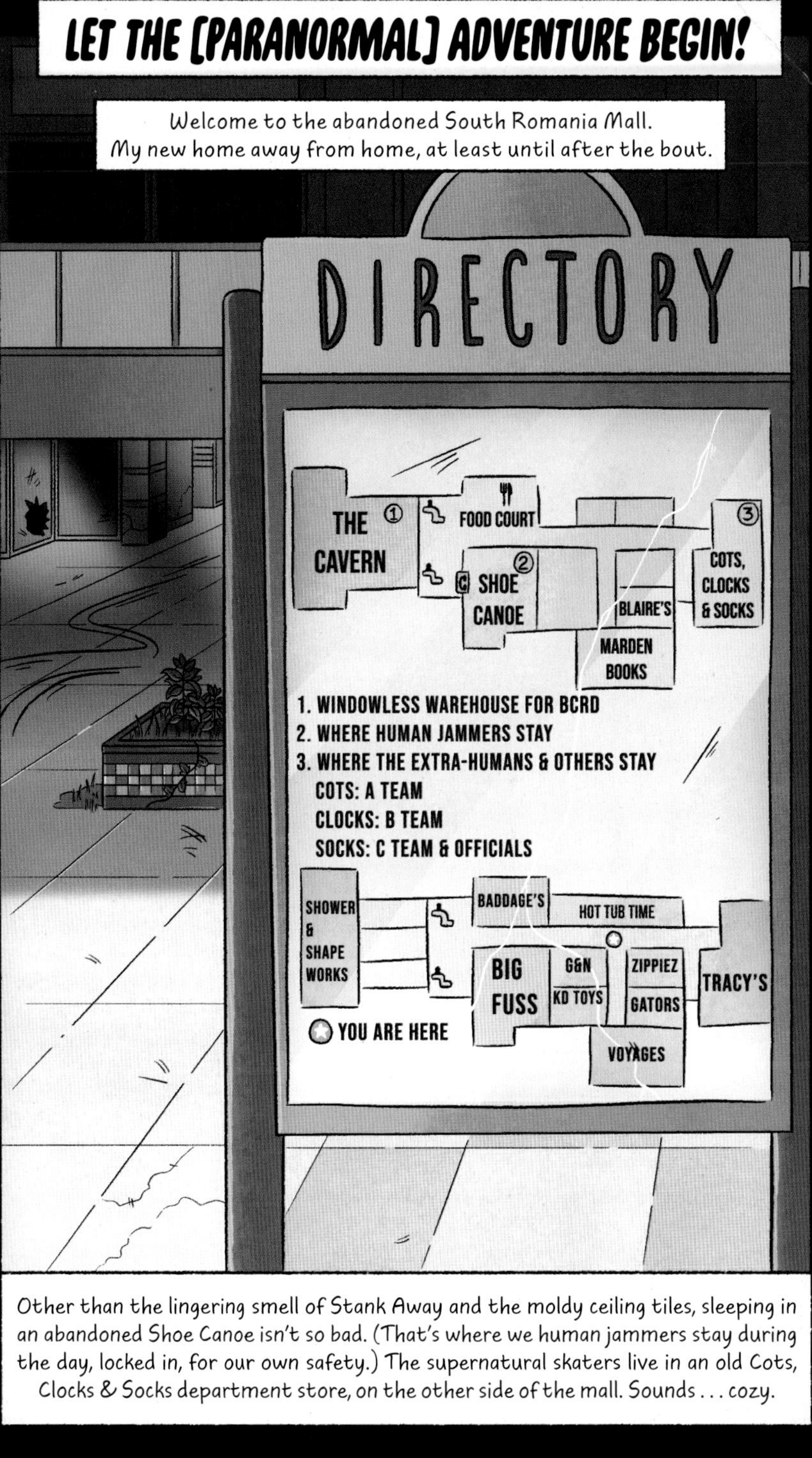
LET THE [PARANORMAL] ADVENTURE BEGIN!
Welcome to the abandoned South Romania Mall. My new home away from home, at least until after the bout.
DIRECTORY
THE CAVERN ①
FOOD COURT
SHOE CANOE ②
BLAIRE'S
MARDEN BOOKS
COTS, CLOCKS & SOCKS ③
1. WINDOWLESS WAREHOUSE FOR BCRD
2. WHERE HUMAN JAMMERS STAY
3. WHERE THE EXTRA-HUMANS & OTHERS STAY
COTS: A TEAM
CLOCKS: B TEAM
SOCKS: C TEAM & OFFICIALS
SHOWER & SHAPE WORKS
BADDAGE'S
HOT TUB TIME
BIG FUSS
G&N
KD TOYS
ZIPPIEZ
GATORS
TRACY'S
VOYAGES
YOU ARE HERE
Other than the lingering smell of Stank Away and the moldy ceiling tiles, sleeping in an abandoned Shoe Canoe isn't so bad. (That's where we human jammers stay during the day, locked in, for our own safety.) The supernatural skaters live in an old Cots, Clocks & Socks department store, on the other side of the mall. Sounds . . . cozy.

Anyway, I have bigger problems than living arrangements.

They said I couldn't go home. They told me there was a chance I could die.

But NOBODY told me there would be HOMEWORK involved.

PRD has a written entrance exam?! Are you serious???

Always.

So, what happens if I don't pass THIS test, and the PRD governing body—Evil on Wheels, EOW or whatever—doesn't let me in? You'll...send me home early?

Certainly.

Alive?

Probably.

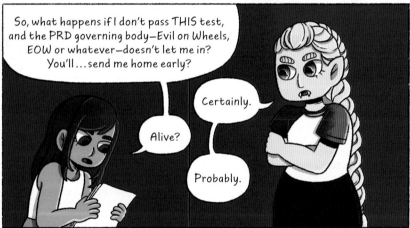

Have I mentioned how much I have grown to appreciate your dry sense of humor?

Enough stalling. You have thirty minutes to complete the test. For every question you get wrong, you owe me ten burpees.

Sigh.

Scenario Four:

Green Blocker initiates a chest-to-chest block against Red Blocker. The force of the impact causes secondary contact of Green Blocker's upper arm to Red Blocker's neck. Red Blocker is decapitated but not killed. Who gets a penalty?

a) Green Blocker, for not controlling their limbs

b) Red Blocker, for failing to react more quickly

c) Neither skater receives a penalty in this case.

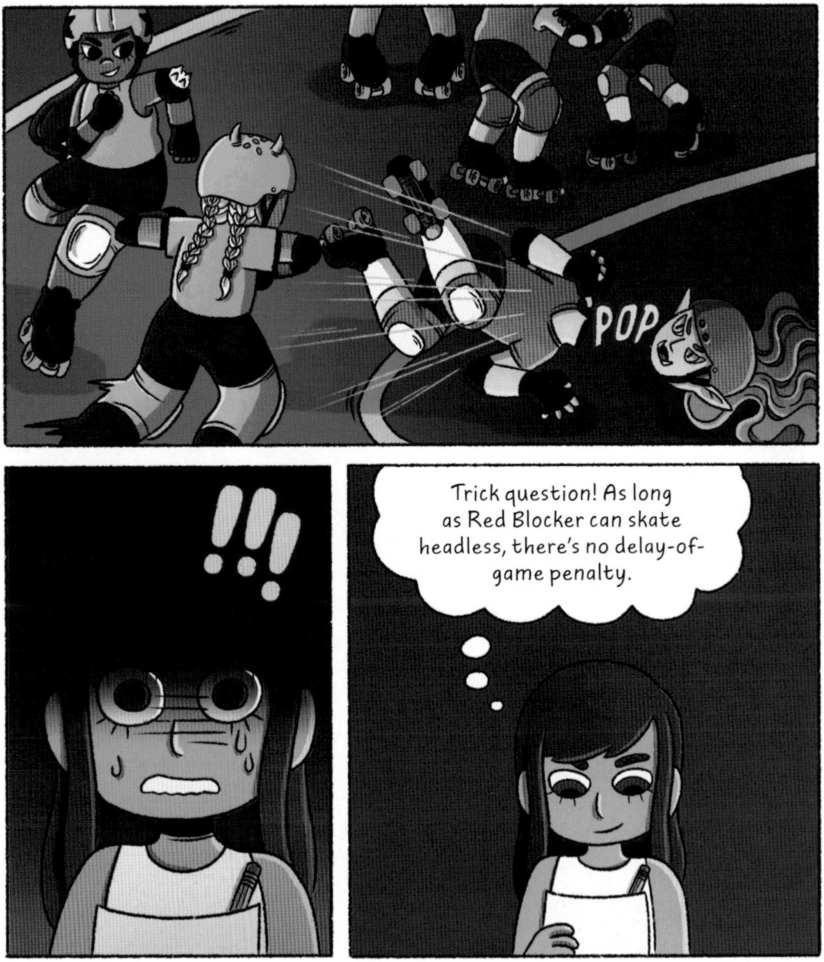
POP
!!!
Trick question! As long as Red Blocker can skate headless, there's no delay-of-game penalty.

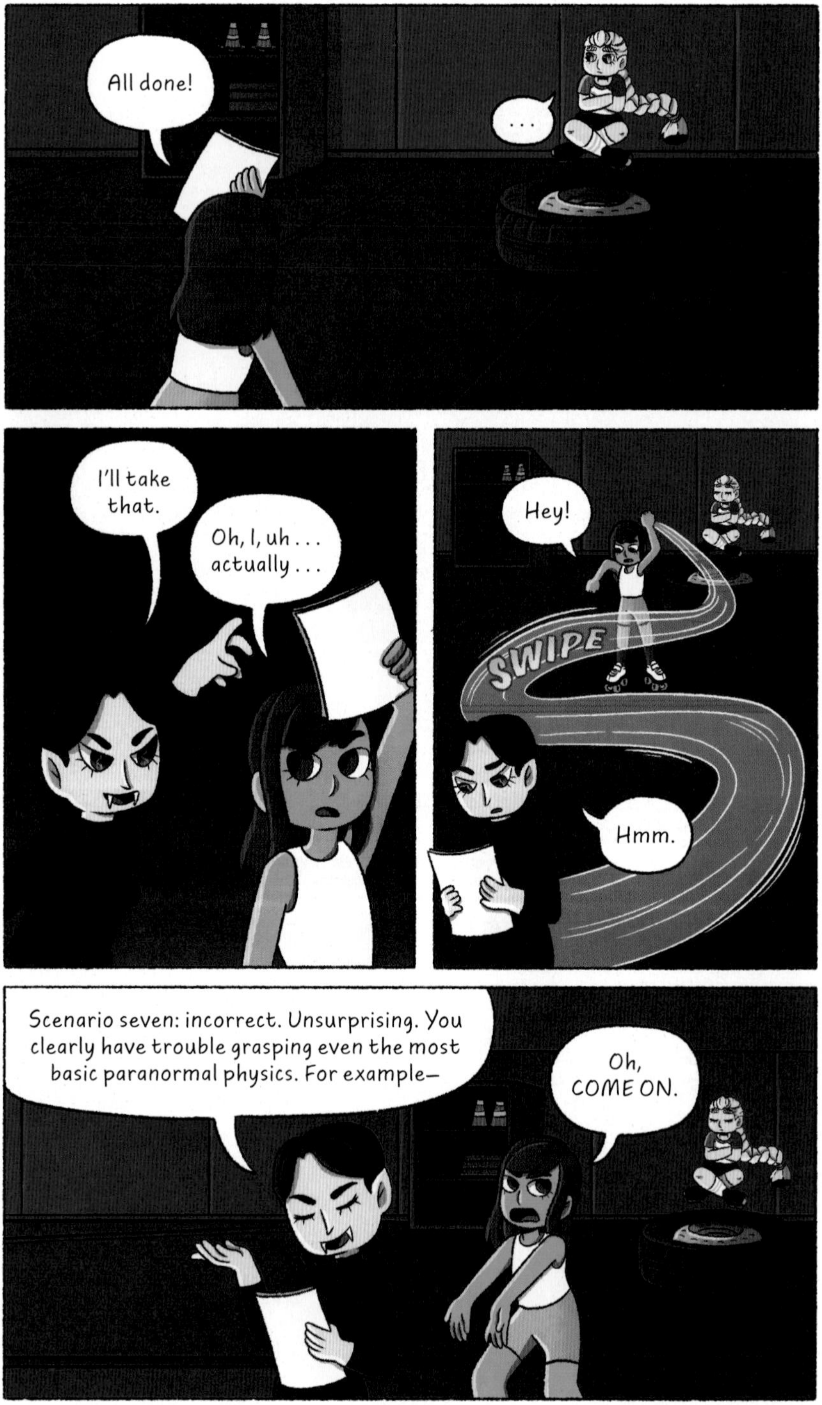
All done!
. . .
I'll take that.
Oh, I, uh . . . actually . . .
Hey!
SWIPE
Hmm.
Scenario seven: incorrect. Unsurprising. You clearly have trouble grasping even the most basic paranormal physics. For example—
Oh, COME ON.

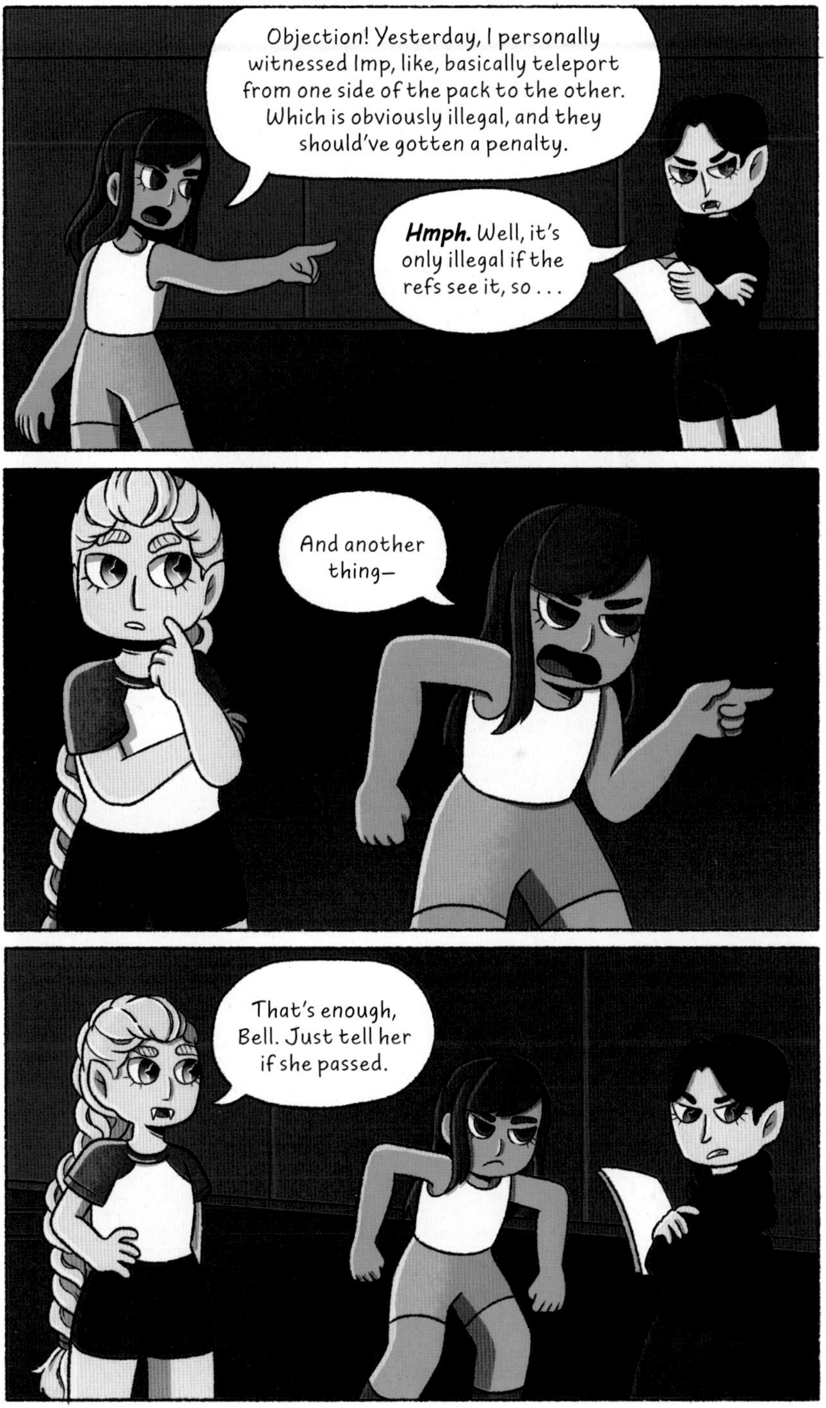

Objection! Yesterday, I personally witnessed Imp, like, basically teleport from one side of the pack to the other. Which is obviously illegal, and they should've gotten a penalty.
Hmph. Well, it's only illegal if the refs see it, so . . .
And another thing—
That's enough, Bell. Just tell her if she passed.

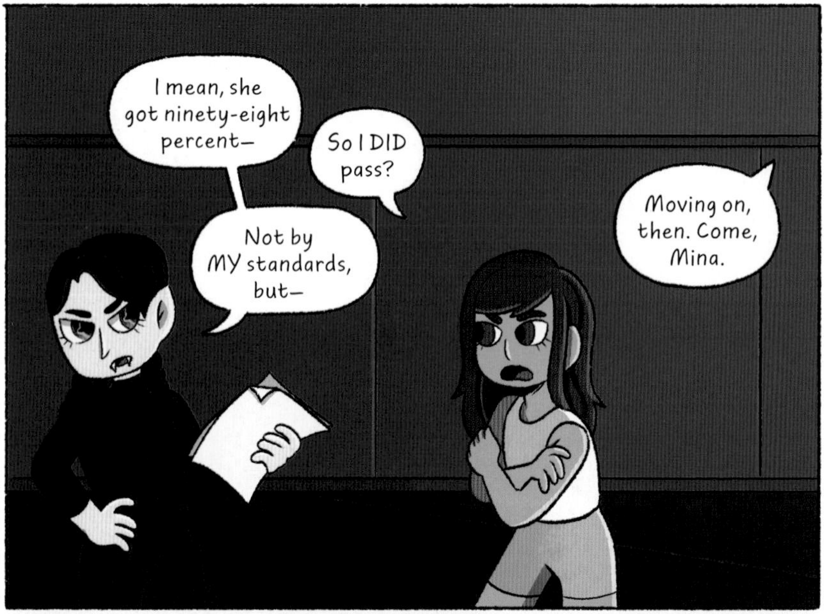

I mean, she got ninety-eight percent—
So I DID pass?
Not by MY standards, but—
Moving on, then. Come, Mina.

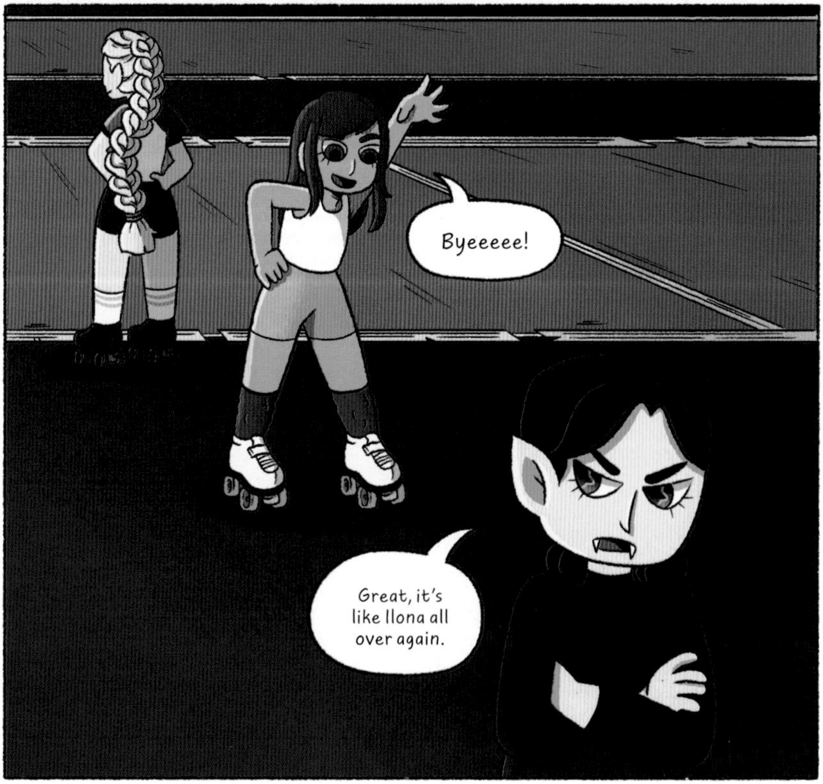

Byeeeee!
Great, it's like Ilona all over again.

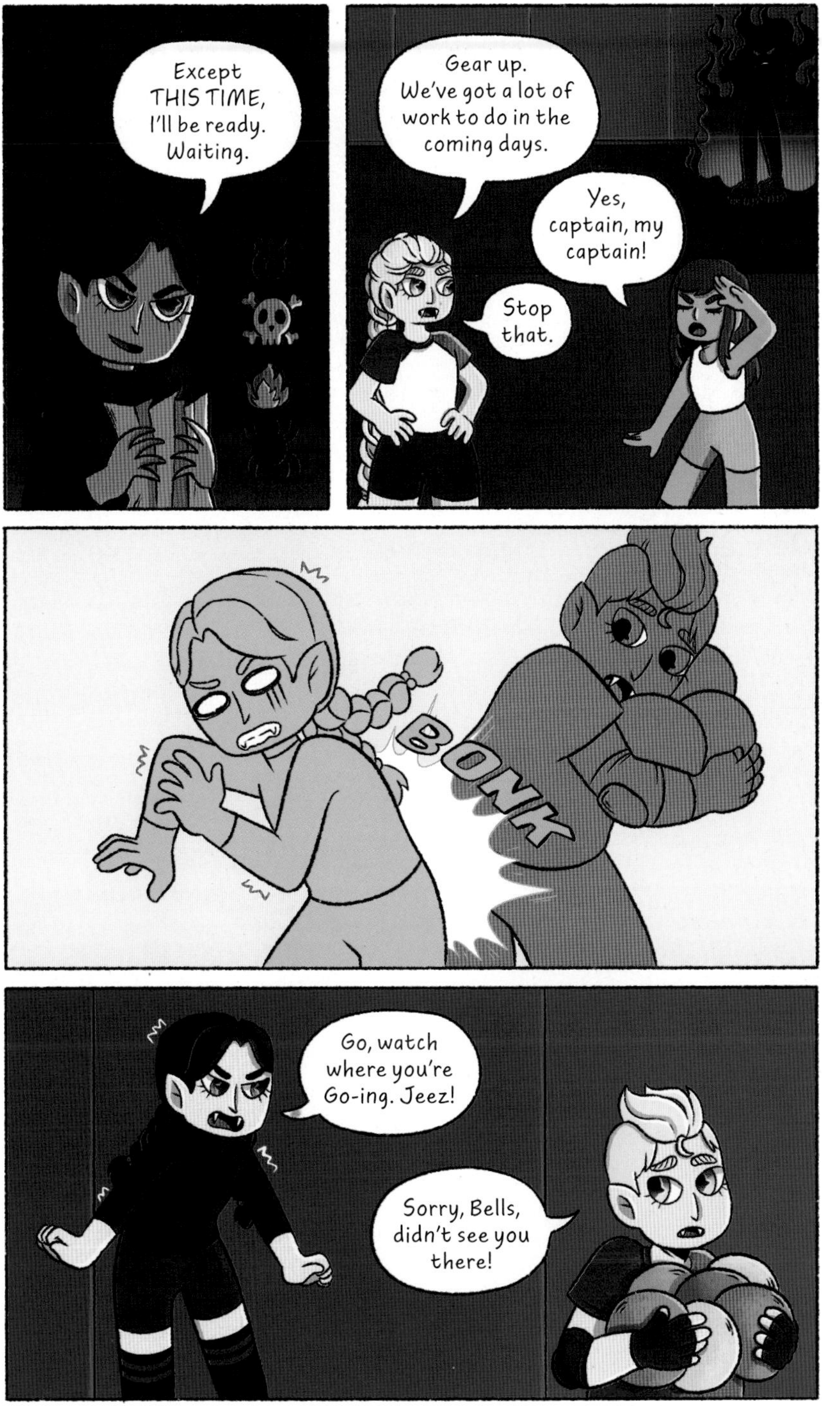
Except THIS TIME, I'll be ready. Waiting.
Gear up. We've got a lot of work to do in the coming days.
Yes, captain, my captain!
Stop that.
BONK
Go, watch where you're Go-ing. Jeez!
Sorry, Bells, didn't see you there!

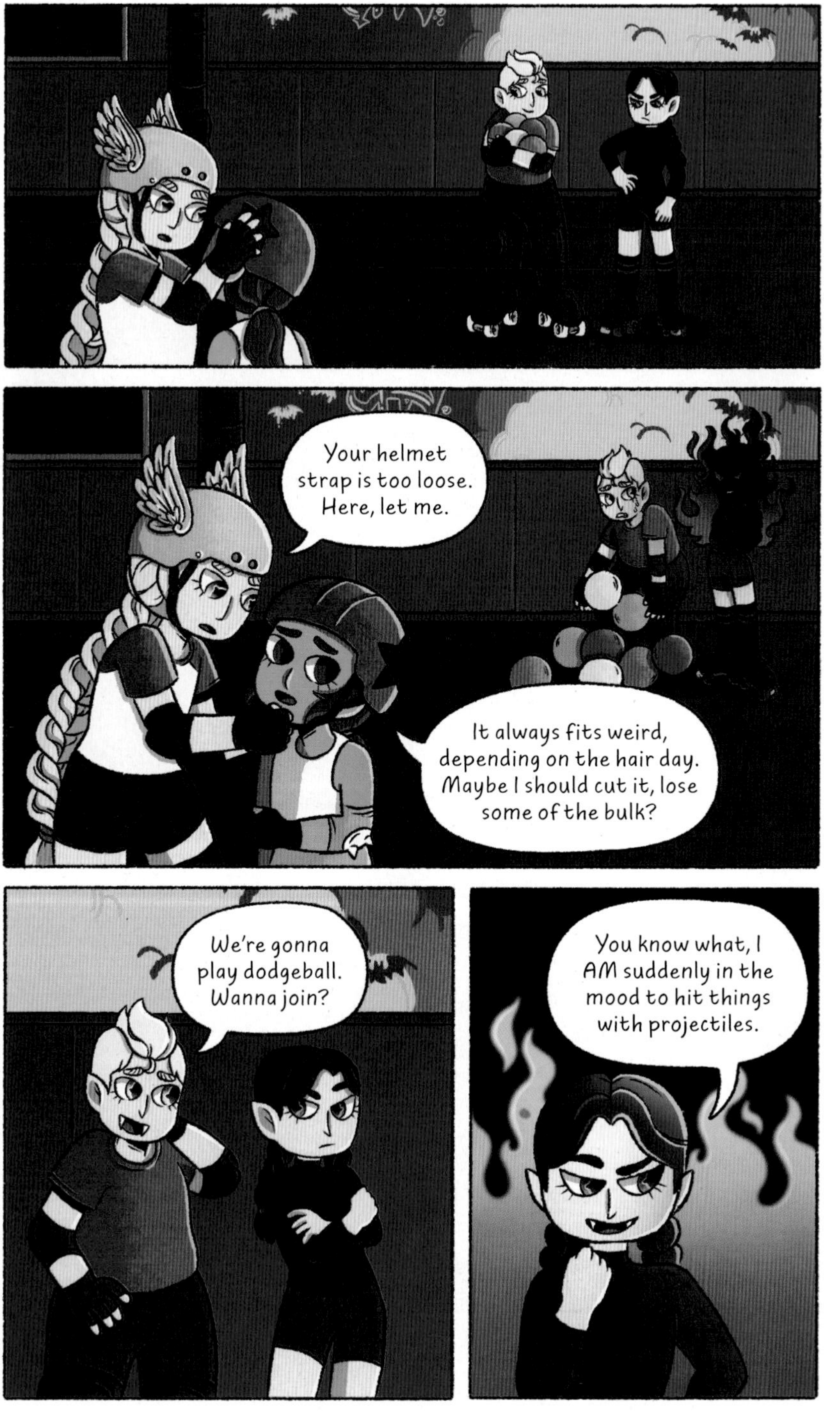

Your helmet strap is too loose. Here, let me.
It always fits weird, depending on the hair day. Maybe I should cut it, lose some of the bulk?
We're gonna play dodgeball. Wanna join?
You know what, I AM suddenly in the mood to hit things with projectiles.

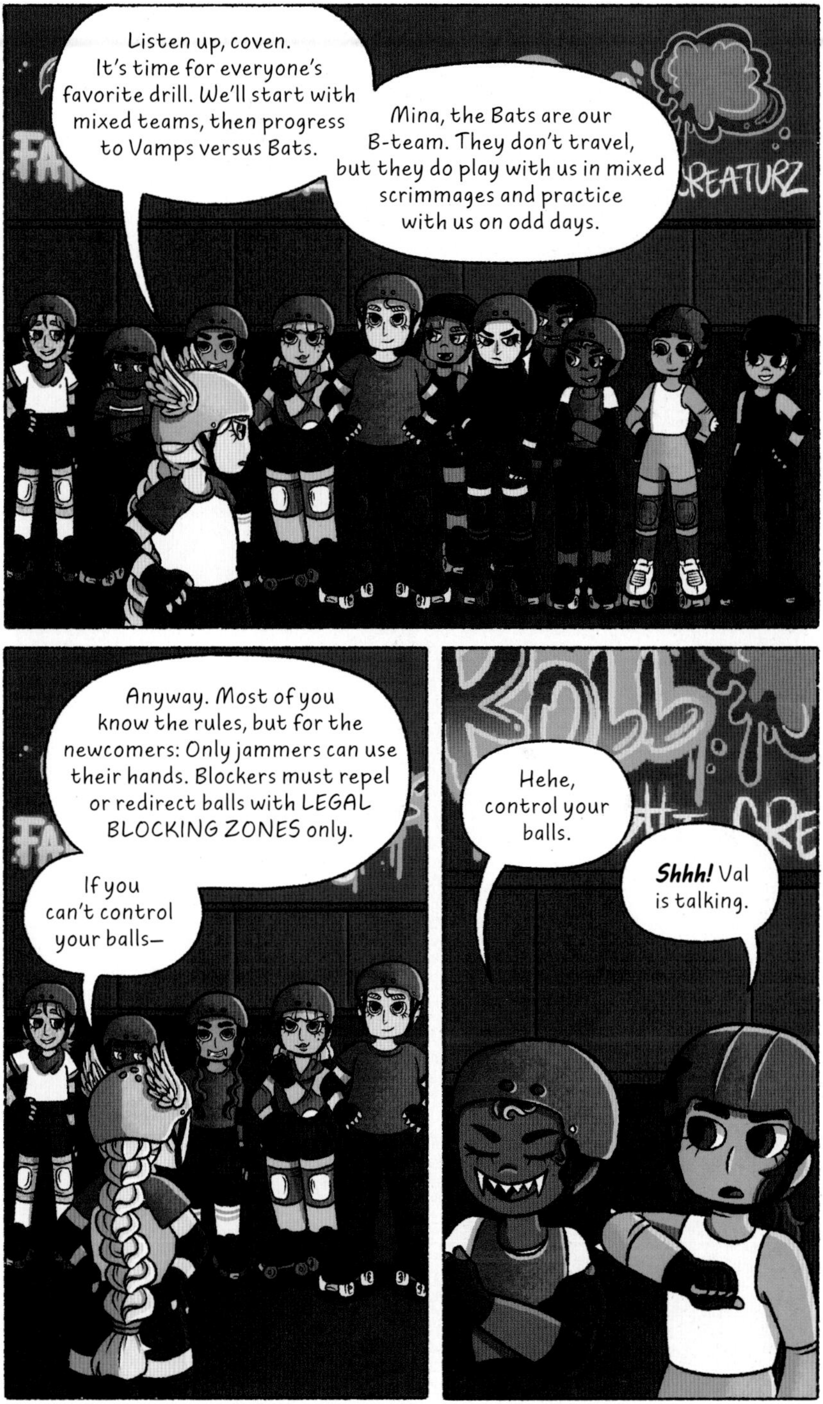
Listen up, coven. It's time for everyone's favorite drill. We'll start with mixed teams, then progress to Vamps versus Bats.
Mina, the Bats are our B-team. They don't travel, but they do play with us in mixed scrimmages and practice with us on odd days.
CREATURZ
Anyway. Most of you know the rules, but for the newcomers: Only jammers can use their hands. Blockers must repel or redirect balls with LEGAL BLOCKING ZONES only.
If you can't control your balls—
Hehe, control your balls.
Shhh! Val is talking.

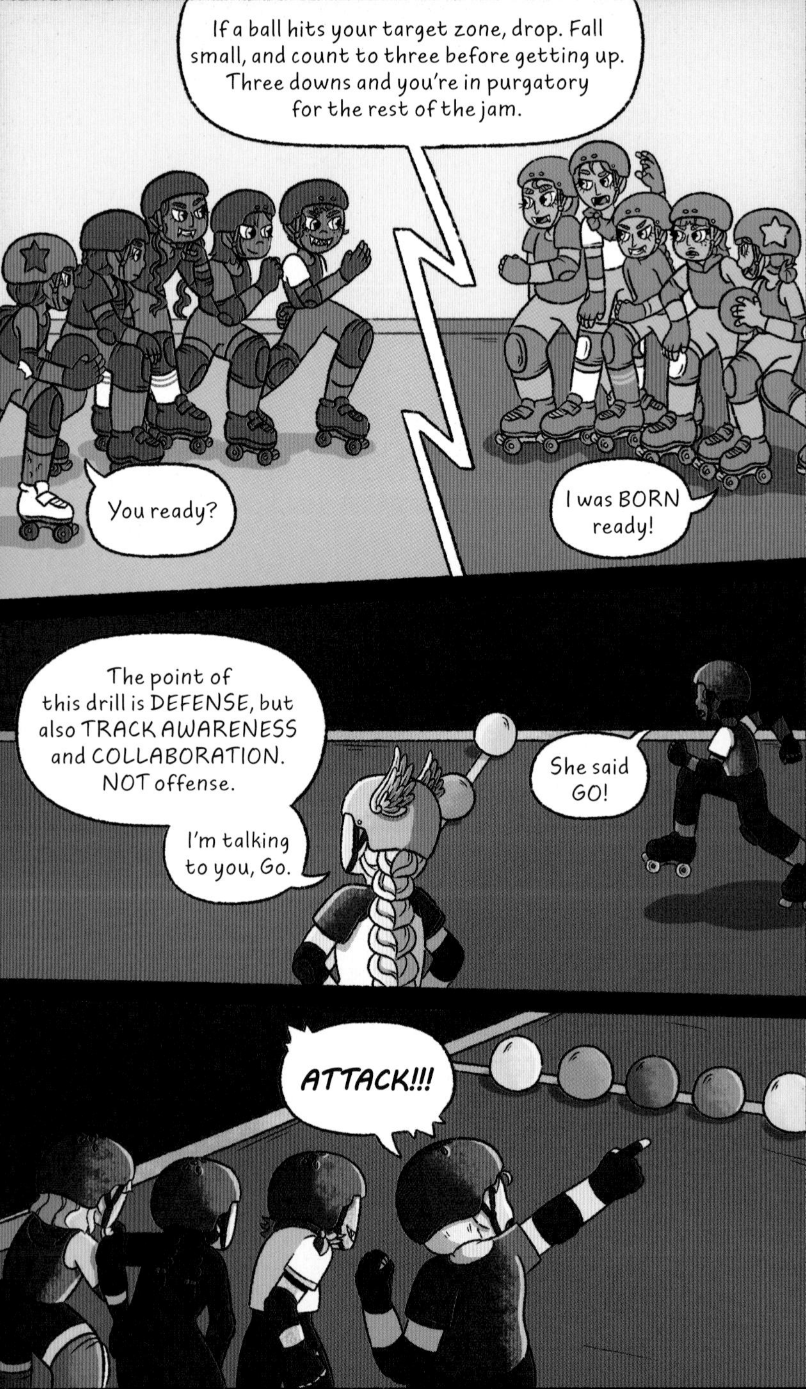

If a ball hits your target zone, drop. Fall small, and count to three before getting up. Three downs and you're in purgatory for the rest of the jam.
You ready?
I was BORN ready!
The point of this drill is DEFENSE, but also TRACK AWARENESS and COLLABORATION. NOT offense.
I'm talking to you, Go.
She said GO!
ATTACK!!!

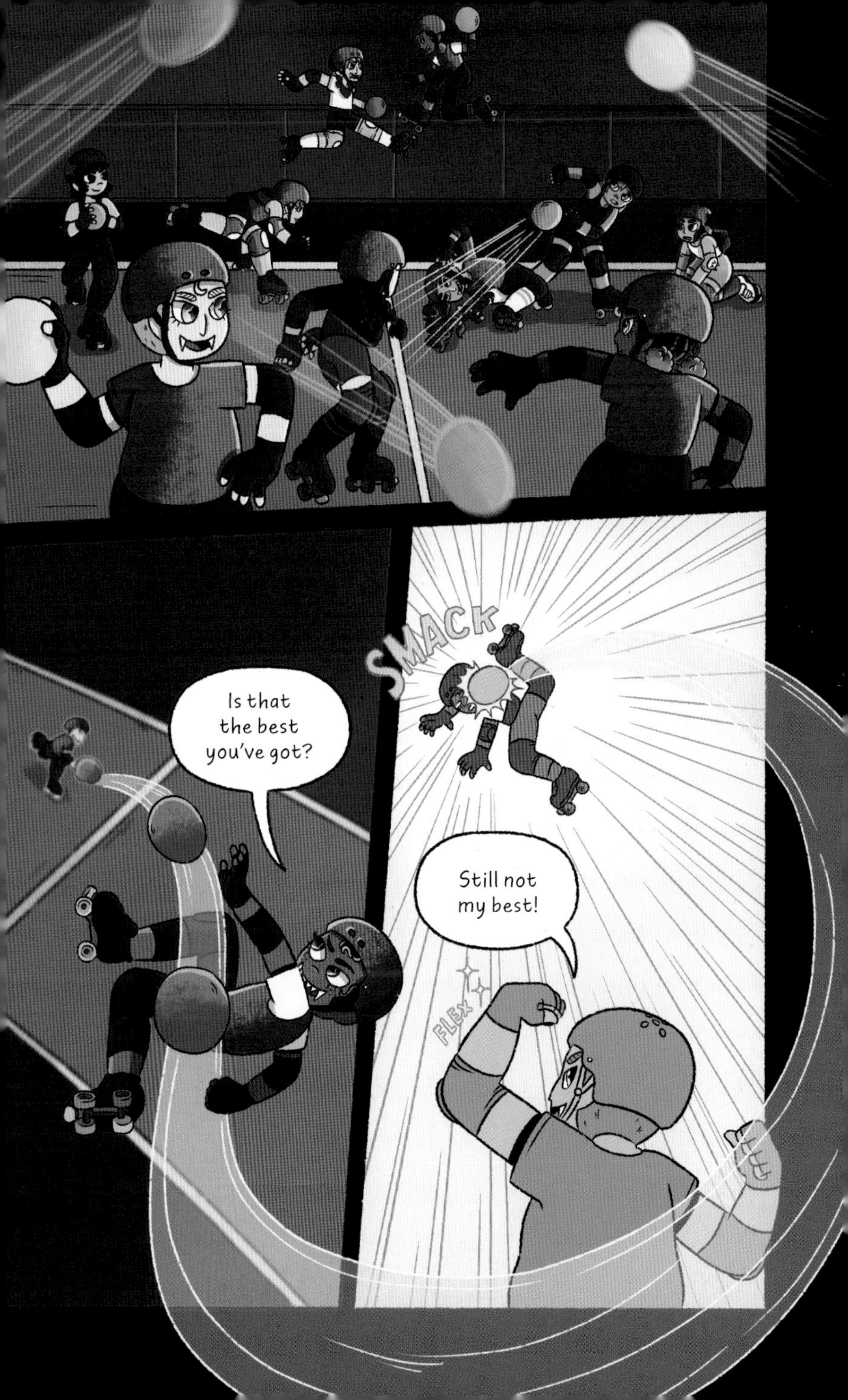
Is that the best you've got?
SMACK
Still not my best!
FLEX

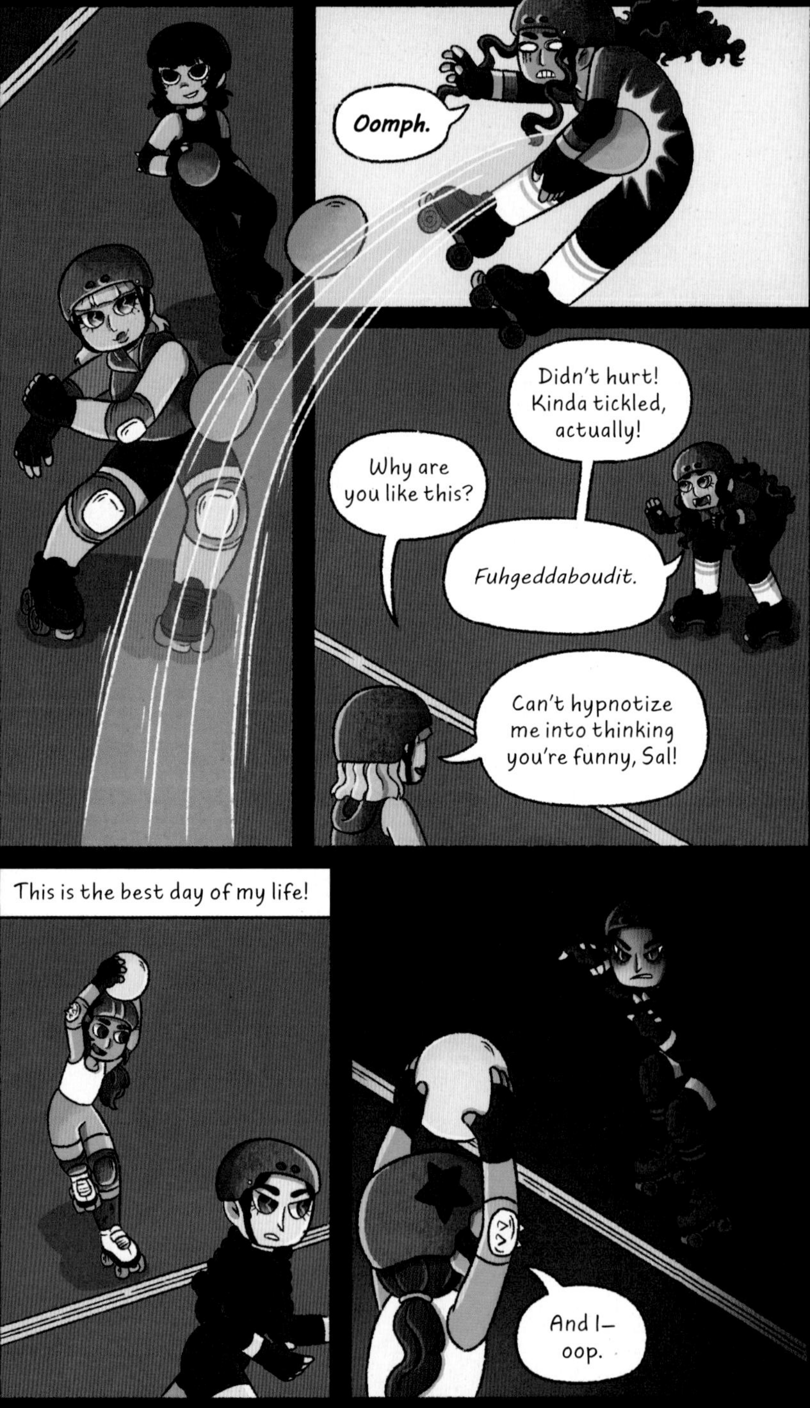
Oomph.
Didn't hurt! Kinda tickled, actually!
Why are you like this?
Fuhgeddaboudit.
Can't hypnotize me into thinking you're funny, Sal!
This is the best day of my life!
And I—
oop.

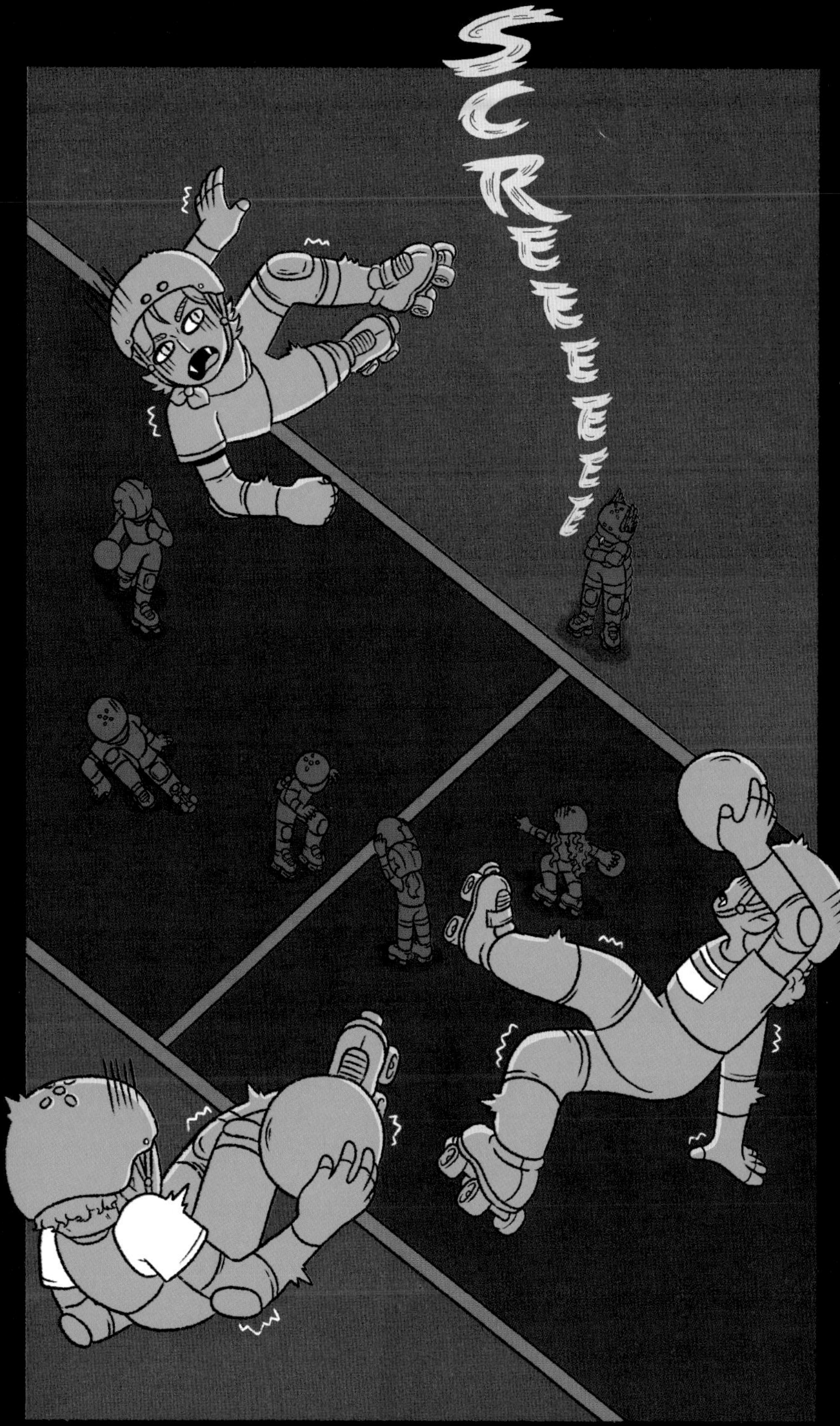
SCREEEEEE

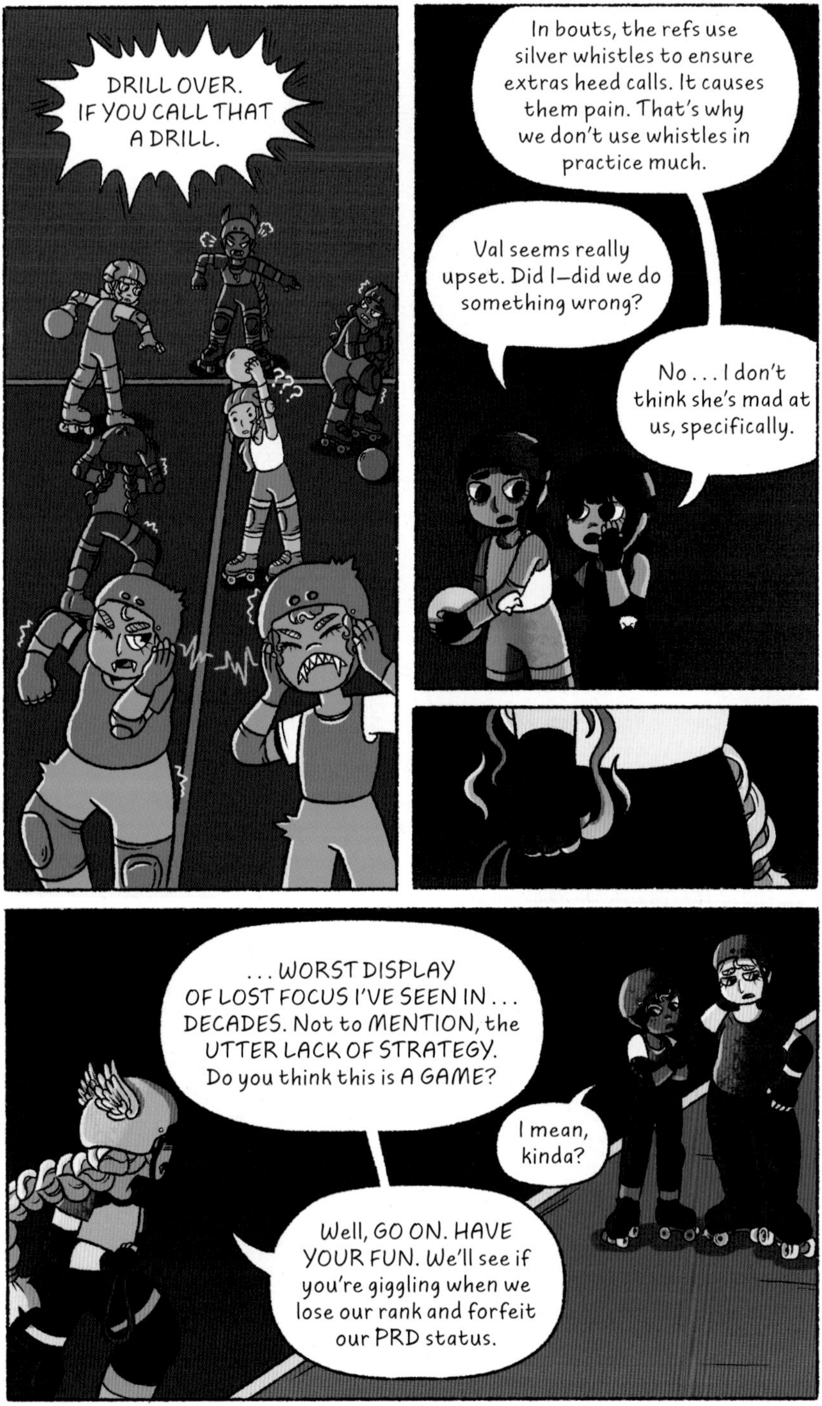
DRILL OVER. IF YOU CALL THAT A DRILL.
In bouts, the refs use silver whistles to ensure extras heed calls. It causes them pain. That's why we don't use whistles in practice much.
Val seems really upset. Did I—did we do something wrong?
No . . . I don't think she's mad at us, specifically.
. . . WORST DISPLAY OF LOST FOCUS I'VE SEEN IN . . . DECADES. Not to MENTION, the UTTER LACK OF STRATEGY. Do you think this is A GAME?
I mean, kinda?
Well, GO ON. HAVE YOUR FUN. We'll see if you're giggling when we lose our rank and forfeit our PRD status.

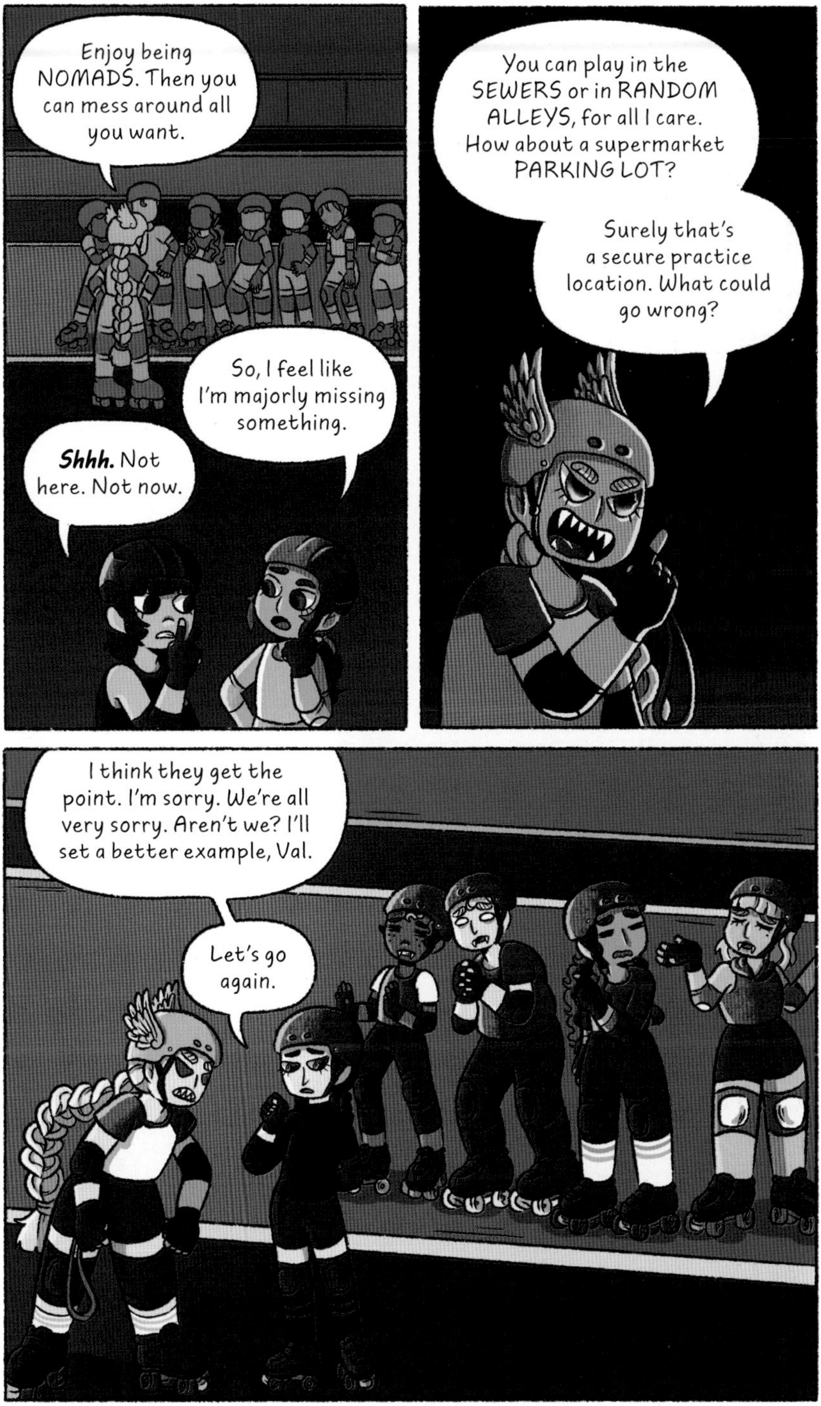
Enjoy being NOMADS. Then you can mess around all you want.
You can play in the SEWERS or in RANDOM ALLEYS, for all I care. How about a supermarket PARKING LOT?
Surely that's a secure practice location. What could go wrong?
So, I feel like I'm majorly missing something.
Shhh. Not here. Not now.
I think they get the point. I'm sorry. We're all very sorry. Aren't we? I'll set a better example, Val.
Let's go again.

Sure. Fine. Go ahead.

Just . . . Bella, you take over for a while. I'll be back.

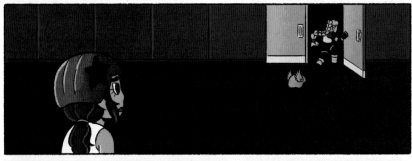

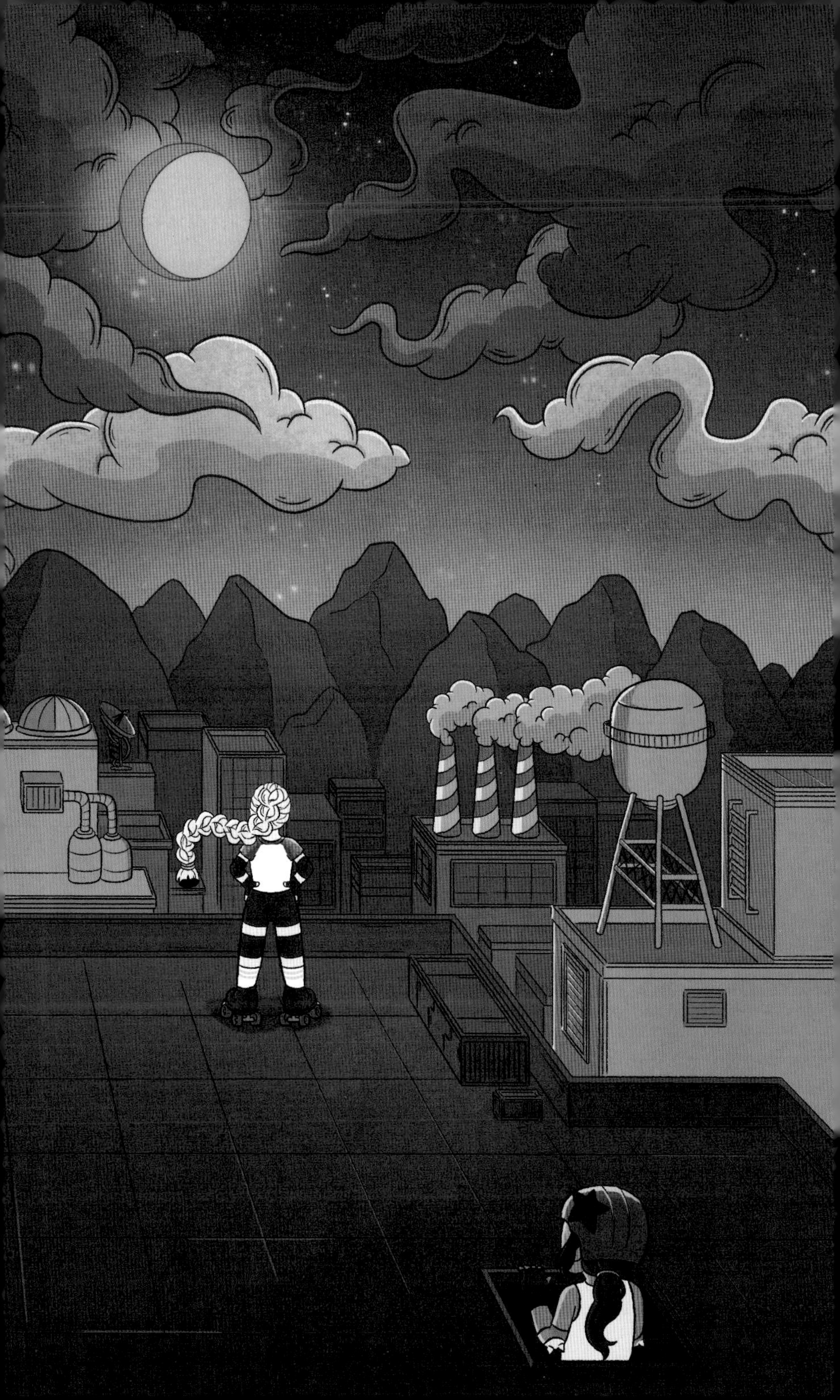

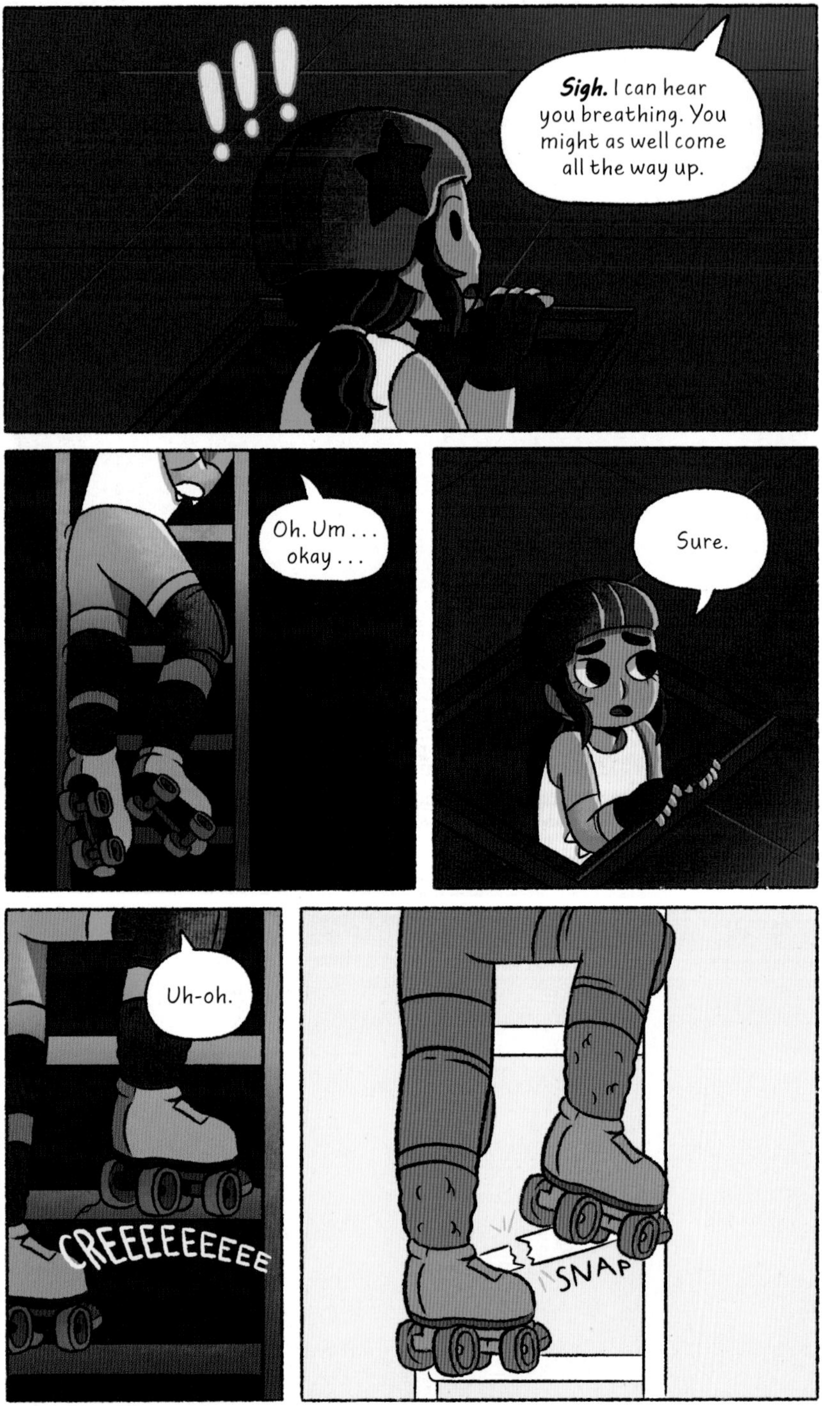
!!!
Sigh. I can hear you breathing. You might as well come all the way up.
Oh. Um . . . okay . . .
Sure.
Uh-oh.
CREEEEEEEEEE
SNAP

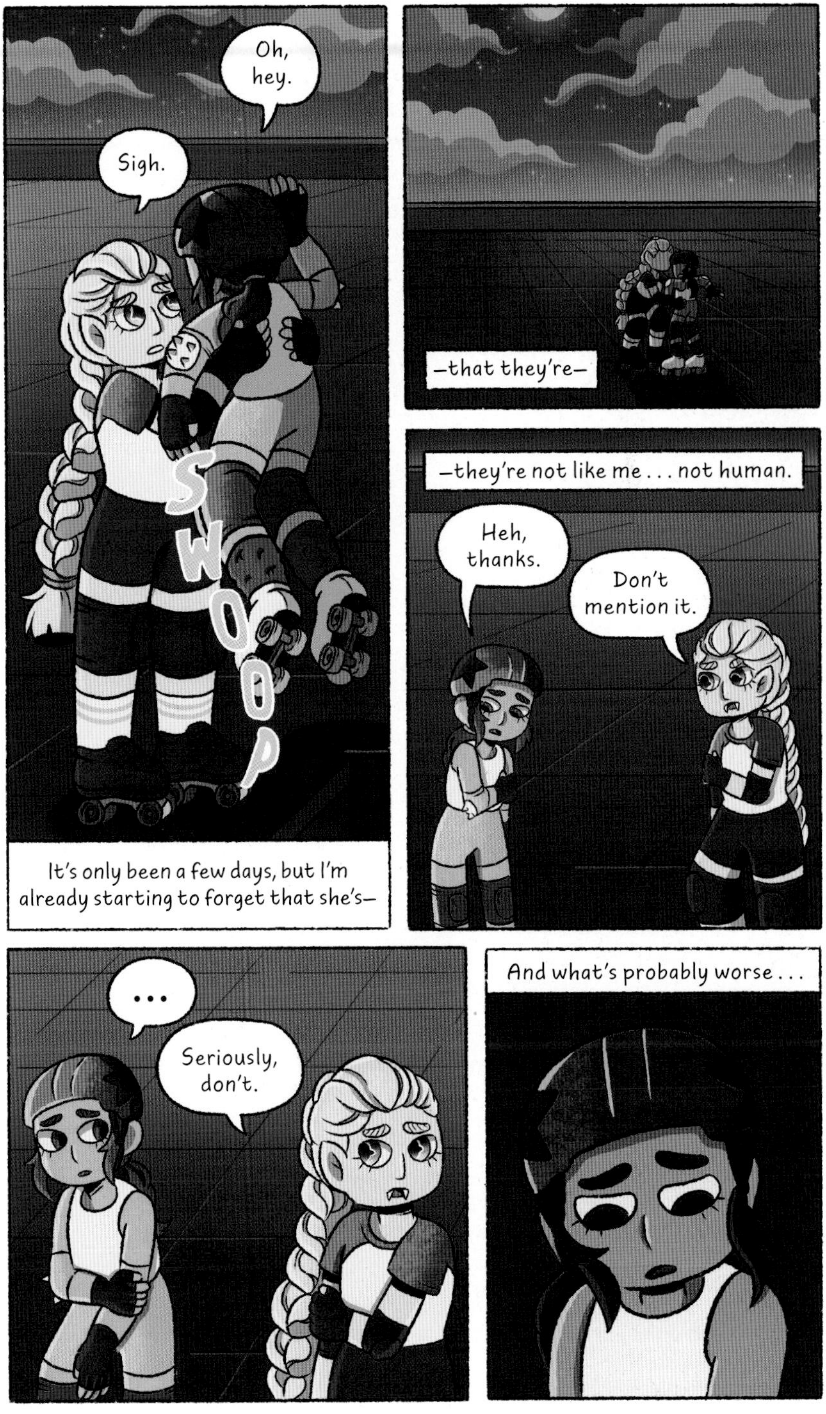

Oh, hey.
Sigh.
SWOOP
It's only been a few days, but I'm already starting to forget that she's—
—that they're—
—they're not like me . . . not human.
Heh, thanks.
Don't mention it.
. . .
Seriously, don't.
And what's probably worse . . .

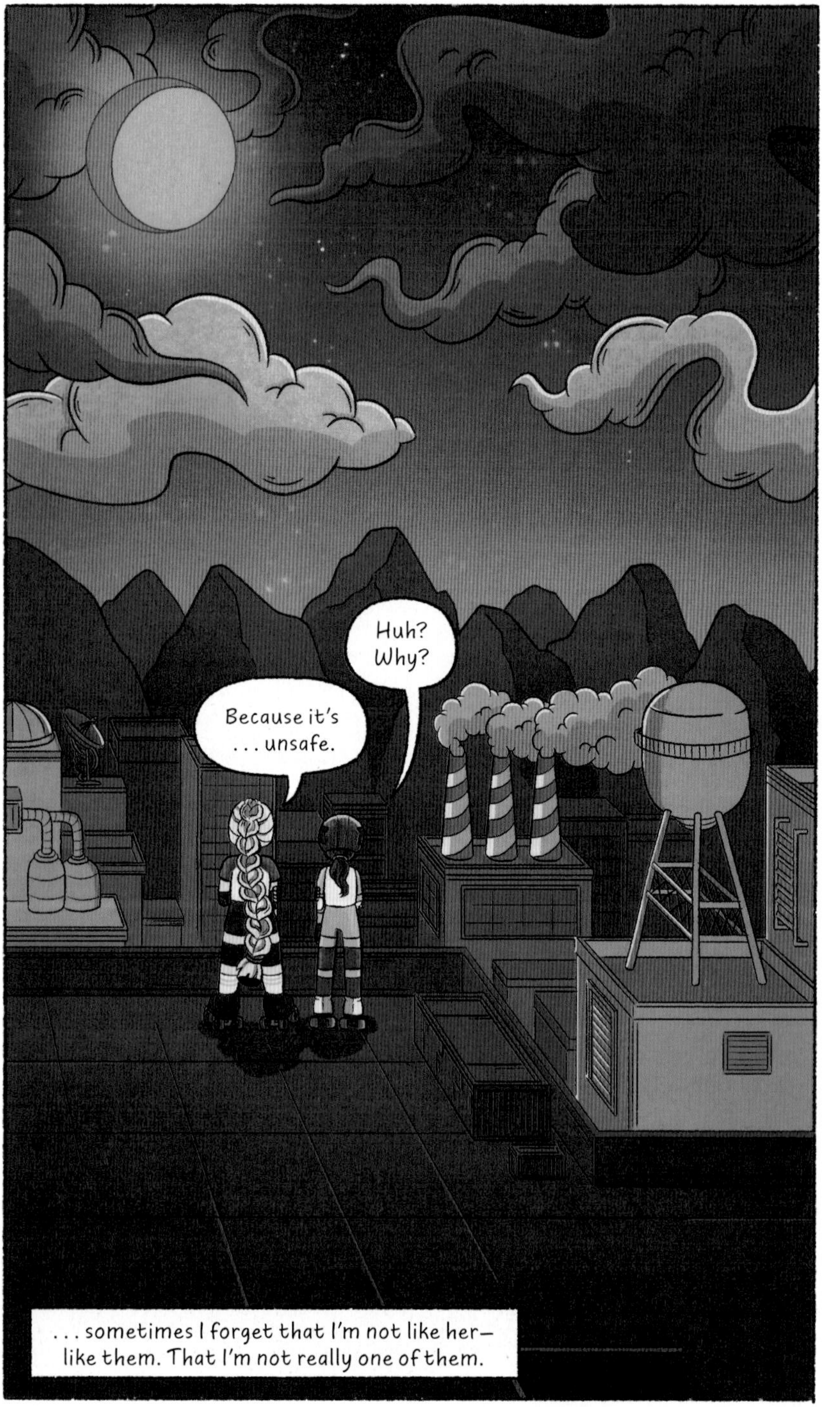
Huh? Why?
Because it's . . . unsafe.
. . . sometimes I forget that I'm not like her—like them. That I'm not really one of them.

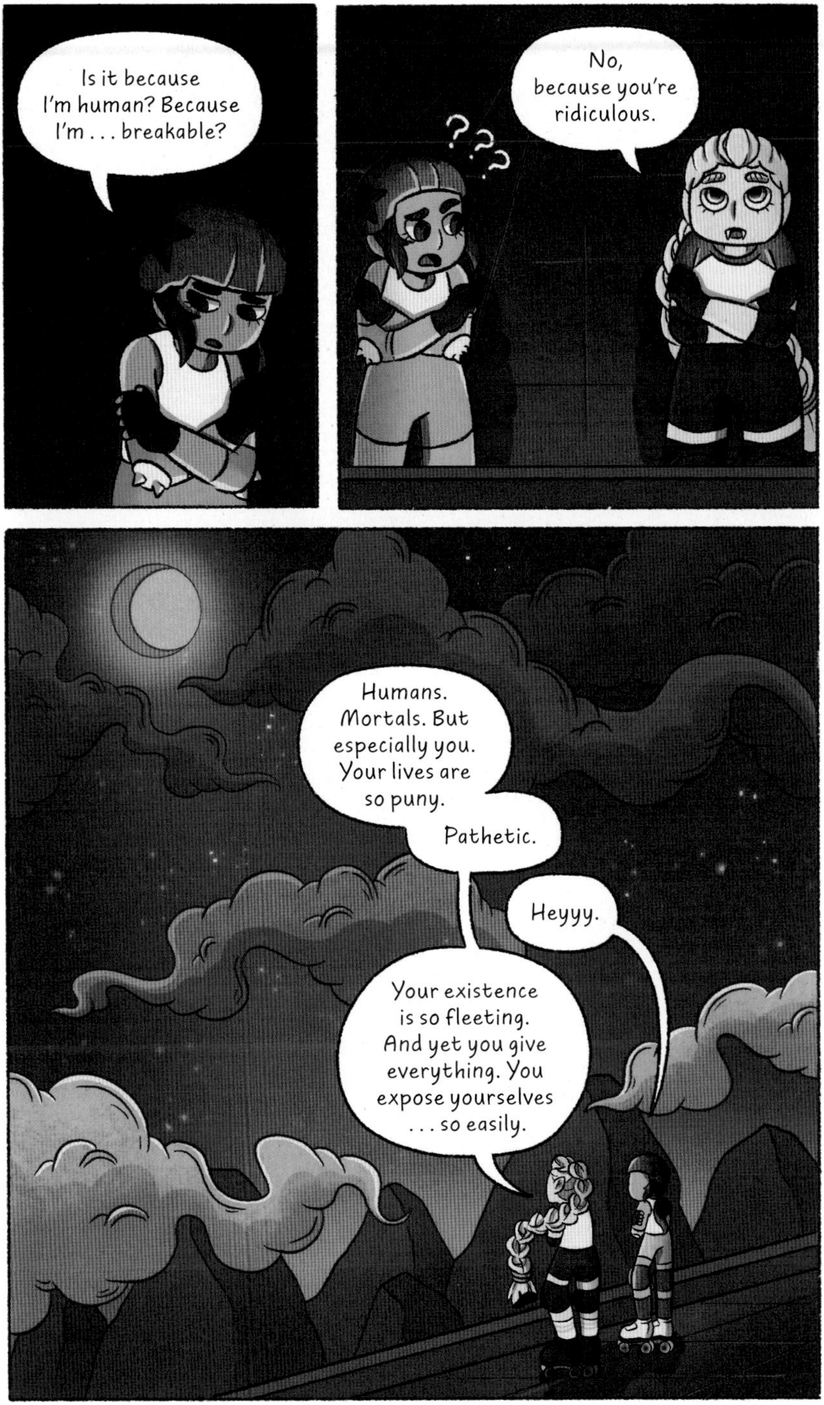
Is it because I'm human? Because I'm . . . breakable?
???
No, because you're ridiculous.
Humans. Mortals. But especially you. Your lives are so puny.
Pathetic.
Heyyy.
Your existence is so fleeting. And yet you give everything. You expose yourselves . . . so easily.

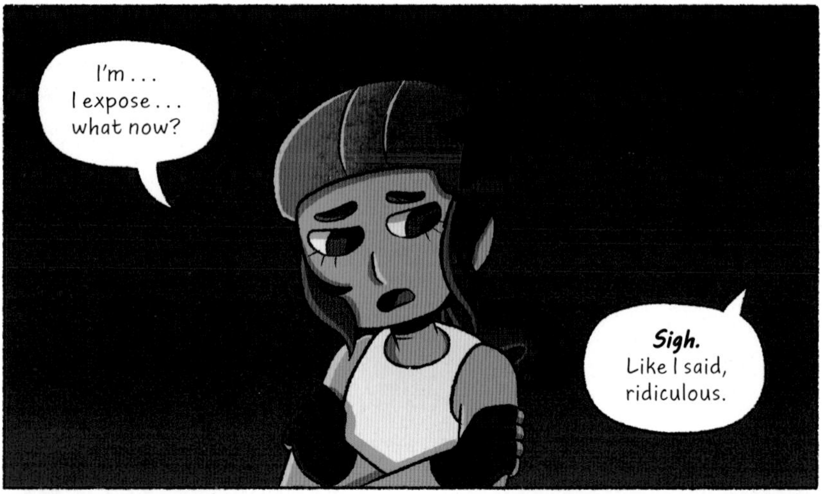
I'm . . .
I expose . . .
what now?
Sigh.
Like I said,
ridiculous.

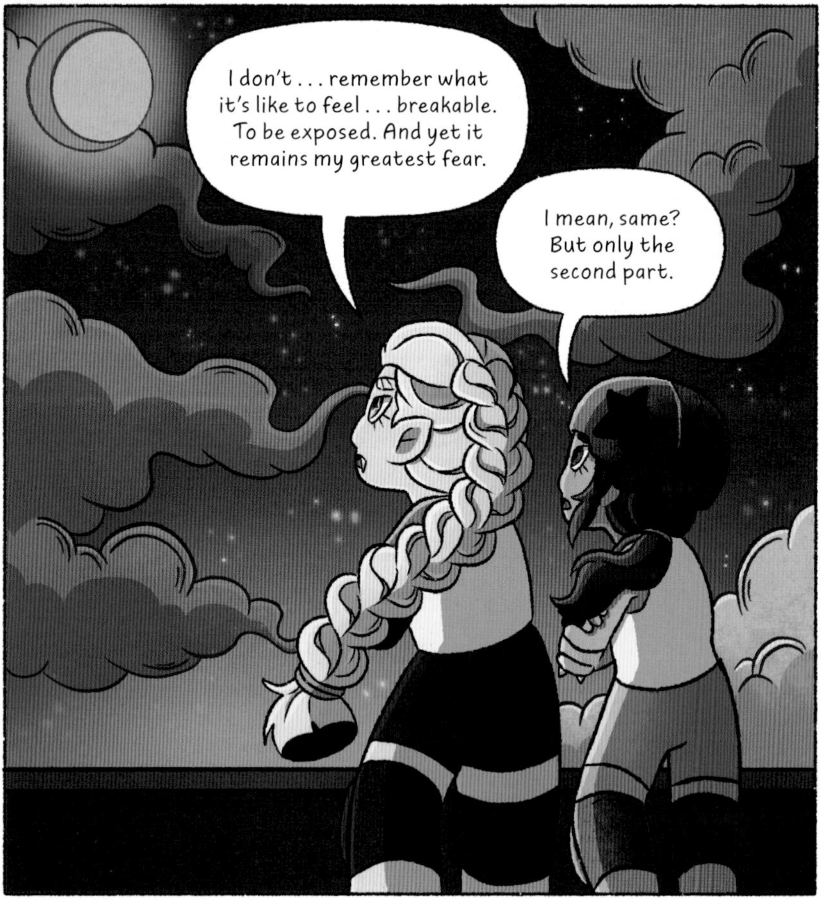
I don't . . . remember what it's like to feel . . . breakable. To be exposed. And yet it remains my greatest fear.
I mean, same? But only the second part.

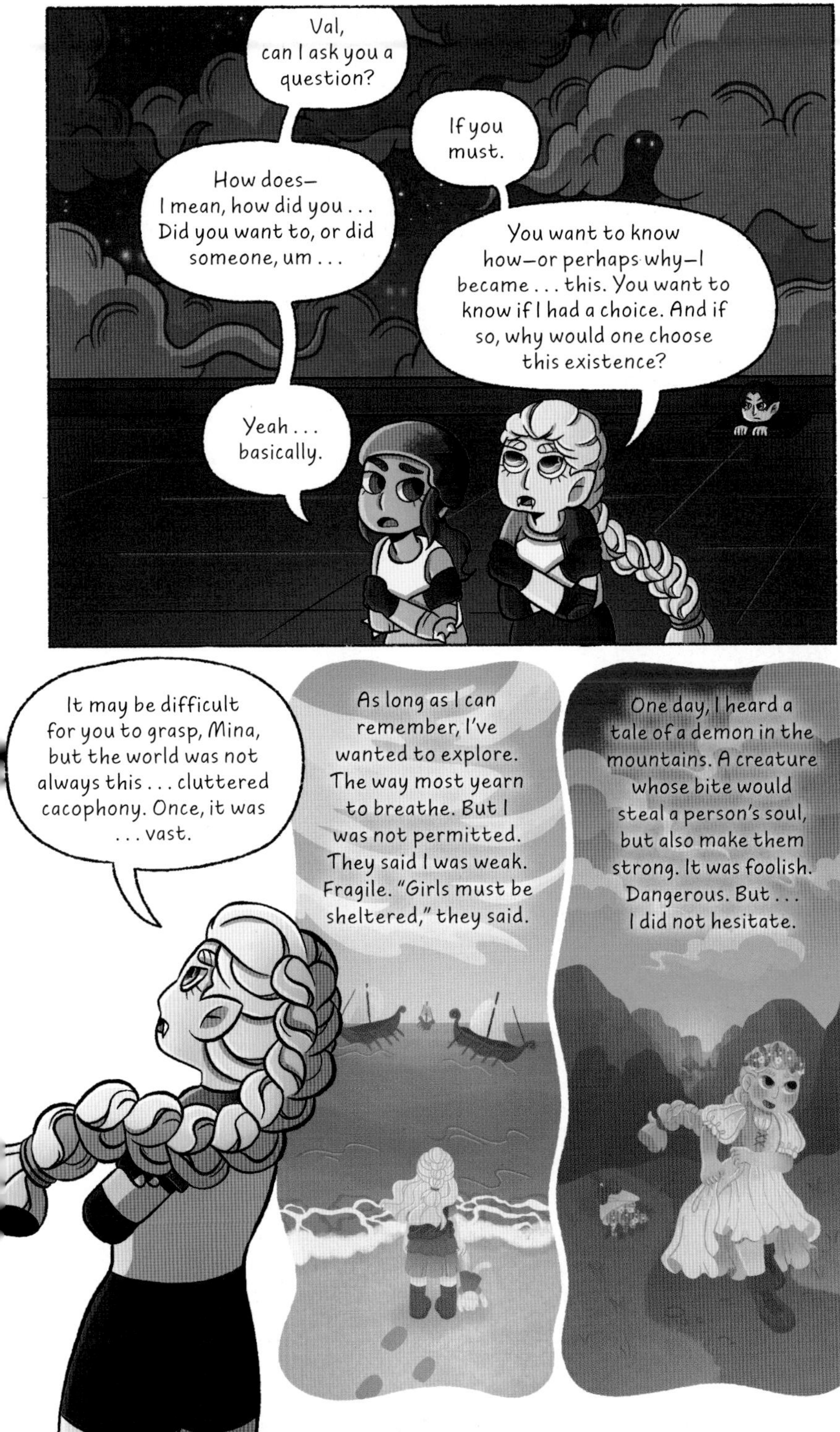
Val, can I ask you a question?
If you must.
How does— I mean, how did you . . . Did you want to, or did someone, um . . .
You want to know how—or perhaps why—I became . . . this. You want to know if I had a choice. And if so, why would one choose this existence?
Yeah . . . basically.
It may be difficult for you to grasp, Mina, but the world was not always this . . . cluttered cacophony. Once, it was . . . vast.
As long as I can remember, I've wanted to explore. The way most yearn to breathe. But I was not permitted. They said I was weak. Fragile. "Girls must be sheltered," they said.
One day, I heard a tale of a demon in the mountains. A creature whose bite would steal a person's soul, but also make them strong. It was foolish. Dangerous. But . . . I did not hesitate.

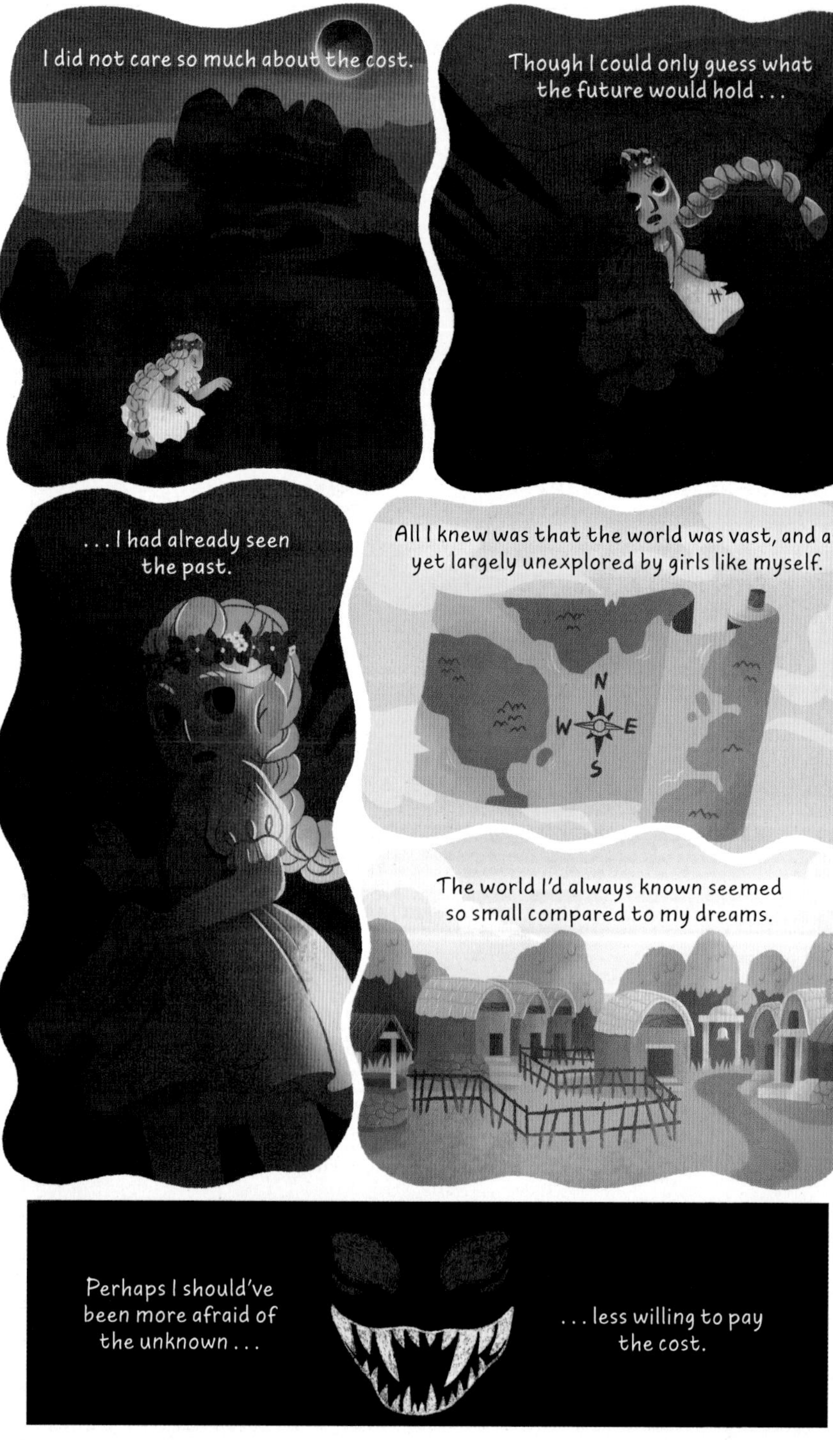
I did not care so much about the cost.
Though I could only guess what the future would hold . . .
. . . I had already seen the past.
All I knew was that the world was vast, and as yet largely unexplored by girls like myself.
N
W
E
S
The world I'd always known seemed so small compared to my dreams.
Perhaps I should've been more afraid of the unknown . . .
. . . less willing to pay the cost.

But then . . . I have learned that we always pay for what we want, one way or another.

Yeah. Hard same. I mean . . . I've learned that . . . too.

In my case, the cost was quite high. But it was also my choice.

Choosing your own path. Your own rules. What—I mean WHO you wanted to be?

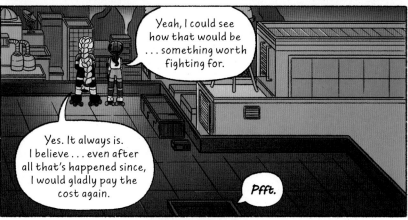

Yeah, I could see how that would be . . . something worth fighting for.

Yes. It always is. I believe . . . even after all that's happened since, I would gladly pay the cost again.

Pfft.

Can I ask—I mean, I know everyone chooses their own derby name. Imp said they're all personal, and you have to earn them. I get that.

But . . . is Val . . . based on, or part of, your real name?

Sigh. That is even more personal, Mina. A closely guarded secret for any vampire, and roller derby players in general, I'm told.

But perhaps one day . . . I will choose to tell you.

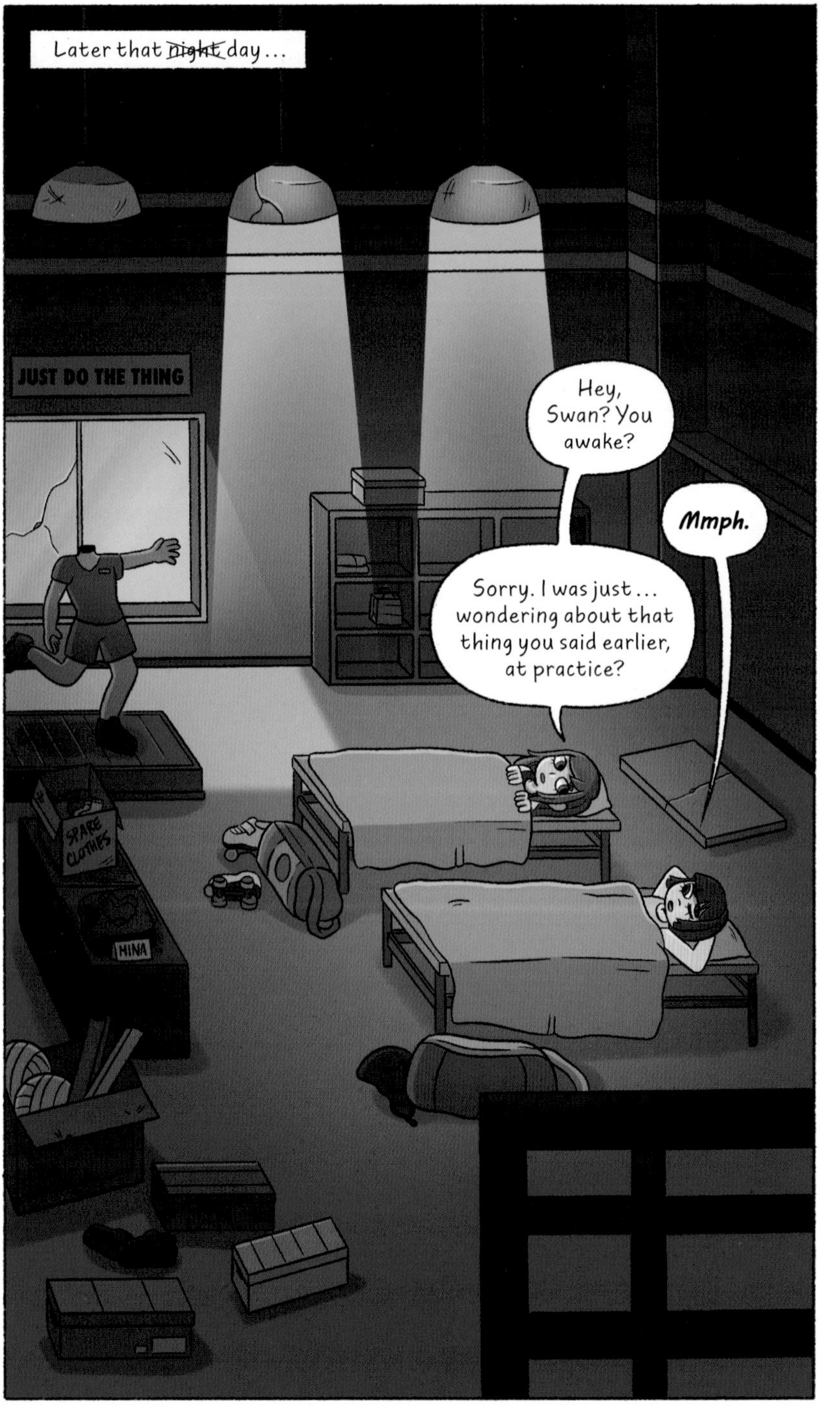
Later that ~~night~~ day...
JUST DO THE THING
Hey, Swan? You awake?
Sorry. I was just... wondering about that thing you said earlier, at practice?
Mmph.
SPARE CLOTHES
HINA

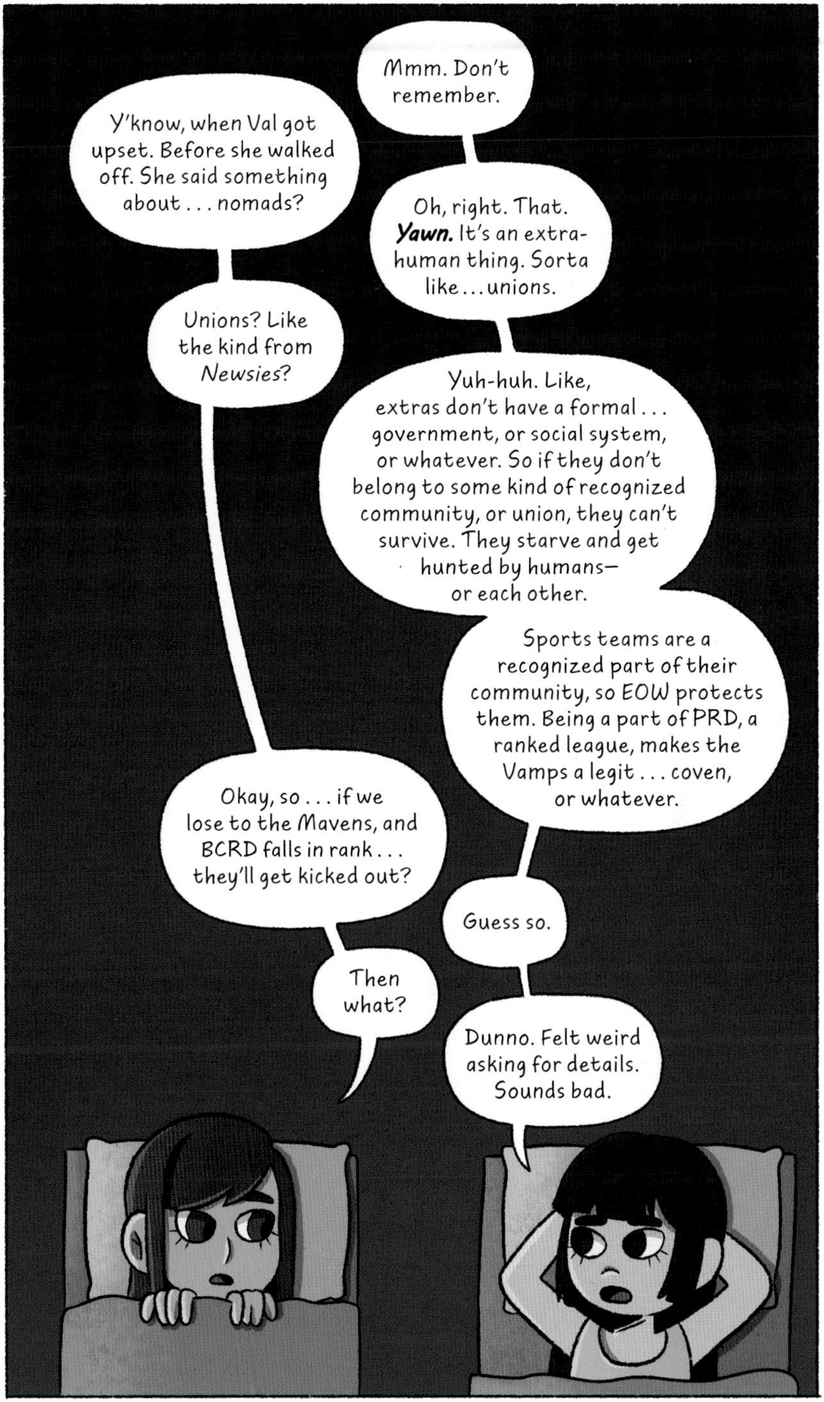
Y'know, when Val got upset. Before she walked off. She said something about . . . nomads?
Mmm. Don't remember.
Oh, right. That. **Yawn.** It's an extra-human thing. Sorta like . . . unions.
Unions? Like the kind from *Newsies*?
Yuh-huh. Like, extras don't have a formal . . . government, or social system, or whatever. So if they don't belong to some kind of recognized community, or union, they can't survive. They starve and get hunted by humans— or each other.
Sports teams are a recognized part of their community, so EOW protects them. Being a part of PRD, a ranked league, makes the Vamps a legit . . . coven, or whatever.
Okay, so . . . if we lose to the Mavens, and BCRD falls in rank . . . they'll get kicked out?
Guess so.
Then what?
Dunno. Felt weird asking for details. Sounds bad.

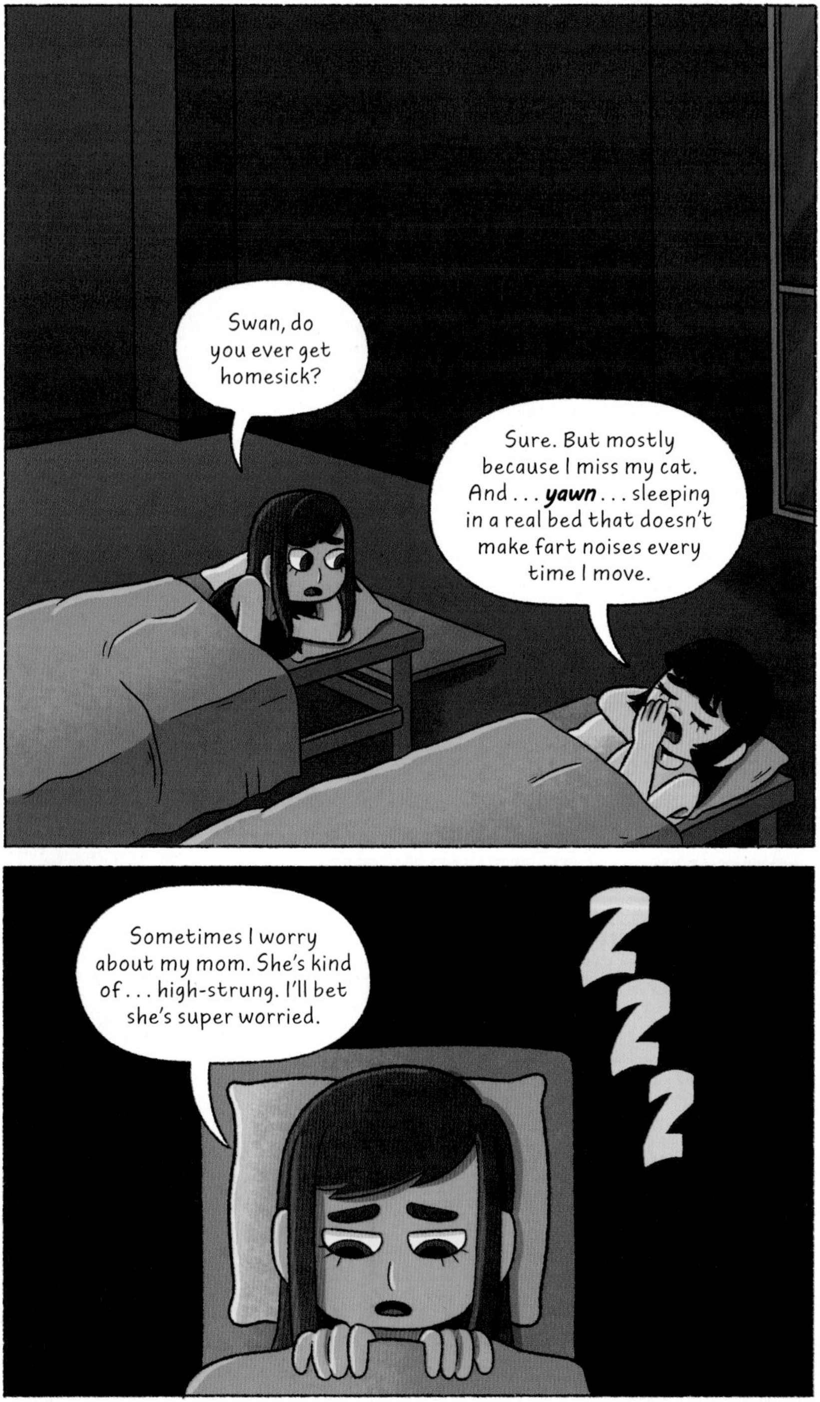
Swan, do you ever get homesick?
Sure. But mostly because I miss my cat. And . . . ***yawn*** . . . sleeping in a real bed that doesn't make fart noises every time I move.
Sometimes I worry about my mom. She's kind of . . . high-strung. I'll bet she's super worried.
ZZZ

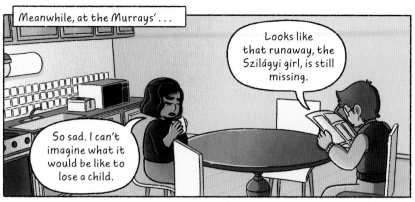

Meanwhile, at the Murrays'...

Looks like that runaway, the Szilágyi girl, is still missing.

So sad. I can't imagine what it would be like to lose a child.

Oh, I'm sure she's fine. They said everything was as it should be.

Speaking of, how is our missing girl doing?

Ah, good. What a fantastic opportunity.

The day Mina went "missing"...

Hi, hello. This is ... South Romania School for Gifted ... um, Skaters. We're pleased to inform you we've accepted Mina for our six-week, EXCLUSIVE training program. Very ELITE ... No tuition necessary. Fantastic opportunity for Mina. You should accept, no questions asked.

Have a good one, Mrs. Murray. Also maybe ... chill, while you're at it. Do some yoga, maybe. Okay, byeeeee.

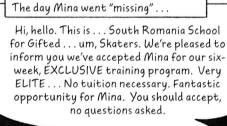

Ha-HA, long-distance hypnosis. NAILED IT.

OMG, we are SO good at doing crimes.

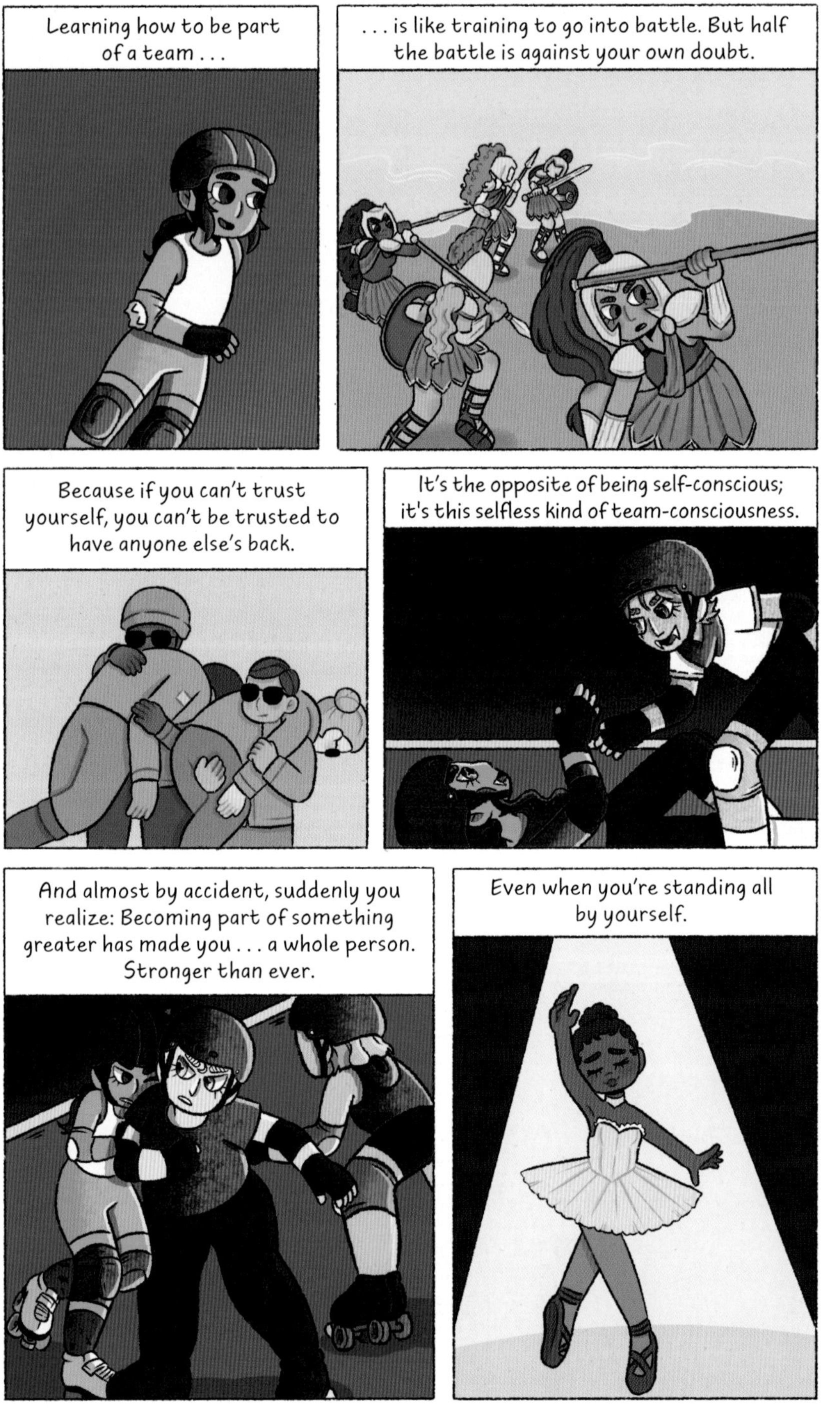
Learning how to be part of a team . . .
. . . is like training to go into battle. But half the battle is against your own doubt.
Because if you can't trust yourself, you can't be trusted to have anyone else's back.
It's the opposite of being self-conscious; it's this selfless kind of team-consciousness.
And almost by accident, suddenly you realize: Becoming part of something greater has made you . . . a whole person. Stronger than ever.
Even when you're standing all by yourself.

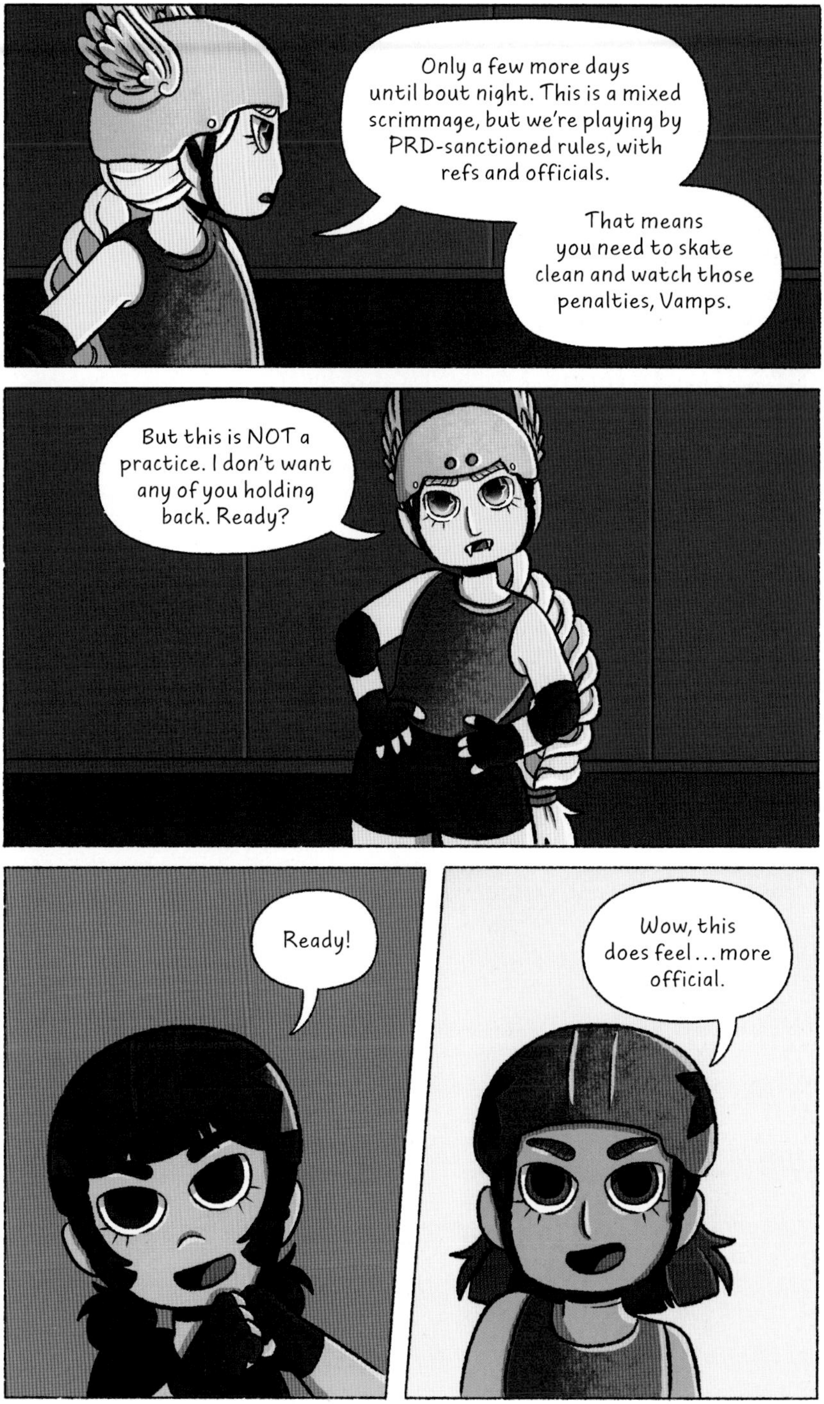
Only a few more days until bout night. This is a mixed scrimmage, but we're playing by PRD-sanctioned rules, with refs and officials.
That means you need to skate clean and watch those penalties, Vamps.
But this is NOT a practice. I don't want any of you holding back. Ready?
Ready!
Wow, this does feel...more official.

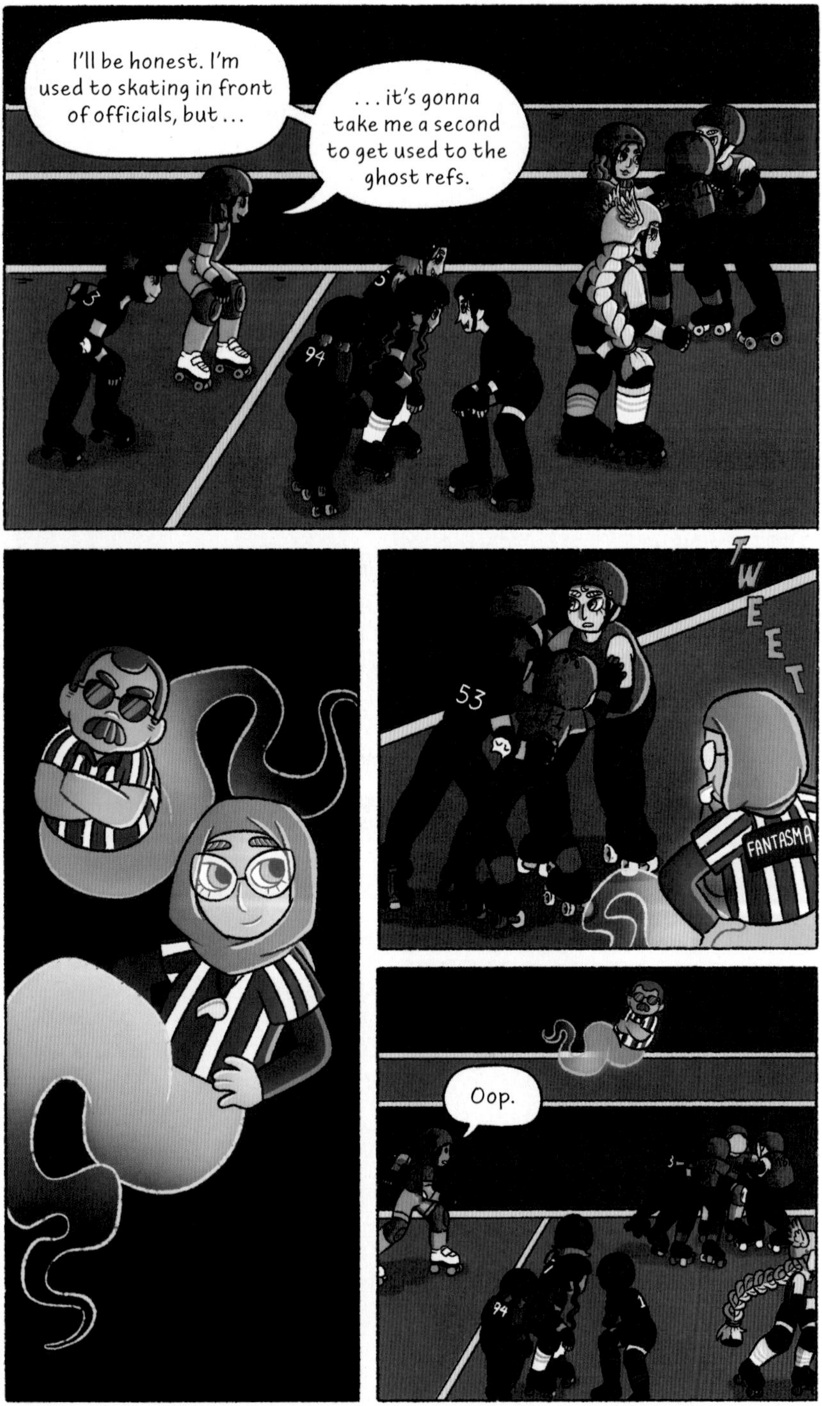
I'll be honest. I'm used to skating in front of officials, but . . .
. . . it's gonna take me a second to get used to the ghost refs.
TWEET
FANTASMA
Oop.

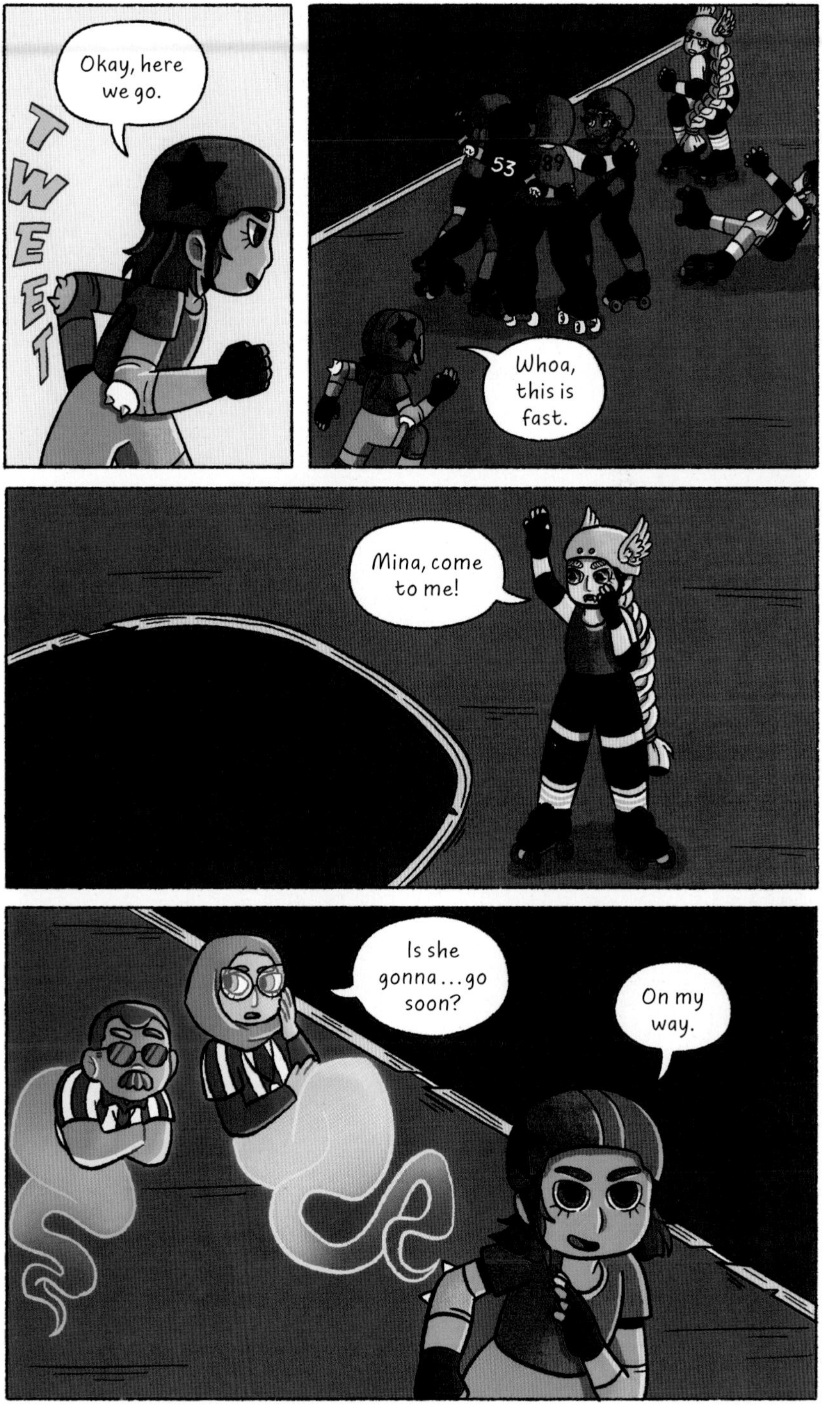

Okay, here we go.
TWEET
53
89
Whoa, this is fast.
Mina, come to me!
Is she gonna...go soon?
On my way.

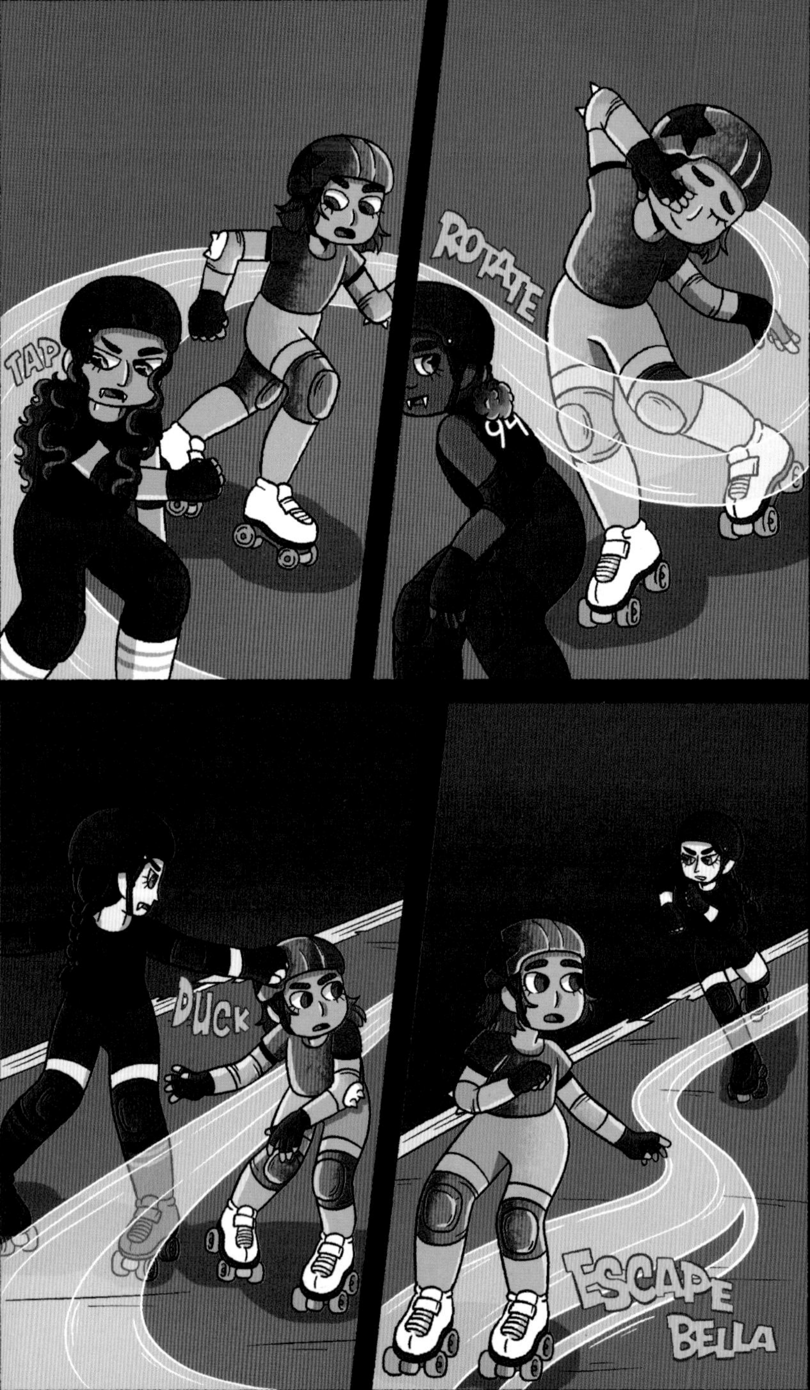
TAP
ROTATE
94
DUCK
ESCAPE
BELLA

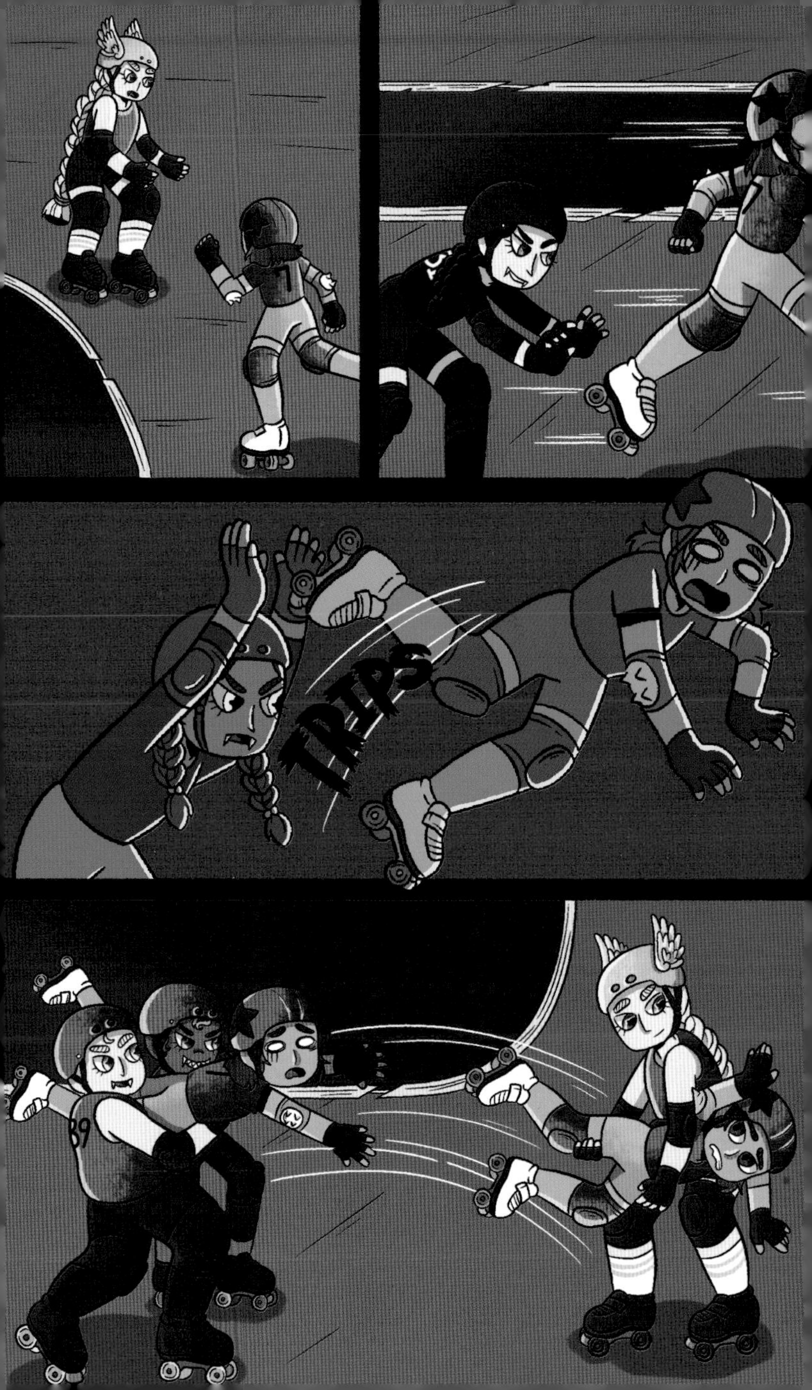
TRIPS

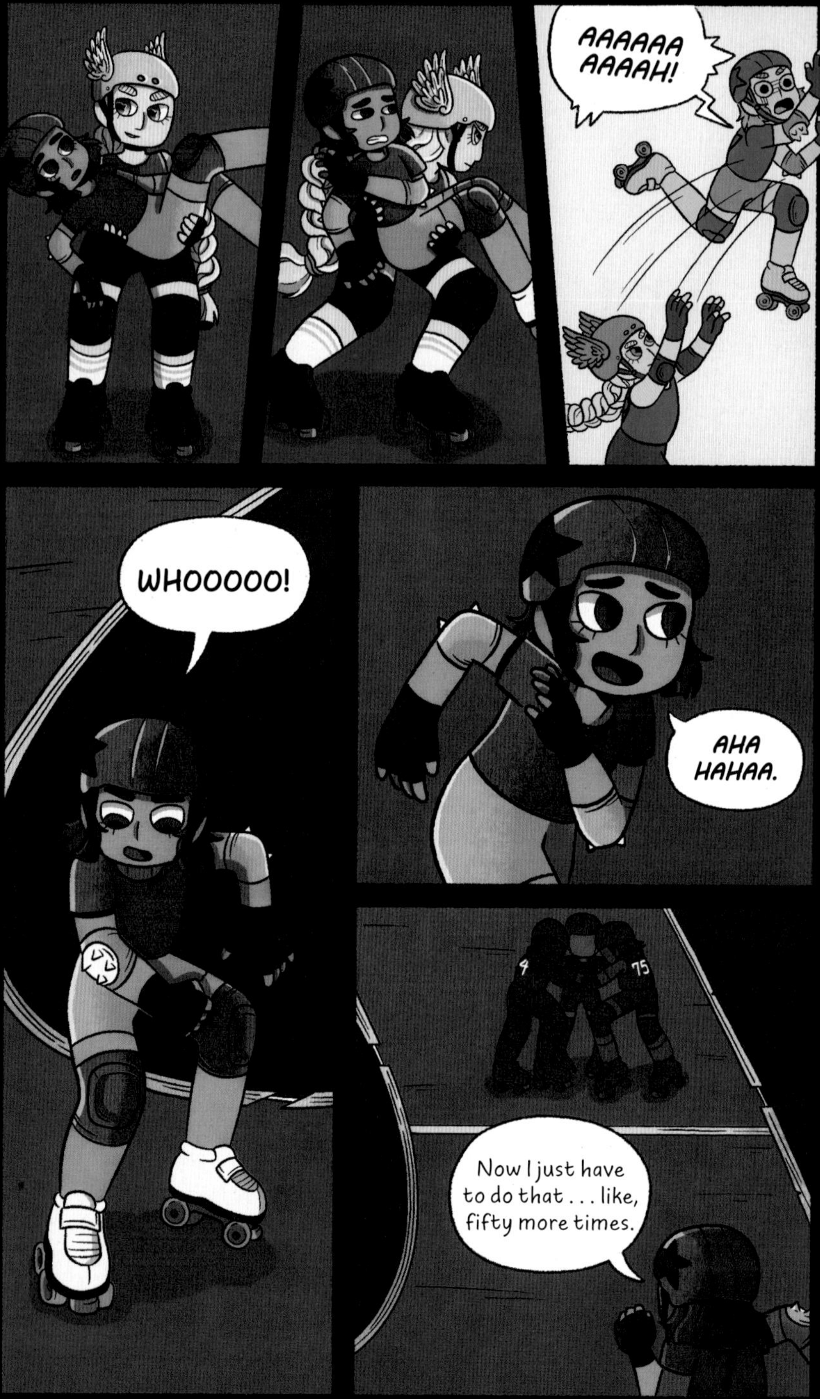
AAAAAA AAAAH!
WHOOOOO!
AHA HAHAA.
4
75
Now I just have to do that . . . like, fifty more times.

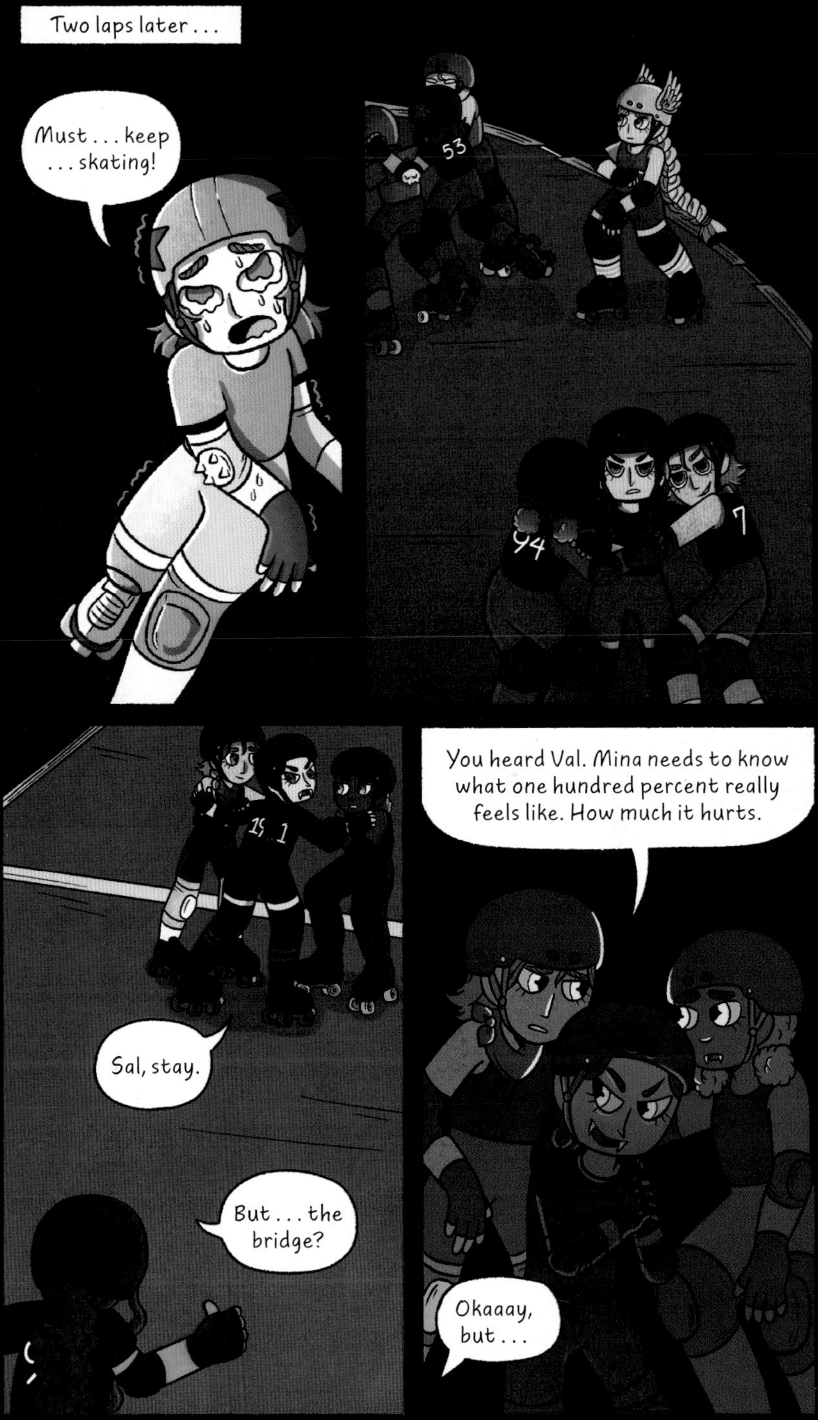
Two laps later . . .
Must . . . keep . . . skating!
53
94
7
You heard Val. Mina needs to know what one hundred percent really feels like. How much it hurts.
Sal, stay.
But . . . the bridge?
Okaaay, but . . .

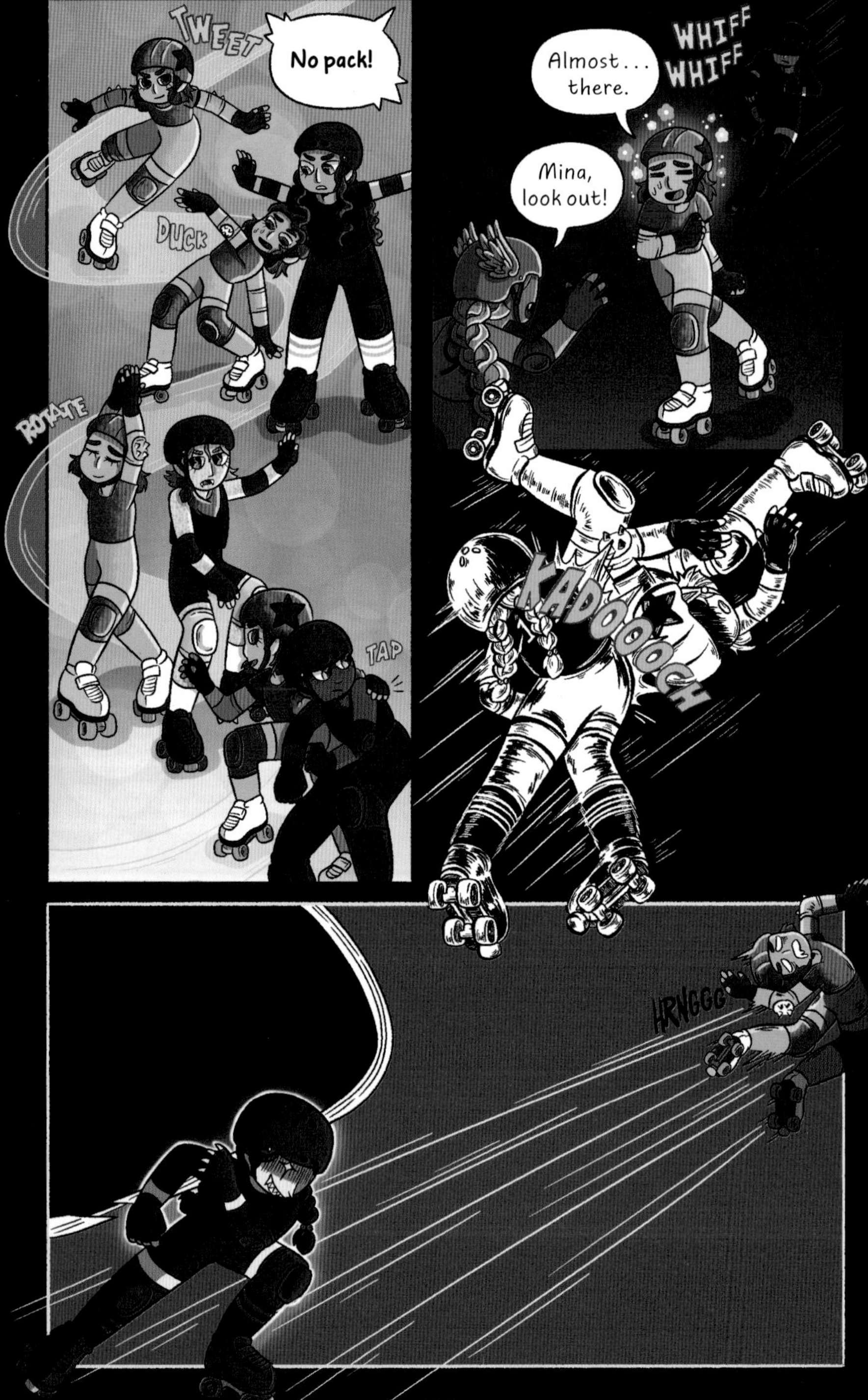
TWEET
No pack!
DUCK
ROTATE
TAP
Almost... there.
WHIFF
WHIFF
Mina, look out!
KADOOOOCH
HRNGGG

Black 1931. Out-of-play hit!

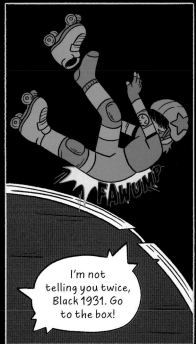

FAWUMP

I'm not telling you twice, Black 1931. Go to the box!

Can't... breathe...

You're all right. You just got the wind knocked out of you.

The wind, and maybe, like, a bit of your soul.

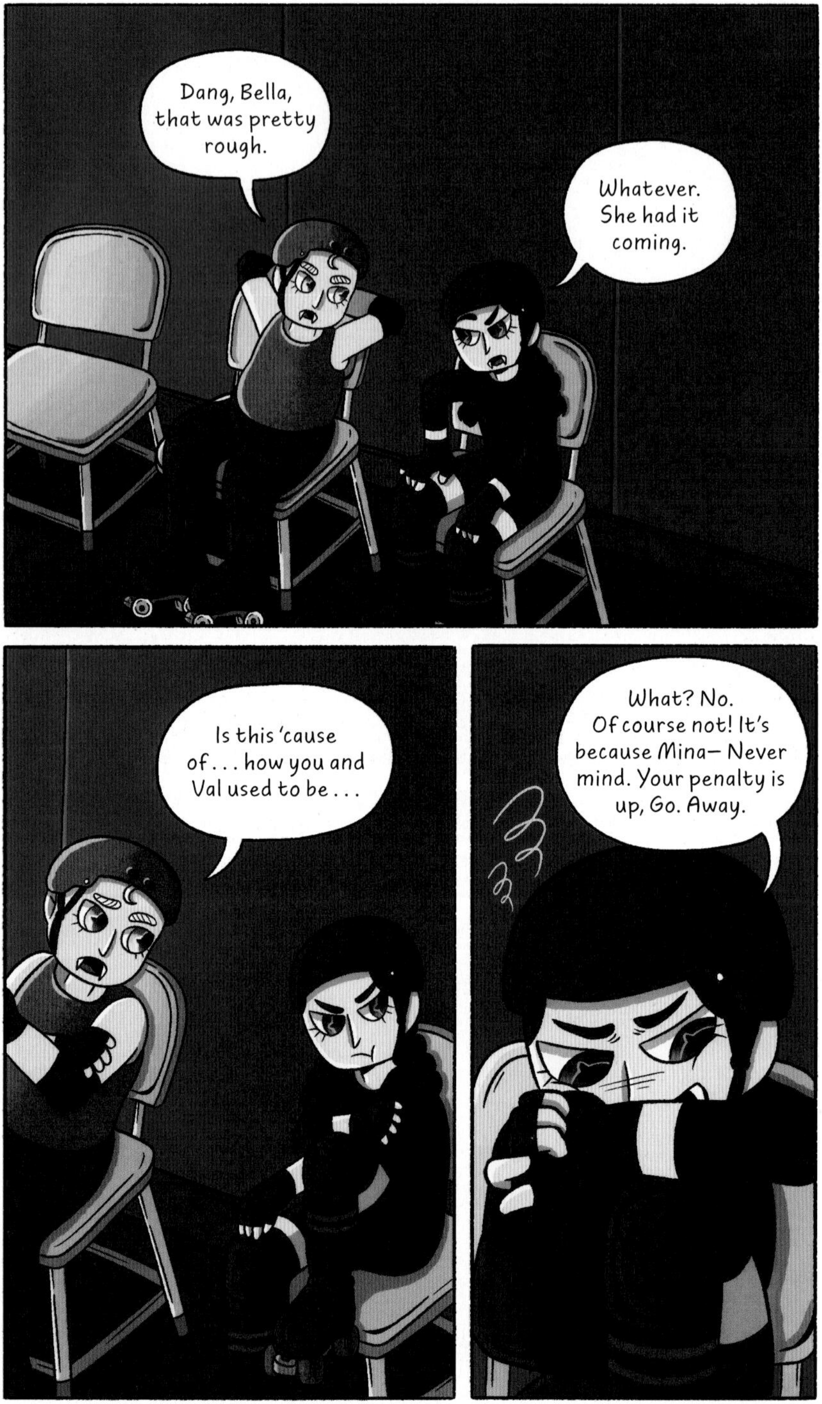
Dang, Bella, that was pretty rough.
Whatever. She had it coming.
Is this 'cause of . . . how you and Val used to be . . .
What? No. Of course not! It's because Mina— Never mind. Your penalty is up, Go. Away.

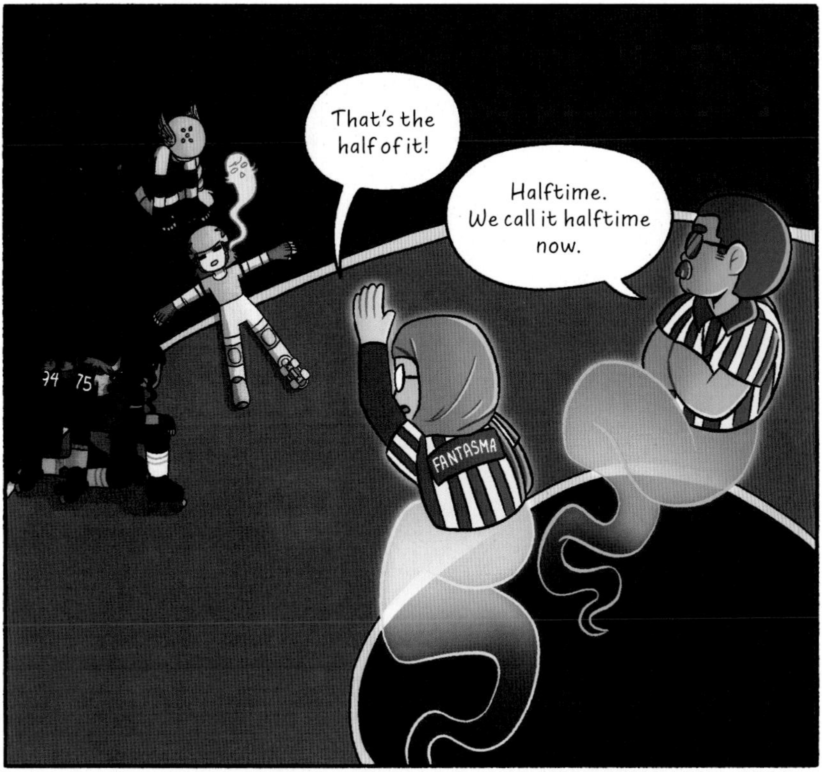
That's the
half of it!
Halftime.
We call it halftime
now.
74 75
FANTASMA

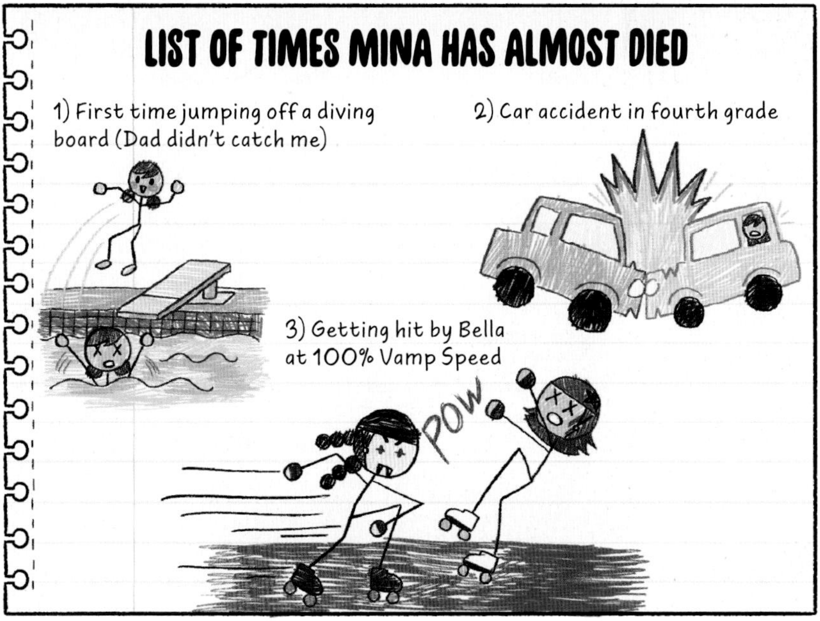
LIST OF TIMES MINA HAS ALMOST DIED
1) First time jumping off a diving board (Dad didn't catch me)
2) Car accident in fourth grade
3) Getting hit by Bella at 100% Vamp Speed
POW

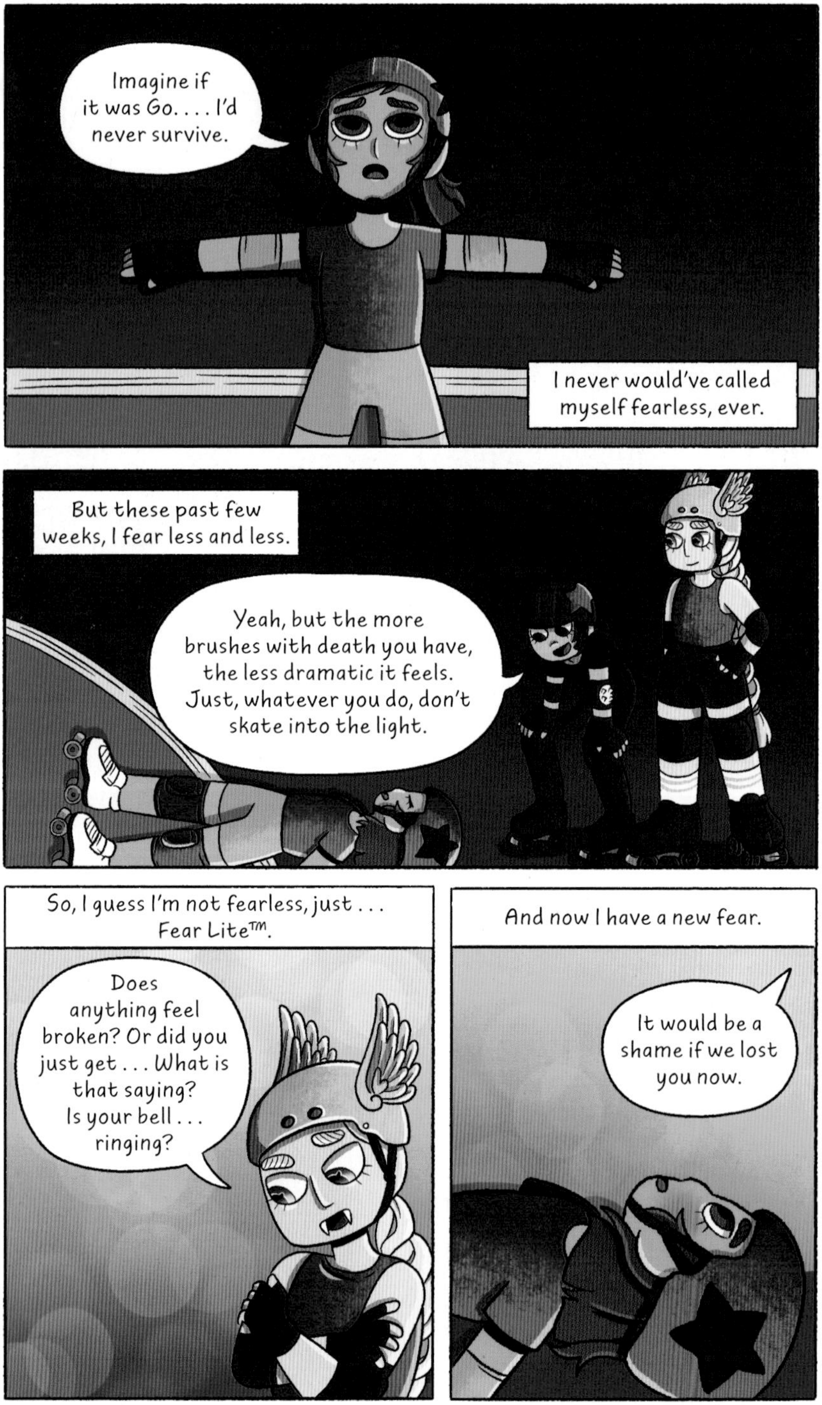

Imagine if it was Go. . . . I'd never survive.
I never would've called myself fearless, ever.
But these past few weeks, I fear less and less.
Yeah, but the more brushes with death you have, the less dramatic it feels. Just, whatever you do, don't skate into the light.
So, I guess I'm not fearless, just . . . Fear Lite™.
Does anything feel broken? Or did you just get . . . What is that saying? Is your bell . . . ringing?
And now I have a new fear.
It would be a shame if we lost you now.

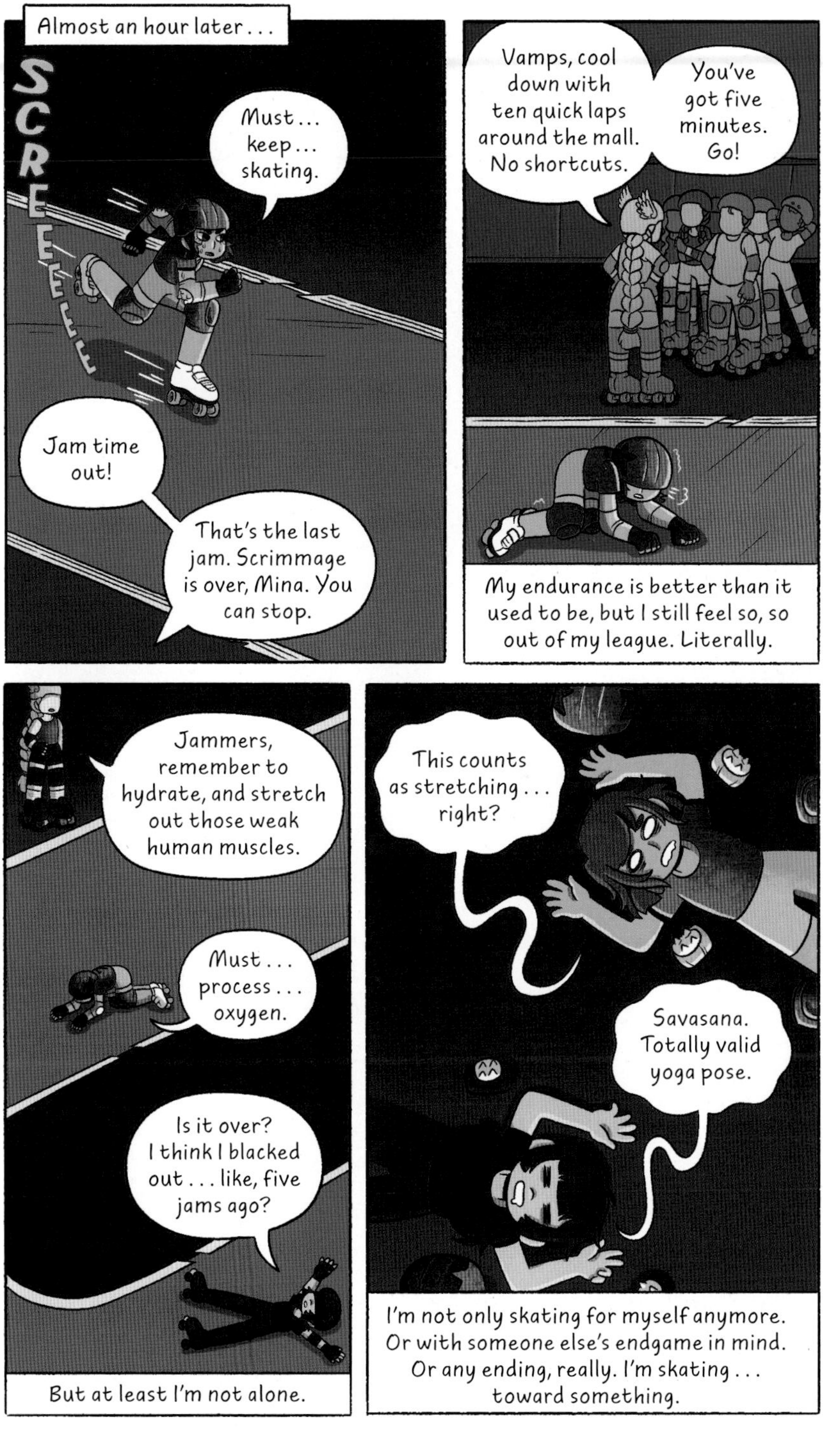

Almost an hour later . . .
SCREEEEEE
Must . . . keep . . . skating.
Jam time out!
That's the last jam. Scrimmage is over, Mina. You can stop.
Vamps, cool down with ten quick laps around the mall. No shortcuts.
You've got five minutes. Go!
My endurance is better than it used to be, but I still feel so, so out of my league. Literally.
Jammers, remember to hydrate, and stretch out those weak human muscles.
Must . . . process . . . oxygen.
Is it over? I think I blacked out . . . like, five jams ago?
But at least I'm not alone.
This counts as stretching . . . right?
Savasana. Totally valid yoga pose.
I'm not only skating for myself anymore. Or with someone else's endgame in mind. Or any ending, really. I'm skating . . . toward something.

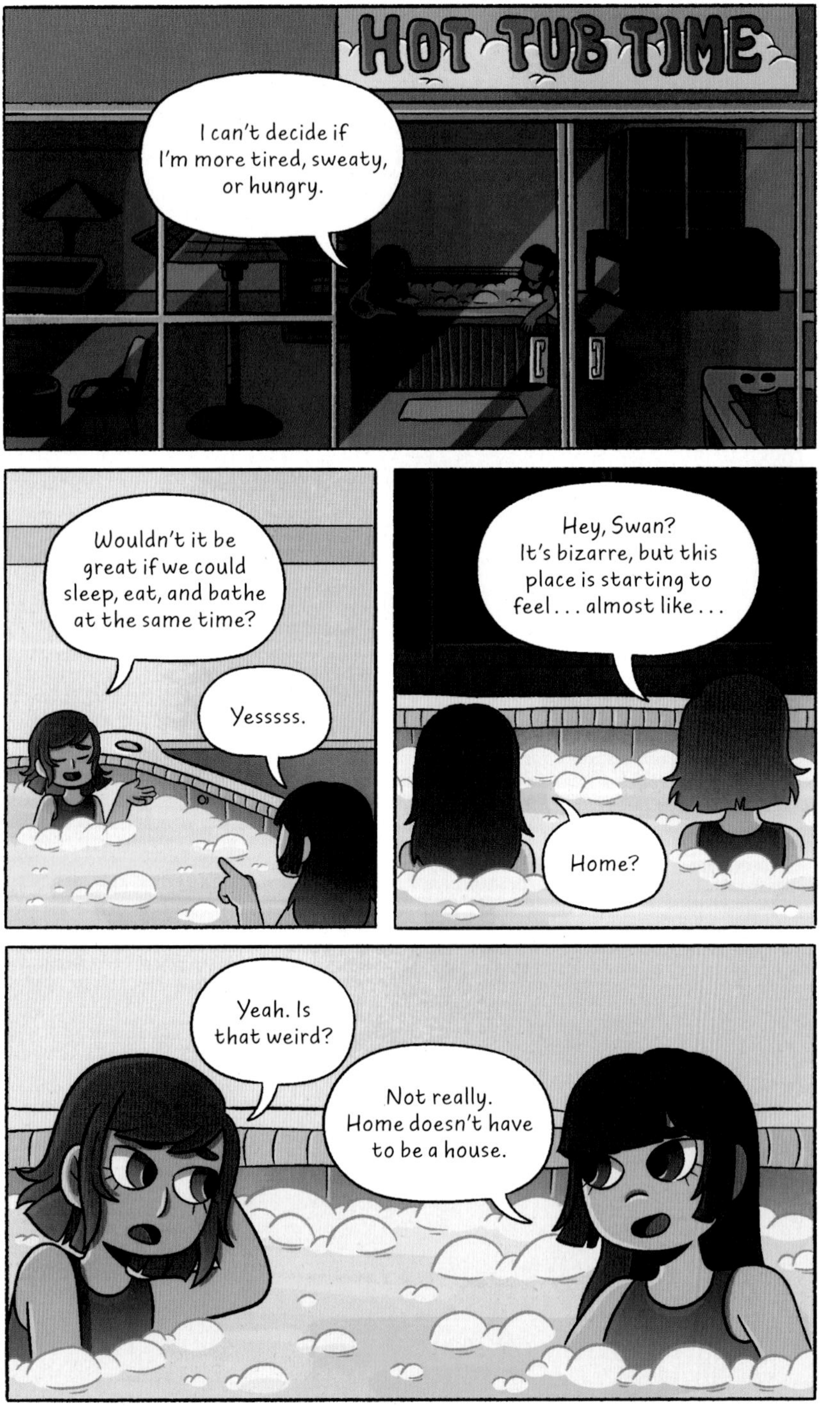
HOT TUB TIME
I can't decide if I'm more tired, sweaty, or hungry.
Wouldn't it be great if we could sleep, eat, and bathe at the same time?
Yesssss.
Hey, Swan? It's bizarre, but this place is starting to feel . . . almost like . . .
Home?
Yeah. Is that weird?
Not really. Home doesn't have to be a house.

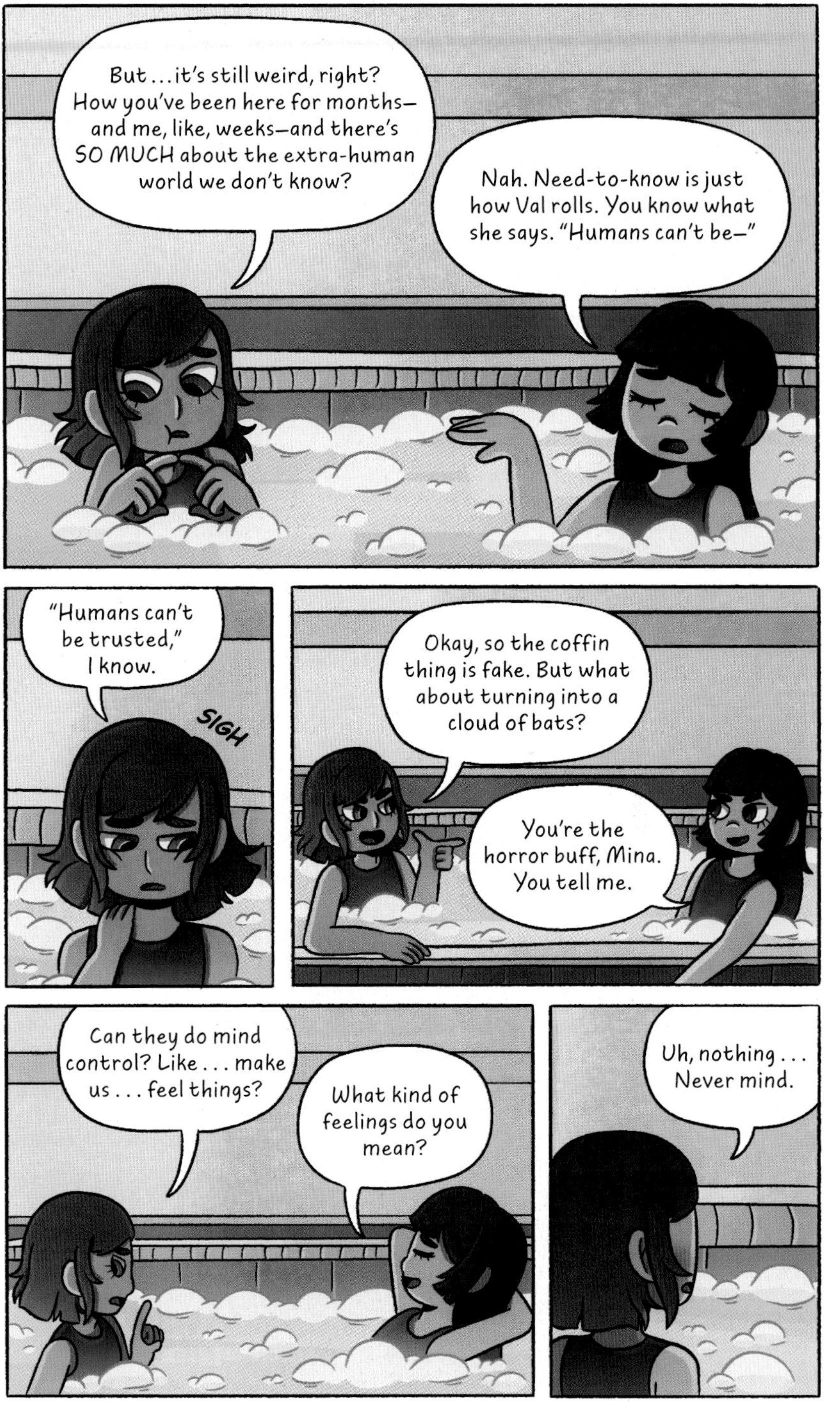
But . . . it's still weird, right? How you've been here for months—and me, like, weeks—and there's SO MUCH about the extra-human world we don't know?
Nah. Need-to-know is just how Val rolls. You know what she says. "Humans can't be—"
"Humans can't be trusted," I know.
SIGH
Okay, so the coffin thing is fake. But what about turning into a cloud of bats?
You're the horror buff, Mina. You tell me.
Can they do mind control? Like . . . make us . . . feel things?
What kind of feelings do you mean?
Uh, nothing . . . Never mind.

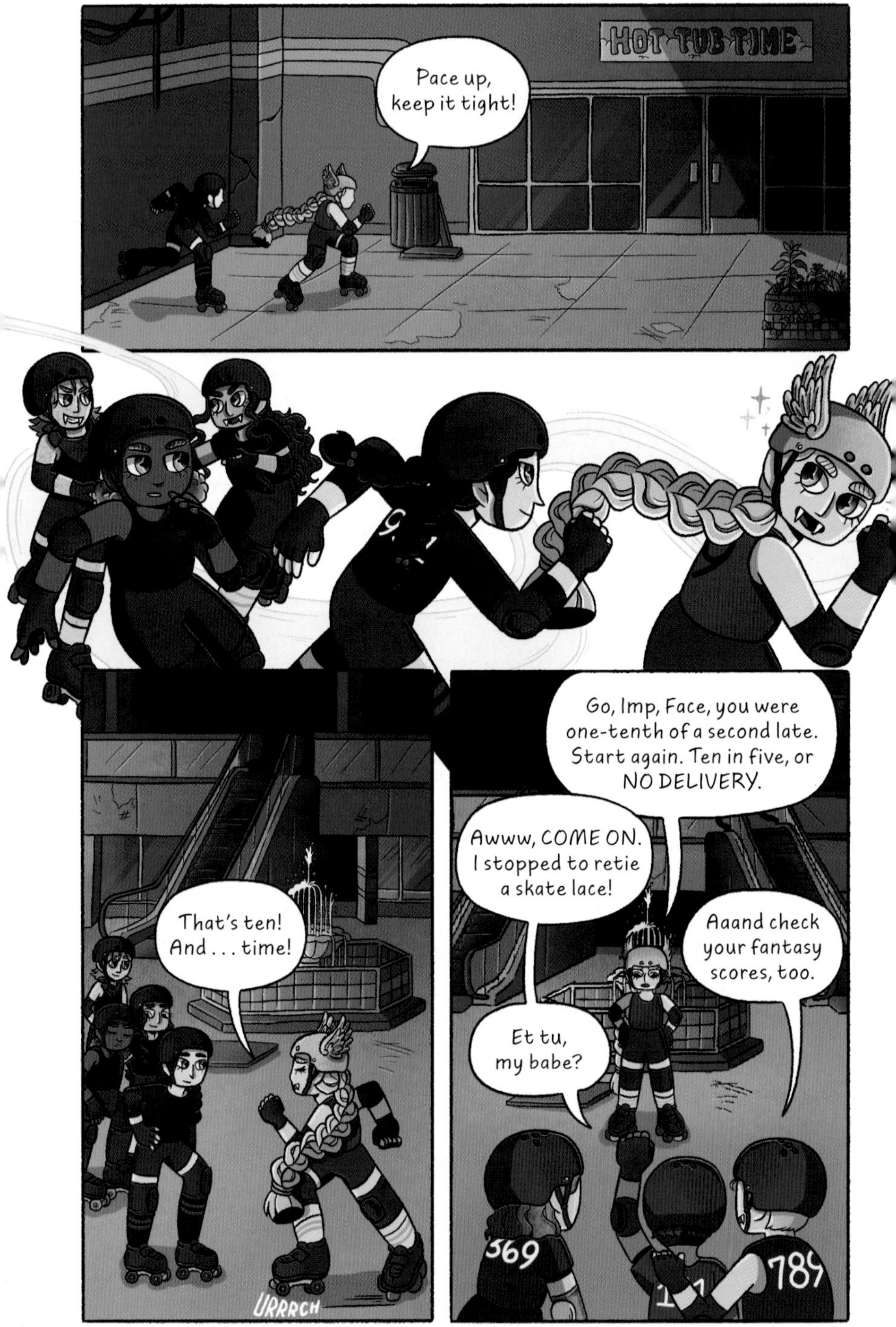
HOT TUB TIME
Pace up, keep it tight!
That's ten! And . . . time!
URRRCH
Go, Imp, Face, you were one-tenth of a second late. Start again. Ten in five, or NO DELIVERY.
Awww, COME ON. I stopped to retie a skate lace!
Et tu, my babe?
Aaand check your fantasy scores, too.
369
789

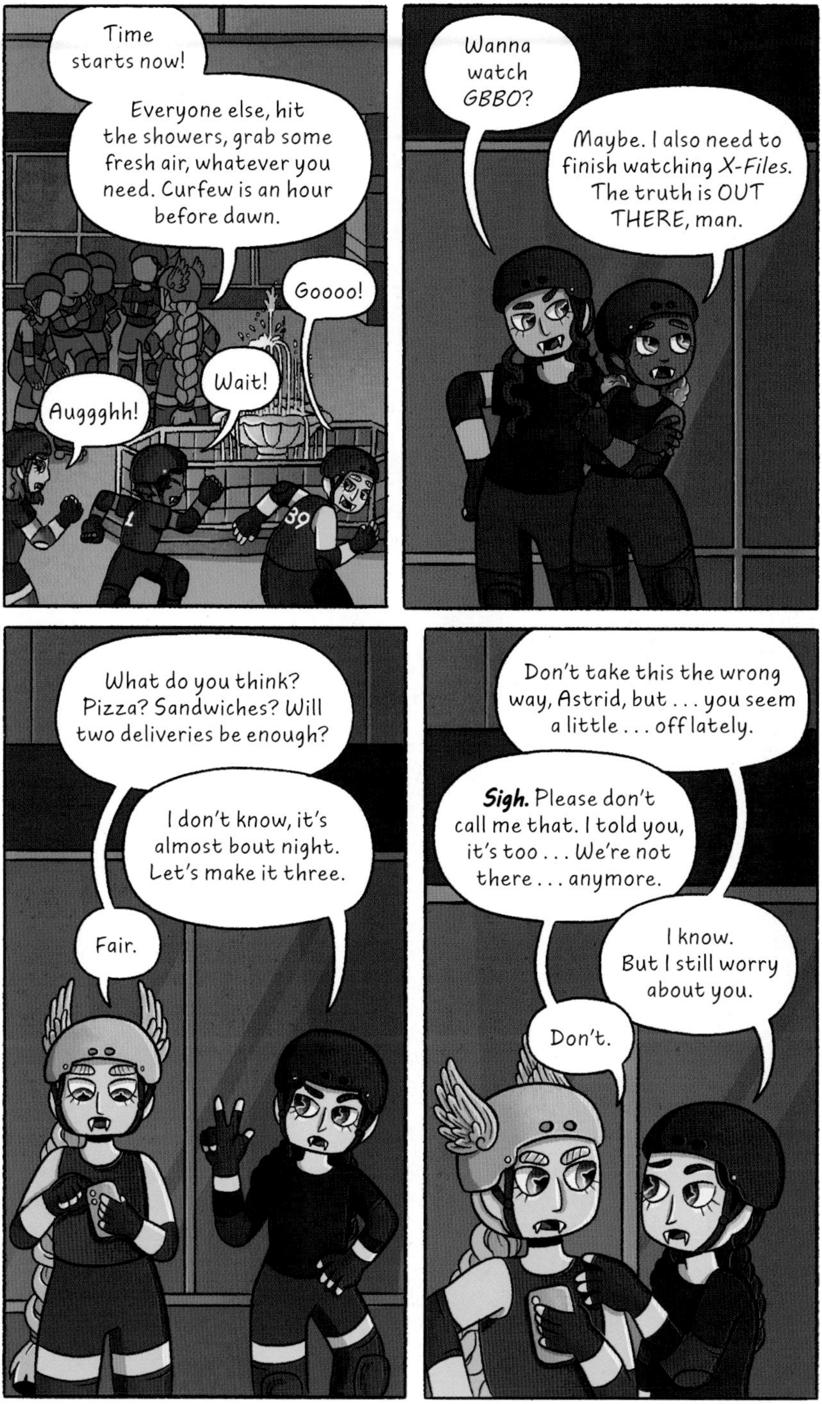
Time starts now!
Everyone else, hit the showers, grab some fresh air, whatever you need. Curfew is an hour before dawn.
Goooo!
Wait!
Auggghh!
Wanna watch GBBO?
Maybe. I also need to finish watching X-Files. The truth is OUT THERE, man.
What do you think? Pizza? Sandwiches? Will two deliveries be enough?
I don't know, it's almost bout night. Let's make it three.
Fair.
Don't take this the wrong way, Astrid, but . . . you seem a little . . . off lately.
Sigh. Please don't call me that. I told you, it's too . . . We're not there . . . anymore.
I know. But I still worry about you.
Don't.

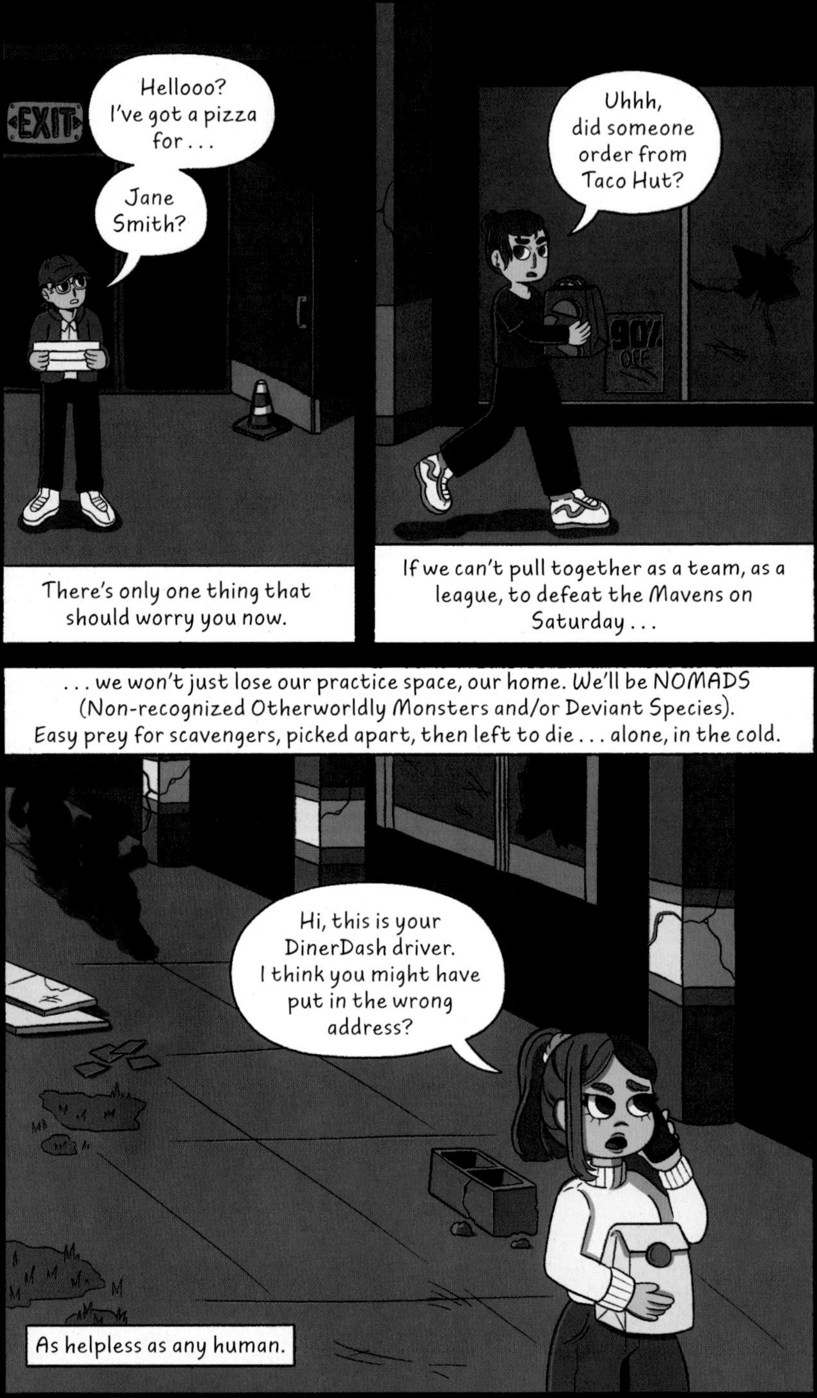
Hellooo?
I've got a pizza for . . .
Jane Smith?
EXIT
There's only one thing that should worry you now.
Uhhh, did someone order from Taco Hut?
90% OFF
If we can't pull together as a team, as a league, to defeat the Mavens on Saturday . . .
. . . we won't just lose our practice space, our home. We'll be NOMADS (Non-recognized Otherworldly Monsters and/or Deviant Species). Easy prey for scavengers, picked apart, then left to die . . . alone, in the cold.
Hi, this is your DinerDash driver. I think you might have put in the wrong address?
As helpless as any human.

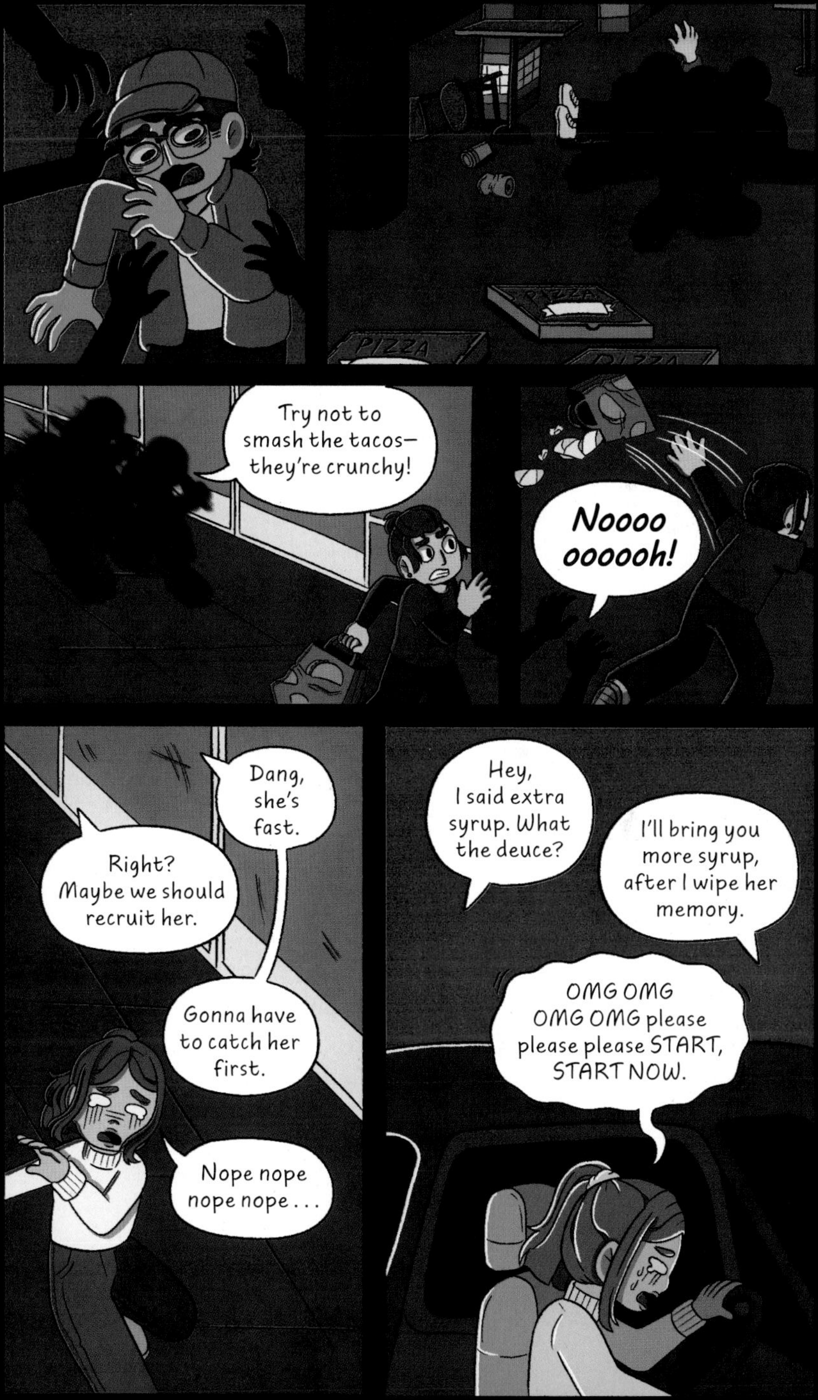
Try not to smash the tacos—they're crunchy!
Noooo ooooh!
Dang, she's fast.
Right? Maybe we should recruit her.
Gonna have to catch her first.
Nope nope nope nope . . .
Hey, I said extra syrup. What the deuce?
I'll bring you more syrup, after I wipe her memory.
OMG OMG OMG OMG please please please START, START NOW.

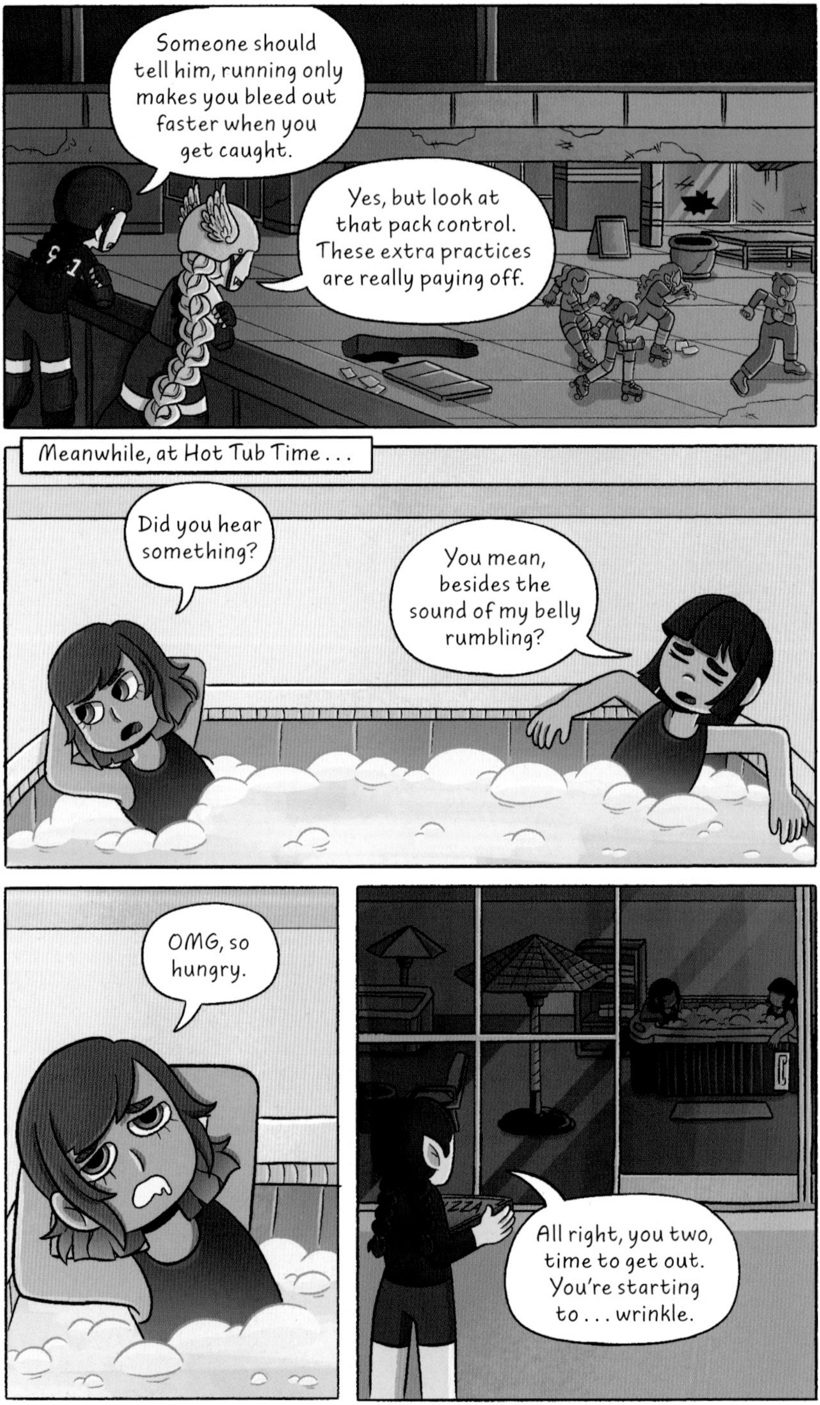
Someone should tell him, running only makes you bleed out faster when you get caught.
Yes, but look at that pack control. These extra practices are really paying off.
Meanwhile, at Hot Tub Time . . .
Did you hear something?
You mean, besides the sound of my belly rumbling?
OMG, so hungry.
All right, you two, time to get out. You're starting to . . . wrinkle.

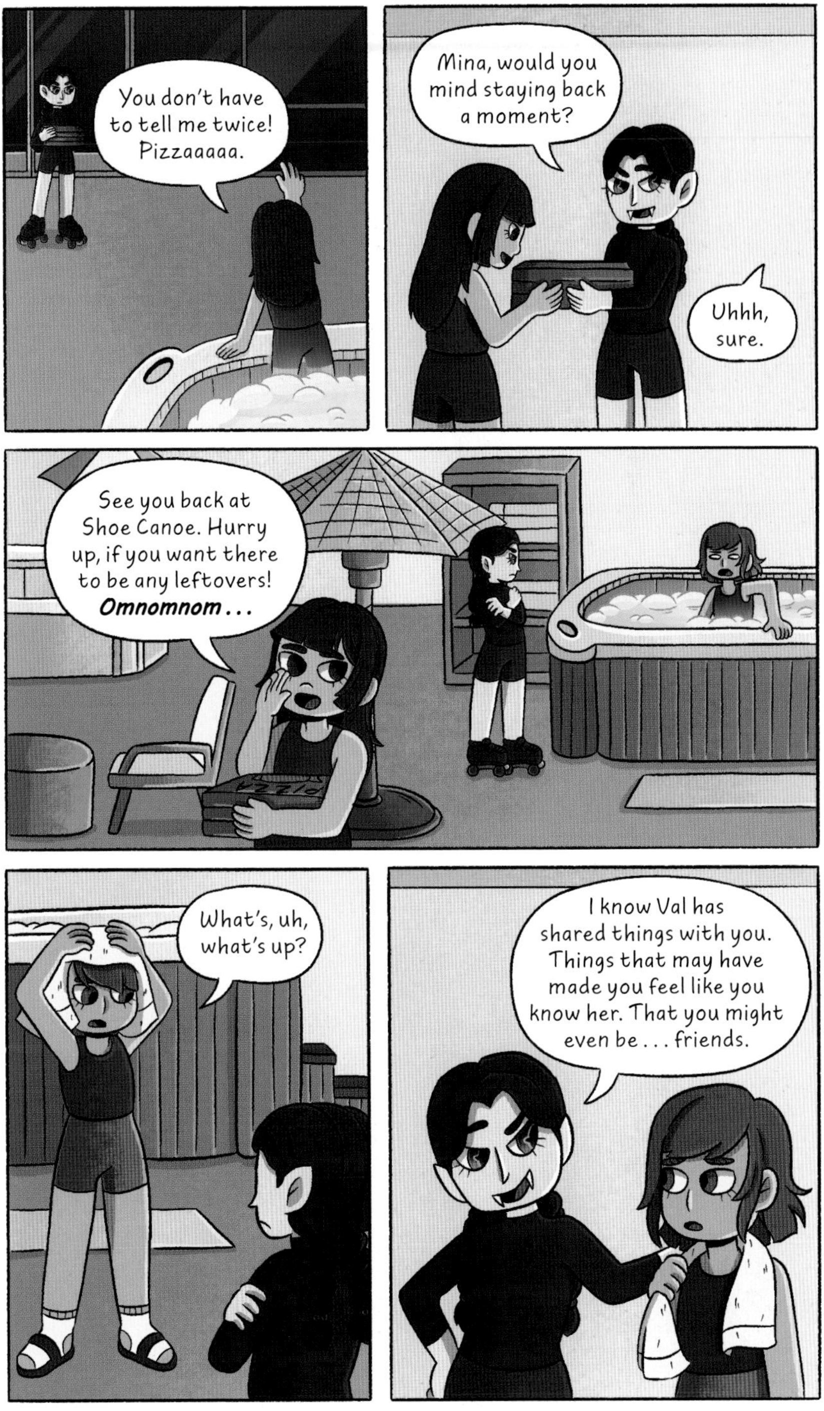
You don't have to tell me twice! Pizzaaaaa.
Mina, would you mind staying back a moment?
Uhhh, sure.
PIZZA
See you back at Shoe Canoe. Hurry up, if you want there to be any leftovers! **Omnomnom . . .**
What's, uh, what's up?
I know Val has shared things with you. Things that may have made you feel like you know her. That you might even be . . . friends.

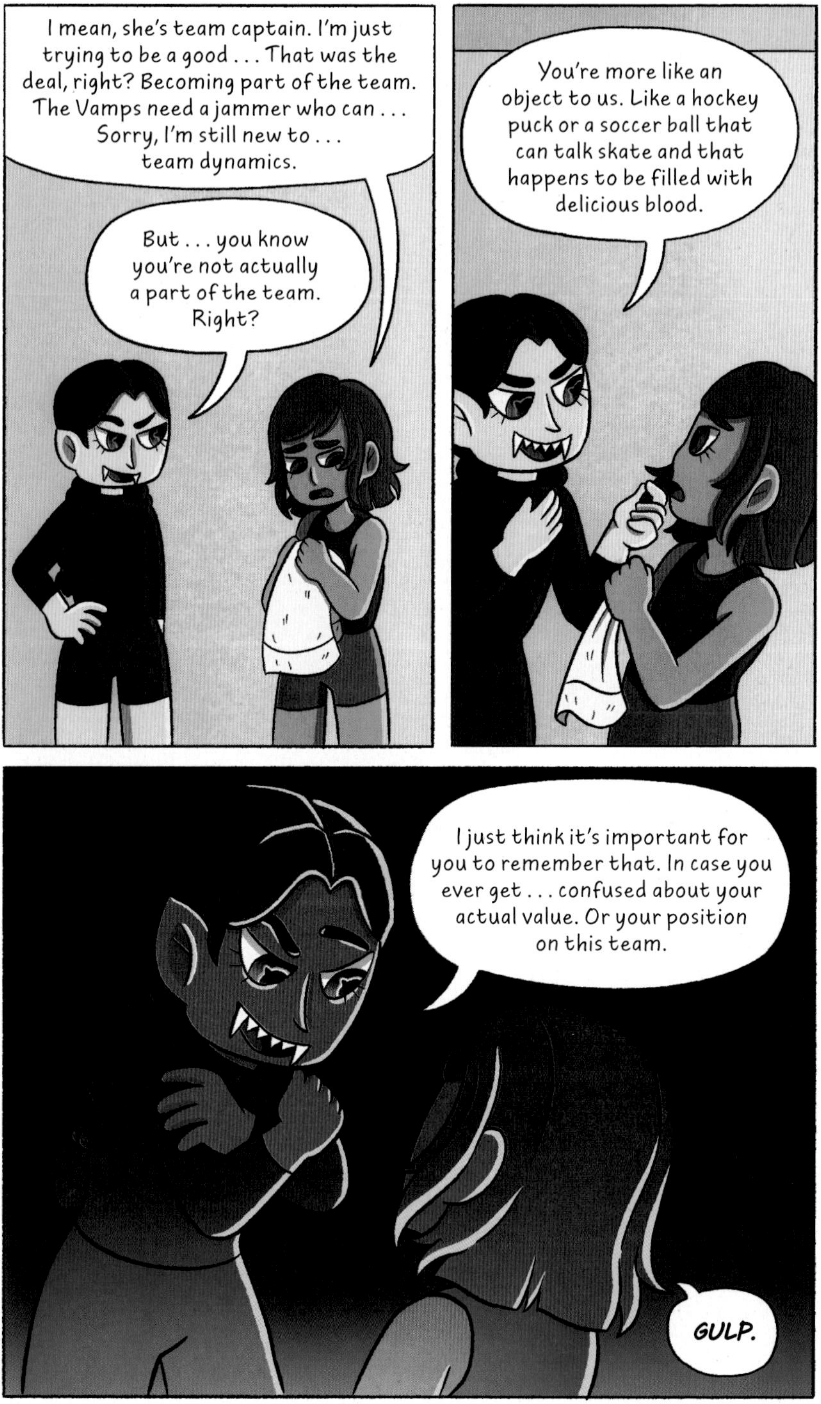
I mean, she's team captain. I'm just trying to be a good . . . That was the deal, right? Becoming part of the team. The Vamps need a jammer who can . . . Sorry, I'm still new to . . . team dynamics.
But . . . you know you're not actually a part of the team. Right?
You're more like an object to us. Like a hockey puck or a soccer ball that can talk skate and that happens to be filled with delicious blood.
I just think it's important for you to remember that. In case you ever get . . . confused about your actual value. Or your position on this team.
GULP.

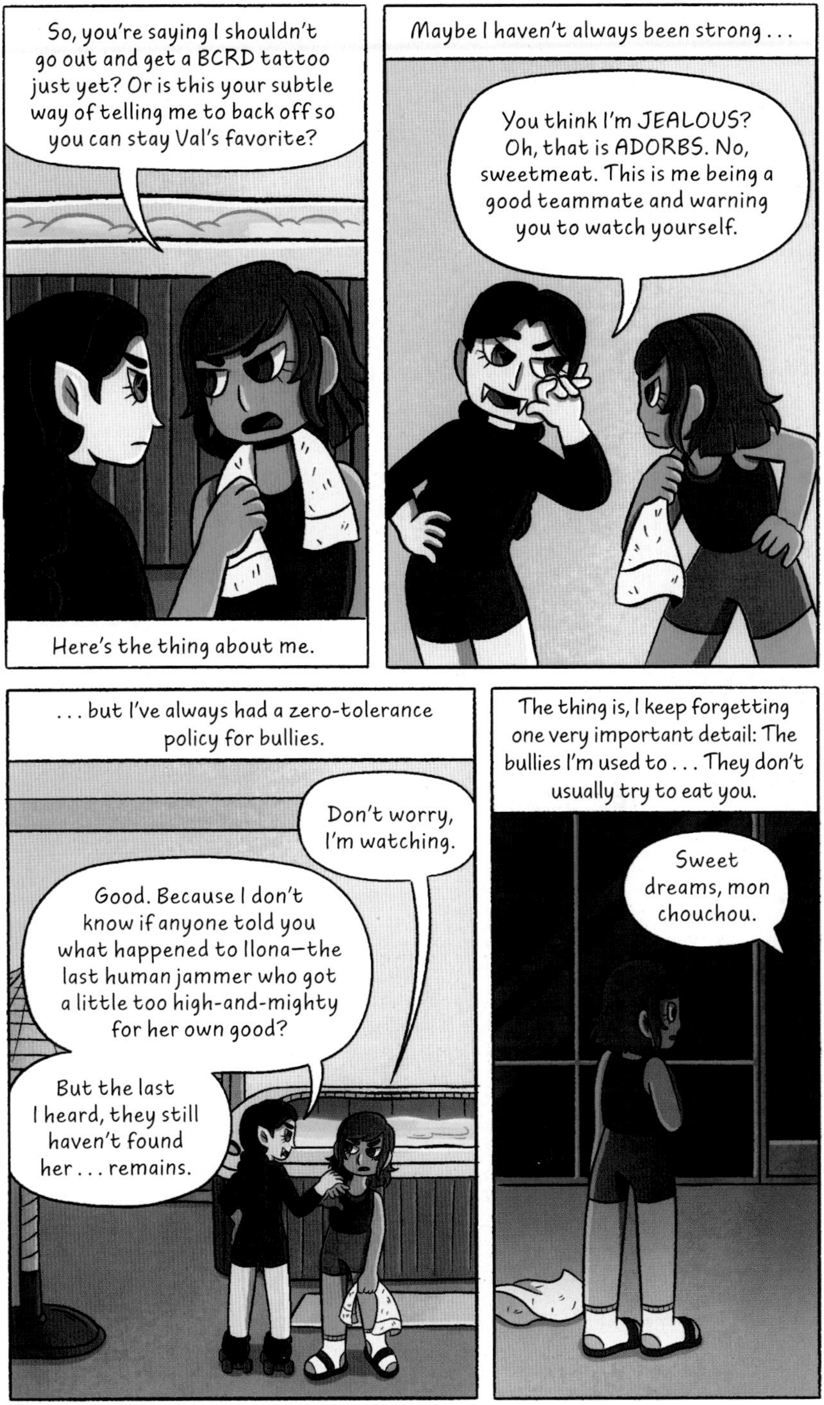
So, you're saying I shouldn't go out and get a BCRD tattoo just yet? Or is this your subtle way of telling me to back off so you can stay Val's favorite?
Here's the thing about me.
Maybe I haven't always been strong . . .
You think I'm JEALOUS? Oh, that is ADORBS. No, sweetmeat. This is me being a good teammate and warning you to watch yourself.
. . . but I've always had a zero-tolerance policy for bullies.
Don't worry, I'm watching.
Good. Because I don't know if anyone told you what happened to Ilona—the last human jammer who got a little too high-and-mighty for her own good?
But the last I heard, they still haven't found her . . . remains.
The thing is, I keep forgetting one very important detail: The bullies I'm used to . . . They don't usually try to eat you.
Sweet dreams, mon chouchou.

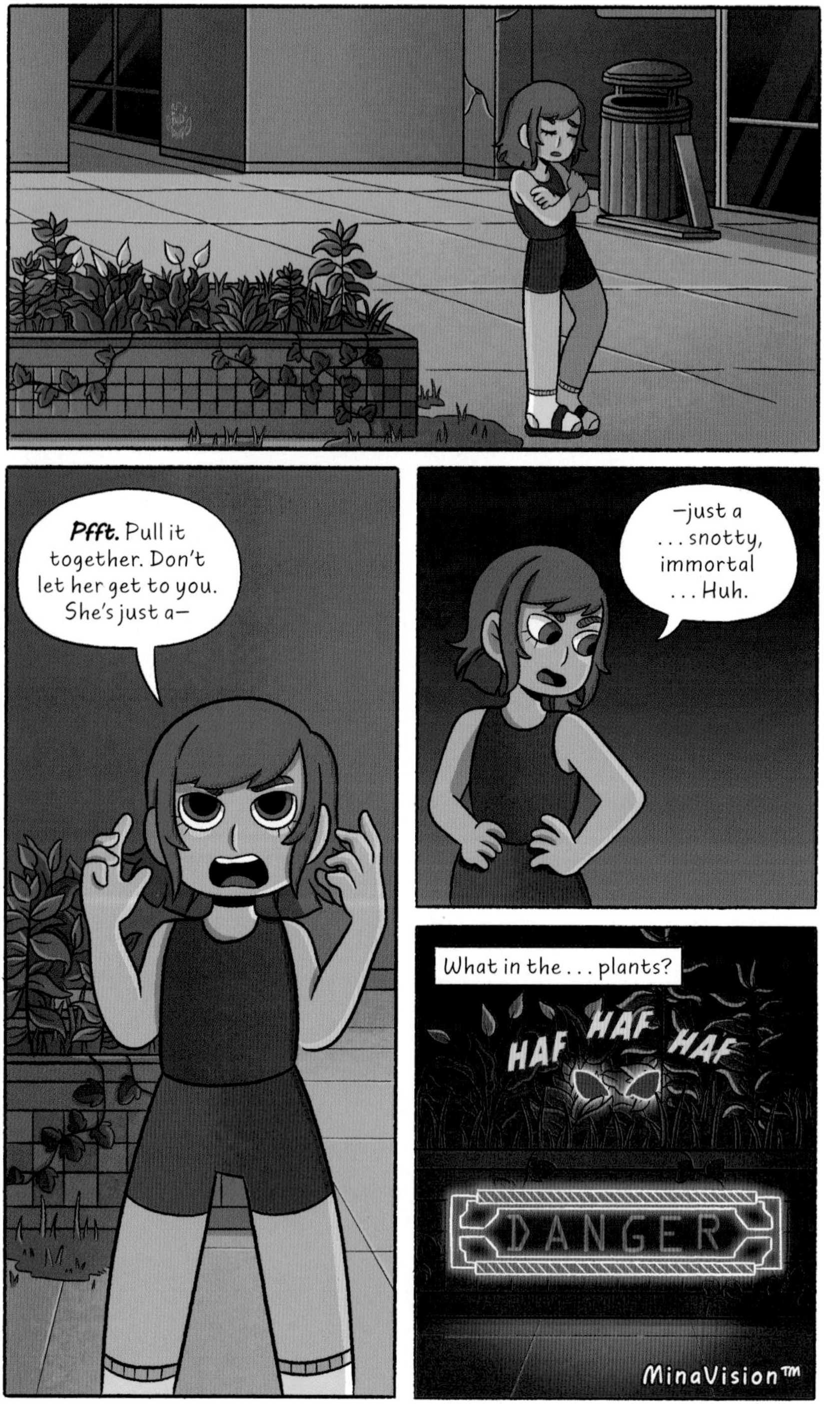
Pfft. Pull it together. Don't let her get to you. She's just a—
—just a . . . snotty, immortal . . . Huh.
What in the . . . plants?
HAF HAF HAF
DANGER
MinaVision™

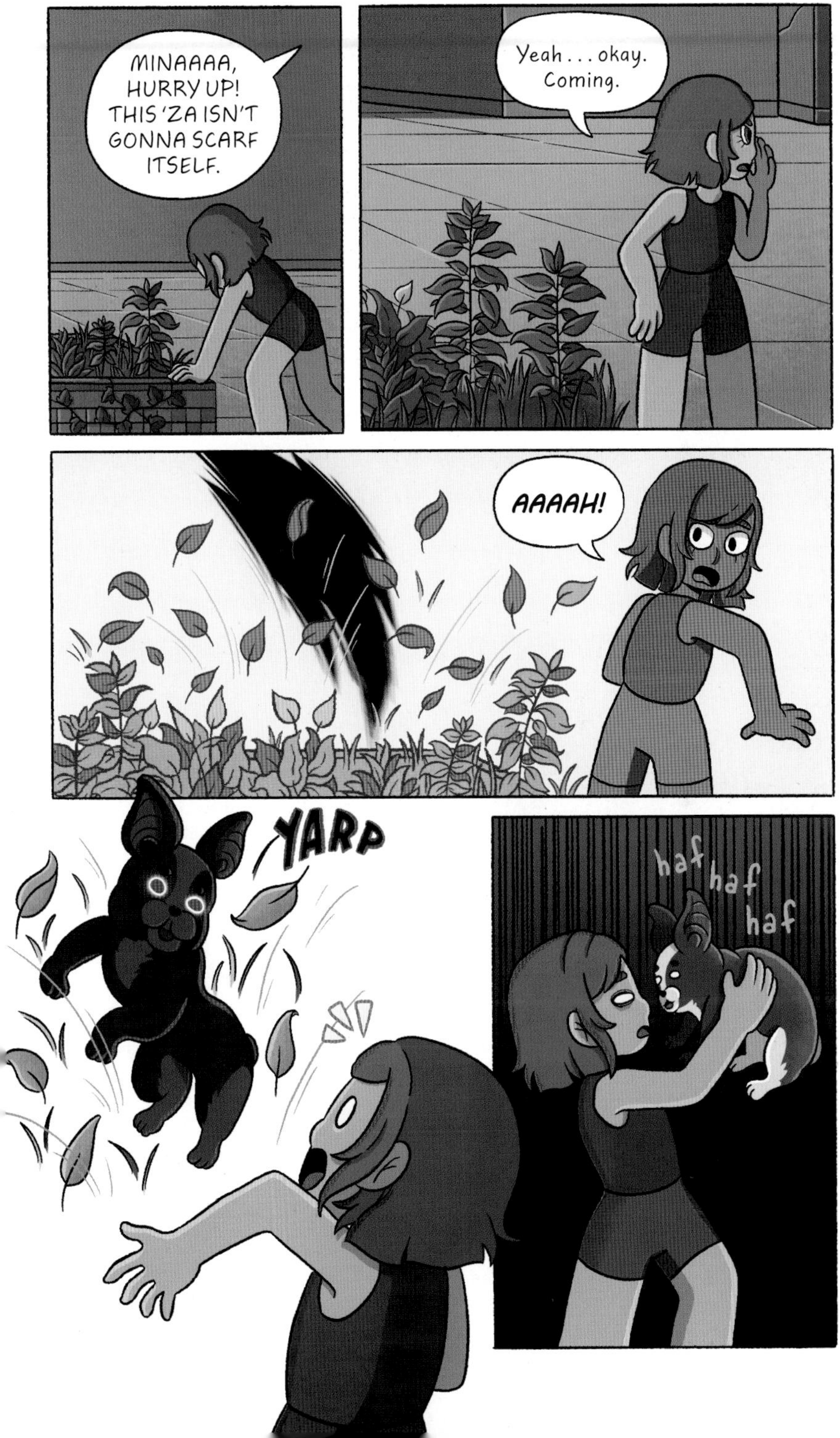
MINAAAA, HURRY UP! THIS 'ZA ISN'T GONNA SCARF ITSELF.
Yeah . . . okay. Coming.
AAAAH!
YARP
haf haf haf

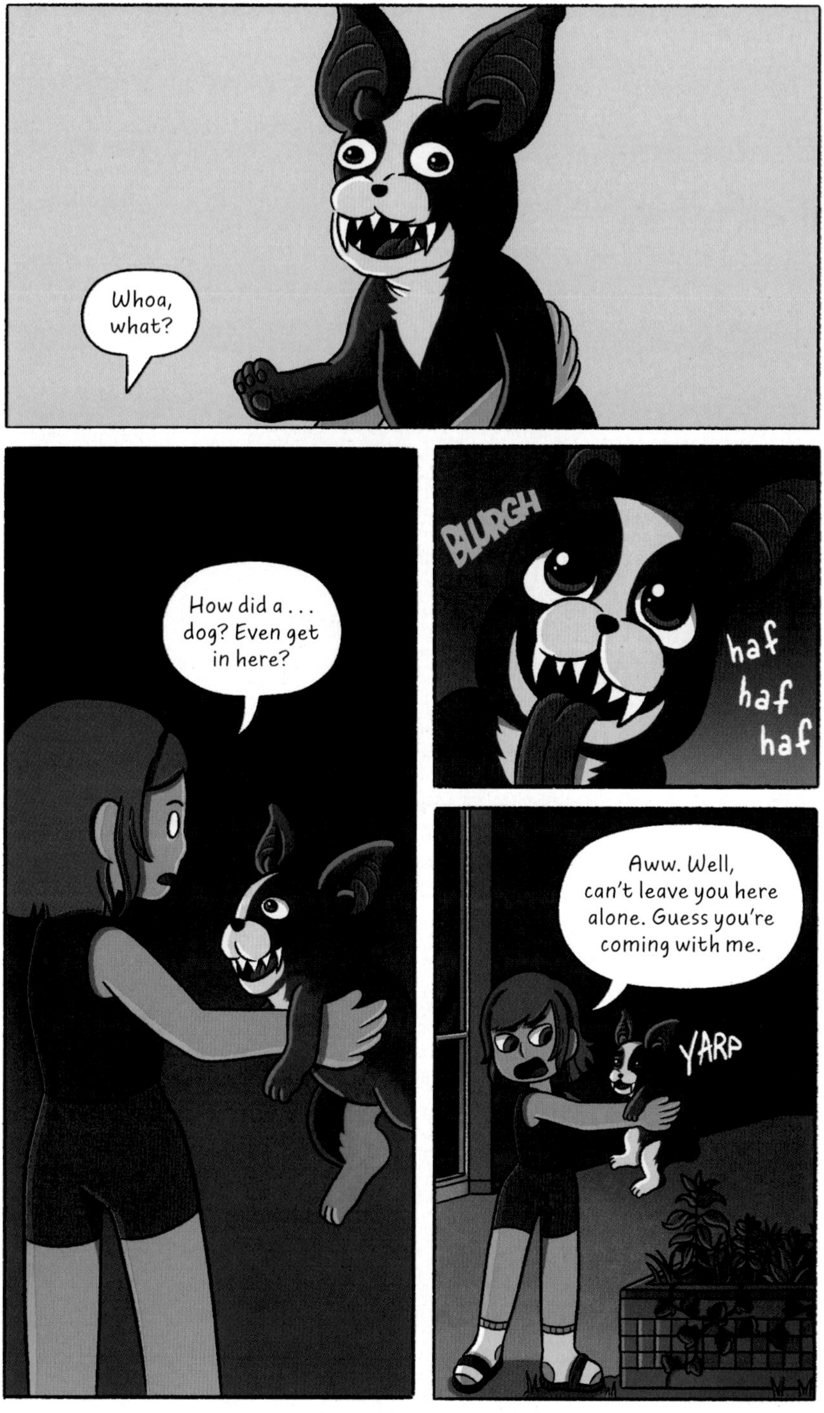
Whoa, what?
How did a . . . dog? Even get in here?
BLURGH
haf
haf
haf
Aww. Well, can't leave you here alone. Guess you're coming with me.
YARP

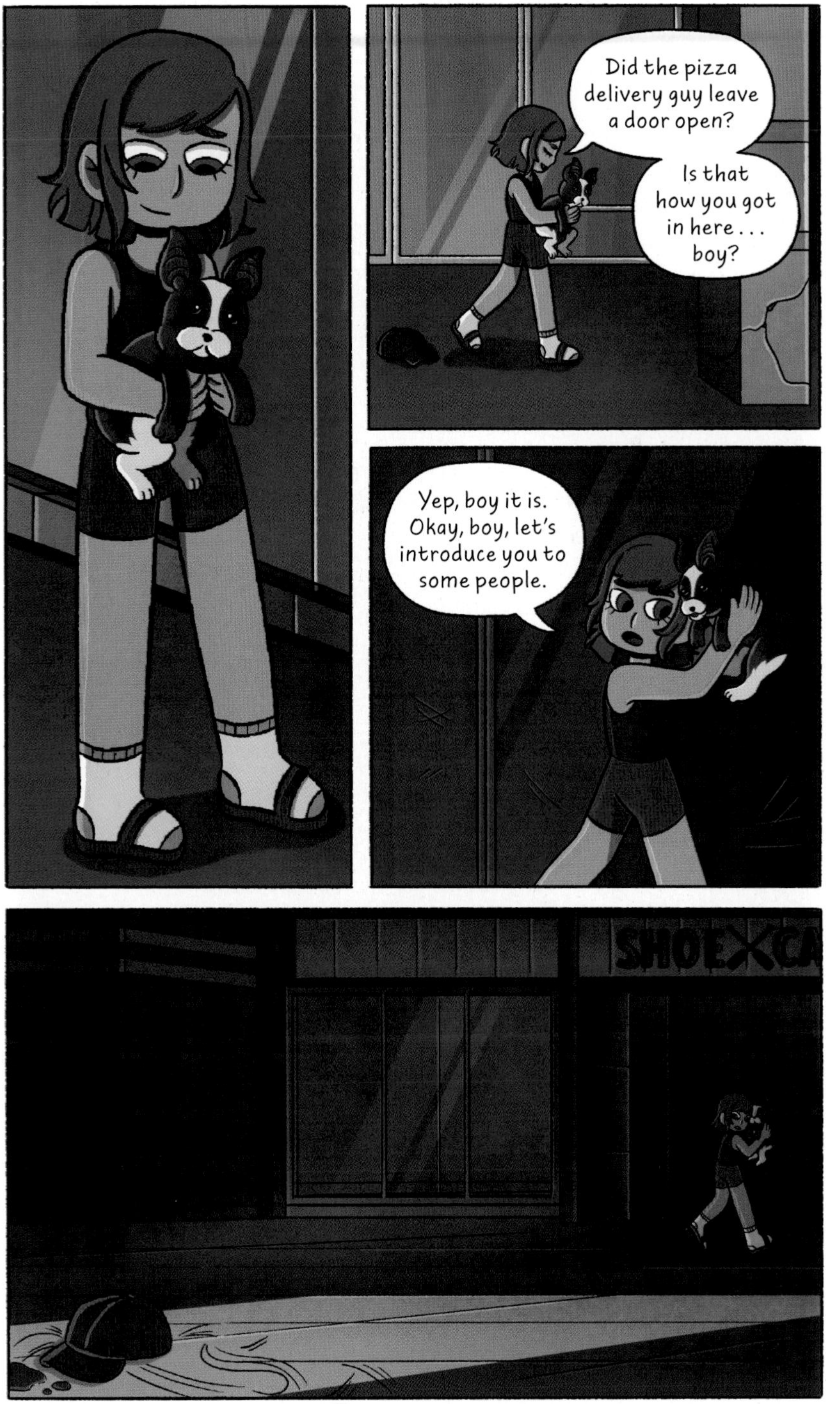
Did the pizza delivery guy leave a door open?
Is that how you got in here . . . boy?
Yep, boy it is. Okay, boy, let's introduce you to some people.
SHOE

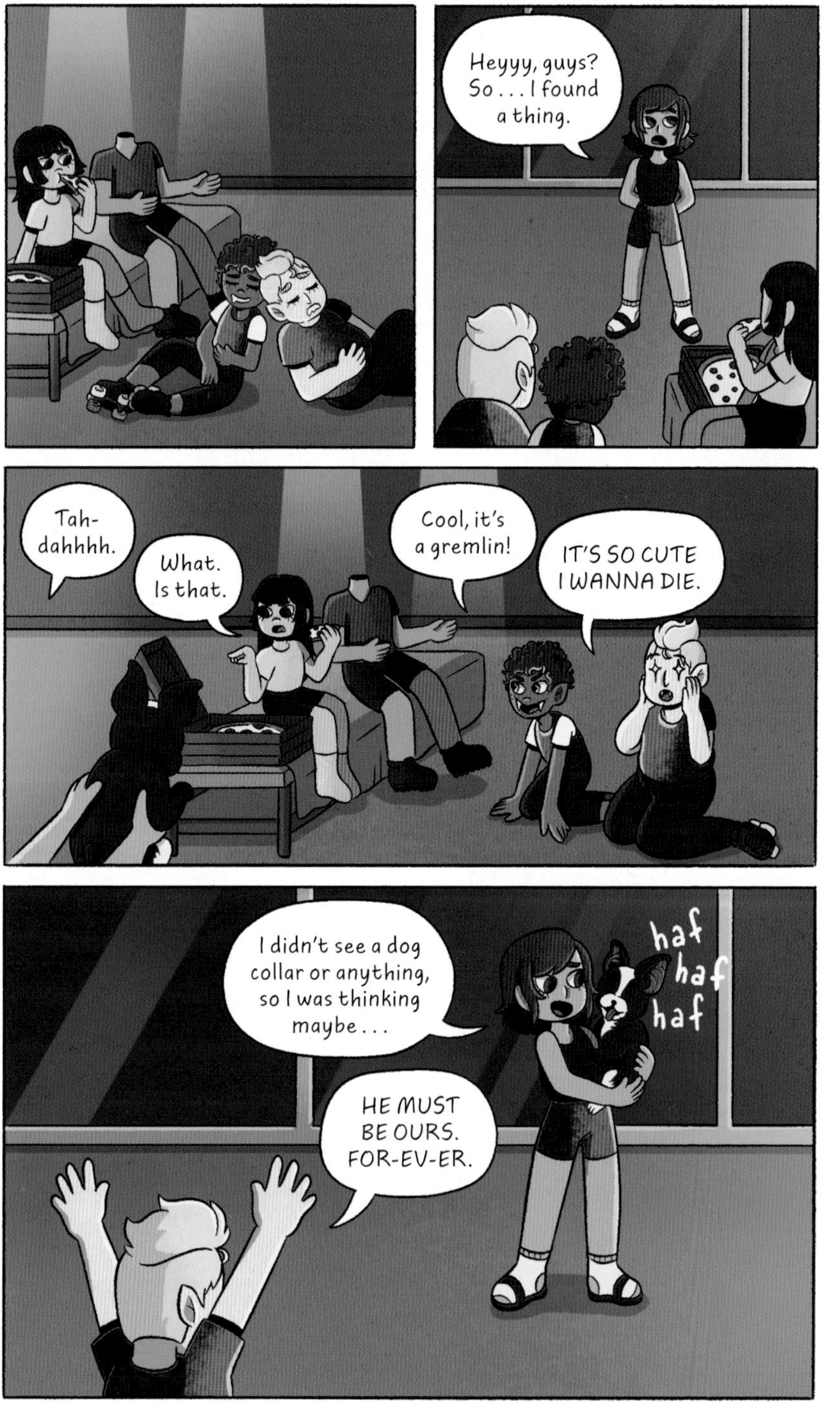

Heyyy, guys? So . . . I found a thing.
Tah-dahhhh.
What. Is that.
Cool, it's a gremlin!
IT'S SO CUTE I WANNA DIE.
I didn't see a dog collar or anything, so I was thinking maybe . . .
haf haf haf
HE MUST BE OURS. FOR-EV-ER.

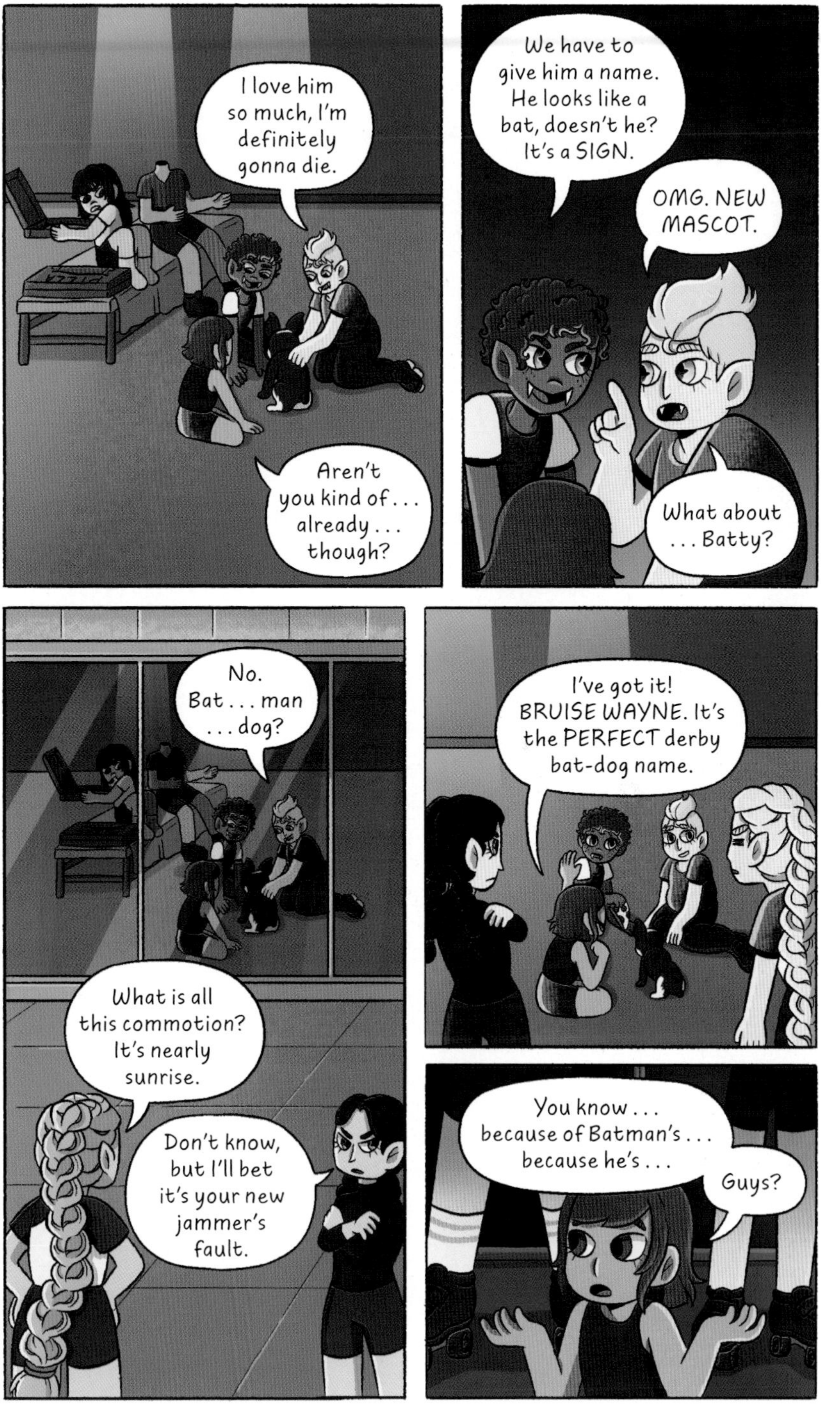
I love him so much, I'm definitely gonna die.
Aren't you kind of . . . already . . . though?
We have to give him a name. He looks like a bat, doesn't he? It's a SIGN.
OMG. NEW MASCOT.
What about . . . Batty?
No. Bat . . . man . . . dog?
What is all this commotion? It's nearly sunrise.
Don't know, but I'll bet it's your new jammer's fault.
I've got it! BRUISE WAYNE. It's the PERFECT derby bat-dog name.
You know . . . because of Batman's . . . because he's . . .
Guys?

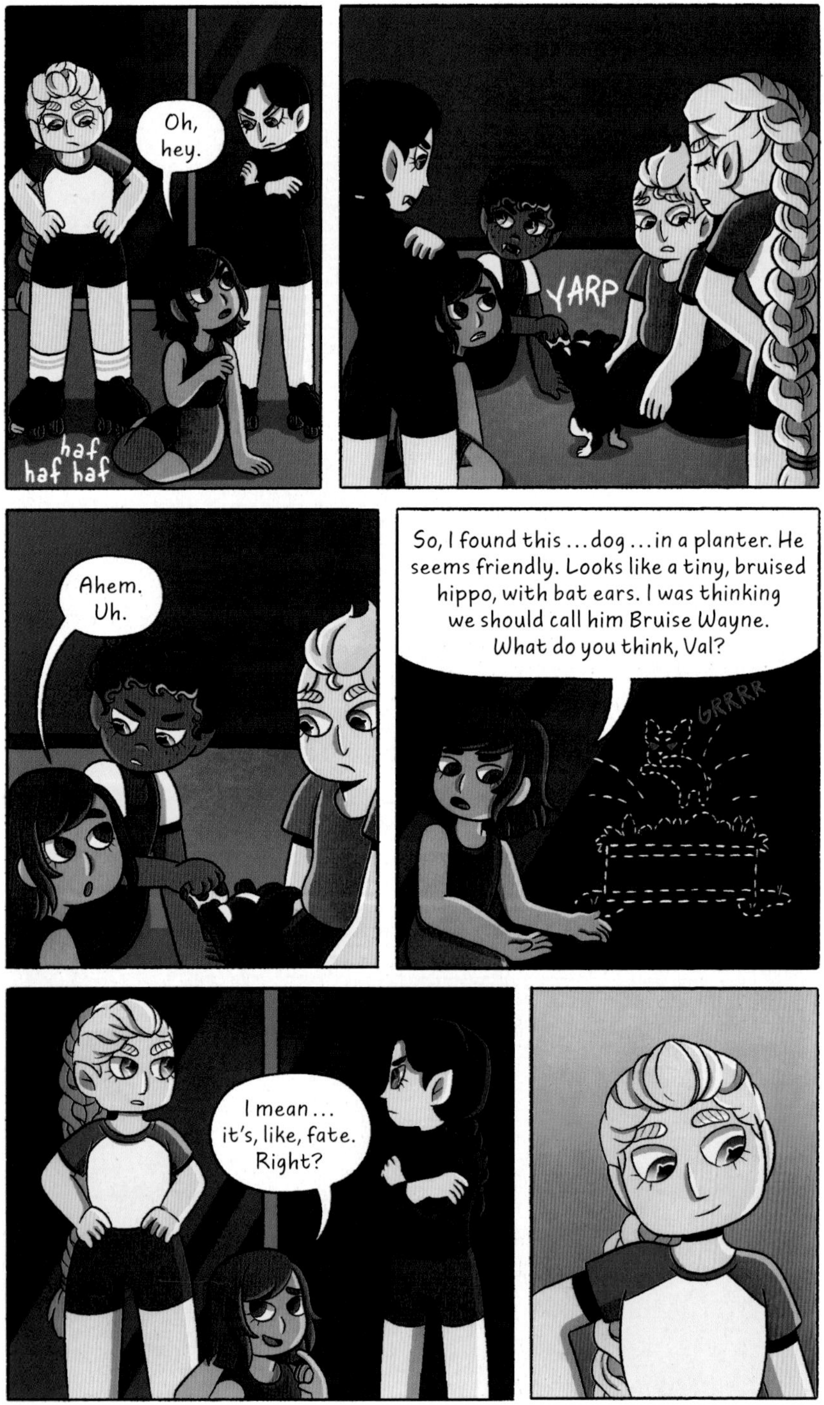
Oh, hey.
haf haf haf
YARP
Ahem. Uh.
So, I found this ... dog ... in a planter. He seems friendly. Looks like a tiny, bruised hippo, with bat ears. I was thinking we should call him Bruise Wayne. What do you think, Val?
GRRRR
I mean... it's, like, fate. Right?

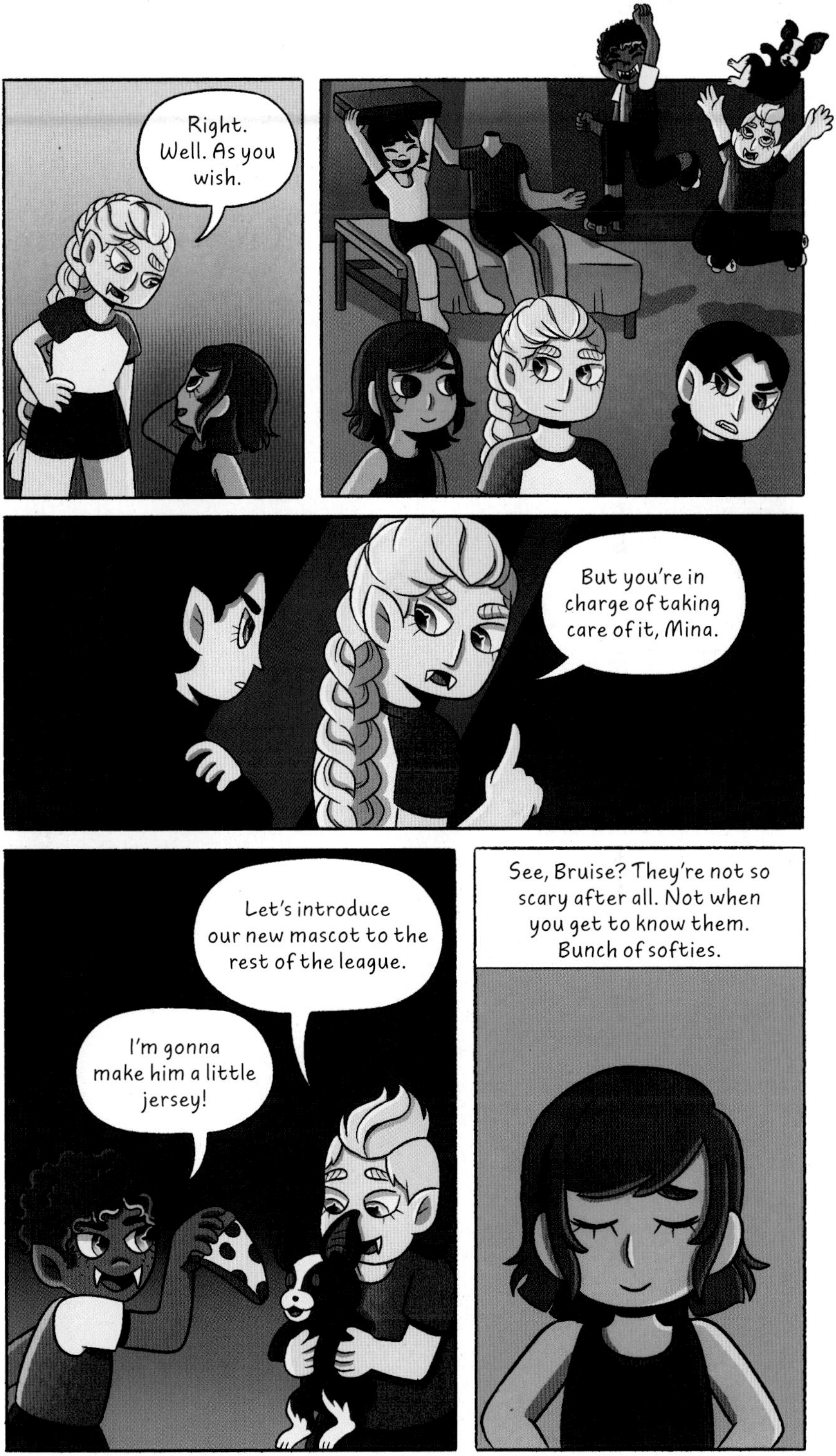
Right. Well. As you wish.
But you're in charge of taking care of it, Mina.
Let's introduce our new mascot to the rest of the league.
I'm gonna make him a little jersey!
See, Bruise? They're not so scary after all. Not when you get to know them. Bunch of softies.

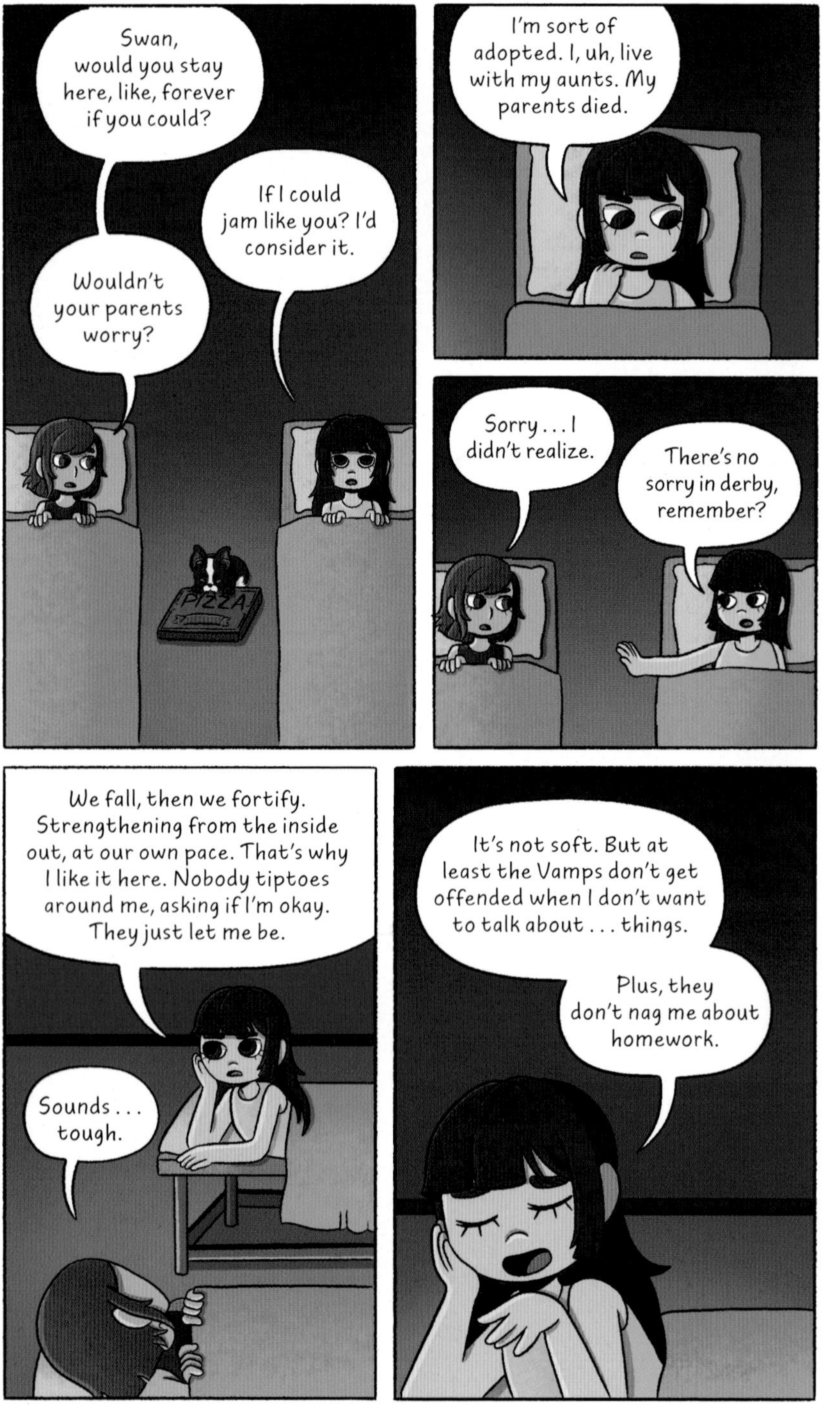
Swan, would you stay here, like, forever if you could?
If I could jam like you? I'd consider it.
Wouldn't your parents worry?
PIZZA
I'm sort of adopted. I, uh, live with my aunts. My parents died.
Sorry . . . I didn't realize.
There's no sorry in derby, remember?
We fall, then we fortify. Strengthening from the inside out, at our own pace. That's why I like it here. Nobody tiptoes around me, asking if I'm okay. They just let me be.
Sounds . . . tough.
It's not soft. But at least the Vamps don't get offended when I don't want to talk about . . . things.
Plus, they don't nag me about homework.

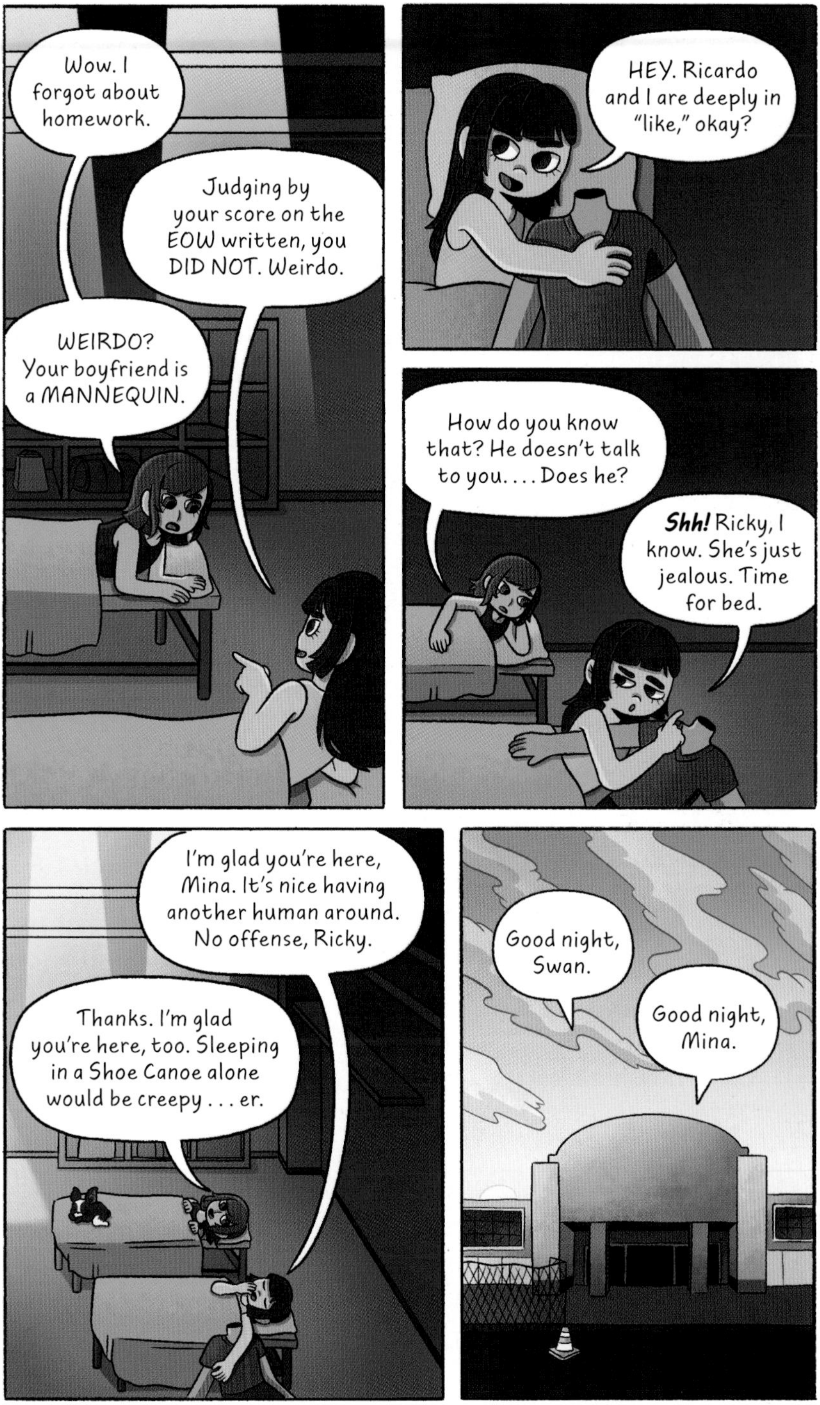
Wow. I forgot about homework.
Judging by your score on the EOW written, you DID NOT. Weirdo.
WEIRDO? Your boyfriend is a MANNEQUIN.
HEY. Ricardo and I are deeply in "like," okay?
How do you know that? He doesn't talk to you. . . . Does he?
Shh! Ricky, I know. She's just jealous. Time for bed.
I'm glad you're here, Mina. It's nice having another human around. No offense, Ricky.
Thanks. I'm glad you're here, too. Sleeping in a Shoe Canoe alone would be creepy . . . er.
Good night, Swan.
Good night, Mina.

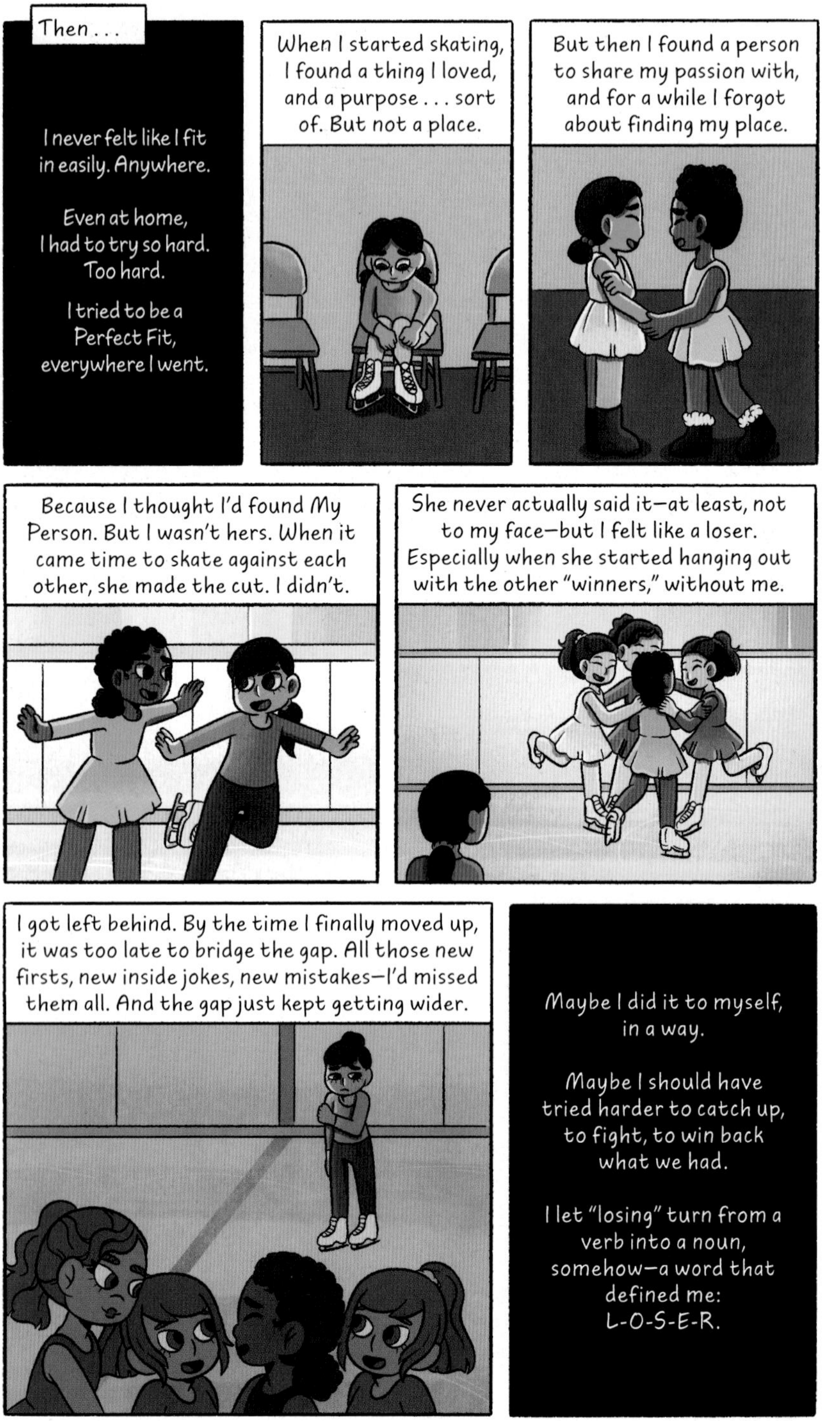
Then . . .
I never felt like I fit in easily. Anywhere.
Even at home, I had to try so hard. Too hard.
I tried to be a Perfect Fit, everywhere I went.
When I started skating, I found a thing I loved, and a purpose . . . sort of. But not a place.
But then I found a person to share my passion with, and for a while I forgot about finding my place.
Because I thought I'd found My Person. But I wasn't hers. When it came time to skate against each other, she made the cut. I didn't.
She never actually said it—at least, not to my face—but I felt like a loser. Especially when she started hanging out with the other "winners," without me.
I got left behind. By the time I finally moved up, it was too late to bridge the gap. All those new firsts, new inside jokes, new mistakes—I'd missed them all. And the gap just kept getting wider.
Maybe I did it to myself, in a way.
Maybe I should have tried harder to catch up, to fight, to win back what we had.
I let "losing" turn from a verb into a noun, somehow—a word that defined me: L-O-S-E-R.

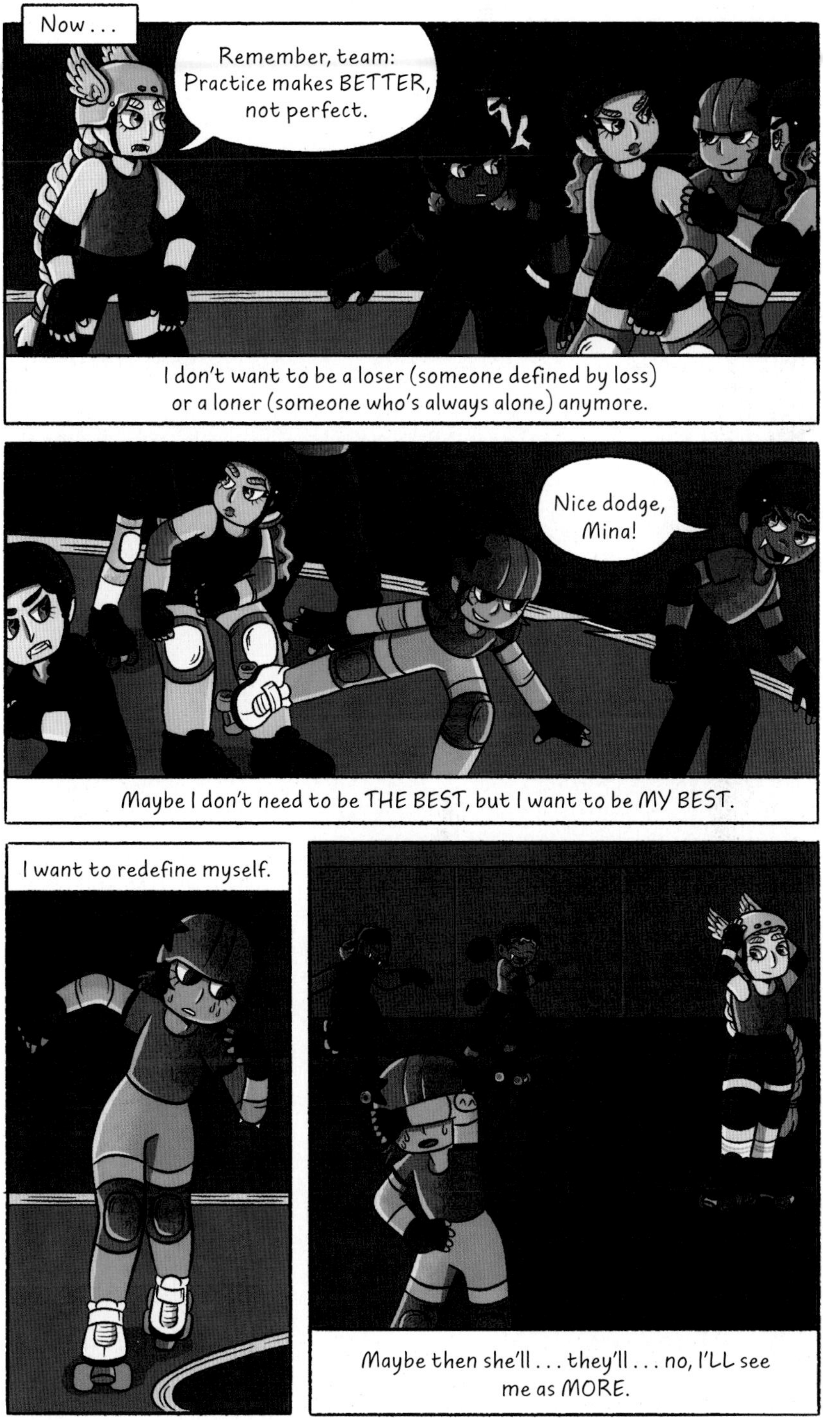
Now . . .
Remember, team: Practice makes BETTER, not perfect.
I don't want to be a loser (someone defined by loss) or a loner (someone who's always alone) anymore.
Nice dodge, Mina!
Maybe I don't need to be THE BEST, but I want to be MY BEST.
I want to redefine myself.
Maybe then she'll . . . they'll . . . no, I'LL see me as MORE.

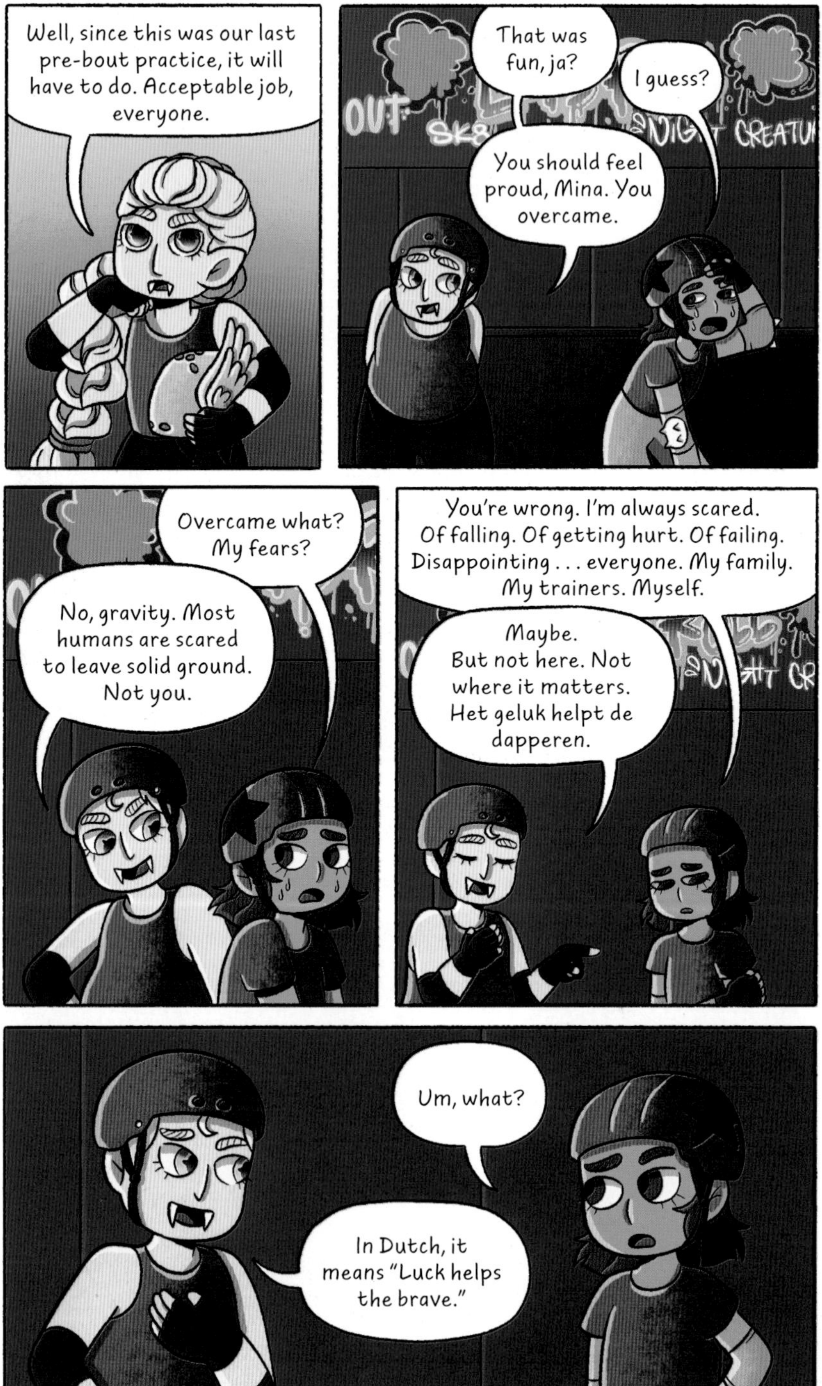
Well, since this was our last pre-bout practice, it will have to do. Acceptable job, everyone.
That was fun, ja?
I guess?
You should feel proud, Mina. You overcame.
OUT SK8 NIGHT CREATU
Overcame what? My fears?
No, gravity. Most humans are scared to leave solid ground. Not you.
You're wrong. I'm always scared. Of falling. Of getting hurt. Of failing. Disappointing . . . everyone. My family. My trainers. Myself.
Maybe. But not here. Not where it matters. Het geluk helpt de dapperen.
Um, what?
In Dutch, it means "Luck helps the brave."

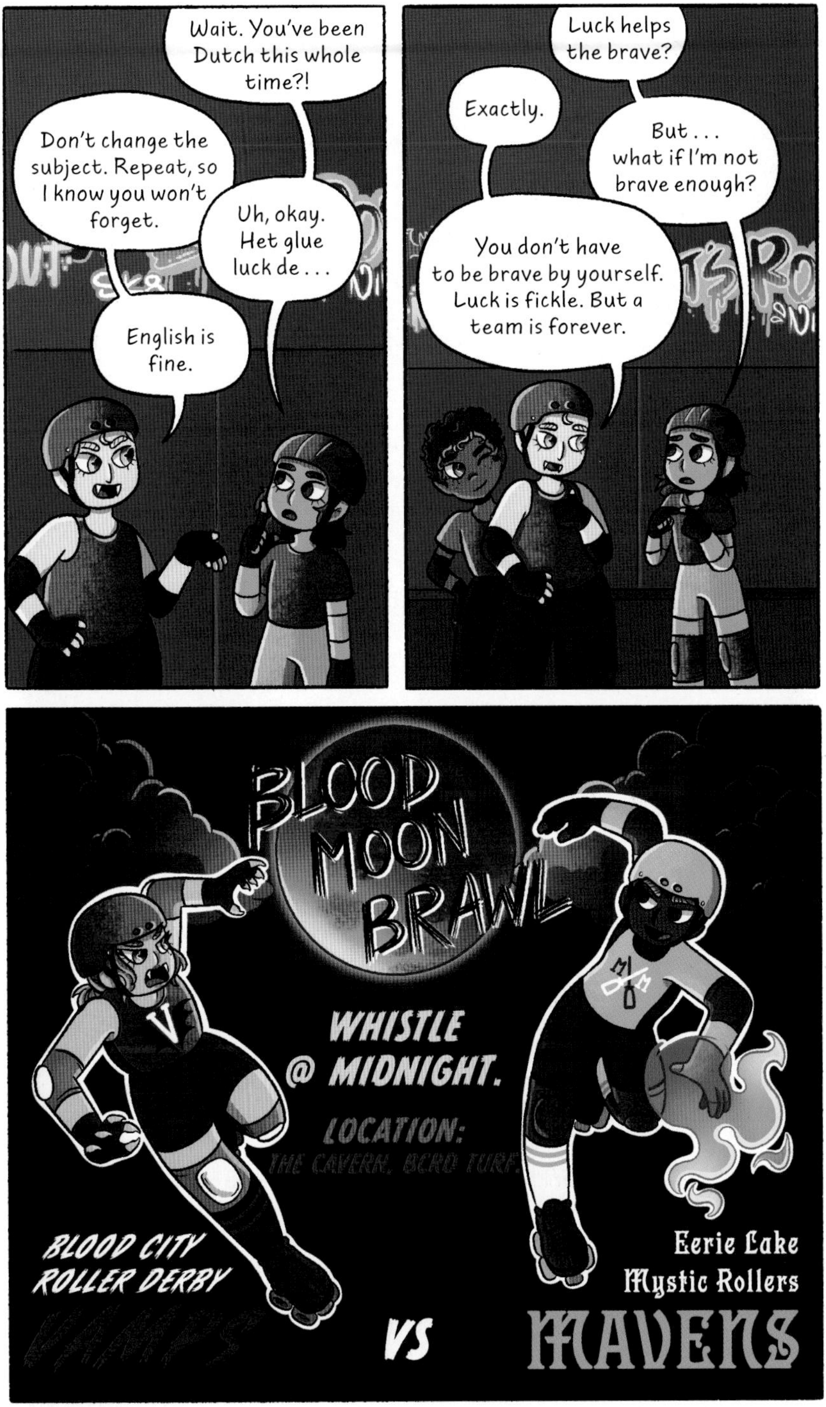
Wait. You've been Dutch this whole time?!
Don't change the subject. Repeat, so I know you won't forget.
Uh, okay. Het glue luck de . . .
English is fine.
Luck helps the brave?
Exactly.
But . . . what if I'm not brave enough?
You don't have to be brave by yourself. Luck is fickle. But a team is forever.
BLOOD MOON BRAWL
WHISTLE @ MIDNIGHT.
LOCATION:
THE CAVERN, BCRD TURF.
BLOOD CITY ROLLER DERBY
VAMPS
VS
Eerie Lake Mystic Rollers
MAVENS

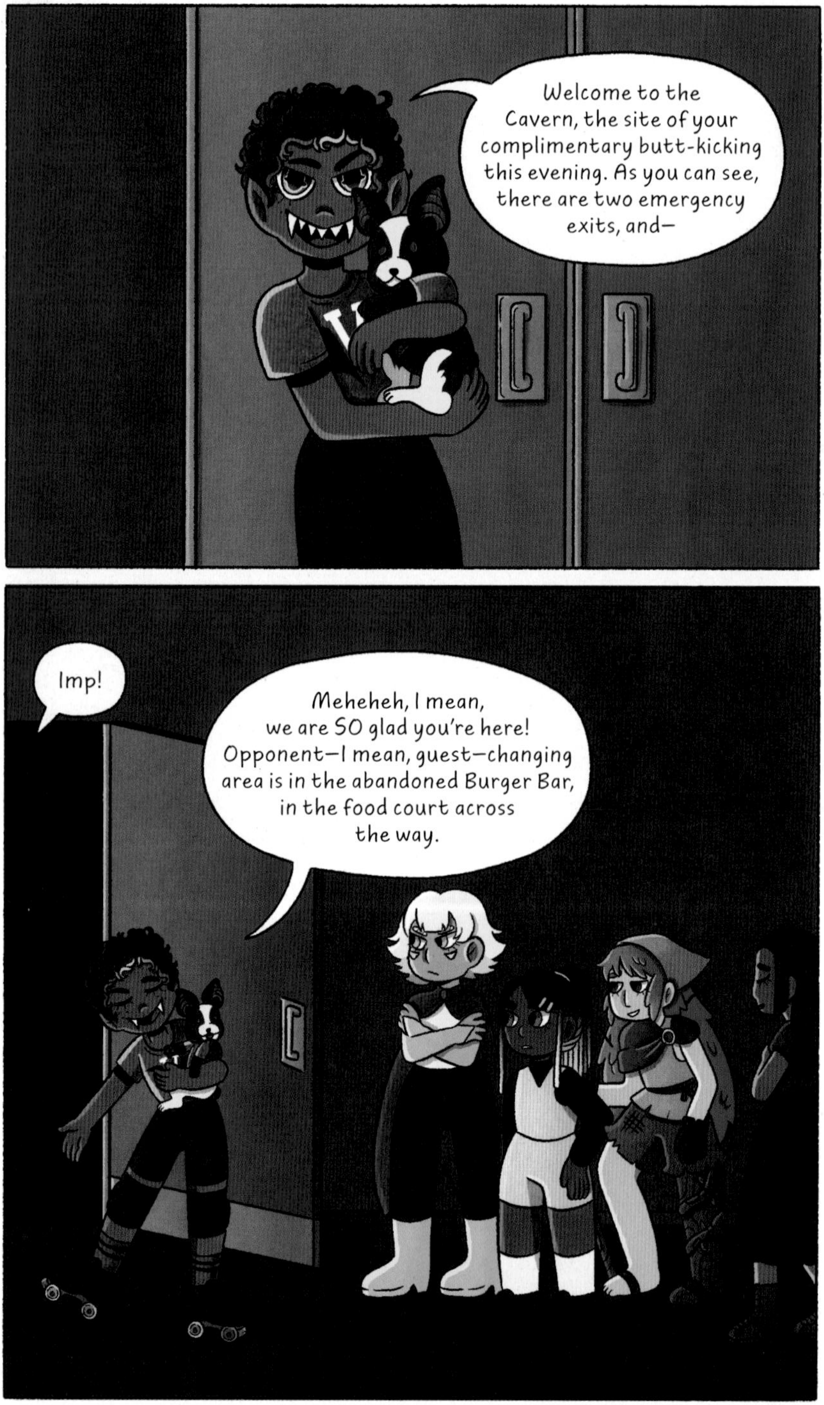
Welcome to the Cavern, the site of your complimentary butt-kicking this evening. As you can see, there are two emergency exits, and—
Imp!
Meheheh, I mean, we are SO glad you're here! Opponent—I mean, guest—changing area is in the abandoned Burger Bar, in the food court across the way.

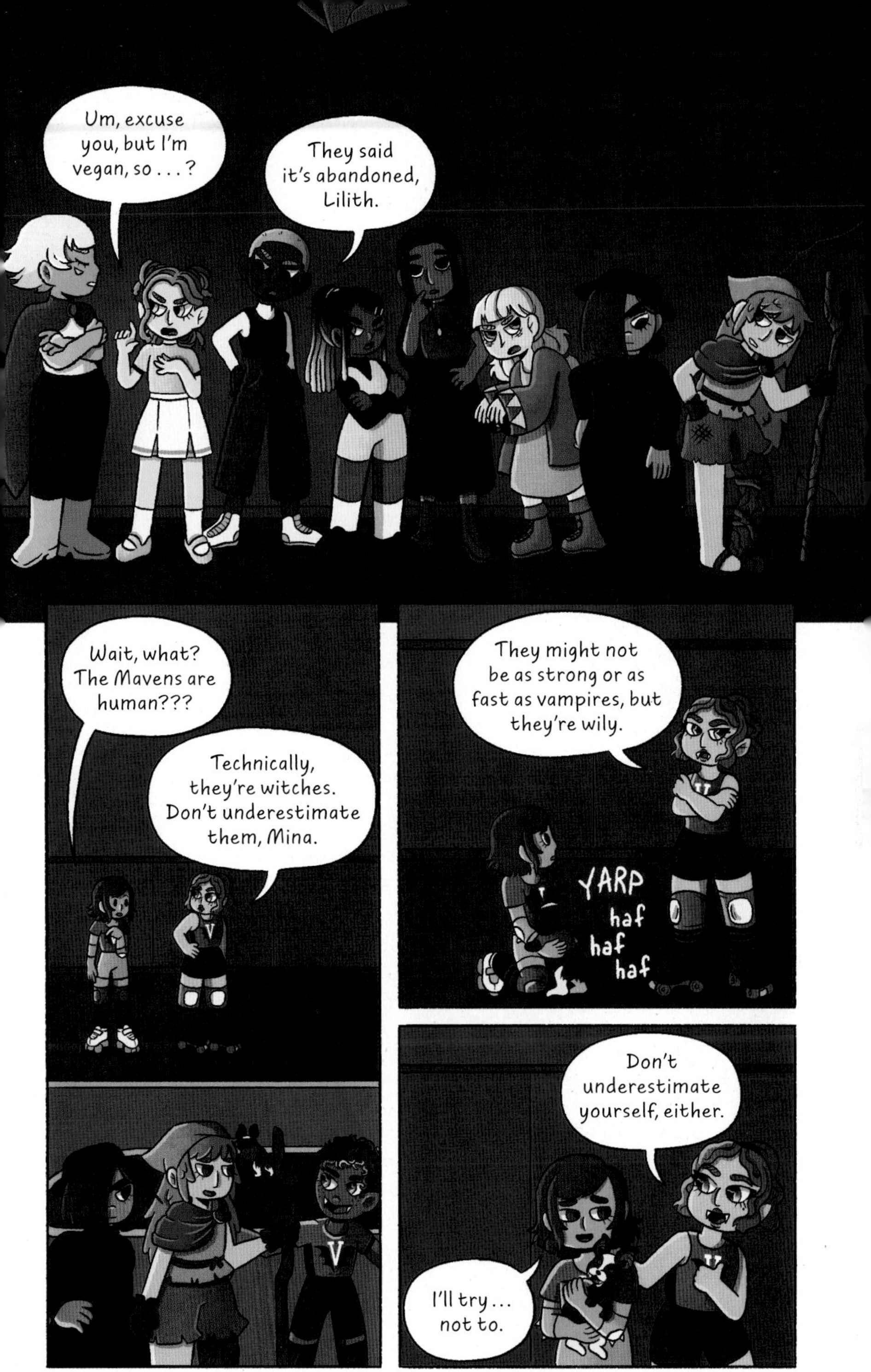
Um, excuse you, but I'm vegan, so . . . ?
They said it's abandoned, Lilith.
Wait, what? The Mavens are human???
Technically, they're witches. Don't underestimate them, Mina.
They might not be as strong or as fast as vampires, but they're wily.
YARP
haf
haf
haf
Don't underestimate yourself, either.
I'll try . . . not to.

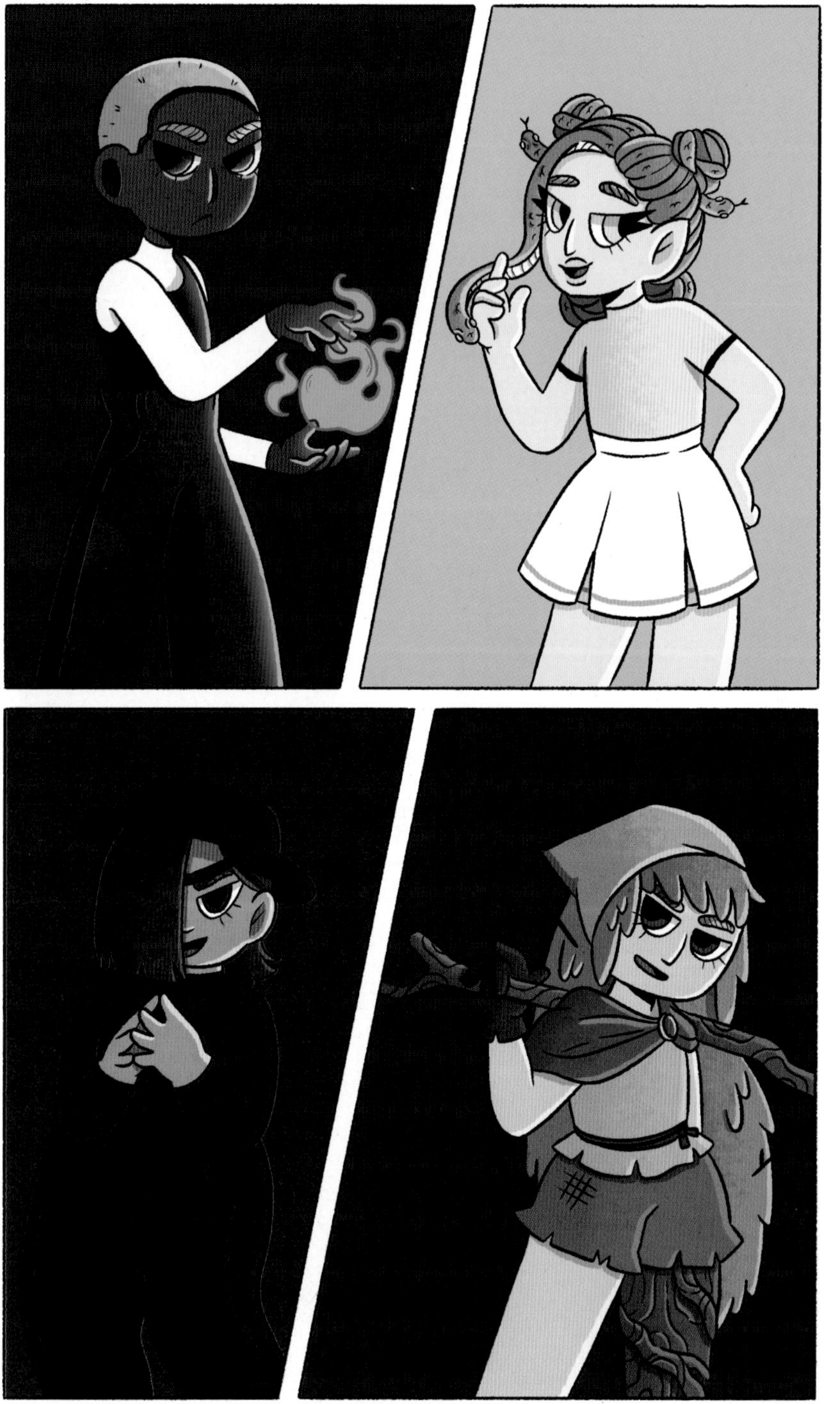

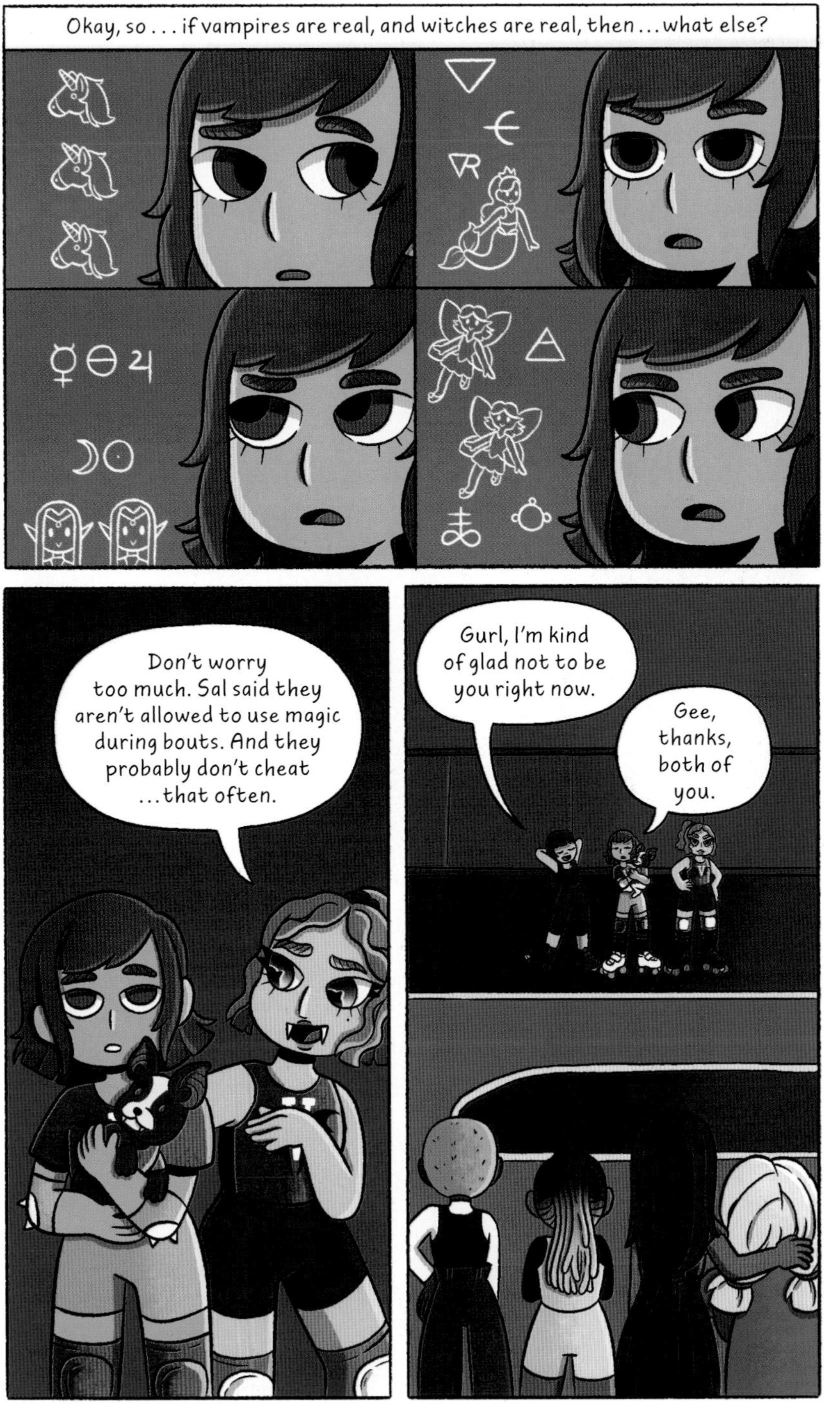
Okay, so . . . if vampires are real, and witches are real, then . . . what else?
Don't worry too much. Sal said they aren't allowed to use magic during bouts. And they probably don't cheat . . . that often.
Gurl, I'm kind of glad not to be you right now.
Gee, thanks, both of you.

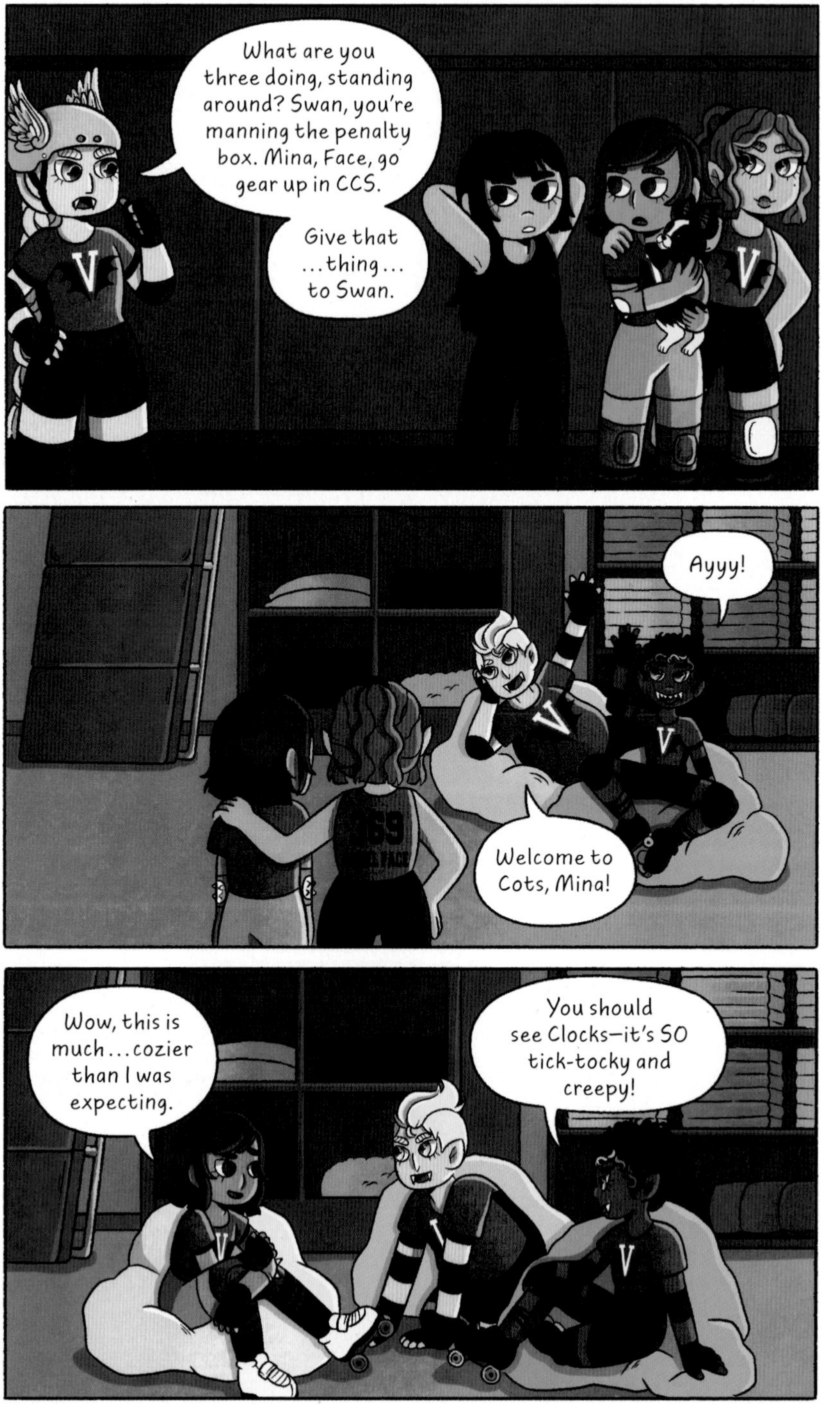
What are you three doing, standing around? Swan, you're manning the penalty box. Mina, Face, go gear up in CCS.
Give that ...thing... to Swan.
Ayyy!
Welcome to Cots, Mina!
Wow, this is much...cozier than I was expecting.
You should see Clocks—it's SO tick-tocky and creepy!

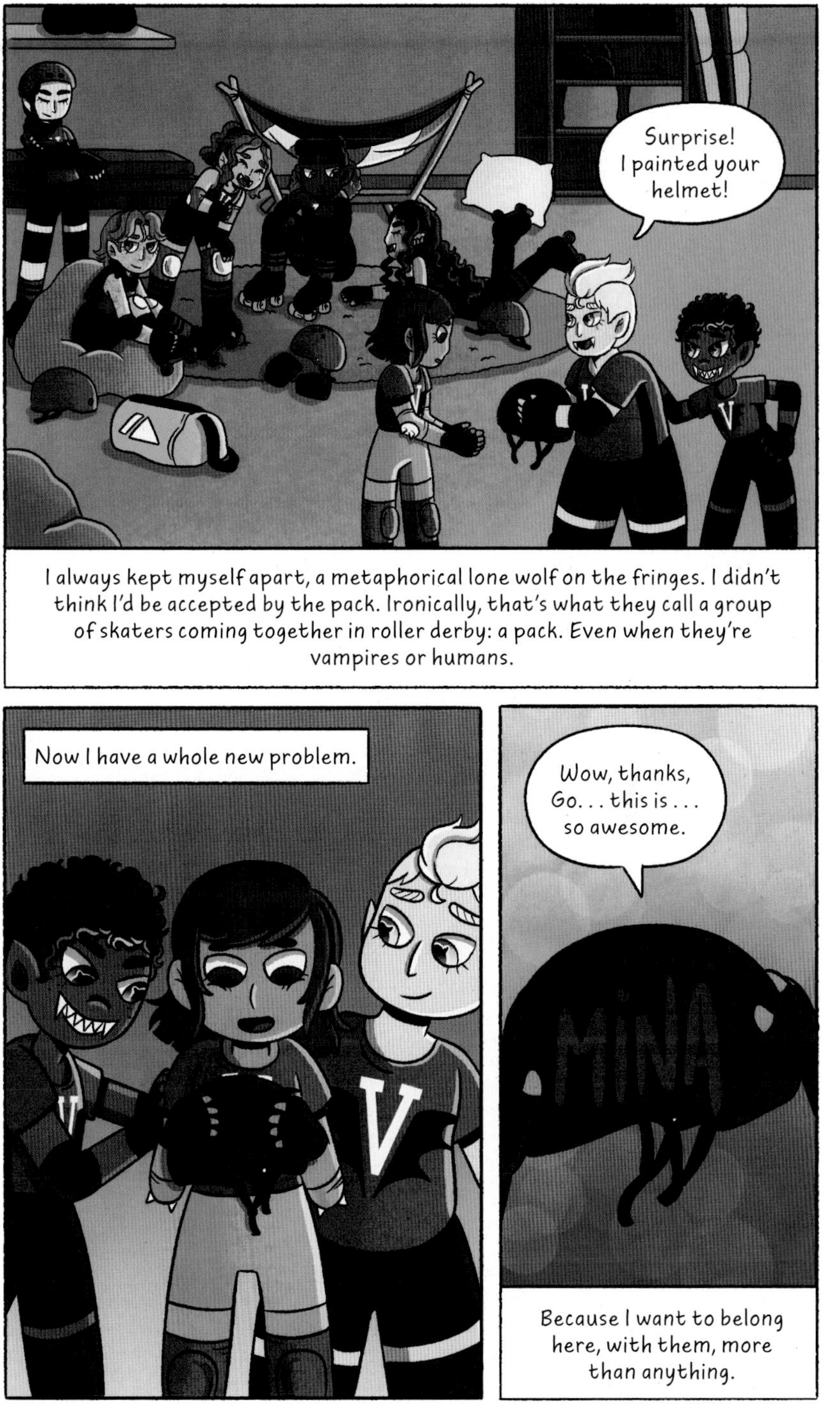
Surprise! I painted your helmet!
I always kept myself apart, a metaphorical lone wolf on the fringes. I didn't think I'd be accepted by the pack. Ironically, that's what they call a group of skaters coming together in roller derby: a pack. Even when they're vampires or humans.
Now I have a whole new problem.
Wow, thanks, Go. . . this is . . . so awesome.
MINA
Because I want to belong here, with them, more than anything.

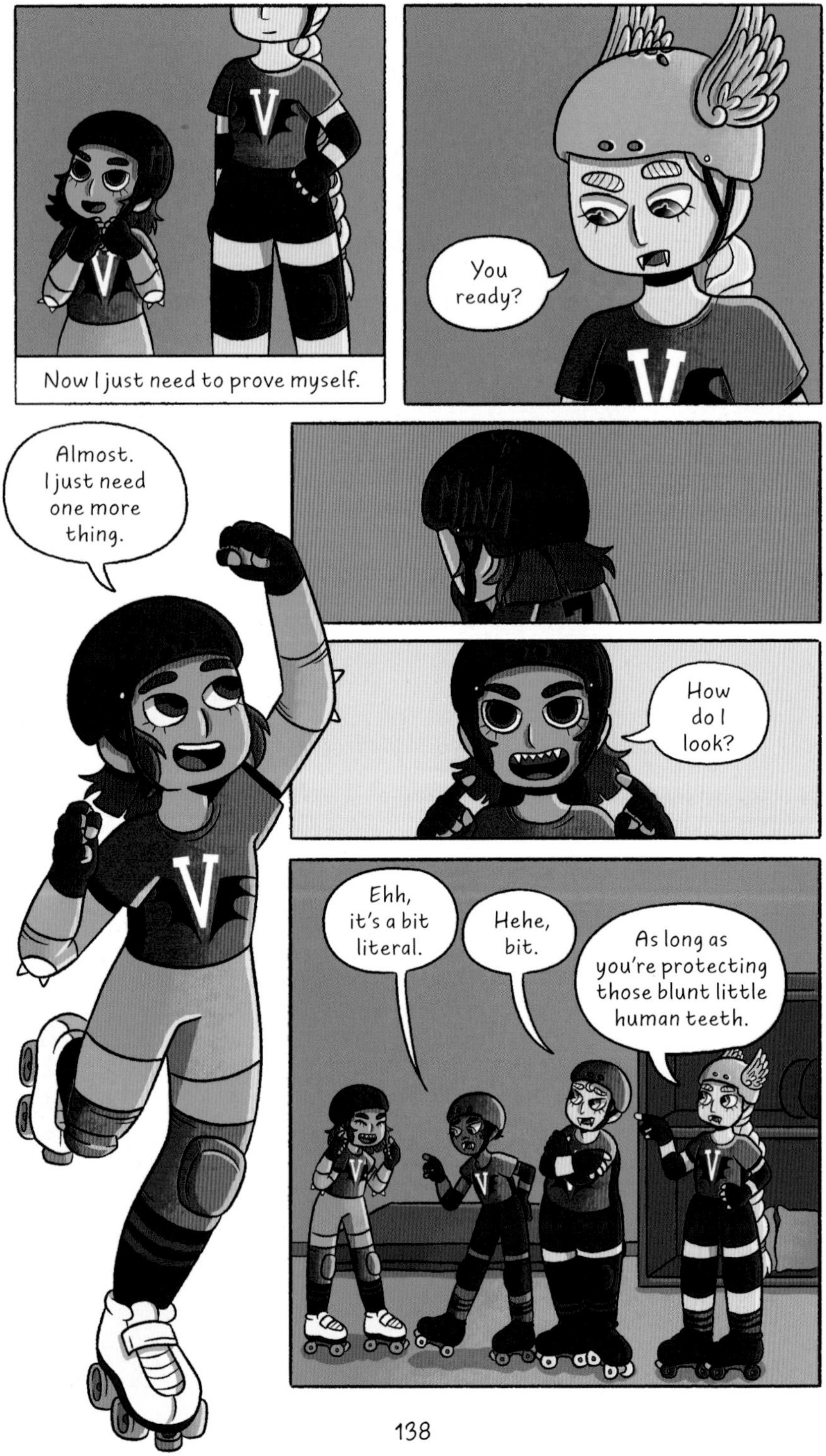
Now I just need to prove myself.
You ready?
Almost. I just need one more thing.
How do I look?
Ehh, it's a bit literal.
Hehe, bit.
As long as you're protecting those blunt little human teeth.

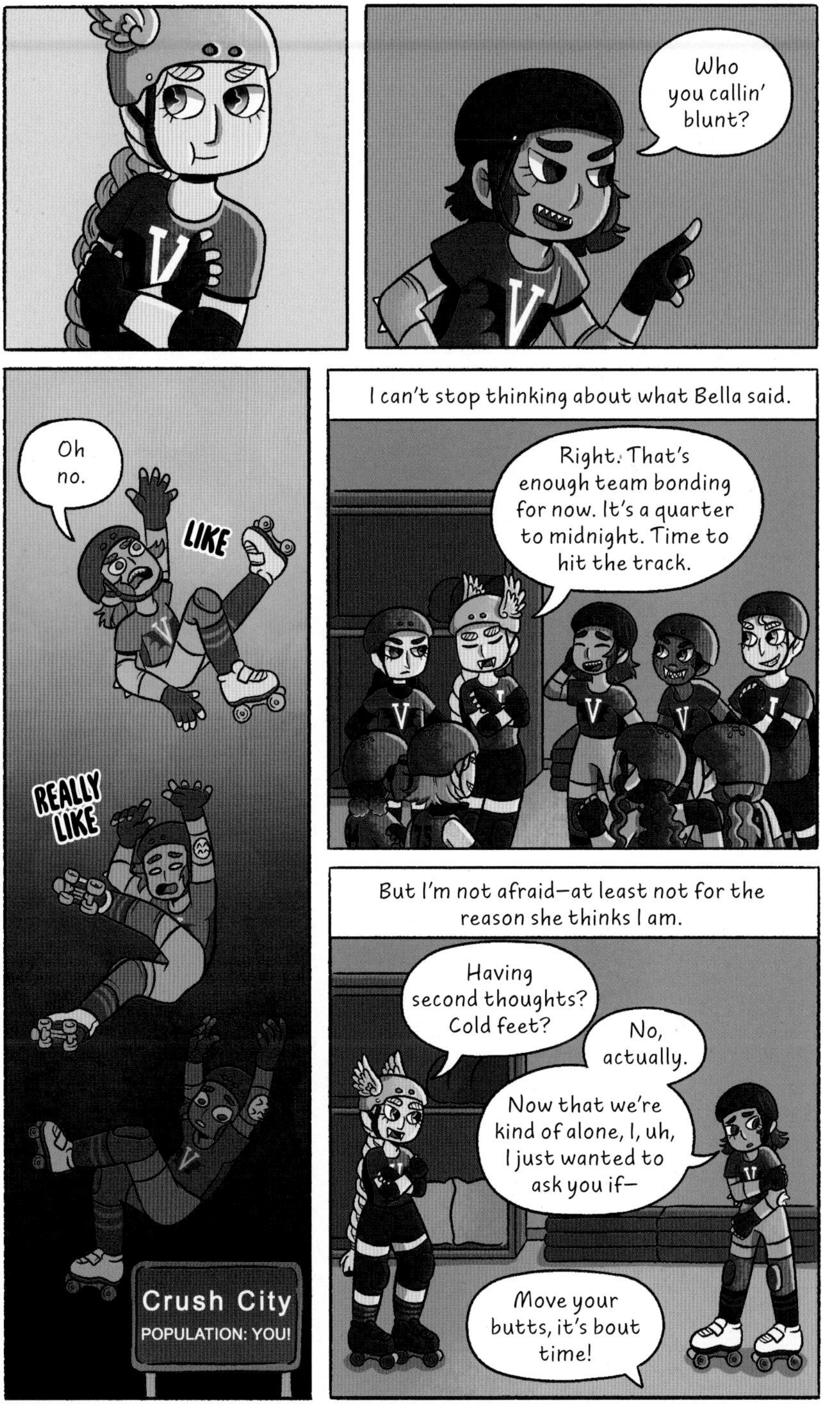
Who you callin' blunt?
Oh no.
LIKE
REALLY LIKE
Crush City
POPULATION: YOU!
I can't stop thinking about what Bella said.
Right. That's enough team bonding for now. It's a quarter to midnight. Time to hit the track.
But I'm not afraid—at least not for the reason she thinks I am.
Having second thoughts? Cold feet?
No, actually.
Now that we're kind of alone, I, uh, I just wanted to ask you if—
Move your butts, it's bout time!

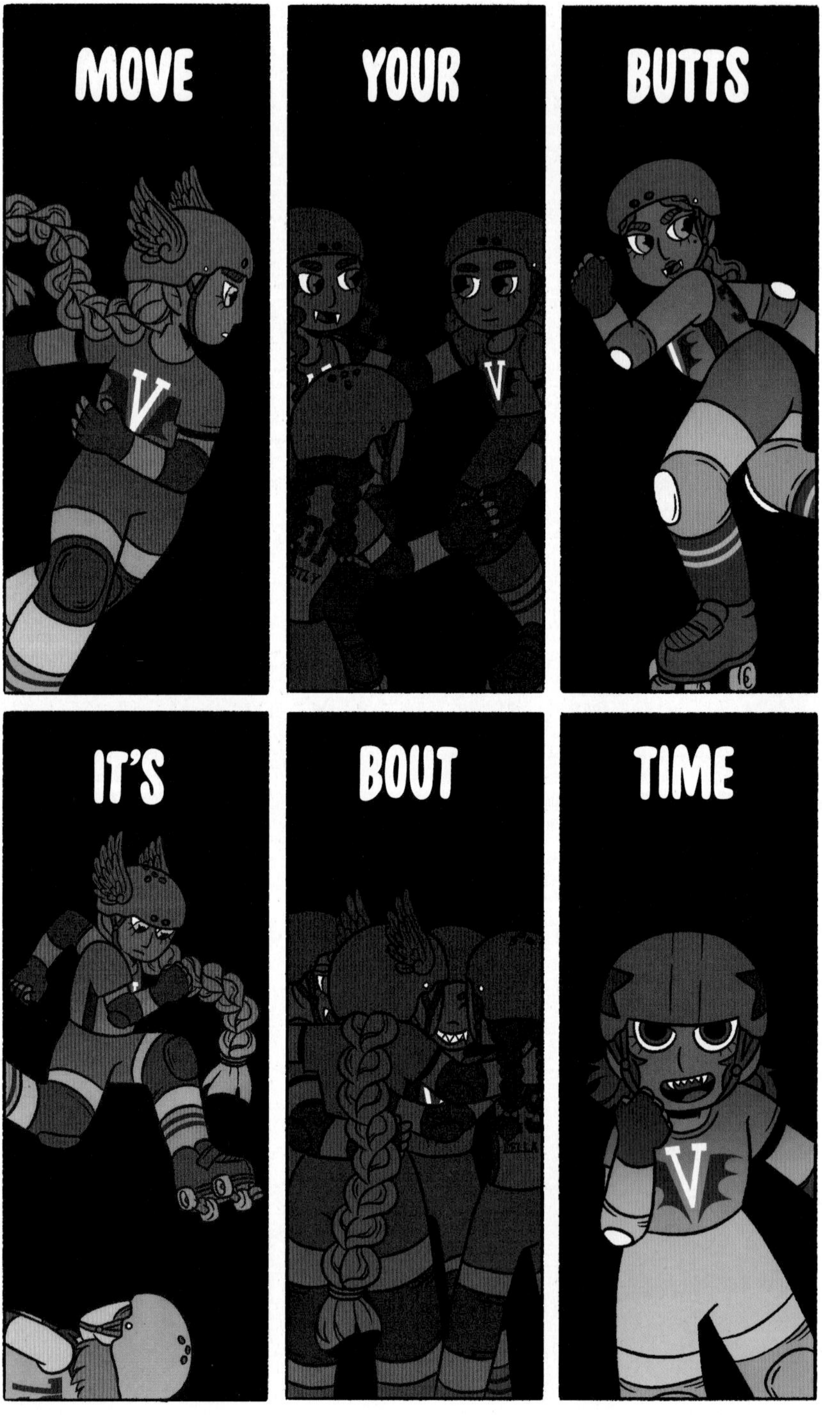
MOVE
YOUR
BUTTS
IT'S
BOUT
TIME

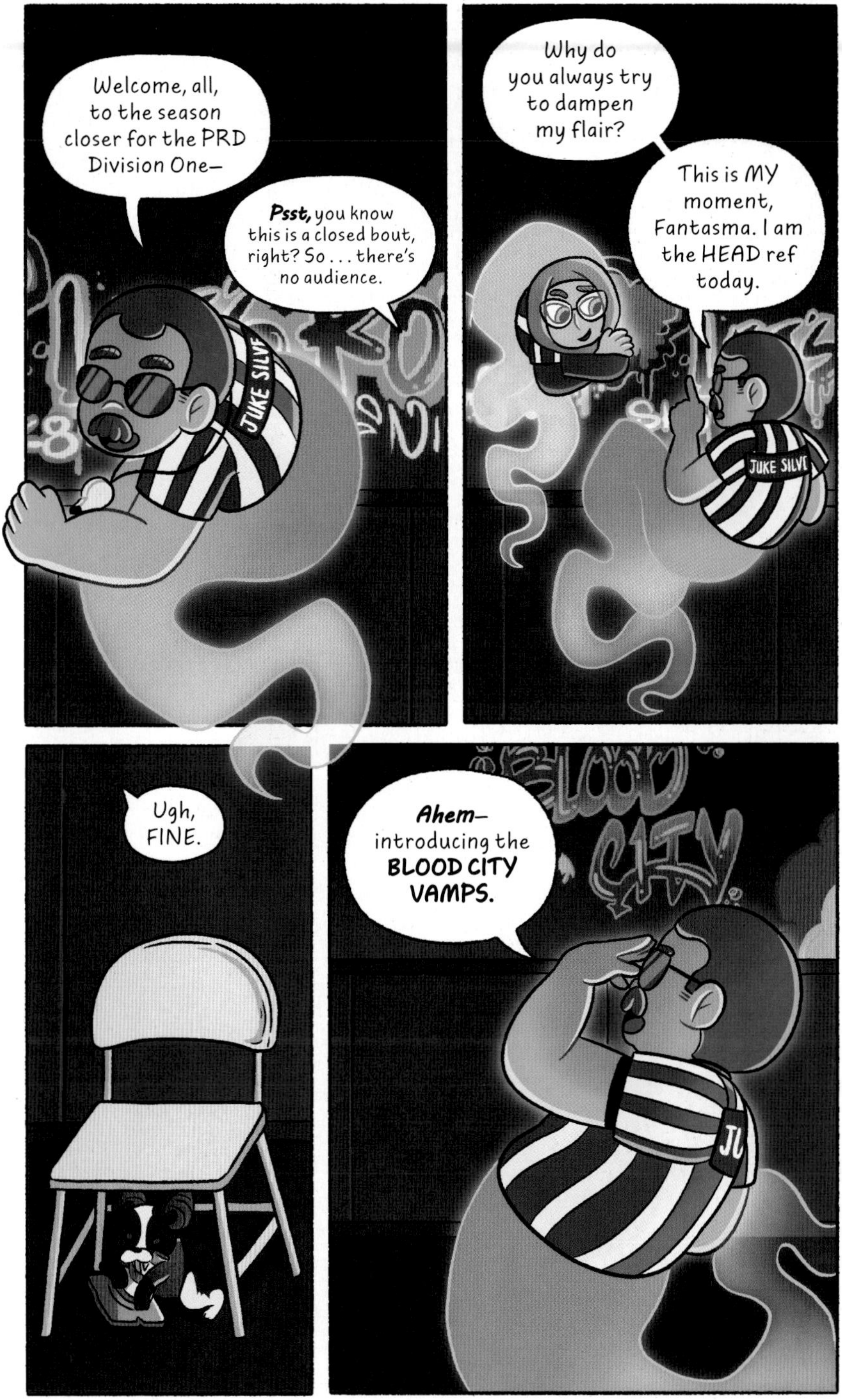
Welcome, all, to the season closer for the PRD Division One—
Psst, you know this is a closed bout, right? So . . . there's no audience.
JUKE SILVE
Why do you always try to dampen my flair?
This is MY moment, Fantasma. I am the HEAD ref today.
JUKE SILVE
Ugh, FINE.
Ahem—introducing the BLOOD CITY VAMPS.
BLOOD CITY

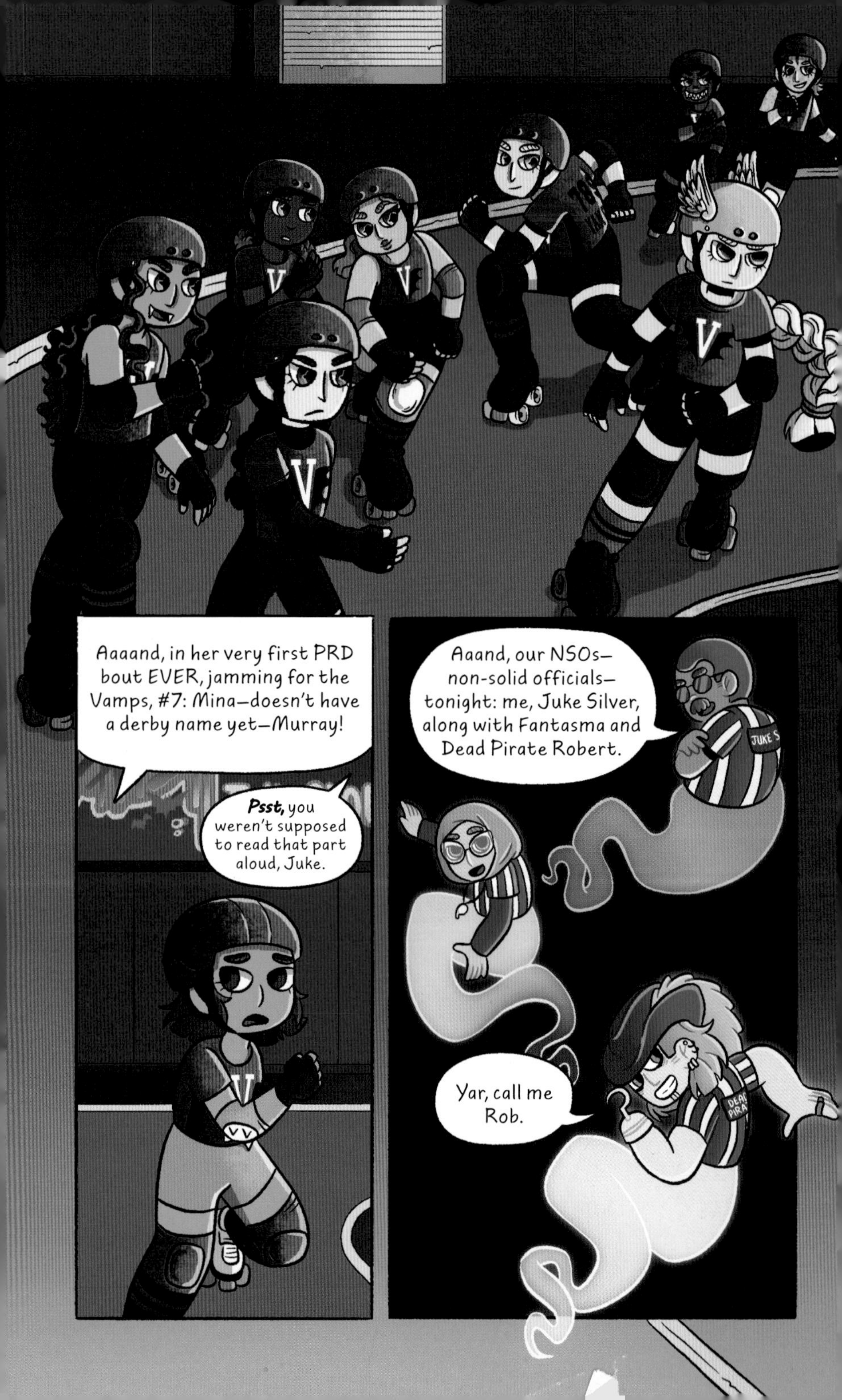
Aaaand, in her very first PRD bout EVER, jamming for the Vamps, #7: Mina—doesn't have a derby name yet—Murray!
Psst, you weren't supposed to read that part aloud, Juke.
Aaand, our NSOs—non-solid officials—tonight: me, Juke Silver, along with Fantasma and Dead Pirate Robert.
JUKE S
Yar, call me Rob.

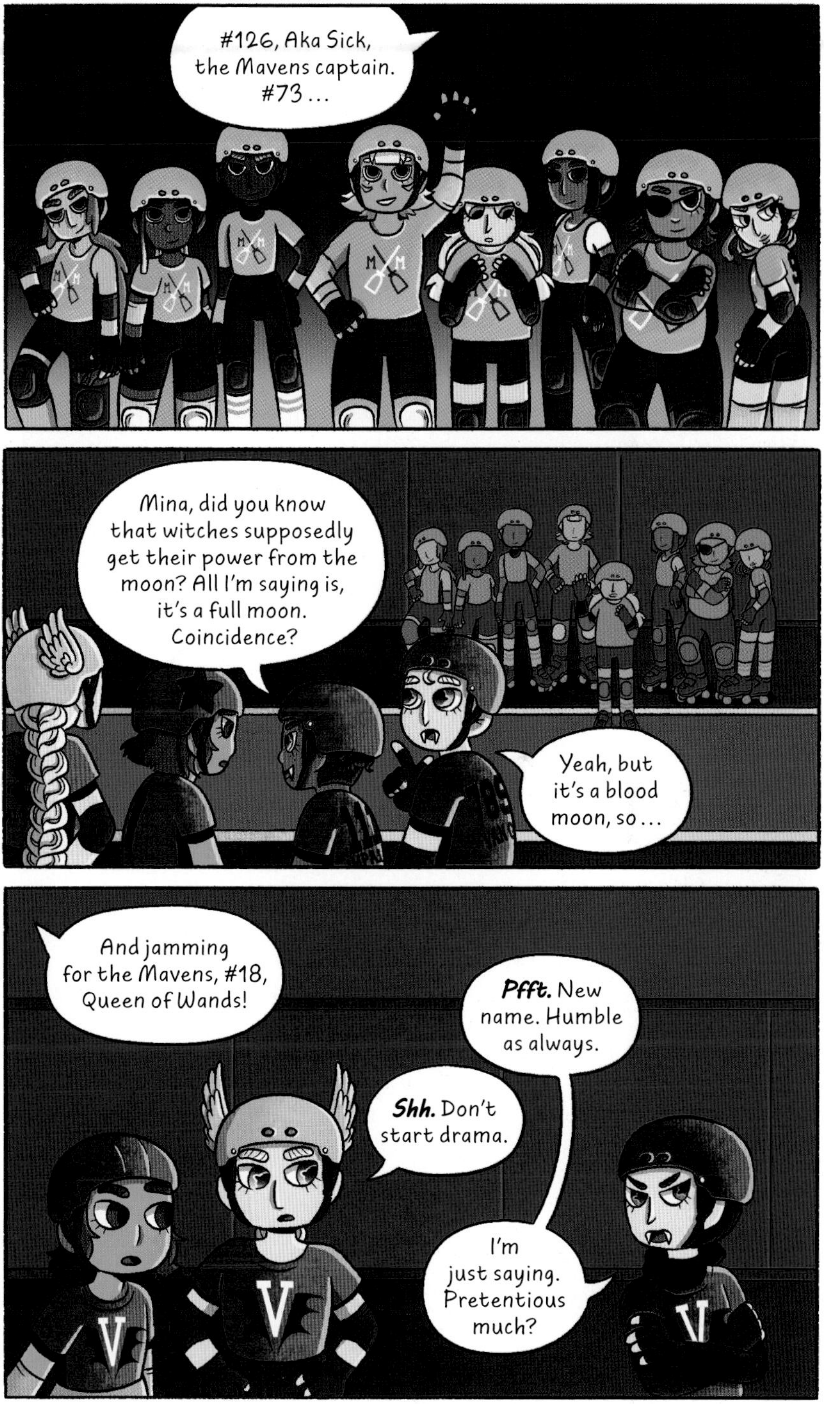

#126, Aka Sick, the Mavens captain. #73 . . .
Mina, did you know that witches supposedly get their power from the moon? All I'm saying is, it's a full moon. Coincidence?
Yeah, but it's a blood moon, so . . .
And jamming for the Mavens, #18, Queen of Wands!
Pfft. New name. Humble as always.
Shh. Don't start drama.
I'm just saying. Pretentious much?

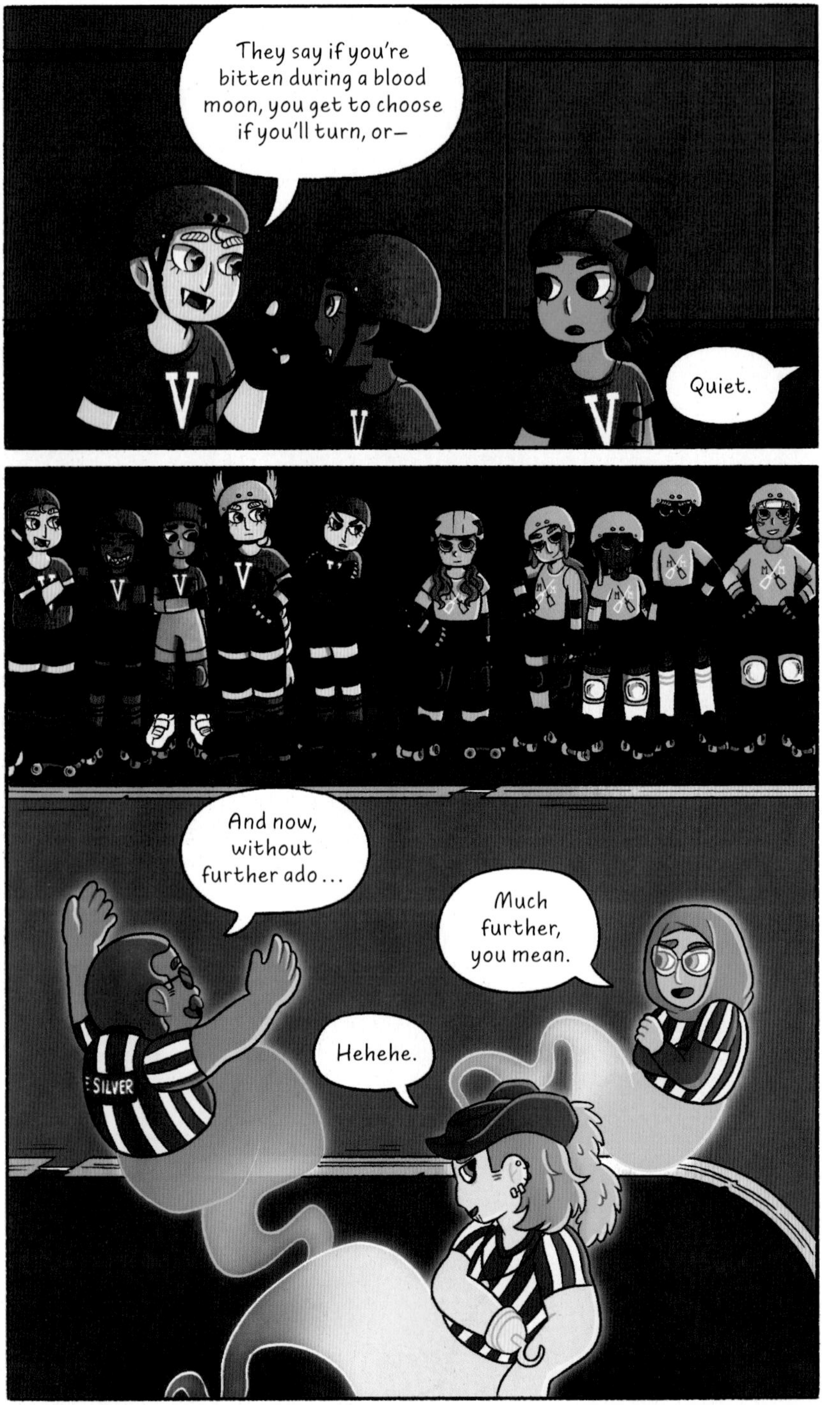
They say if you're bitten during a blood moon, you get to choose if you'll turn, or—
Quiet.
And now, without further ado...
Much further, you mean.
Hehehe.
SILVER

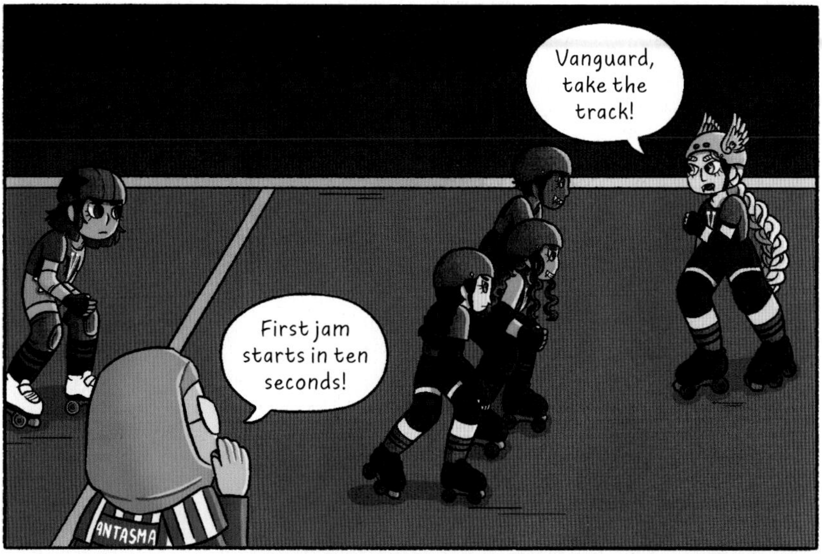
Vanguard, take the track!
First jam starts in ten seconds!
ANTASMA

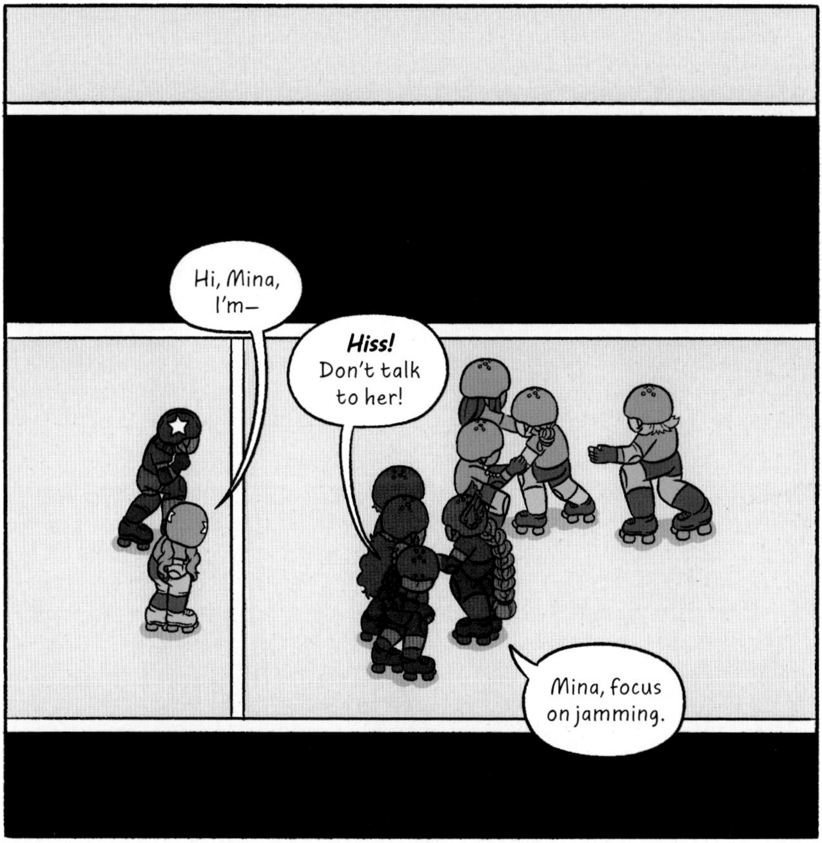
Hi, Mina, I'm—
Hiss! Don't talk to her!
Mina, focus on jamming.

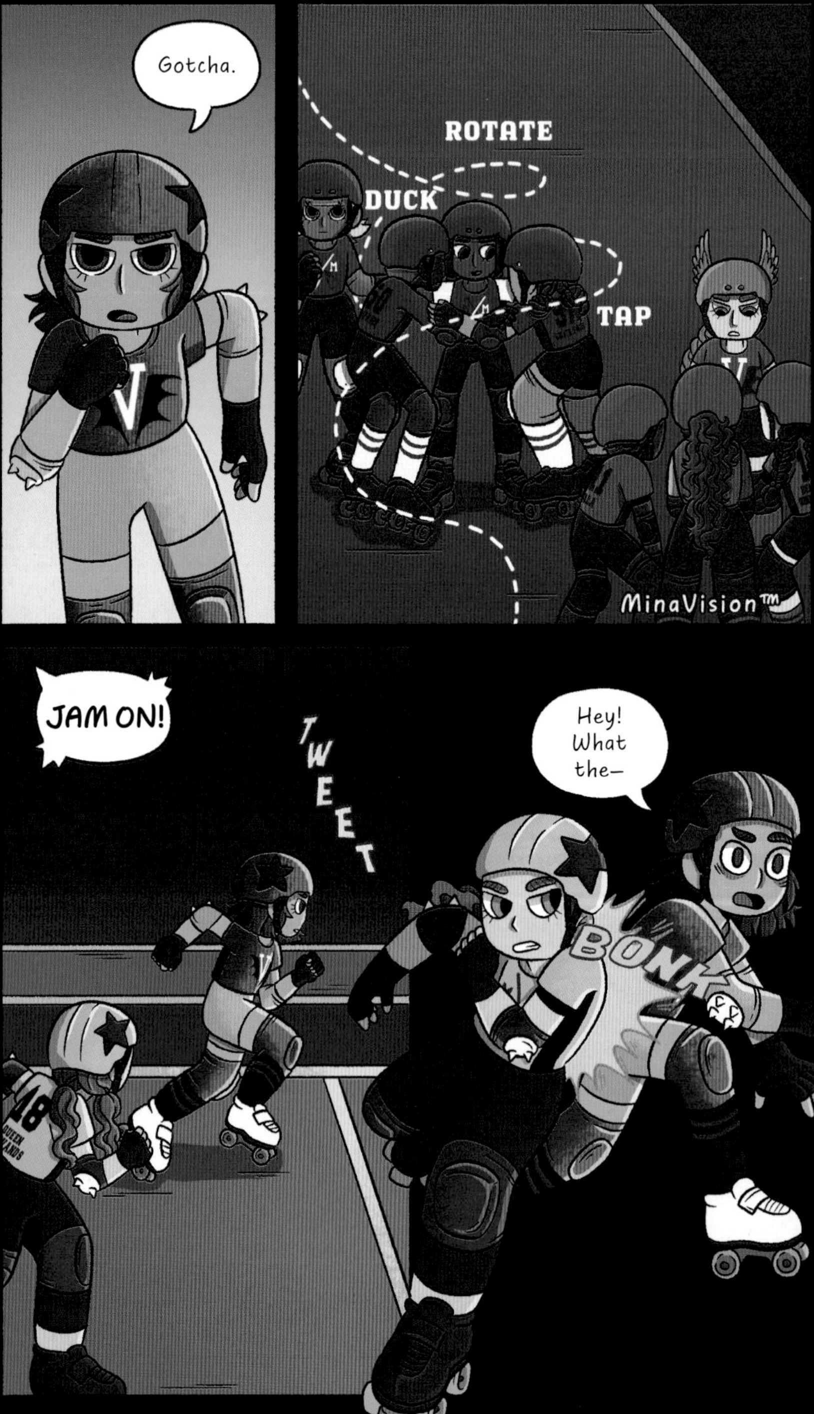
Gotcha.
ROTATE
DUCK
TAP
MinaVision™
JAM ON!
TWEET
Hey! What the—
BONK

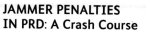

JAMMER PENALTIES IN PRD: A Crash Course

1. Remember on the PRD Rules Test when we mentioned that the only jammer penalty is voluntarily leaving the track during game play?
2. SURPRISE. Human jammers can hit each other, trip each other, elbow each other in the face—basically, do whatever they want—as long as they stay on the track and keep skating in derby direction, counterclockwise.
3. TL;DR: All's fair when it comes to outscoring the opposing jammer.
4. Welcome to the school of hard knocks, fresh meat.

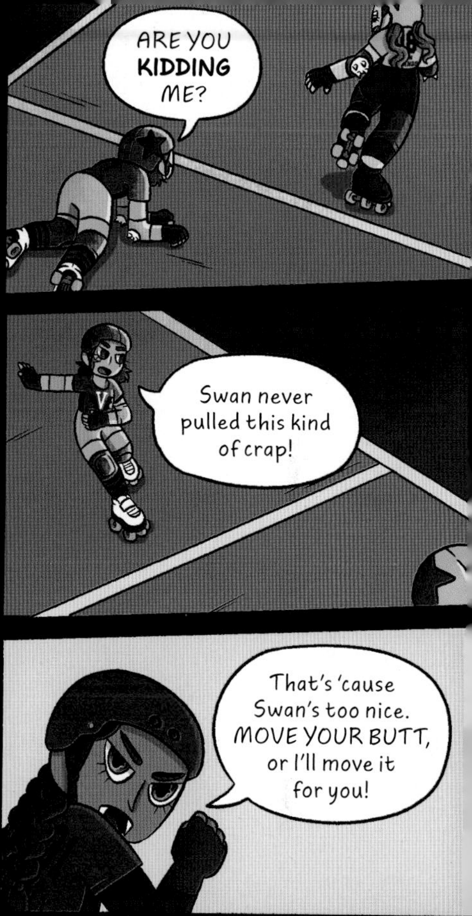
ARE YOU KIDDING ME?
Swan never pulled this kind of crap!
That's 'cause Swan's too nice. MOVE YOUR BUTT, or I'll move it for you!

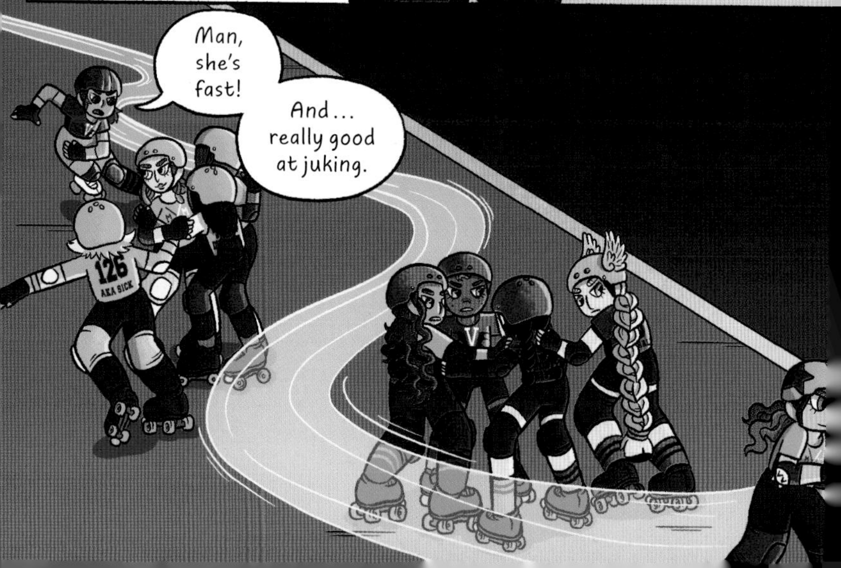
Man, she's fast!
And... really good at juking.
126
AKA SICK

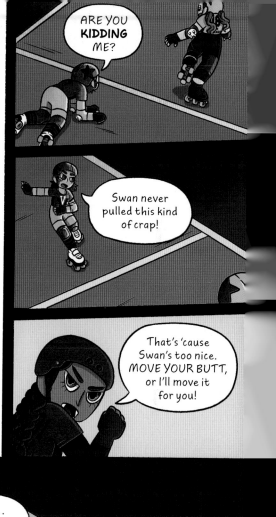

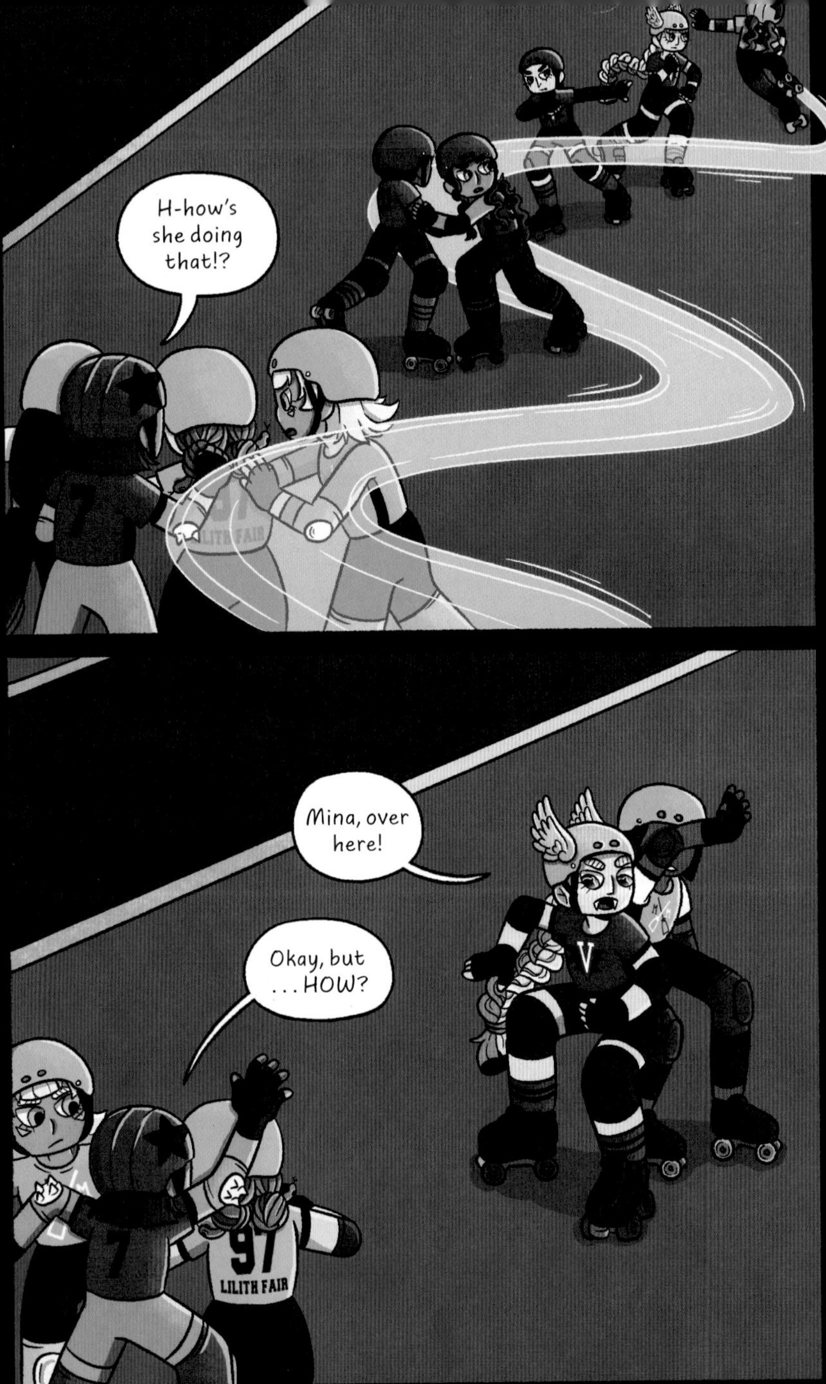
H-how's she doing that!?
7
97
LILITH FAIR
Mina, over here!
Okay, but ...HOW?
V
7
97
LILITH FAIR

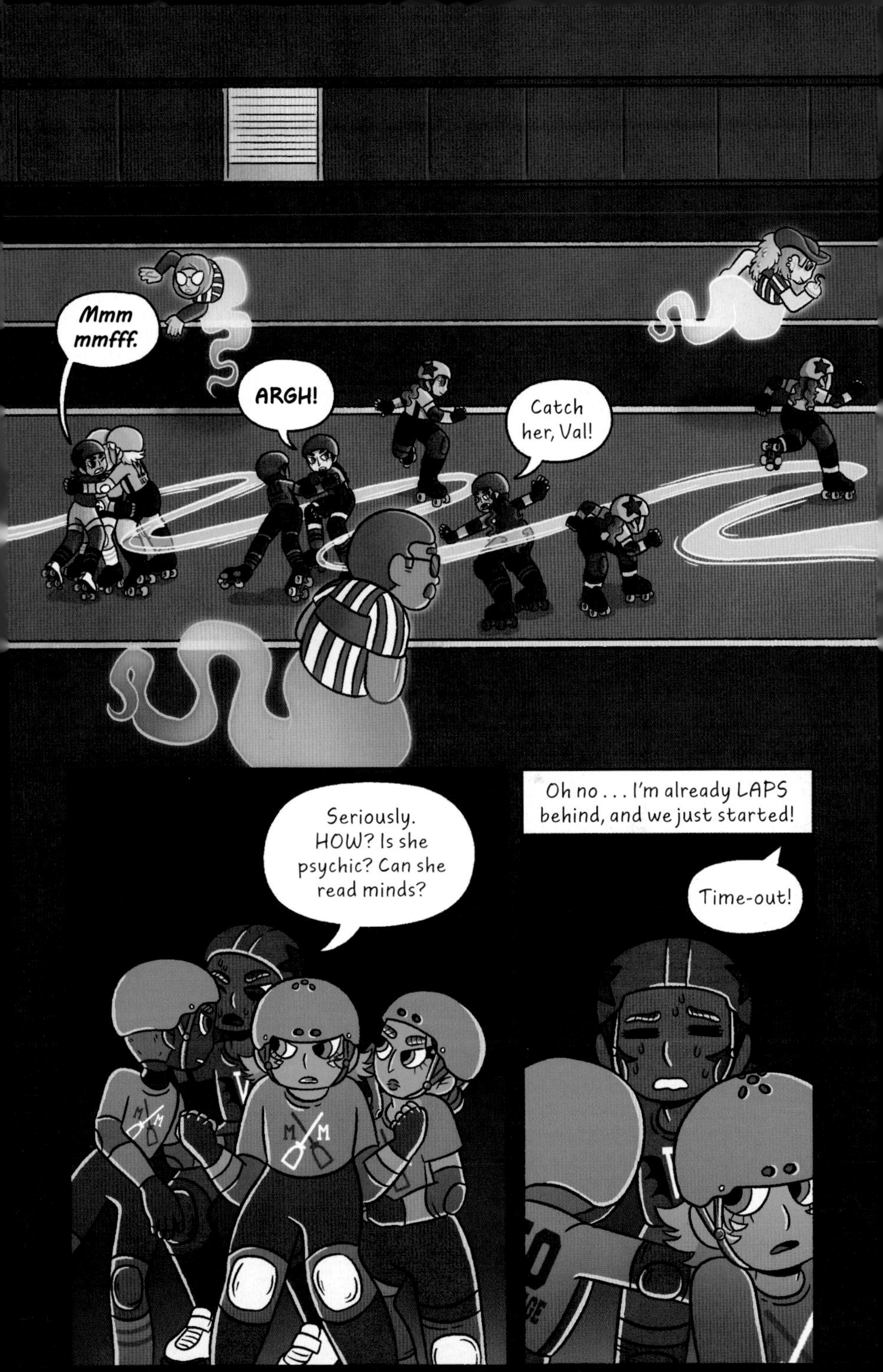
Mmm mmfff.
ARGH!
Catch her, Val!
Seriously. HOW? Is she psychic? Can she read minds?
Oh no . . . I'm already LAPS behind, and we just started!
Time-out!

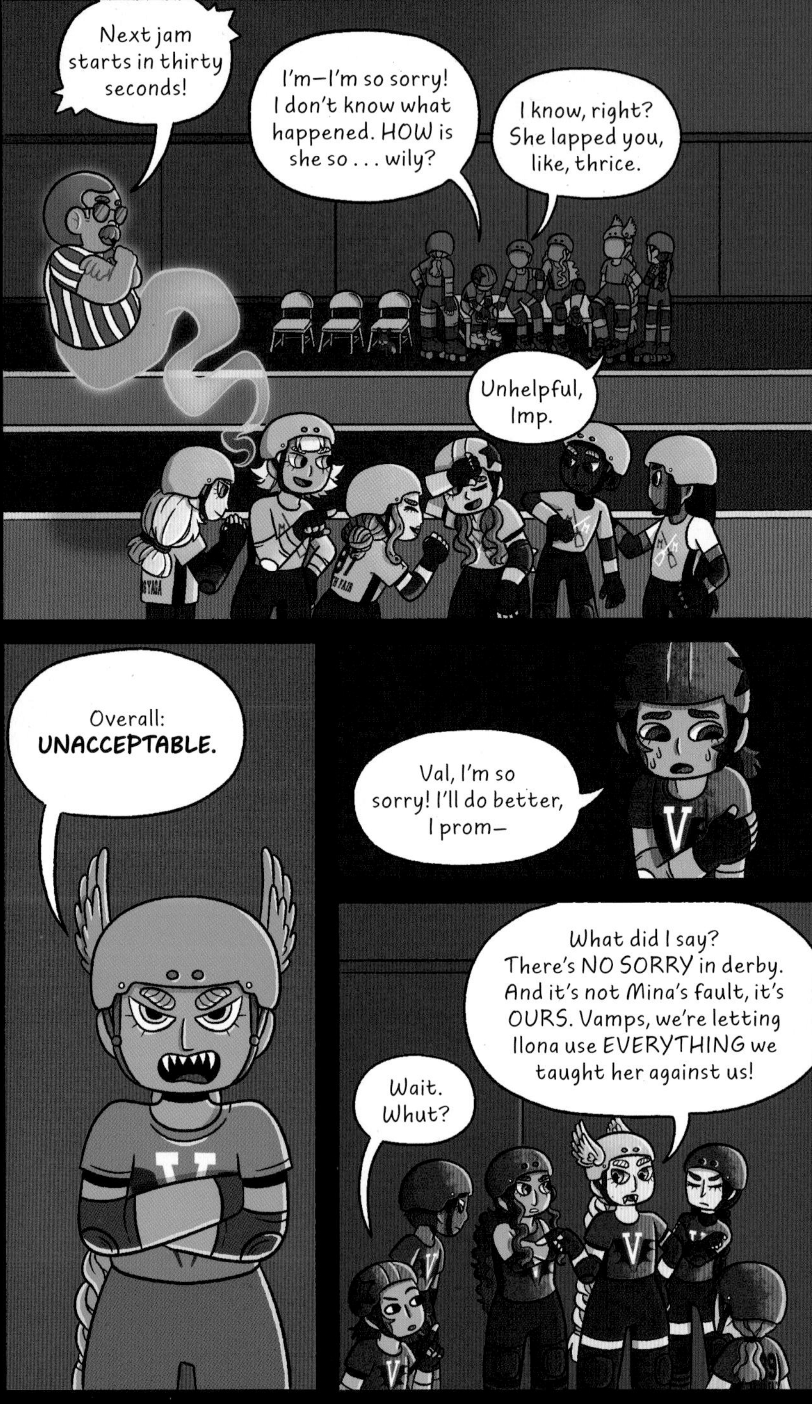
Next jam starts in thirty seconds!
I'm—I'm so sorry! I don't know what happened. HOW is she so . . . wily?
I know, right? She lapped you, like, thrice.
Unhelpful, Imp.
Overall: **UNACCEPTABLE.**
Val, I'm so sorry! I'll do better, I prom—
What did I say? There's NO SORRY in derby. And it's not Mina's fault, it's OURS. Vamps, we're letting Ilona use EVERYTHING we taught her against us!
Wait. Whut?

MEET THE MAVENS

Captain	Blocker	Blocker	Blocker

Aka Sick #126
She/Her

New Rage #50
They/Them

Meta Fizzick #010
They/Them

Blocker

Blocker

Blocker

Lilith Fair #97
She/Her

Babs Yaga #73
She/Her

Dharma #4815
She/Her

Blocker

Blocker

Ex-Vamps Jammer?!

Rich Yule #575
They/Them

Blessed Bee #28
She/They

Ilona Szilágyi, aka
"**Queen of Wands**" #18
She/Her

Sal, you're overreacting out there! You need to time your hits based on where she's actually going—not on where you THINK she's going.

And, Bella, you HAVE to keep that temper in check....

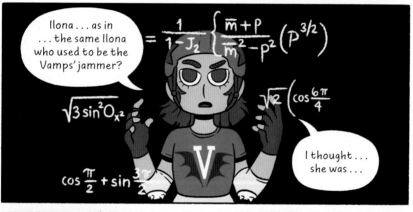

Ilona...as in ...the same Ilona who used to be the Vamps' jammer?

$$= \frac{1}{1-J_2} \left\{ \frac{\bar{m}+P}{\bar{m}^2-P^2} \left(P^{3/2}\right) \right.$$

$$\sqrt{3\sin^2 O_{x^2}}$$

$$\sqrt{2}\left(\cos\frac{6\pi}{4}\right)$$

$$\cos\frac{\pi}{2} + \sin\frac{3\pi}{2}$$

I thought... she was...

YOU. You said your last jammer died, or whatever!

No, I said they'd never found any REMAINS. Which they never will, if I ever get her alone...

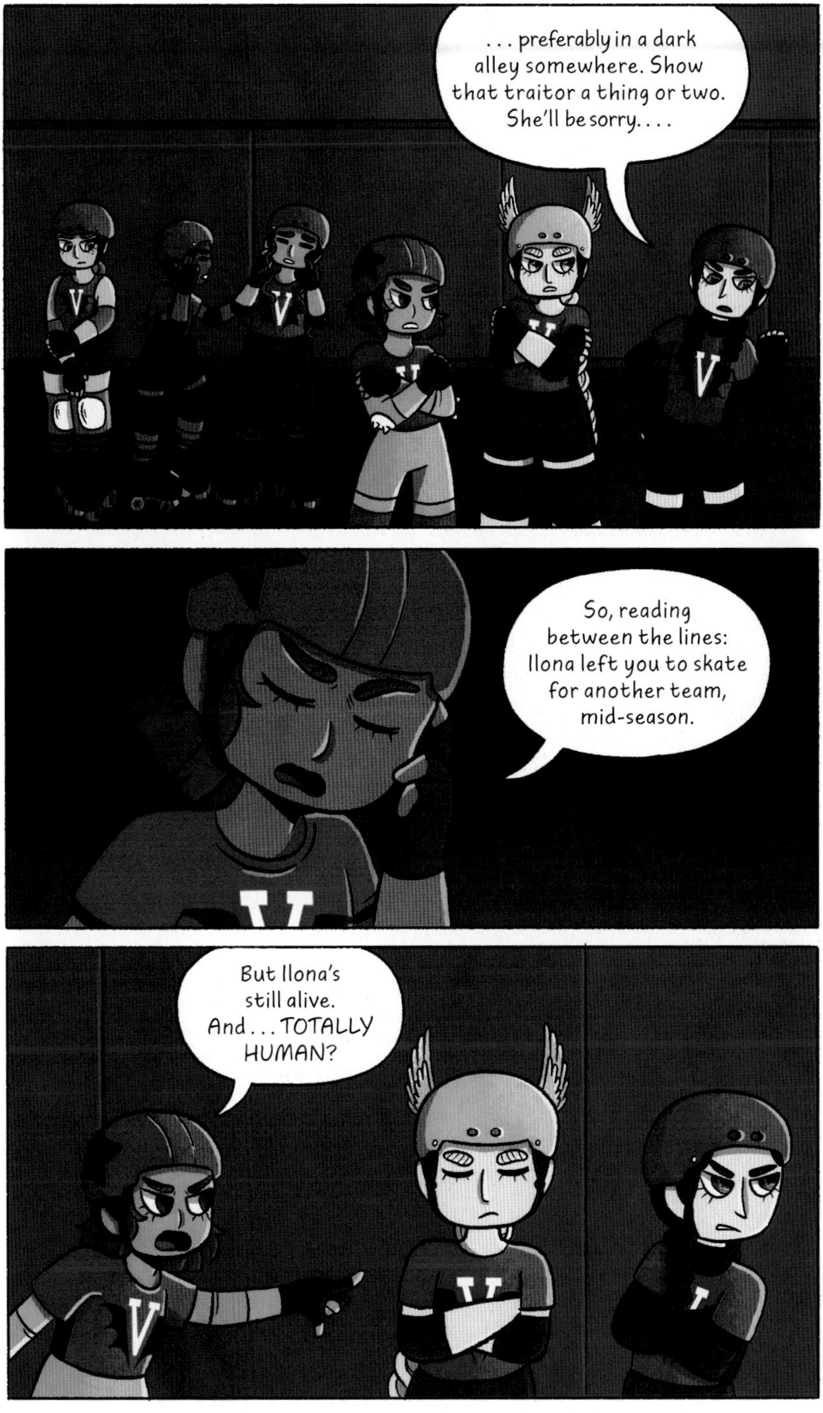
. . . preferably in a dark alley somewhere. Show that traitor a thing or two. She'll be sorry. . . .
So, reading between the lines: Ilona left you to skate for another team, mid-season.
But Ilona's still alive. And . . . TOTALLY HUMAN?

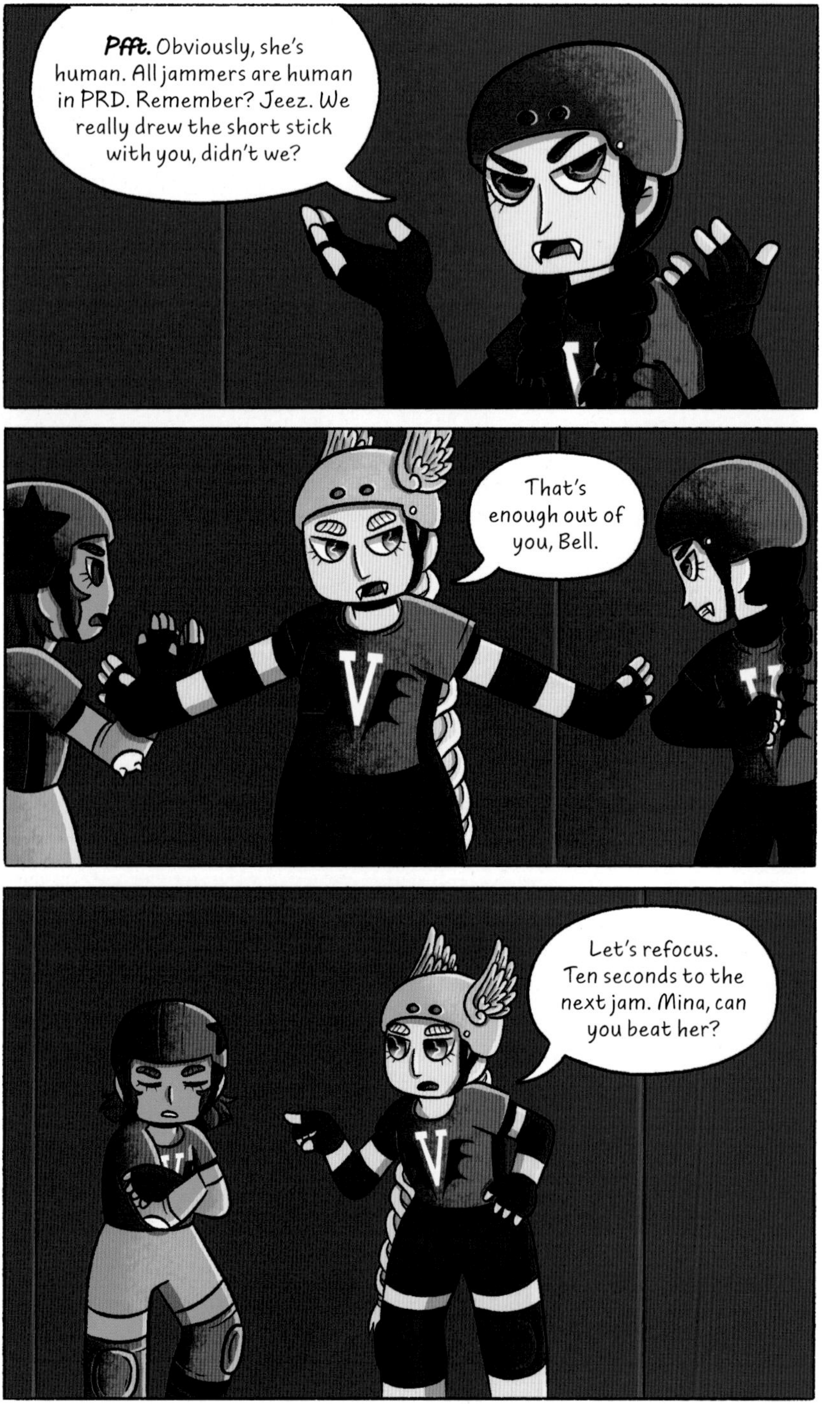
Pfft. Obviously, she's human. All jammers are human in PRD. Remember? Jeez. We really drew the short stick with you, didn't we?
That's enough out of you, Bell.
Let's refocus. Ten seconds to the next jam. Mina, can you beat her?

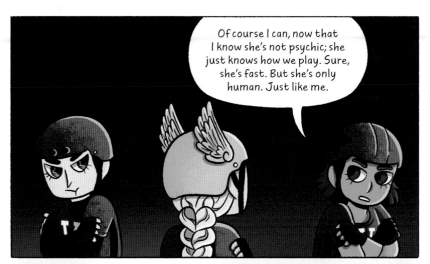

Of course I can, now that I know she's not psychic; she just knows how we play. Sure, she's fast. But she's only human. Just like me.

Besides, now I'm mad. NOBODY betrays MY team and gets away with it!

Wow, okay.

THERE it is.

Five seconds!

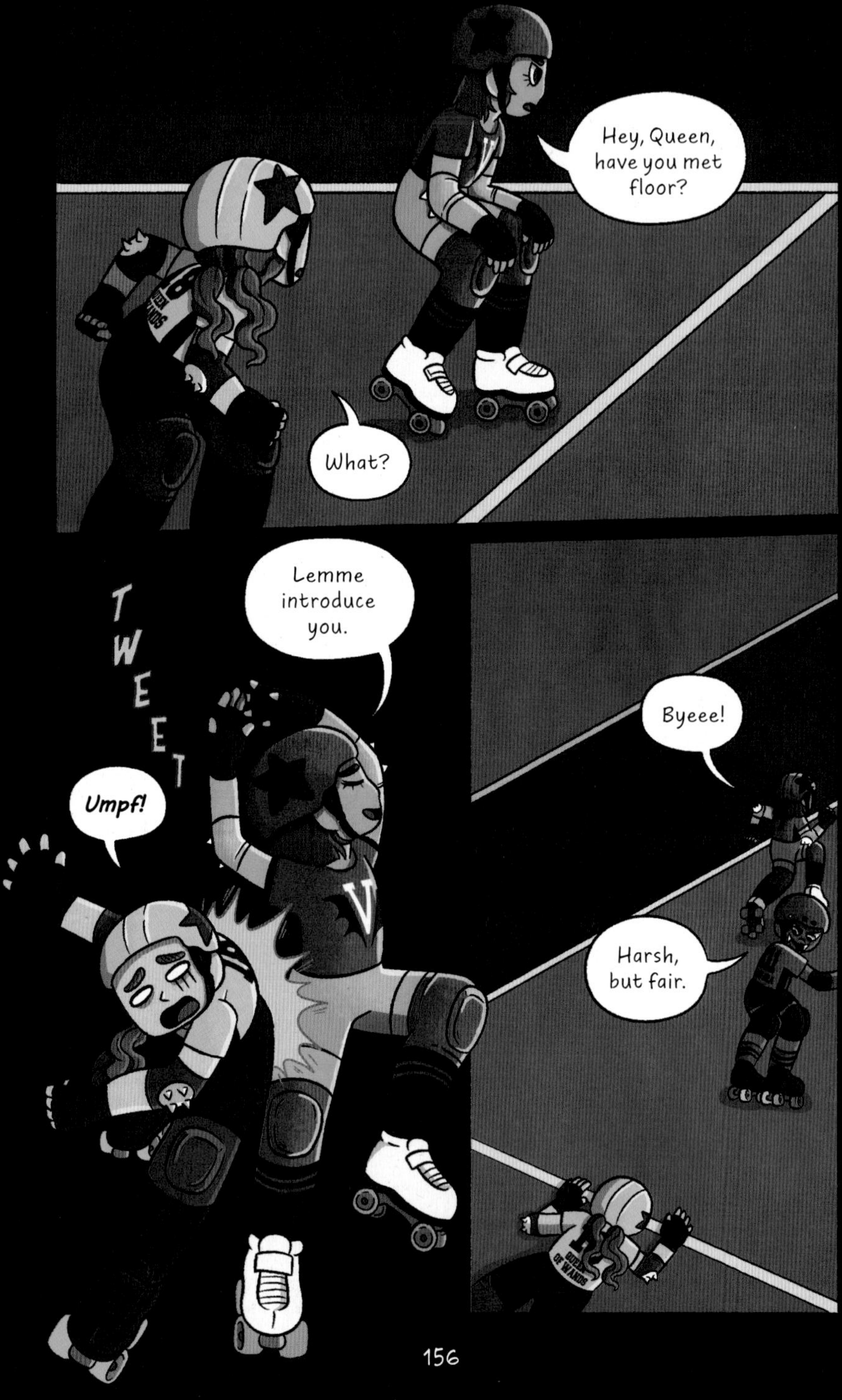
Hey, Queen, have you met floor?
What?
Lemme introduce you.
TWEET
Umpf!
Byeee!
Harsh, but fair.

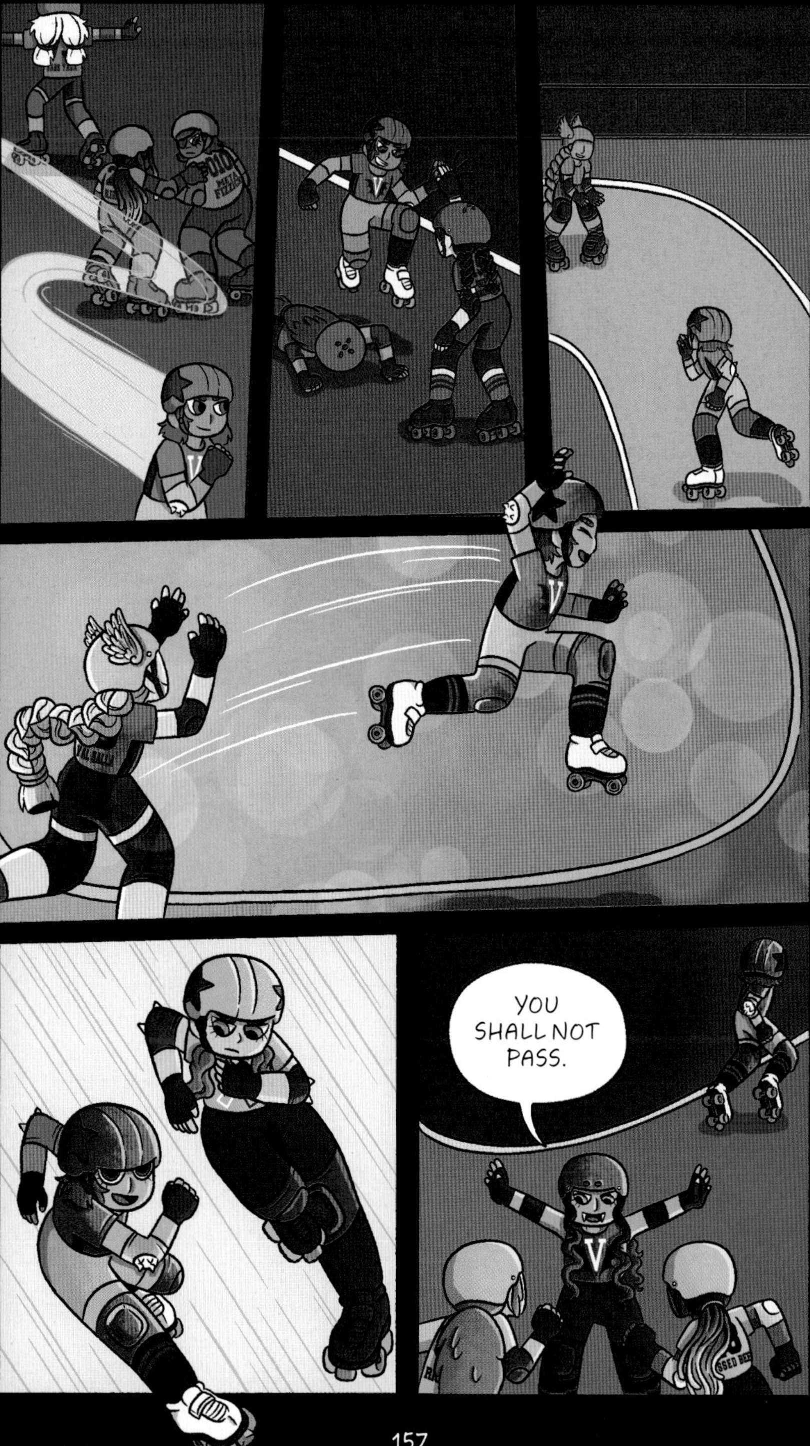
YOU SHALL NOT PASS.

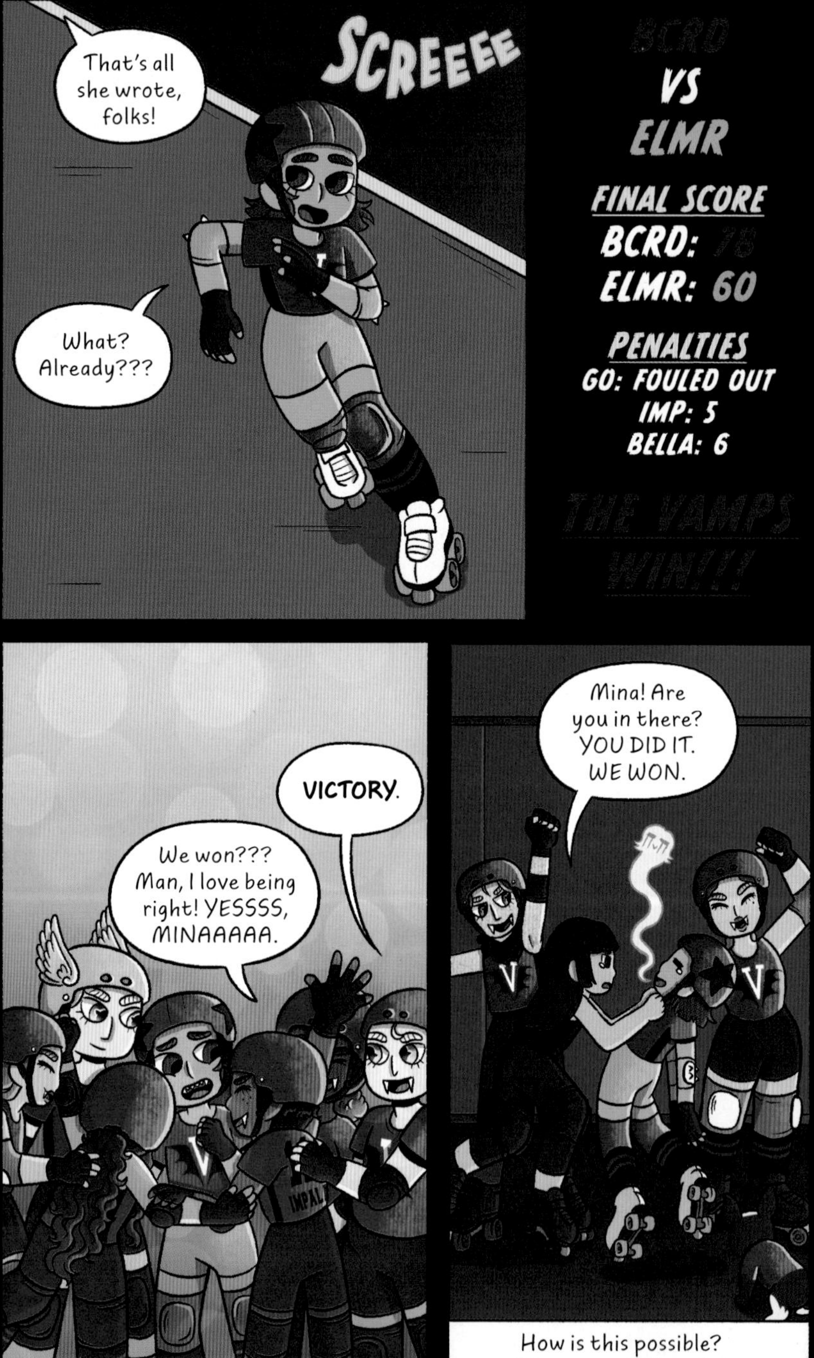
SCREEEEE
That's all she wrote, folks!
What? Already???
BCRD
VS
ELMR
FINAL SCORE
BCRD: 78
ELMR: 60
PENALTIES
GO: FOULED OUT
IMP: 5
BELLA: 6
THE VAMPS WIN!!
VICTORY.
We won??? Man, I love being right! YESSSS, MINAAAAA.
Mina! Are you in there? YOU DID IT. WE WON.
How is this possible? It's . . . over? Already?

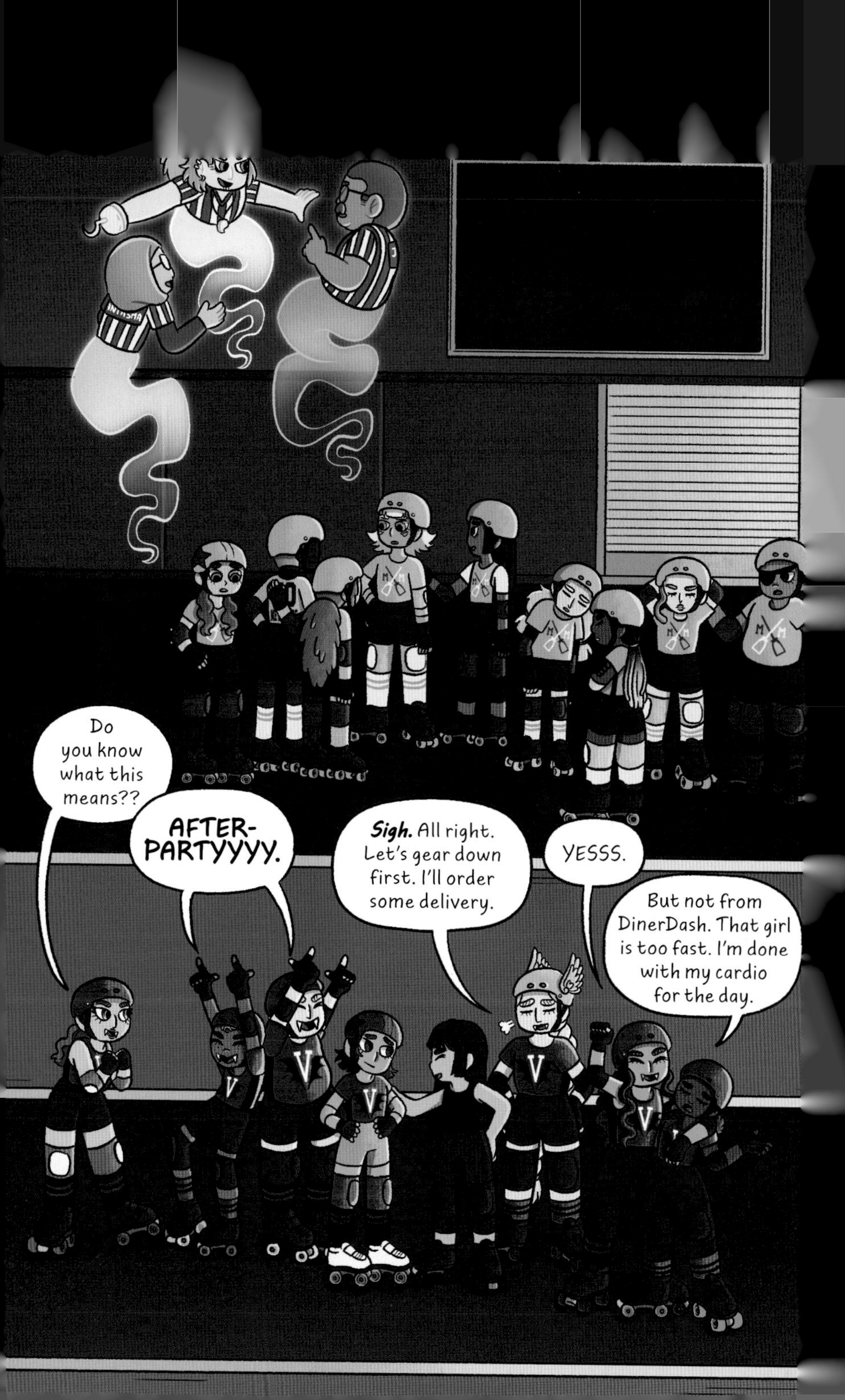
Do you know what this means??
AFTER-PARTYYYY.
Sigh. All right. Let's gear down first. I'll order some delivery.
YESSS.
But not from DinerDash. That girl is too fast. I'm done with my cardio for the day.

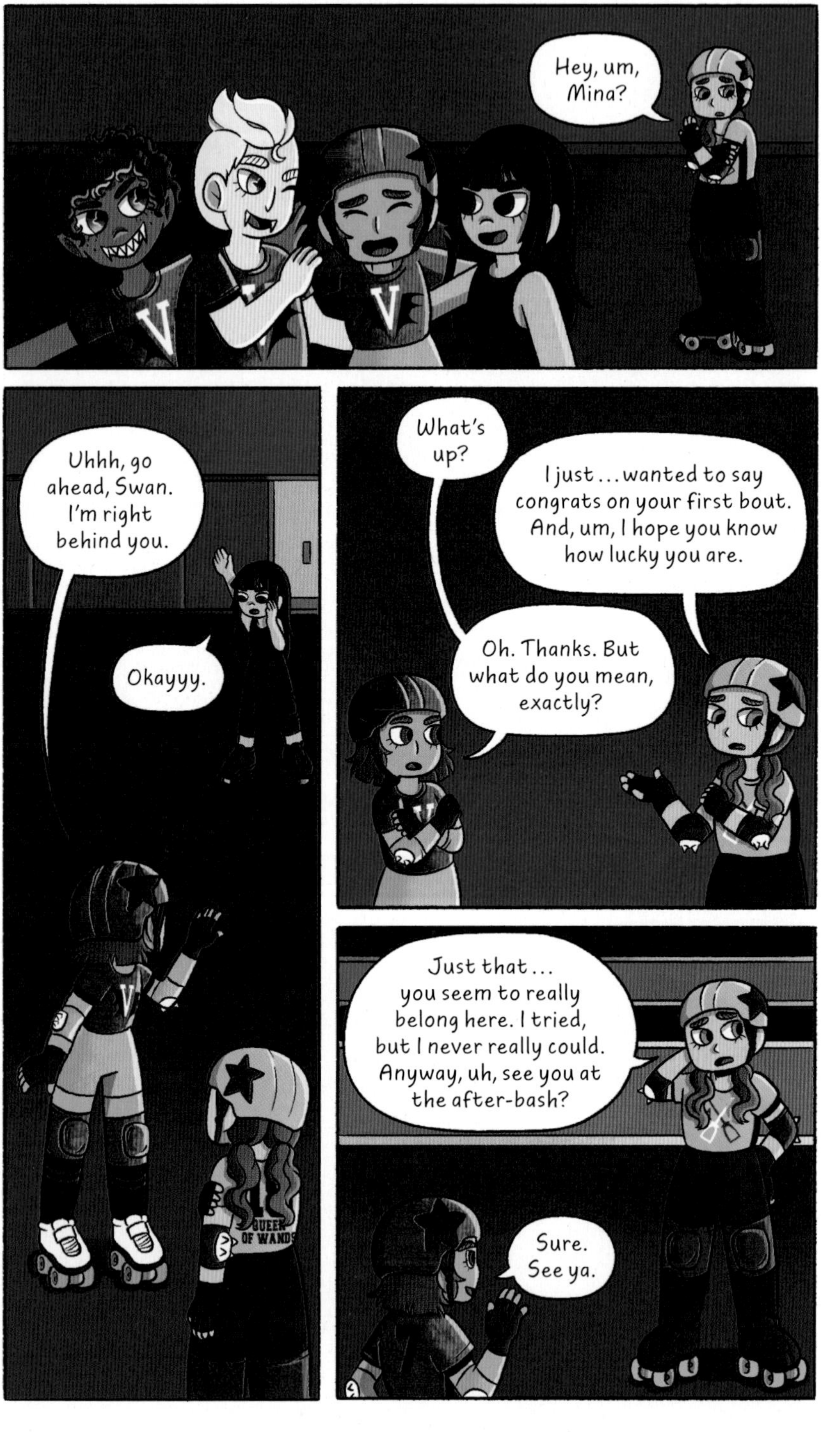
Hey, um, Mina?
Uhhh, go ahead, Swan. I'm right behind you.
Okayyy.
What's up?
I just . . . wanted to say congrats on your first bout. And, um, I hope you know how lucky you are.
Oh. Thanks. But what do you mean, exactly?
QUEEN OF WANDS
Just that . . . you seem to really belong here. I tried, but I never really could. Anyway, uh, see you at the after-bash?
Sure. See ya.

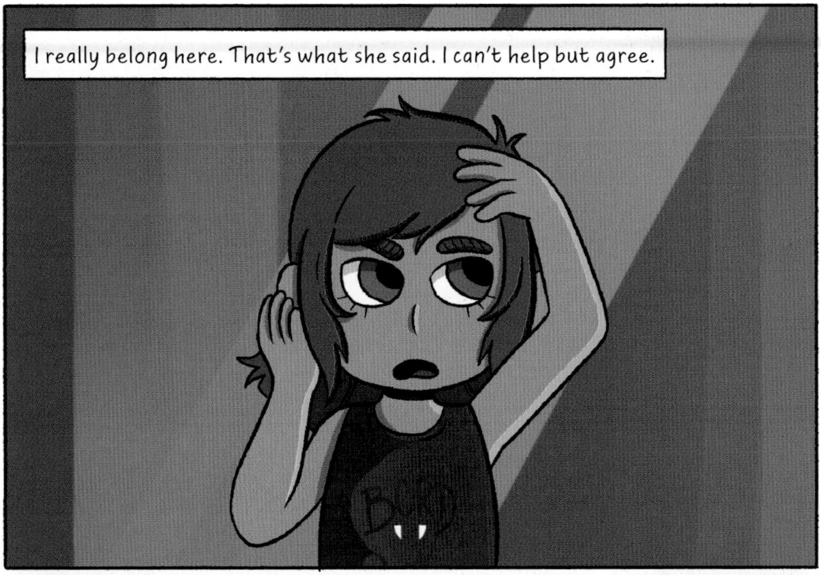
I really belong here. That's what she said. I can't help but agree.

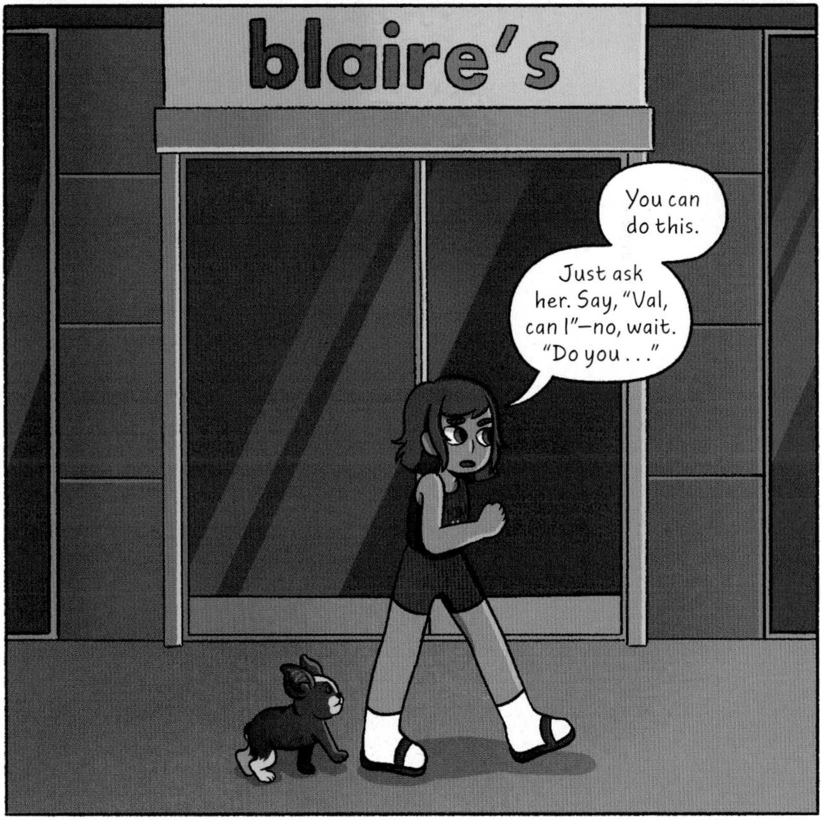
blaire's
You can do this.
Just ask her. Say, "Val, can I"—no, wait. "Do you . . ."

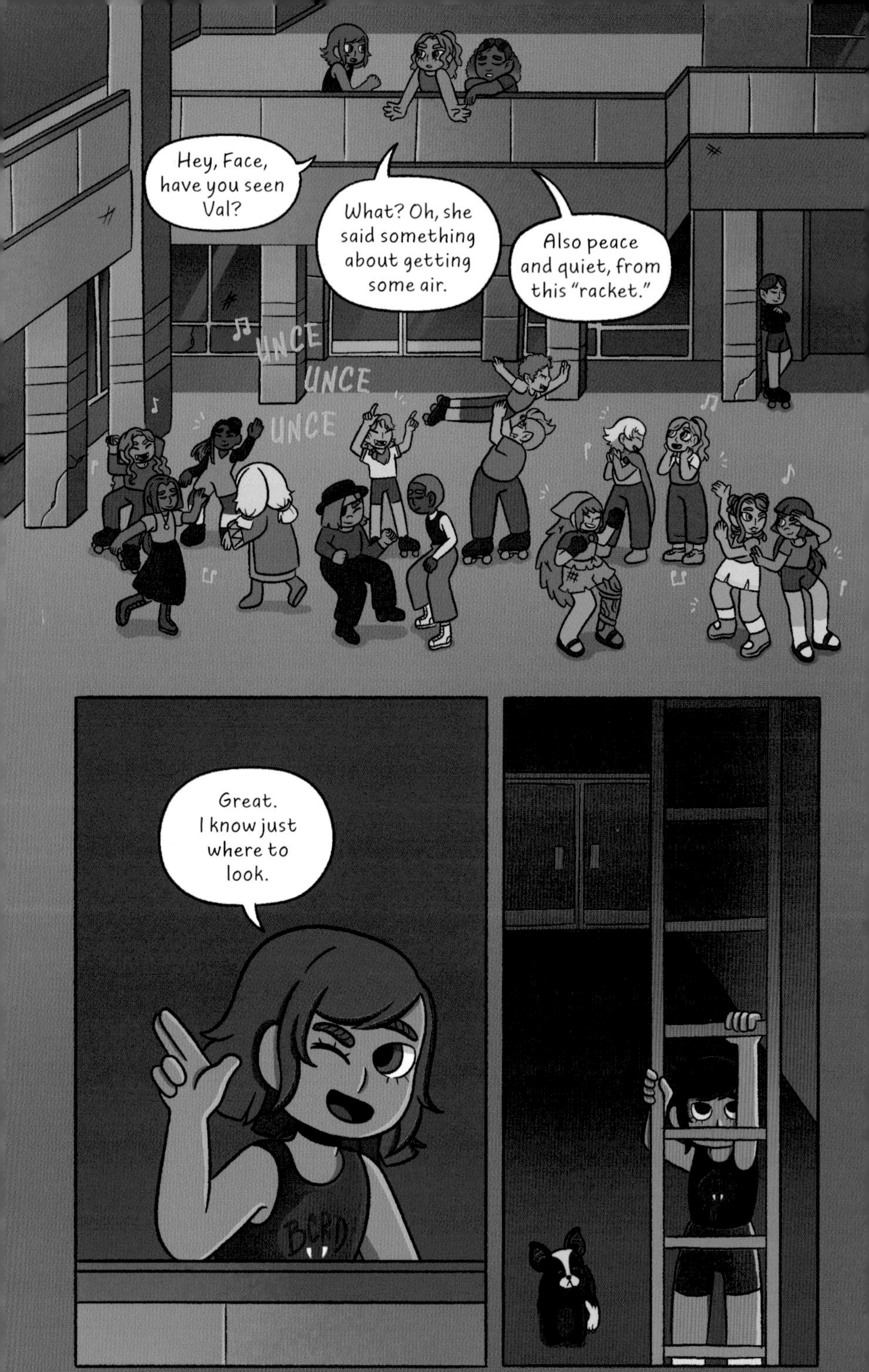
Hey, Face, have you seen Val?
What? Oh, she said something about getting some air.
Also peace and quiet, from this "racket."
UNCE
UNCE
UNCE
Great. I know just where to look.
BCRD

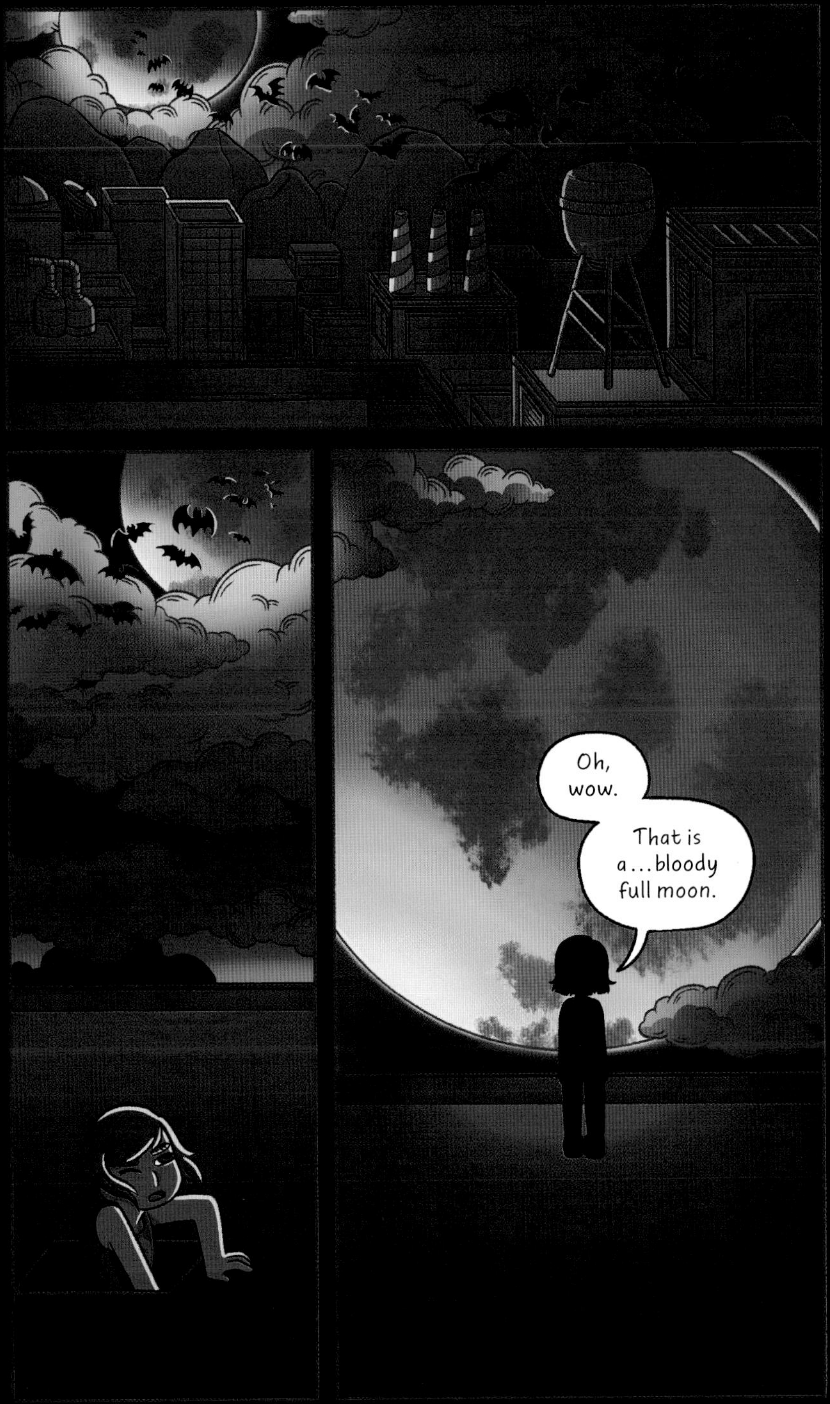
Oh, wow.
That is a...bloody full moon.

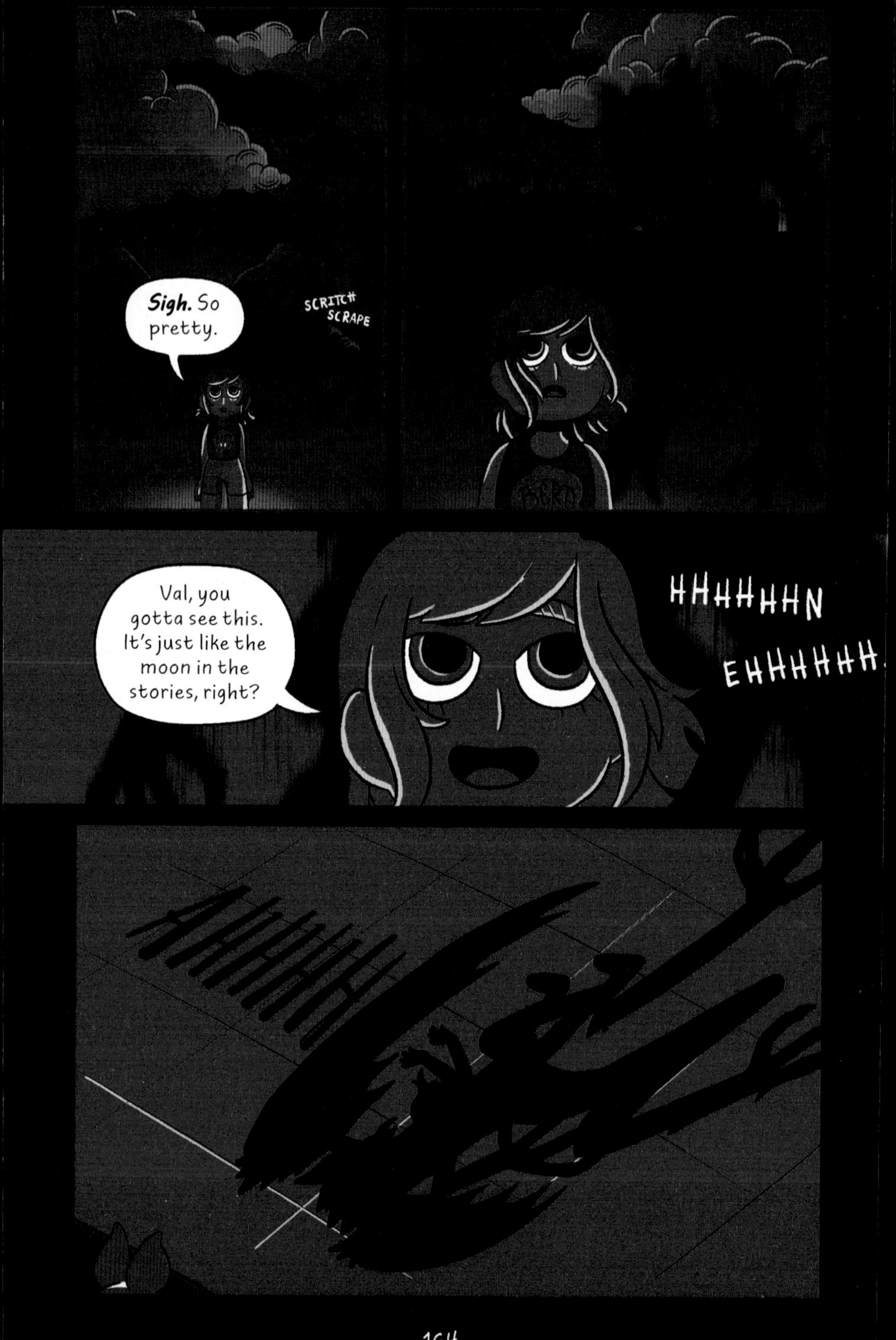
Sigh. So pretty.
SCRITCH SCRAPE
Val, you gotta see this. It's just like the moon in the stories, right?
HHHHHHN
EHHHHHH
AHHHH!

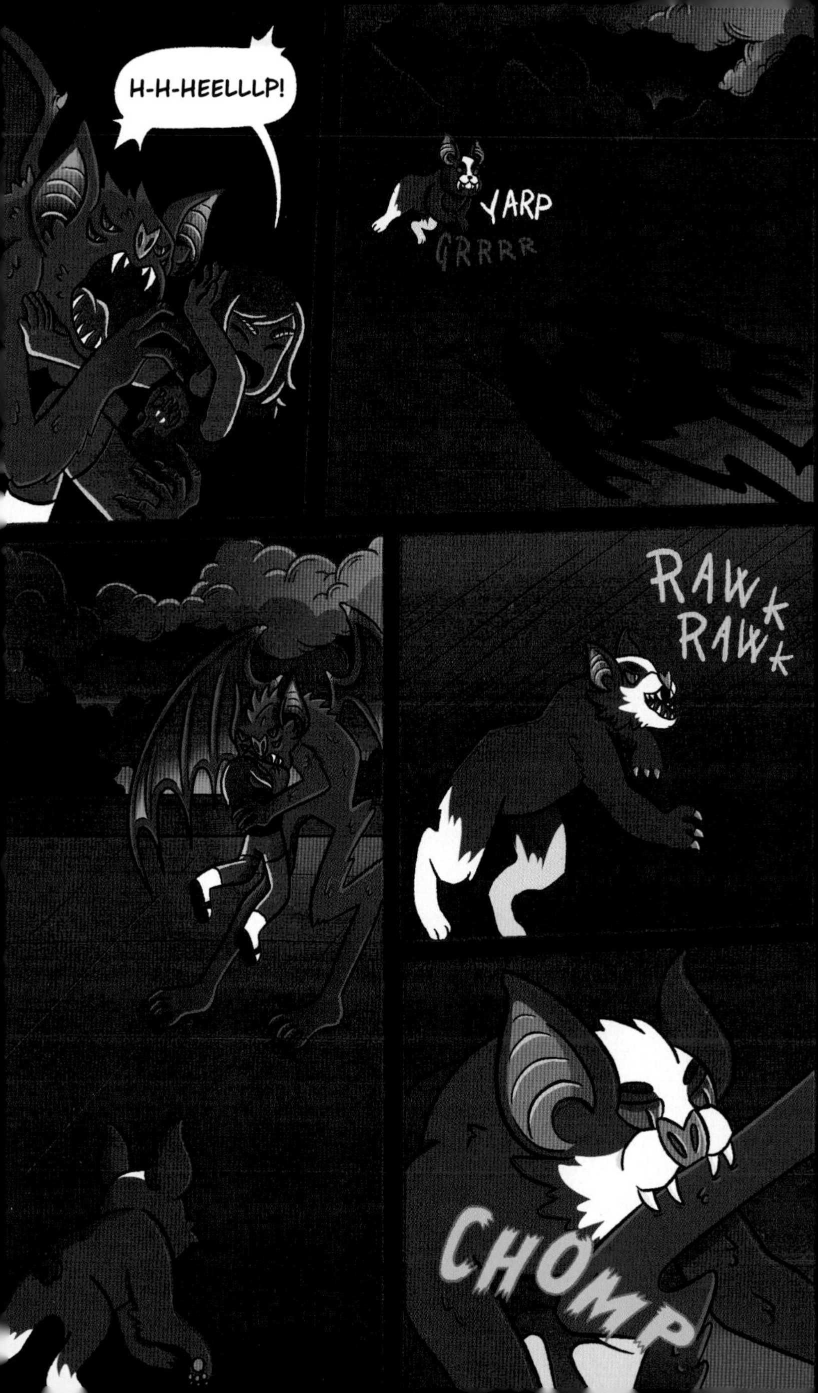
H-H-HEELLLLP!
YARP
GRRRR
RAWK RAWK
CHOMP

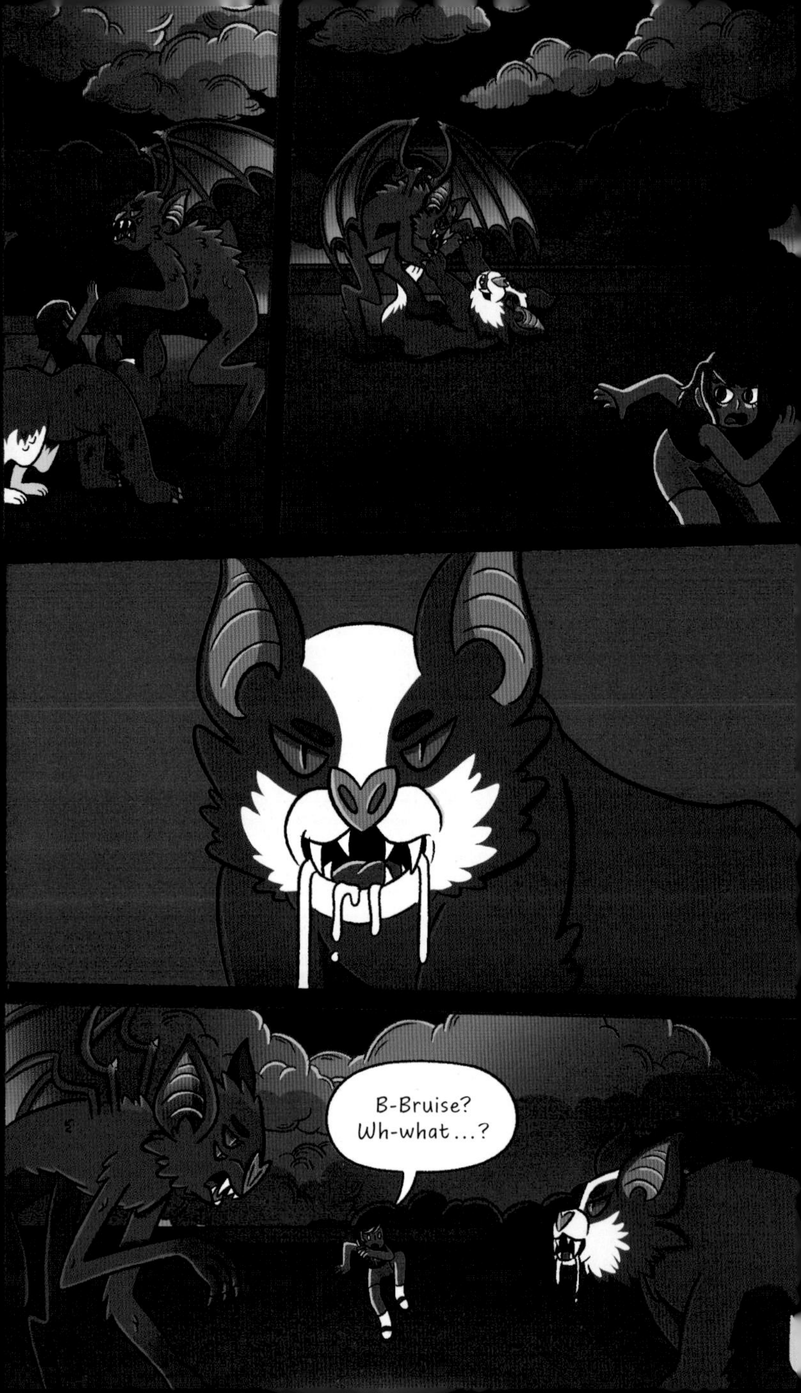
B-Bruise?
Wh-what...?

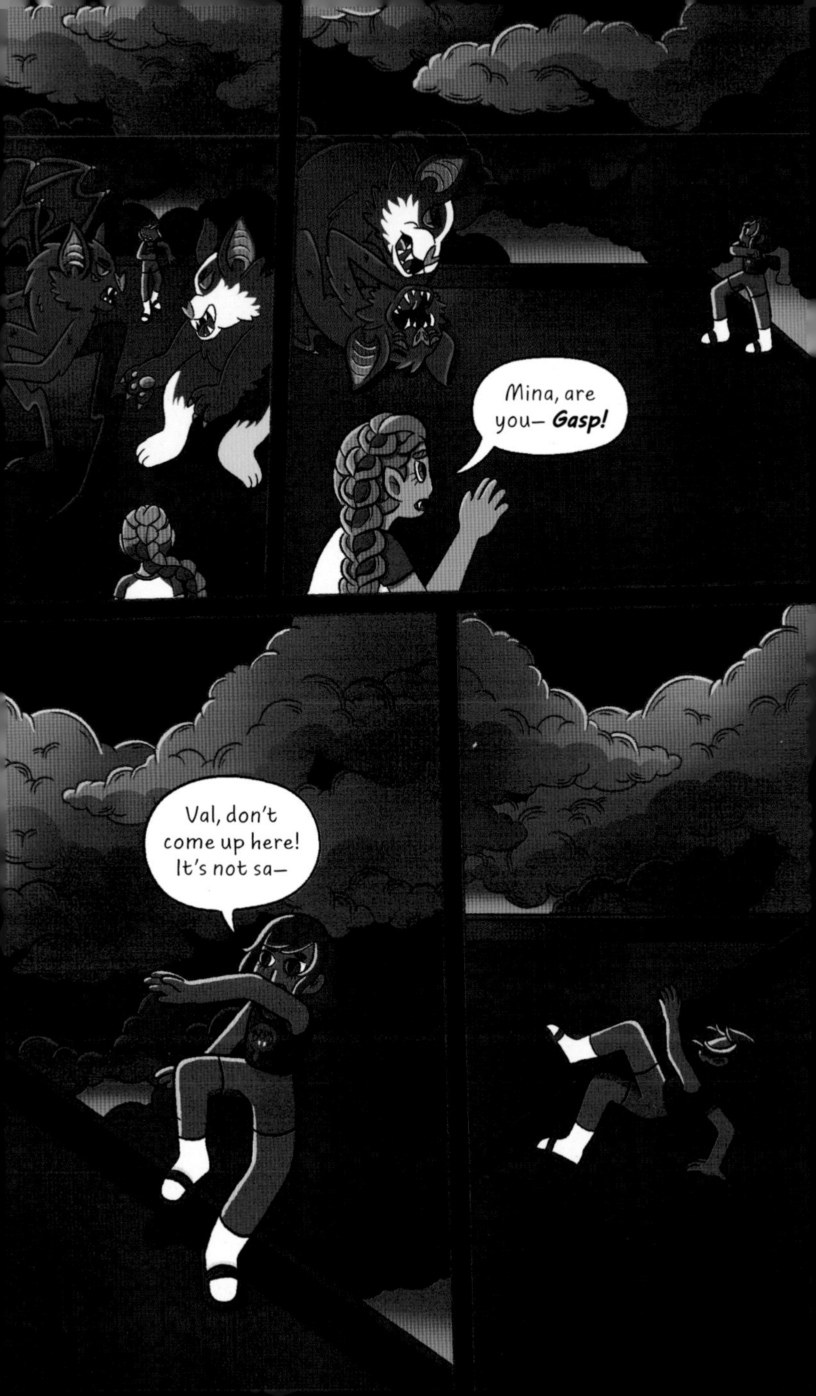
Mina, are you— **Gasp!**
Val, don't come up here! It's not sa—

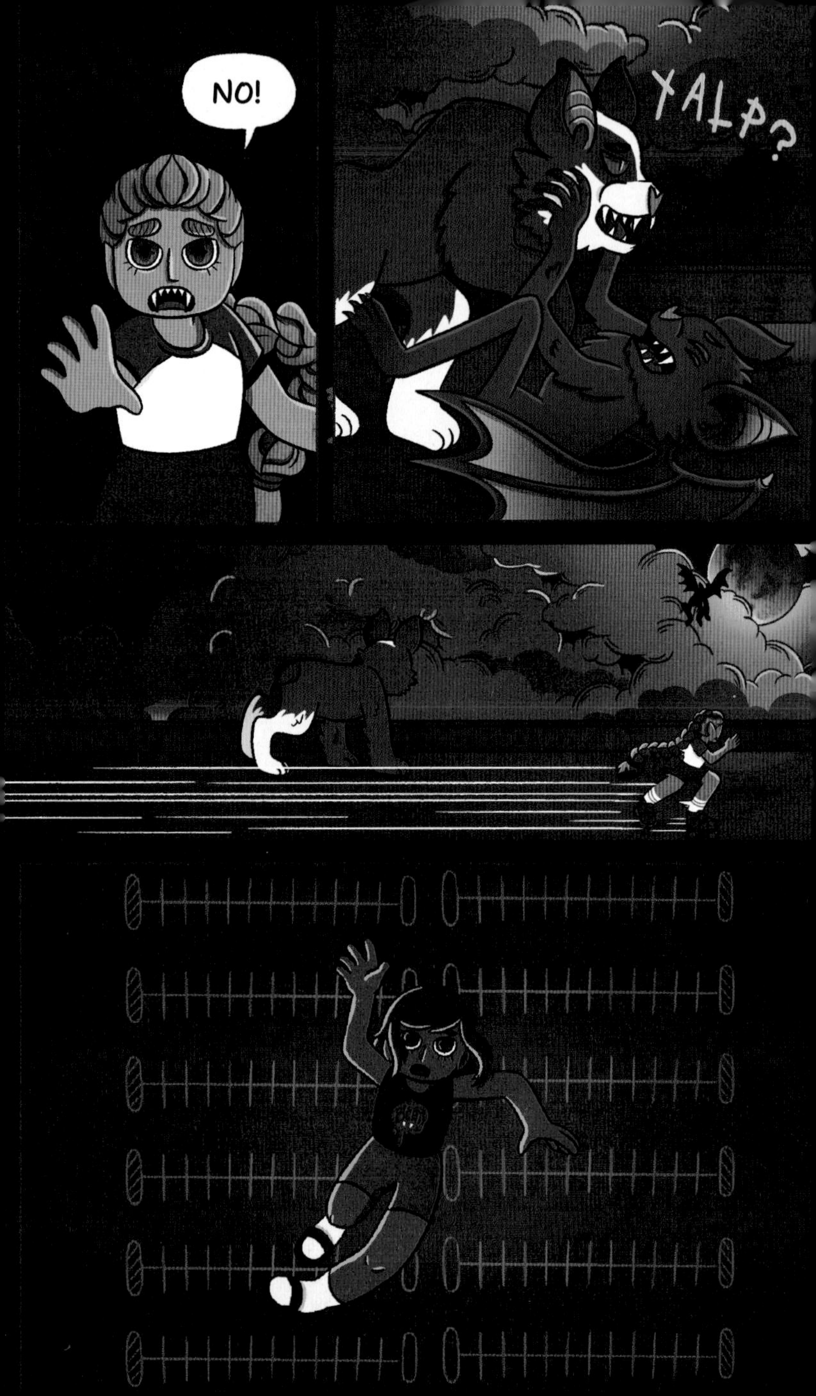
NO!
YALP?

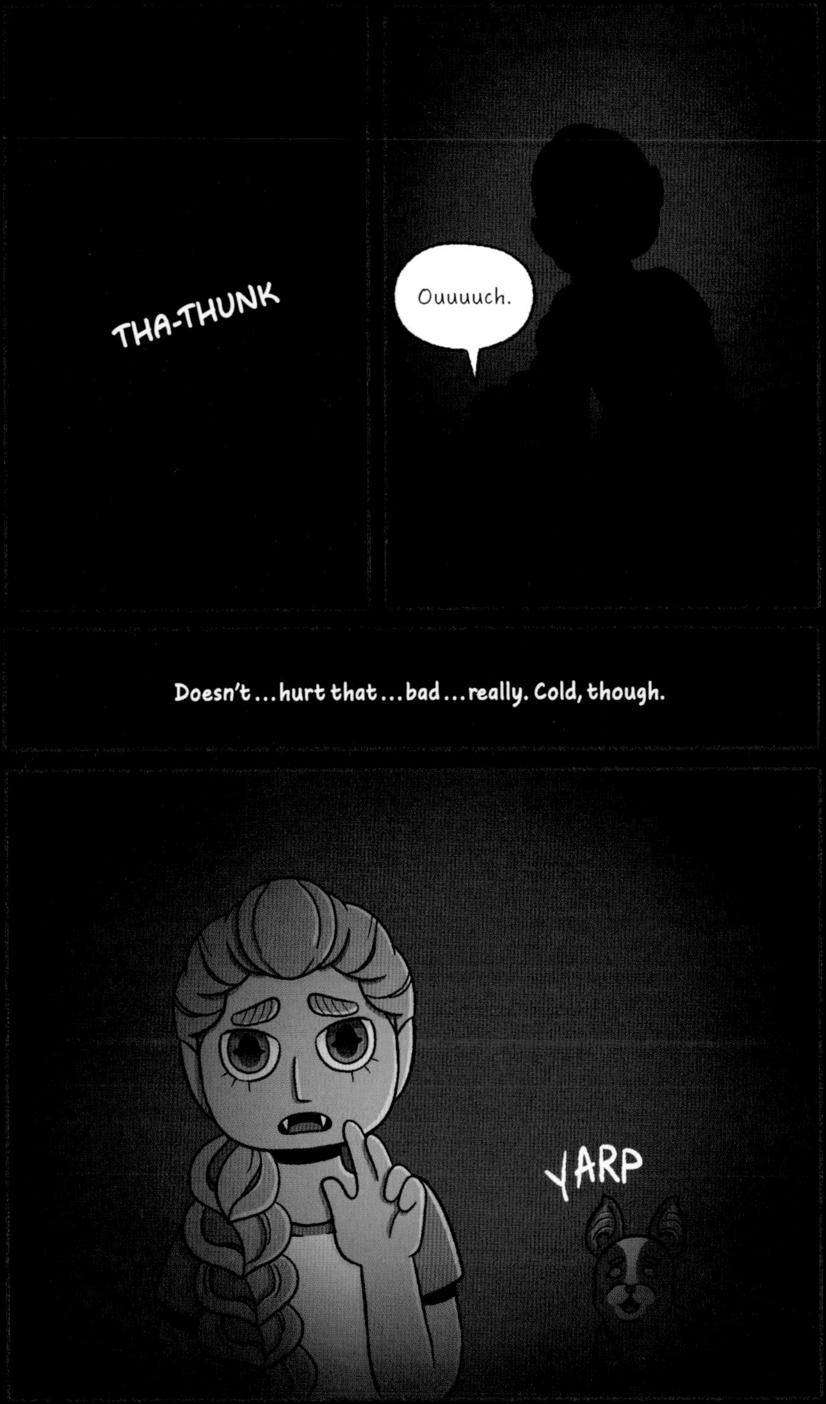
THA-THUNK
Ouuuuch.
Doesn't...hurt that...bad...really. Cold, though.
YARP

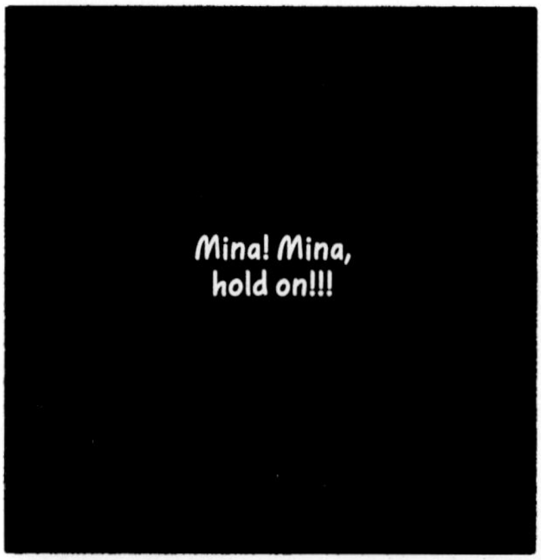
Mina! Mina,
hold on!!!

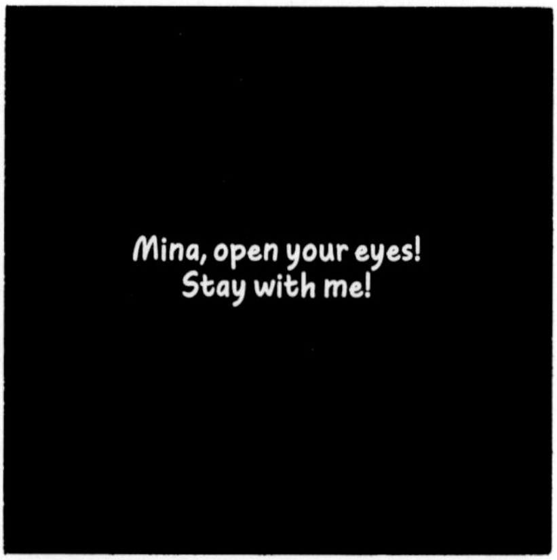
Mina, open your eyes!
Stay with me!

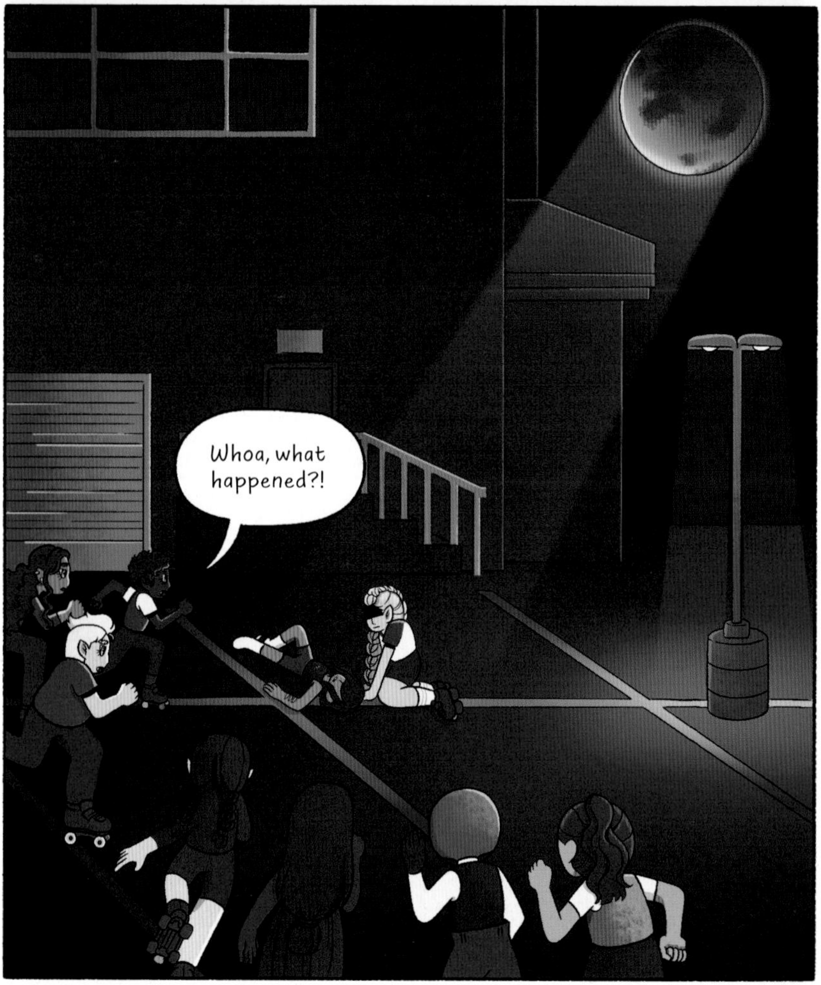
Whoa, what happened?!

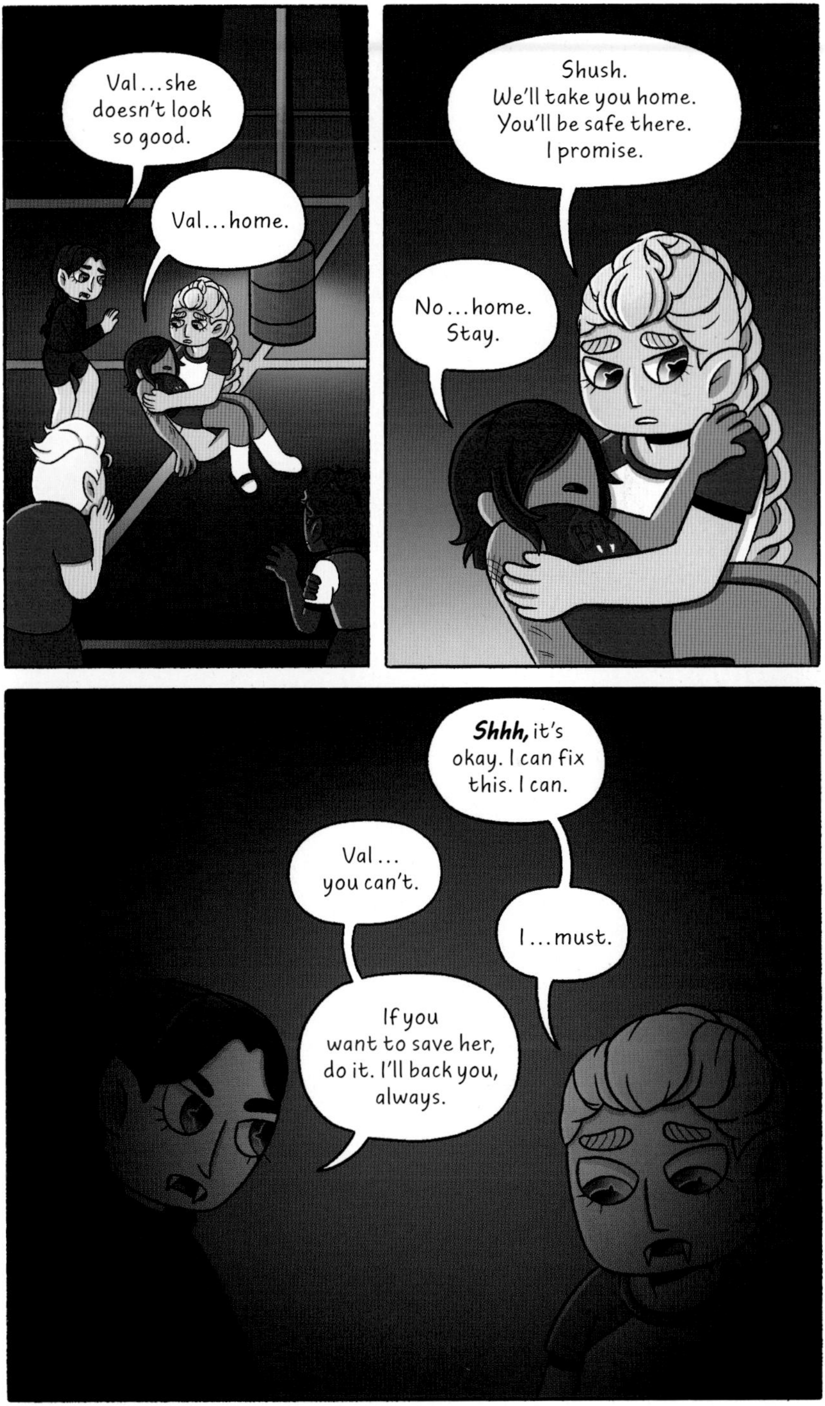
Val...she doesn't look so good.
Val...home.
Shush. We'll take you home. You'll be safe there. I promise.
No...home. Stay.
Shhh, it's okay. I can fix this. I can.
Val... you can't.
I...must.
If you want to save her, do it. I'll back you, always.

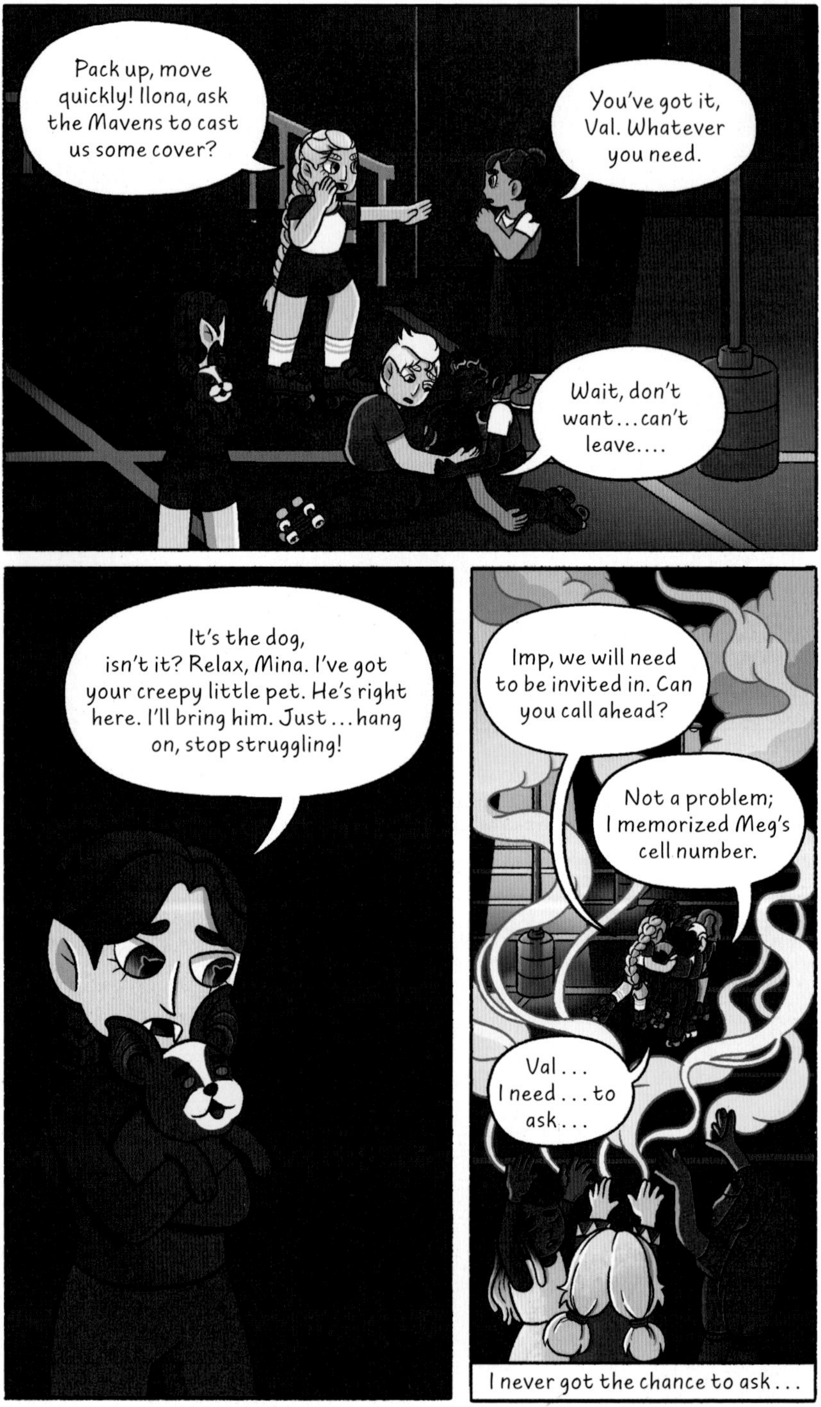
Pack up, move quickly! Ilona, ask the Mavens to cast us some cover?
You've got it, Val. Whatever you need.
Wait, don't want...can't leave....
It's the dog, isn't it? Relax, Mina. I've got your creepy little pet. He's right here. I'll bring him. Just...hang on, stop struggling!
Imp, we will need to be invited in. Can you call ahead?
Not a problem; I memorized Meg's cell number.
Val... I need... to ask...
I never got the chance to ask...

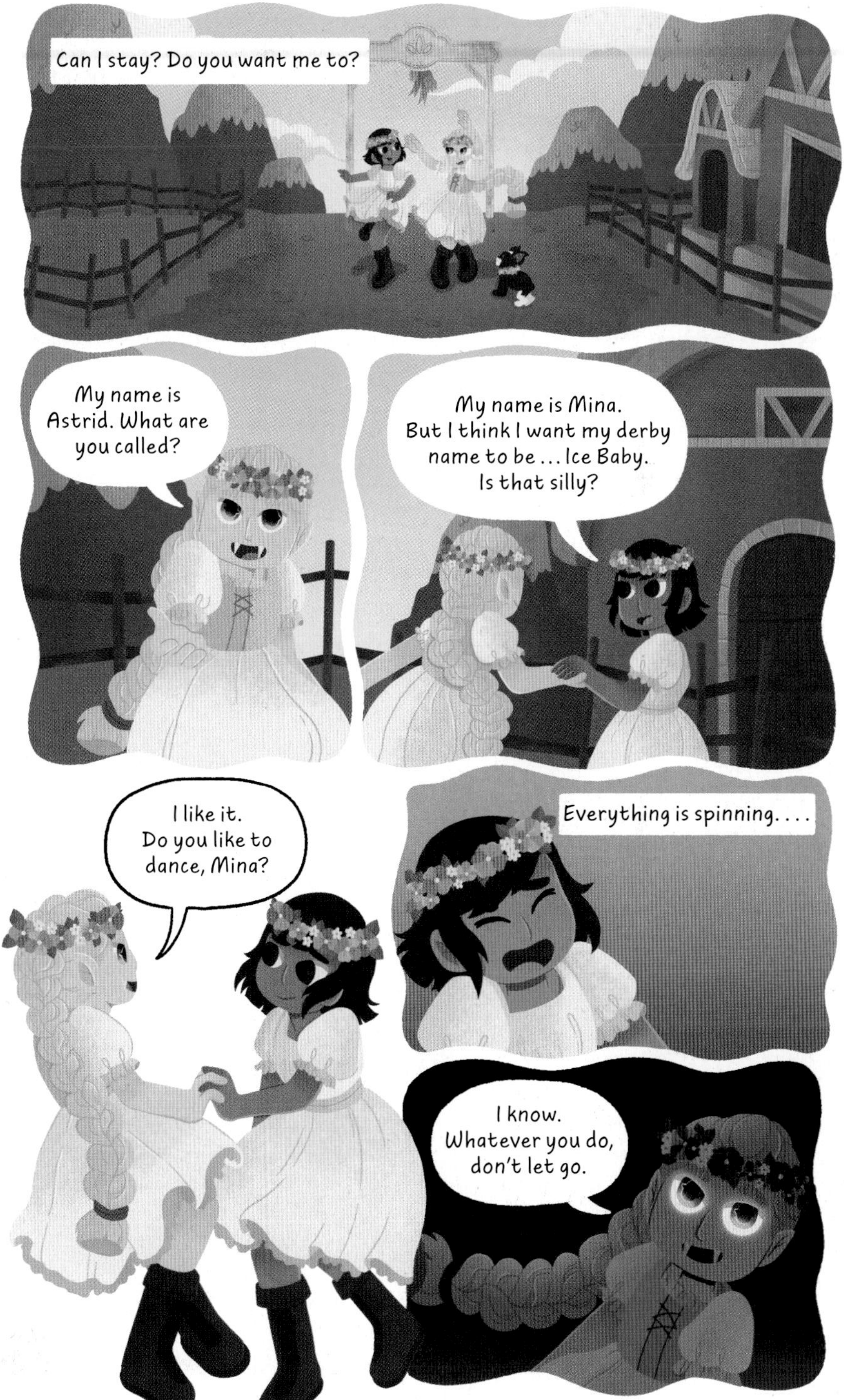

Can I stay? Do you want me to?
My name is Astrid. What are you called?
My name is Mina. But I think I want my derby name to be . . . Ice Baby. Is that silly?
I like it. Do you like to dance, Mina?
Everything is spinning. . . .
I know. Whatever you do, don't let go.

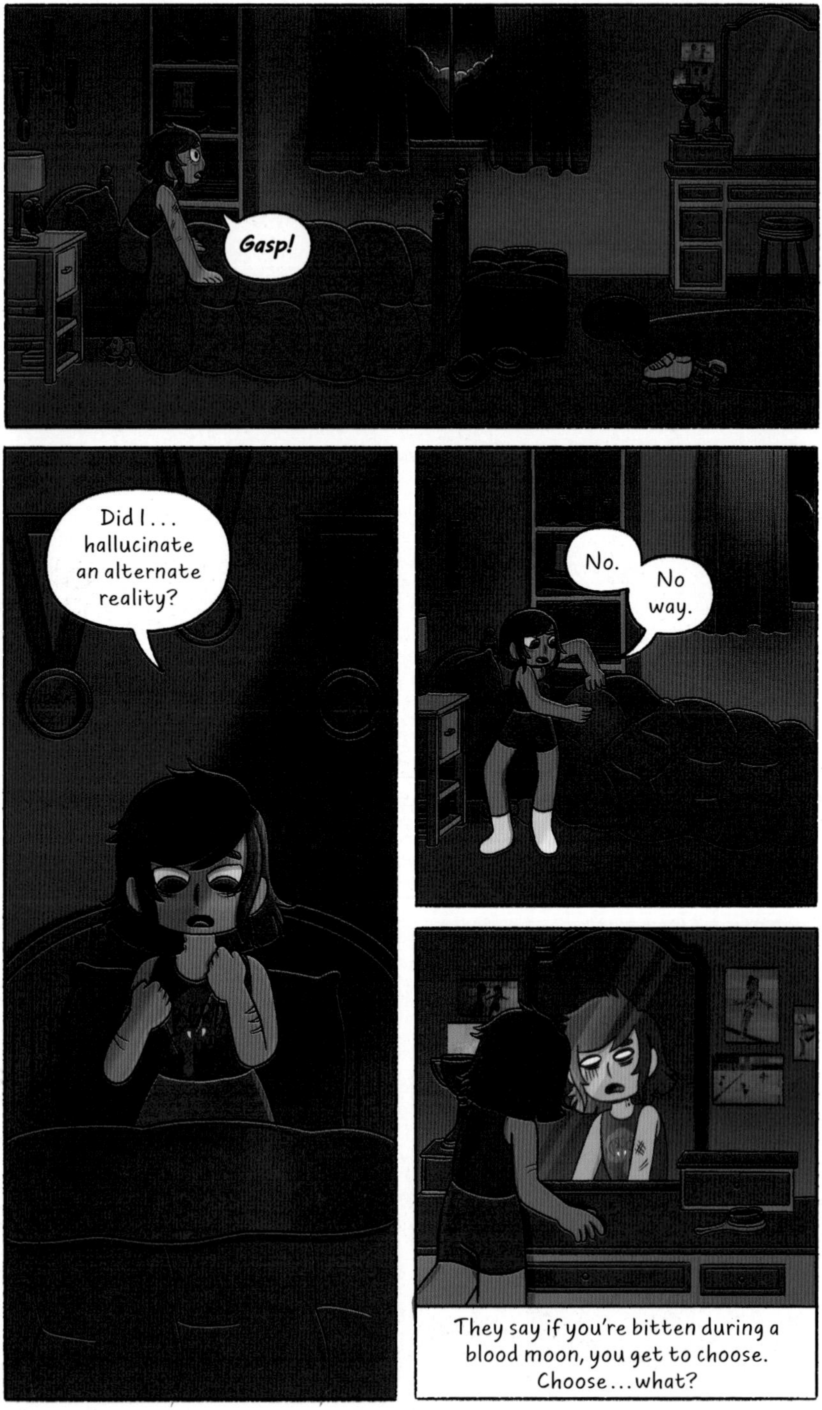
Gasp!
Did I . . . hallucinate an alternate reality?
No.
No way.
They say if you're bitten during a blood moon, you get to choose. Choose . . . what?

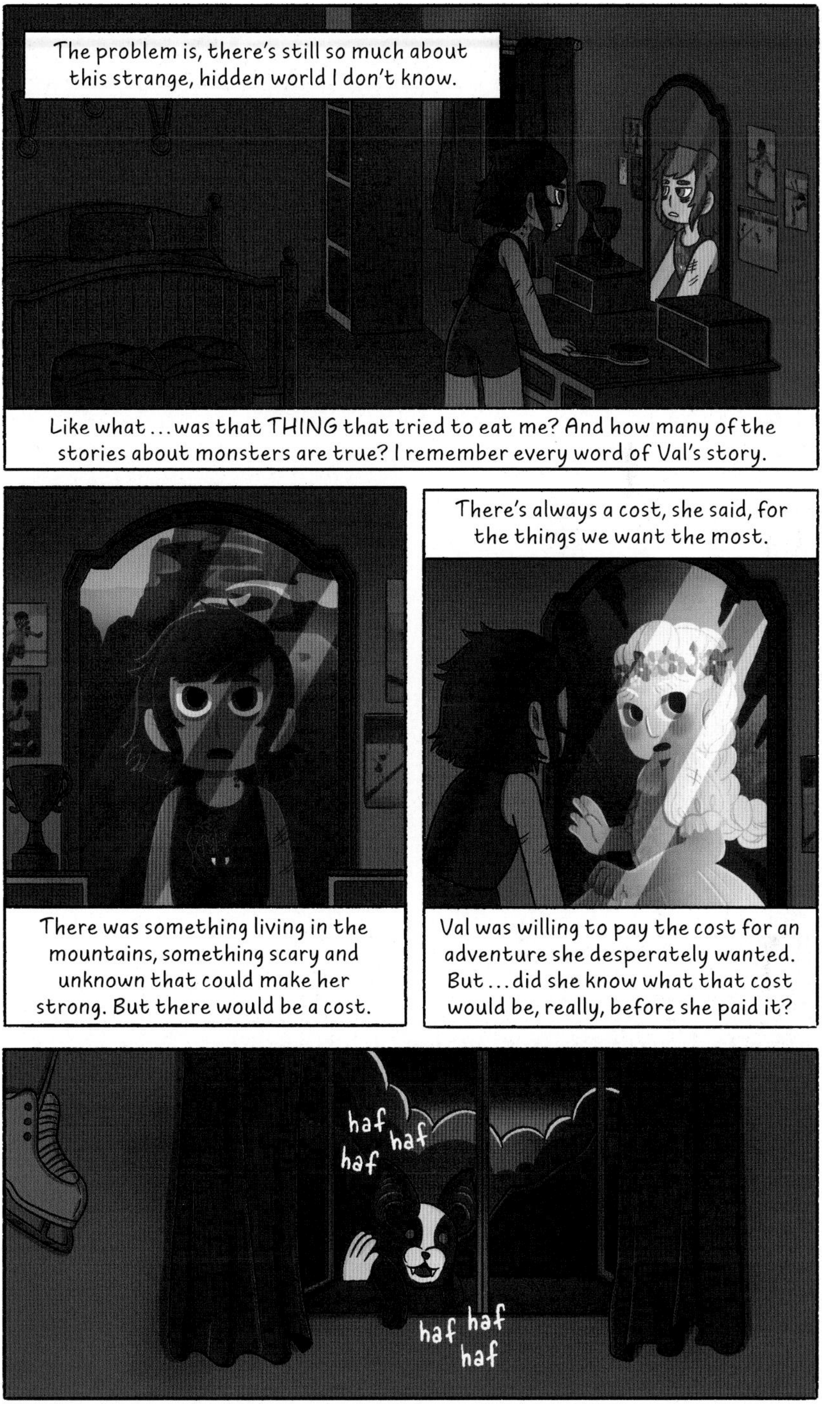
The problem is, there's still so much about this strange, hidden world I don't know.
Like what... was that THING that tried to eat me? And how many of the stories about monsters are true? I remember every word of Val's story.
There was something living in the mountains, something scary and unknown that could make her strong. But there would be a cost.
There's always a cost, she said, for the things we want the most.
Val was willing to pay the cost for an adventure she desperately wanted. But... did she know what that cost would be, really, before she paid it?
haf haf haf
haf haf haf

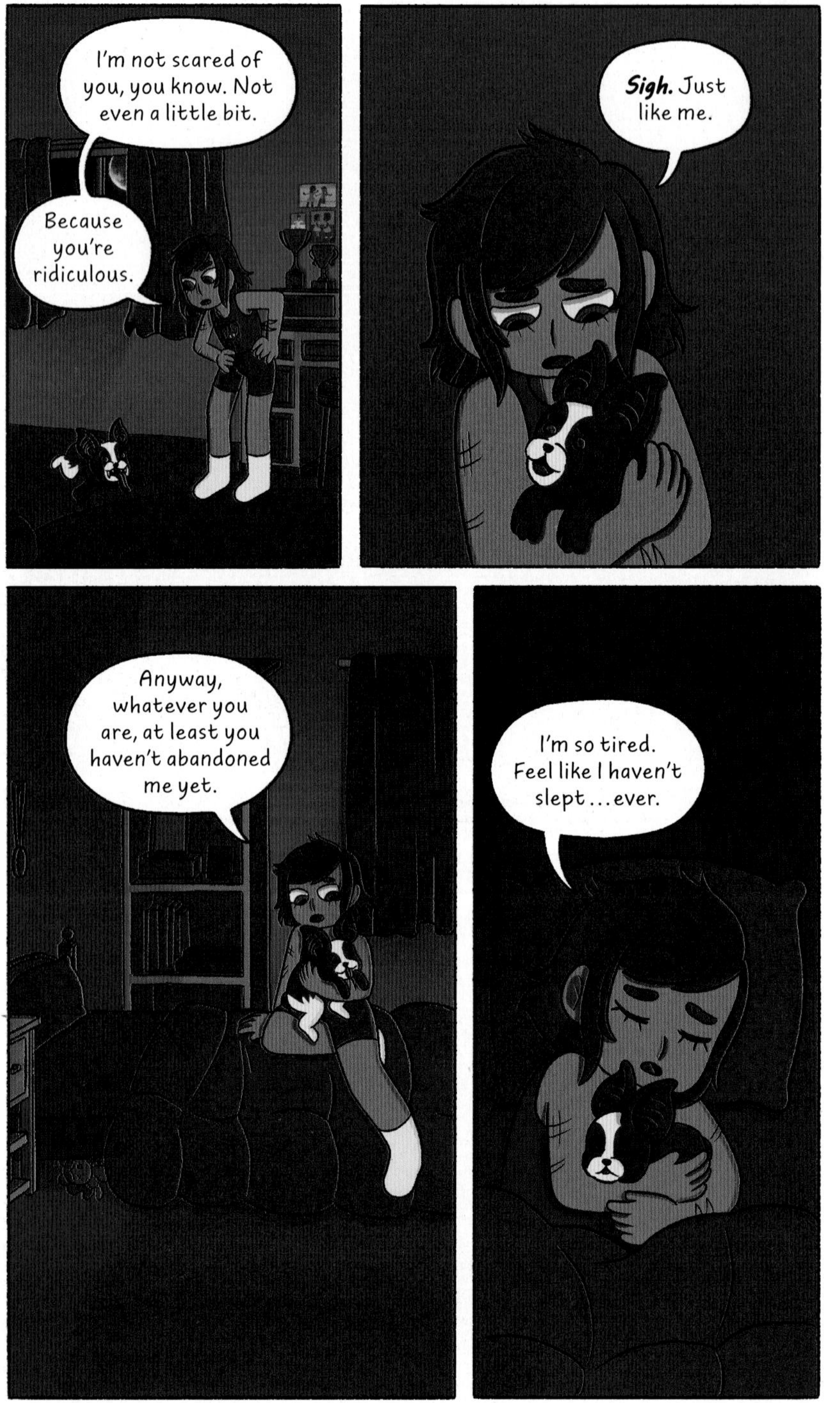
I'm not scared of you, you know. Not even a little bit.
Because you're ridiculous.
Sigh. Just like me.
Anyway, whatever you are, at least you haven't abandoned me yet.
I'm so tired. Feel like I haven't slept . . . ever.

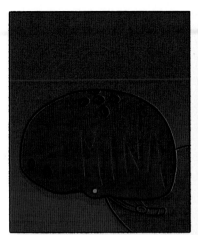

Nobody ever asked me what
I wanted, and it didn't occur to
me to push back or pivot away.
Or choose...or even dream...
anything else.

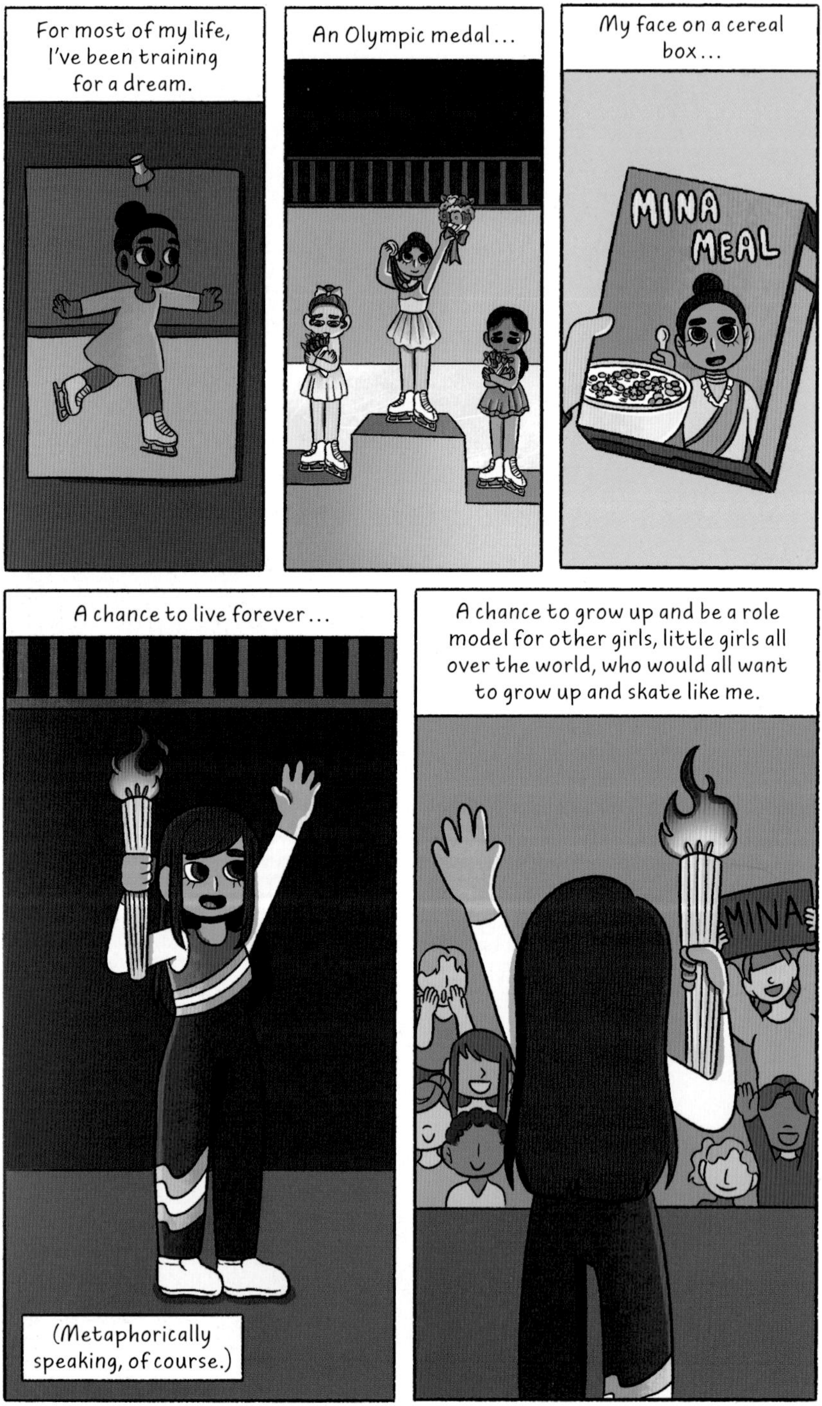
For most of my life, I've been training for a dream.
An Olympic medal...
My face on a cereal box...
MINA MEAL
A chance to live forever...
(Metaphorically speaking, of course.)
A chance to grow up and be a role model for other girls, little girls all over the world, who would all want to grow up and skate like me.
MINA

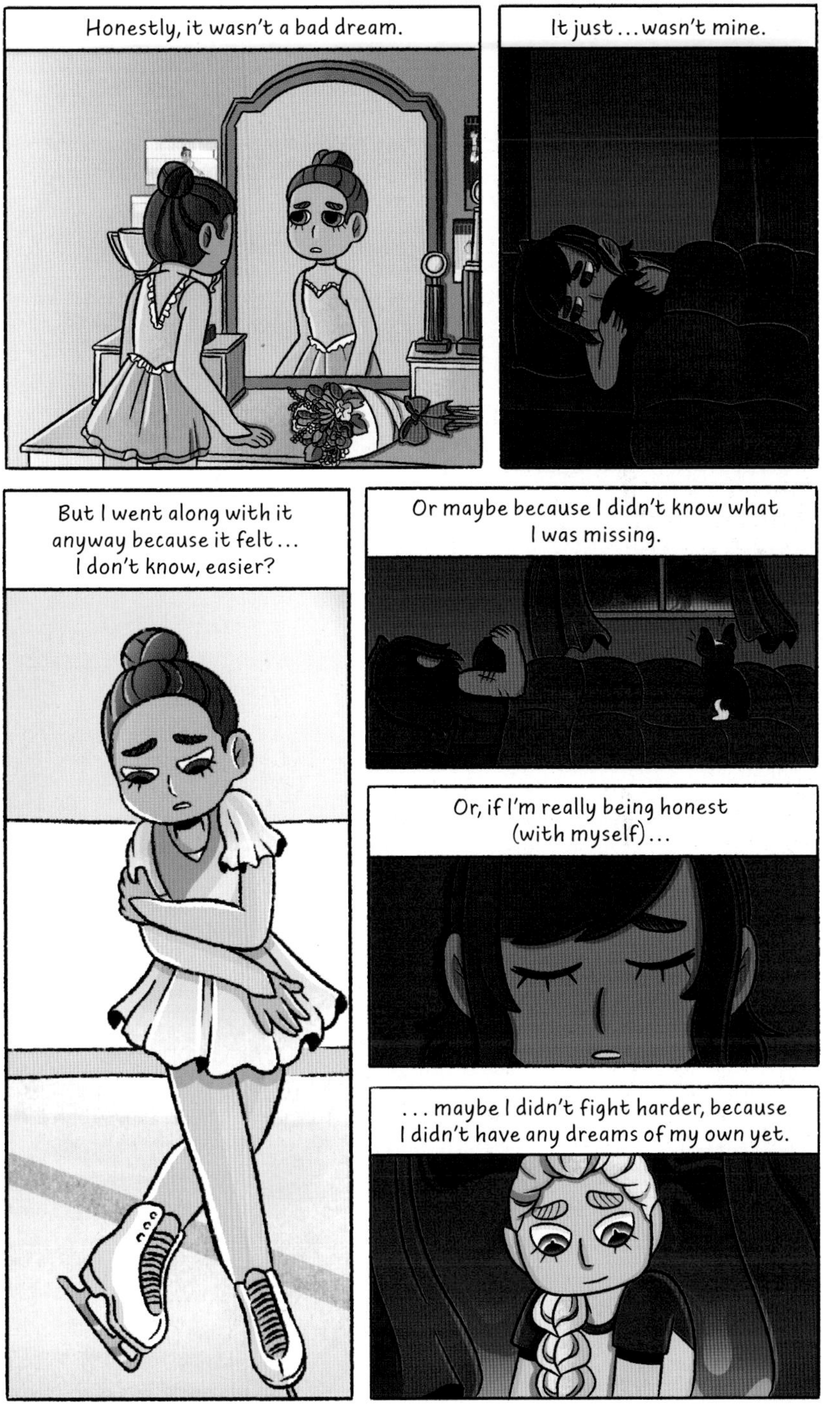
Honestly, it wasn't a bad dream.
It just . . . wasn't mine.
But I went along with it anyway because it felt . . . I don't know, easier?
Or maybe because I didn't know what I was missing.
Or, if I'm really being honest (with myself) . . .
. . . maybe I didn't fight harder, because I didn't have any dreams of my own yet.

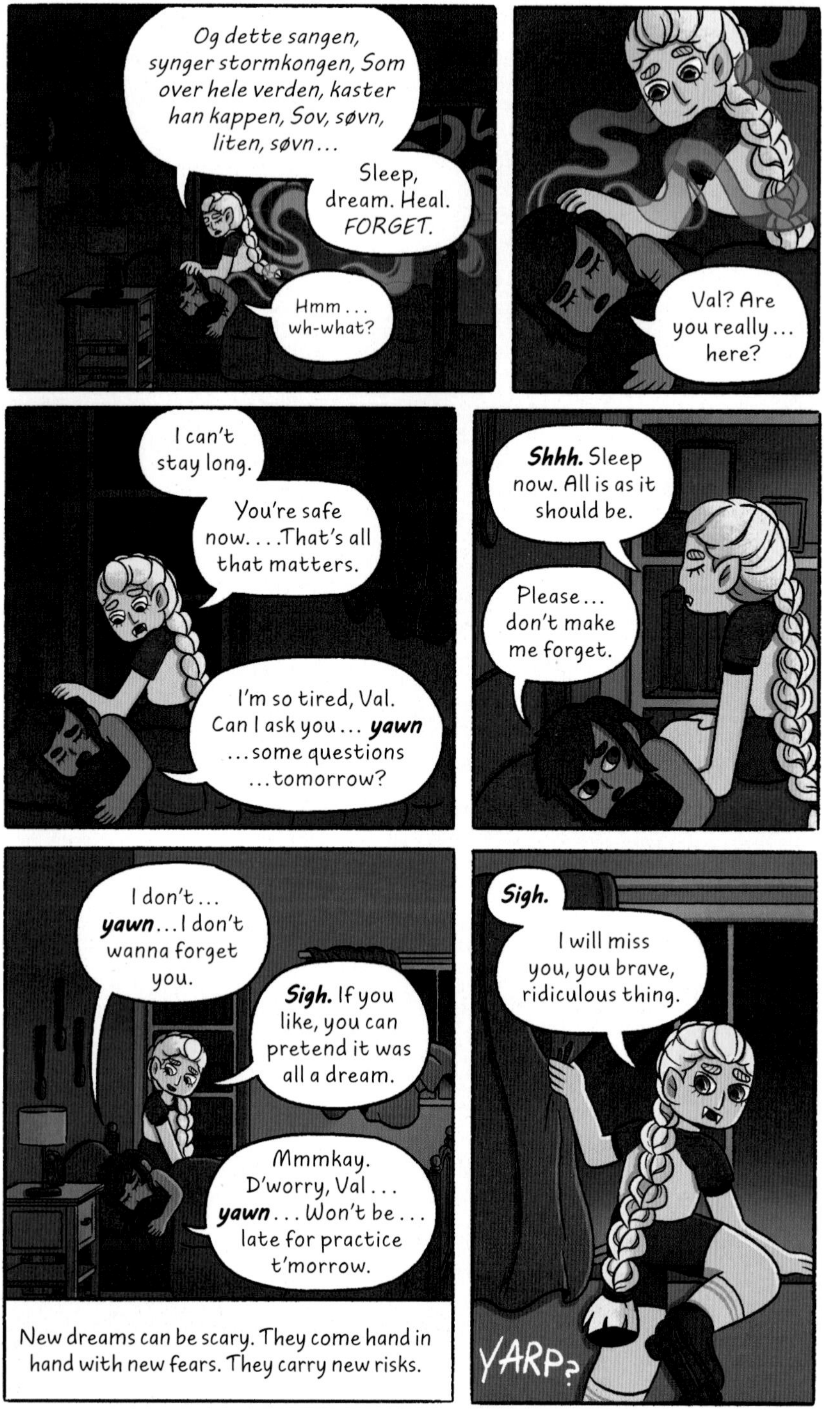
Og dette sangen, synger stormkongen, Som over hele verden, kaster han kappen, Sov, søvn, liten, søvn...
Sleep, dream. Heal. FORGET.
Hmm... wh-what?
Val? Are you really... here?
I can't stay long.
You're safe now. . . .That's all that matters.
I'm so tired, Val. Can I ask you... **yawn** ...some questions ...tomorrow?
Shhh. Sleep now. All is as it should be.
Please... don't make me forget.
I don't... **yawn**...I don't wanna forget you.
Sigh. If you like, you can pretend it was all a dream.
Mmmkay. D'worry, Val... **yawn**... Won't be... late for practice t'morrow.
New dreams can be scary. They come hand in hand with new fears. They carry new risks.
Sigh.
I will miss you, you brave, ridiculous thing.
YARP?

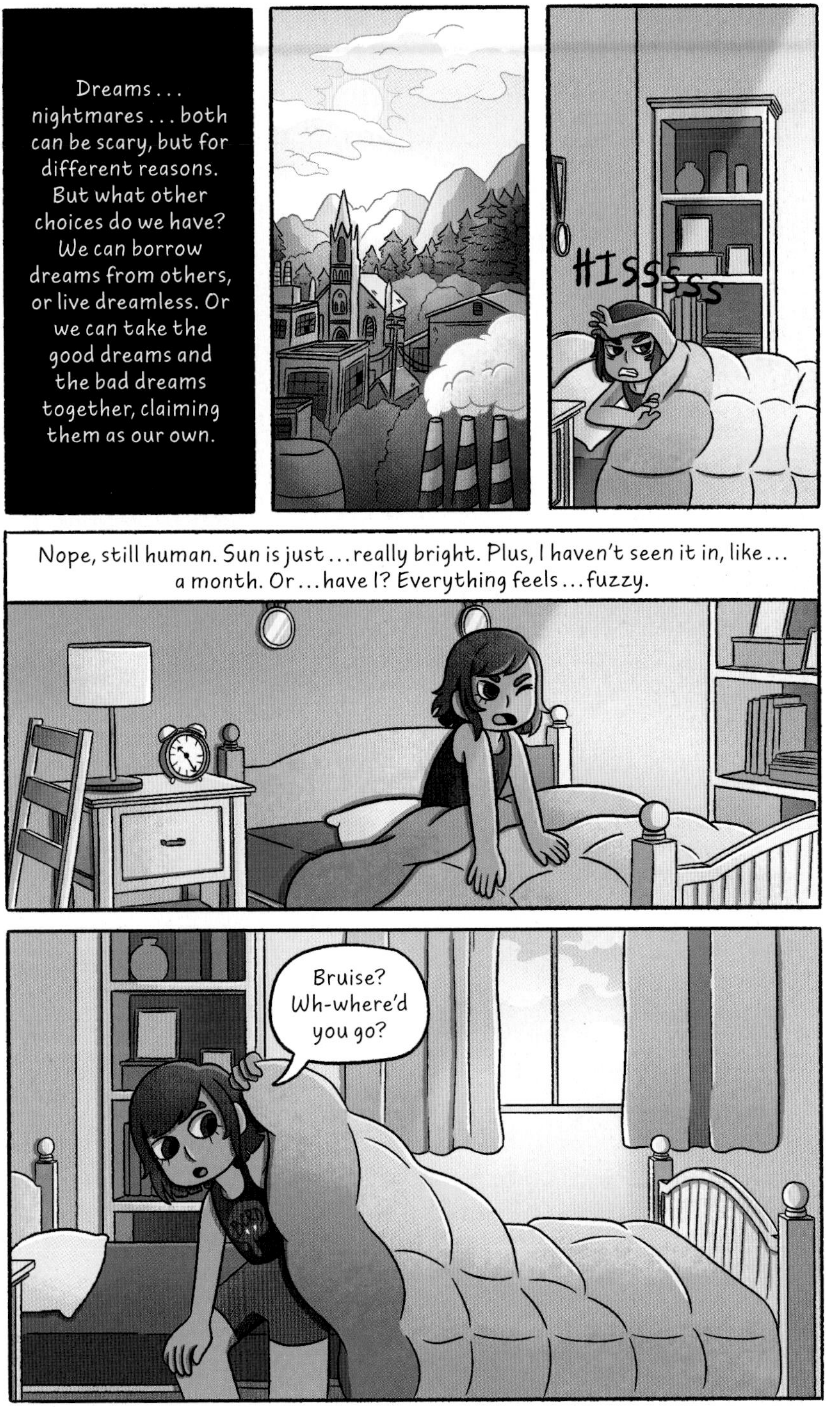
Dreams . . . nightmares . . . both can be scary, but for different reasons. But what other choices do we have? We can borrow dreams from others, or live dreamless. Or we can take the good dreams and the bad dreams together, claiming them as our own.
HISSSSSS
Nope, still human. Sun is just . . . really bright. Plus, I haven't seen it in, like . . . a month. Or . . . have I? Everything feels . . . fuzzy.
Bruise? Wh-where'd you go?

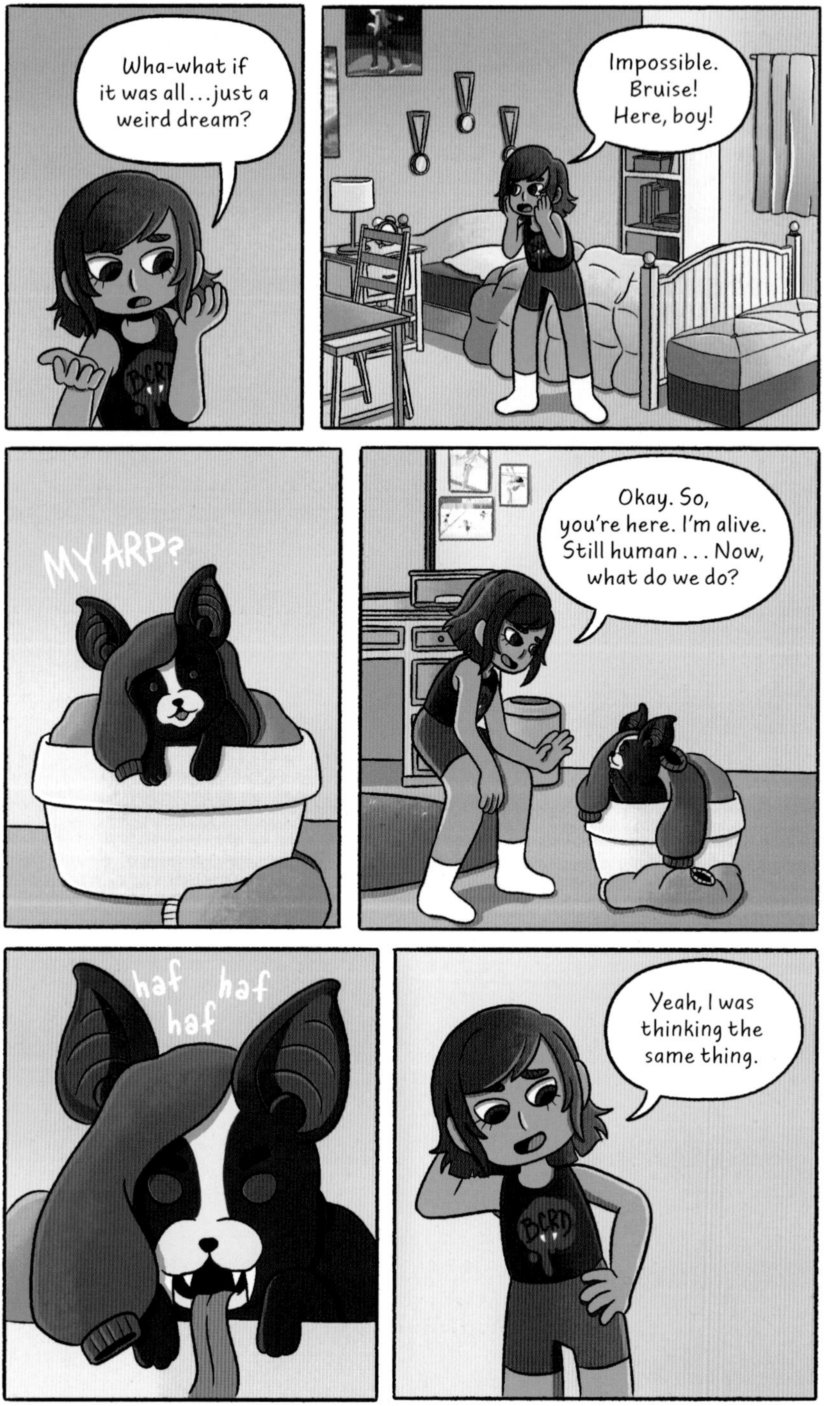
Wha-what if it was all . . . just a weird dream?
Impossible. Bruise! Here, boy!
MY ARP?
Okay. So, you're here. I'm alive. Still human . . . Now, what do we do?
haf haf haf
Yeah, I was thinking the same thing.

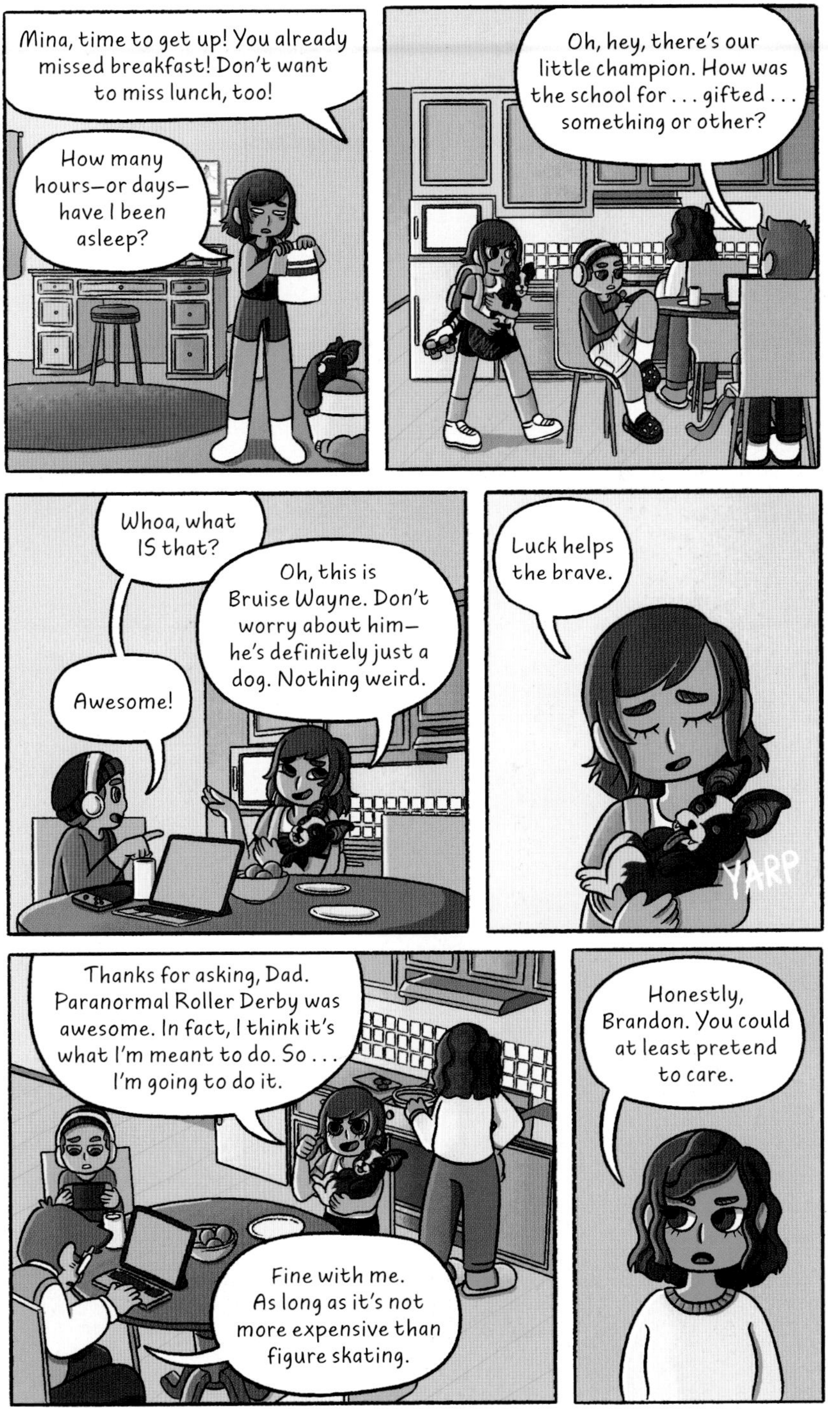
Mina, time to get up! You already missed breakfast! Don't want to miss lunch, too!
How many hours—or days—have I been asleep?
Oh, hey, there's our little champion. How was the school for . . . gifted . . . something or other?
Whoa, what IS that?
Awesome!
Oh, this is Bruise Wayne. Don't worry about him—he's definitely just a dog. Nothing weird.
Luck helps the brave.
YARP
Thanks for asking, Dad. Paranormal Roller Derby was awesome. In fact, I think it's what I'm meant to do. So . . . I'm going to do it.
Fine with me. As long as it's not more expensive than figure skating.
Honestly, Brandon. You could at least pretend to care.

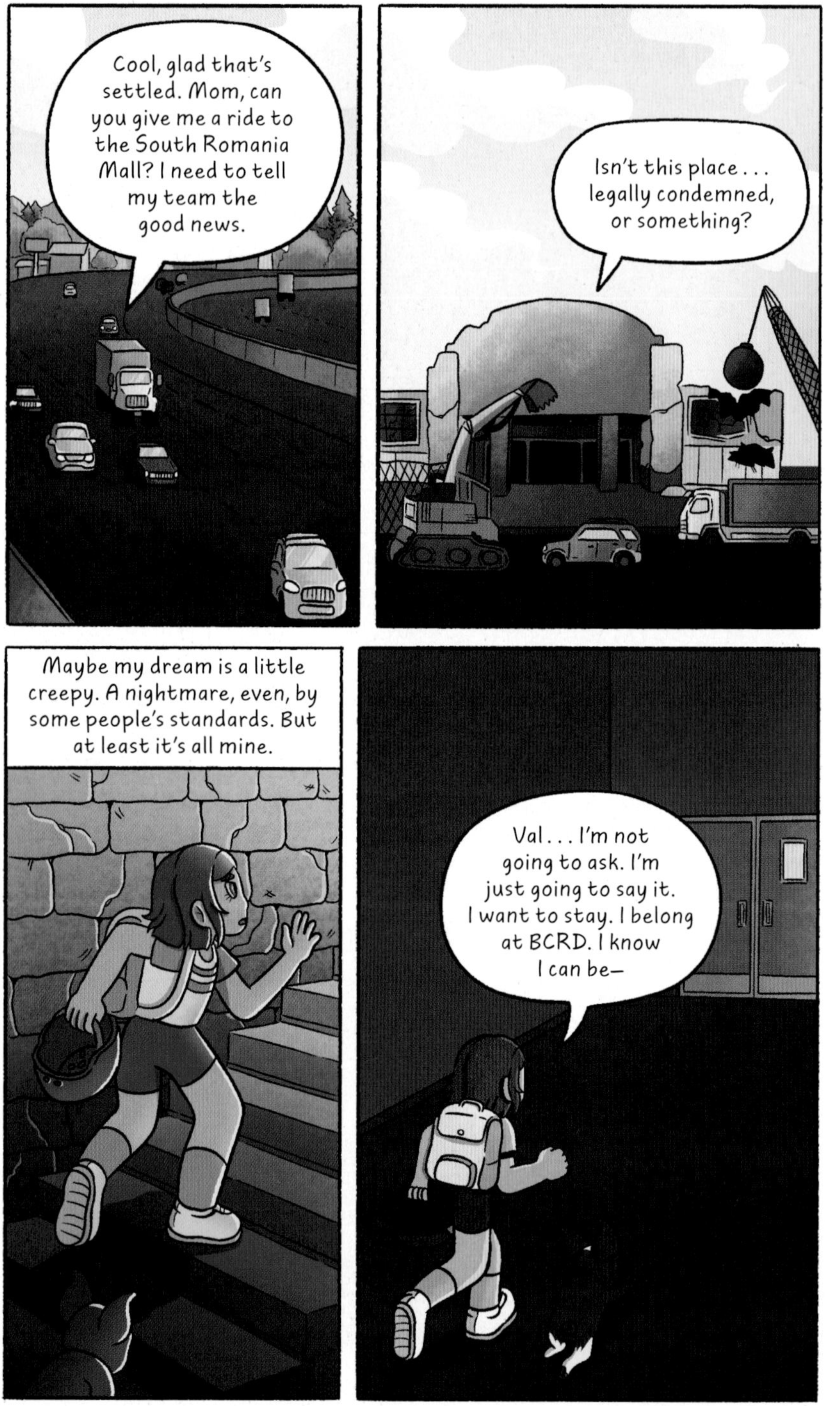
Cool, glad that's settled. Mom, can you give me a ride to the South Romania Mall? I need to tell my team the good news.
Isn't this place . . . legally condemned, or something?
Maybe my dream is a little creepy. A nightmare, even, by some people's standards. But at least it's all mine.
Val . . . I'm not going to ask. I'm just going to say it. I want to stay. I belong at BCRD. I know I can be–

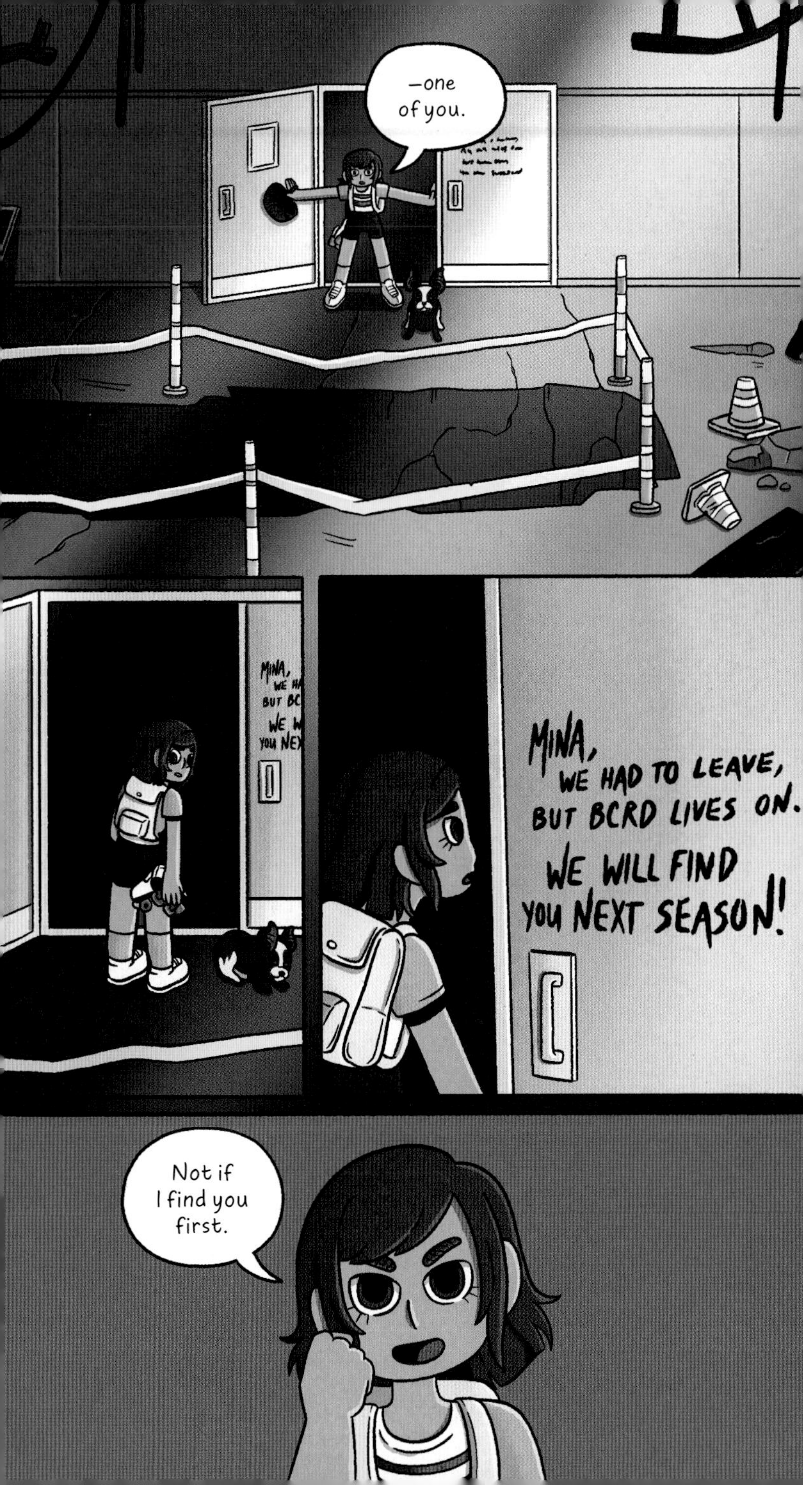
—one of you.
MINA, WE HAD TO LEAVE, BUT BCRD LIVES ON. WE WILL FIND YOU NEXT SEASON!
Not if I find you first.

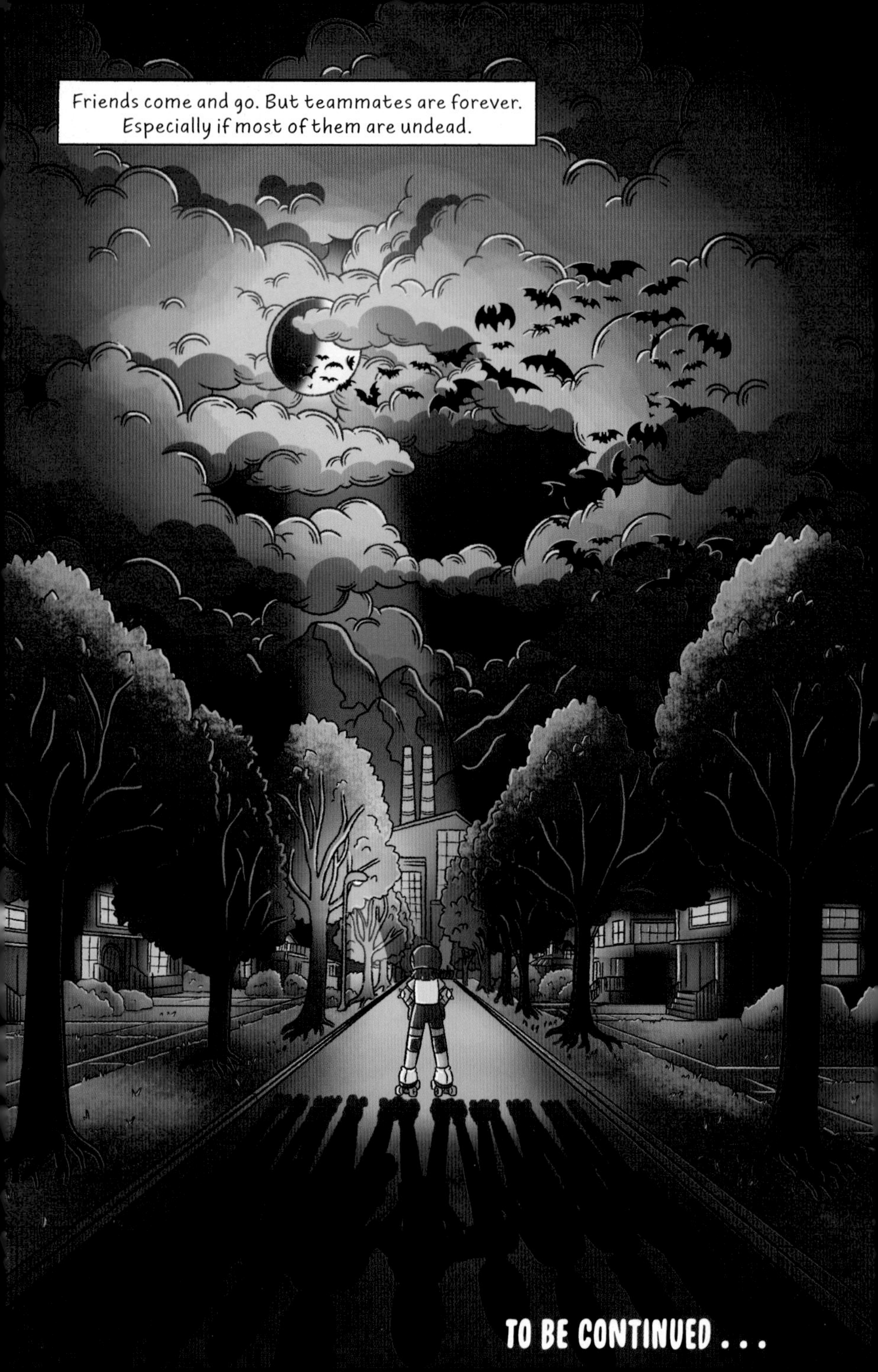
Friends come and go. But teammates are forever.
Especially if most of them are undead.
TO BE CONTINUED . . .

ACKNOWLEDGMENTS

HUMAN SUPPORT TEAM

Cheyenne "Chey
Butterfly" Wells (she/her)

Jake "Sparrow"
Anderson (he/him)

Jonathan "Sparky"
Hernandez (he/him)

Kelly "Philly Queen"
Peterson (she/her)

Rey "Glitter Prince"
Noble (he/they)

PRE-PUBLISHING & PUBLISHING TEAM

Mandy "The Hub"
Hubbard (she/her)

Moe "Haggle Rock"
Ferrara (she/her)

Liesa "Baltimore Bruiser"
Abrams (she/her)

Emily "Titanic Rose"
Harburg (she/her)

Juliet "Crash Capulet"
Goodman (she/her)

April "Ape Wilde"
Ward (she/her)

Barbara "Lil BowOwski"
Bakowski (she/her)

Rebecca "Sharp Cheddah"
Vitkus (she/her)

Debra "Deb Utaunt"
DeFord Minerva (she/her)

Janine "High Bar" Barlow
(she/her)

Amy "Pixie Sic" Bowman
(she/her)

THE TEAMS THAT INSPIRED & TRAINED US

Queen City Roller Derby
Buffalo, NY
(they/them)

Roc City Roller Derby
Rochester, NY
(they/them)

Salt City Roller Derby
Syracuse, NY
(they/them)

SFV Roller Derby
Sylmar, CA
(they/them)

The Derby Dolls
Los Angeles, CA
(they/them)

MEET THE CREATORS

V Park Anderson aka
"Scarlet Five" #55
She/They

VERONICA PARK (V. P.) ANDERSON (she/they) is a neurodivergent, queer, feminist millennial writer with a résumé that Victor Frankenstein would disown for being "a bit much." V's previous job titles include award-winning community theater actor, professional lecturer on cruise ships, indie film producer, literary agent, and creative project manager; however, writer is the title that always fits. V plays competitive flat track roller derby as "Scarlet Five" #55 and prefers the pivot role, aka "surprise jamming." Born in Alaska and raised in Oregon, she currently lives with her partner in Upstate New York and has two cats, Skeletor and Bo-Catan.

Tatiana Hill aka
"Twisstee" #35
She/Her

TATIANA HILL (she/her) is a Black and Latina illustrator by day and roller skater by night. Her art journey began alongside her love for anime in the early 2000s and culminated with a BA in animation. After receiving awards for best art direction, she applied her skill set in color and design to illustration. Born in Los Angeles and a member of the roller skate community there, Tatiana enjoys participating in a space that celebrates diversity, identity, and found family. She illustrated the Roller World tarot deck, and *Blood City Rollers* is her debut graphic novel as an illustrator.

3 1901 06227 1723